LESSER GODS & DEMONS

Also by Andrew Forrest Baker

NOVEL
The House That Wasn't There

SHORT STORY COLLECTION
We Tremble As We Sink

LESSER GODS & DEMONS

ANDREW FORREST BAKER

PARLYAREE PRESS

Parlyaree Press
Atlanta, Georgia
www.parlyaree.com

Library of Congress Cataloging-in-Publication Data
Names: Baker, Andrew Forrest, 1980, author.
Title: Lesser Gods & Demons / Andrew Forrest Baker
Description: First Edition | Atlanta : Parlyaree Press, 2023
Identifiers: LCCN: 2023907708| ISBN 9781961206014 (paperback)
Subjects: LCGFT: Novels
LC record available at https://lccn.loc.gov/2023907708

Design by Parlyaree Press

Front Cover/Title Typeface is Rig Solid by Jamie Clarke Type.
Cover Imagery (pre-alteration) by Koyash07; Atlanta Skyline (pre-
alteration) by Ray of Light. Licensed from Adobe.
Interior Text Typeface is Baskerville, deisgned in the 1750s by John
Baskerville and cut by punchcutter John Handy.
Interior Ornaments licensed from Yorinworks.

Hardcover ISBN: 978-1-961206-00-7
Paperback ISBN: 978-1-961206-01-4
Ebook ISBN: 987-1-961206-02-1

To my parents.

LESSER GODS & DEMONS

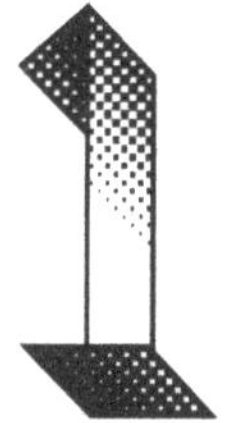

he seasons changed quickly that year. As if on a timer, the sticky sweetness of humidity sank into a frosty morning dew. The leaves of the great trees, only a day before glossy and brilliant and green, yellowed and trilled in the suddenly harsh and oppressive breeze as if it were their final chance to wave goodbye. Those which had overshot their turn leapt in cyclones to trip their browns across the red corrugated roof. It sounded to Daniel, sitting below in what would have been his favorite chair if he allowed himself those sorts of indulgences, exactly the same as the chittering parade of newborn squirrels chasing one another at the onset of Summer, the cracking trickle of the last vestiges of ice as Spring broke, or the clicking lift-off farewell of the final birds moving south when Winter finally set in. The same sound to denote each season. A ticking clock of time lost.

He tried to peer through the window at his untended garden. Over-ripe tomatoes pocked where the skin bruised and sagged heavily against the furry chartreuse stems. The blistering purple of his eggplants bulged black with the solanine promise of nightshade poison. The basil at the base of the vines had long since bolted and bittered. He felt he could taste it on the draft seeping around the window frame. The only plant in the garden still successful was a determined sprig of rosemary which held its color as it advanced and threatened to overtake the grounds, now looking more like a small cypress tree than the gentle, aromatic herb he had dug into his yard.

He tried to focus on anything other than what the day meant, what the sudden change in the outer dynamic foretold. He wanted to keep it as far from his mind as avoidance allowed, but his eyes continued to glaze, and his reflection peered back at him from the window glass: angry and judgmental and urging him to get on with it. His dark hair, still tussled from the pillow he had tossed and turned upon as he failed to find sleep, curled about his head like a halo, like horns. The dark-lined half-moon below his eyes made them appear large and hollow and accusing. He felt his own lips quiver as his reflection balked.

"You know it's time," it said. "This was the deal. This was always the deal."

"Just a moment longer," Daniel pleaded. He just needed a few more minutes, seconds really, to sit in what could have been his favorite chair and stare out at the garden that could have been so perfect had he tended to its needs while the leaves ticked their seconds by on the roof. "I just need a little longer."

His reflected face grew furious, threatening to leap from the glass and drag him to his fate. He braced himself, feet planted firmly against the floor, for the impact of his subconscious on his chest. His reflection frowned and began to count down.

"Forty-five." It said it stoically. A downbeat as the leaves ticked by in triplets above his head. "Forty-four."

Daniel heaved himself to his feet and looked down to study the worn, brown tweed fabric of the chair. The seat cushion had already returned to its full-figured curve, shaking itself free of his weight as if he had never been there to begin with. Like he didn't exist at all, which somewhere, deep down, all evidence to the contrary, he knew was not true. He imagined the sultry stale smell of burnt coffee wafting in from the kitchen. Another memory he needed one more moment to fully embrace.

"Thirty-nine."

He walked stodgily to the basement door. His house had never had a basement before, but now it was necessary for survival. Now it was a matter of fact and nestled in the short nook of a hallway where the linen closet he never used for actual linens and instead filled with the multitude of items purchased and forgotten had been. No real loss there; all the gadgets invented to make life easier and faster and safer were of so little importance now. No, the basement door was better. Without it, he would be as lost as the rolling seasons outside.

"Thirty. Twenty-nine."

The voice was louder now, echoing through his head in seconds which seemed somehow to pick up in speed. He began to descend the long and dark and far too gentle for the width of his house stairwell at a steady pace. He refused to rush. If he made it, great. If he got caught, so be it. He knew the dangers of returning home. A hefty part of him wondered what would happen if he just stayed.

"Fifteen" sounded as he reached the base of the stairs and sent his gaze around. The out of place white marble cube, spotless and brightly lit, did its best to disconnect Daniel from the steel-roofed cottage above him. But that was part of the point. He walked slowly to the center of the room and lifted himself into the metal reclining seat placed there. He flicked an unlabeled switch on the right arm of the chair. A soft whirr skipped across the room: the hum of an air conditioner unable to decide if it wanted to stay on or off. He counted down to five.

Fighting the urge to throw it across the room, Daniel placed the white helmet that looked remarkably like the oversized contraption his mother had made him wear anytime he took his bicycle out as a child over his poofed and knotted hair and leaned back. His eyes shot open as he remembered he had forgotten to say goodbye. But it was too late.

"Three."

Besides, it's not like they would care.

"Two."

Or know, for that matter.

"One."

"You almost didn't make it that time."

Daniel grunted his reply and winced to wet his eyes. The harsh glare of the pure white tile ceiling met him with an unblinking cold, and the steel recliner sent a shiver down his spine.

"You keep doing that, and they won't let you in anymore."

"I found the fucking door," he replied and cleared the gurgle from his throat.

Daniel leveraged himself up and to the floor. He looked sullenly around the room. It was just like his imagined basement except for the gentle whine of machinery stacked against the wall and the bouncing attendant checking boxes on a tablet then winding cables he'd just unhooked from the white helmet Daniel had left lazing in his place on the chair. He stumbled slightly as he attempted to stabilize his footing.

"Be careful, Danny. Give yourself some time to adjust."

"It's Daniel," he groaned as he closed his eyes to center his breathing. Only his mother called him Danny. He hadn't been Danny in years.

"Daniel," the attendant confirmed. They had known each other, peripherally, in the Before, but Daniel couldn't remember exactly how. It seemed a lifetime ago. An altogether different existence. He handed Daniel a brush to attempt to tame his hair, tossed and matted from his time inside the helmet. "Ready for the checklist? Did you experience any nausea within the simulation?"

"No."

Daniel had, indeed, found the door. One, in that he was back in the white room with the bouncing attendant and the stale air which cycled so quickly it sometimes felt as if it was pulling the breath from his lungs, but also in that it was he who had created the door that ensured a way back at all.

"Any anomalies unexplained by the missteps of memory?"

"No."

In the early days of the Haptic Mind Map, only two in five people made it out of the trials with severe headaches and three days of vomiting. The others, all two hundred and ninety-six of them in the end, remained inside, as if locked in a dream. Even with IVs delivering liquid and nutrients to their bloodstreams and their minds registering heightened activity as if in a constant REM state, after twenty-four days and four hours, without fail, their bodies shut down. First the lungs; then the heart; the mind always the last to go. Even with stricter parameters in place, with time limits and simultaneous re-mapping, people only had a 50/50 chance of returning. It was Daniel, using his past as a therapist, who realized the mind would adjust better through transition. That inserting a doorway, a space, a ritual, a pattern would create a bridge to keep the brain intact.

"And now, outside the Map. Any dissociative thoughts?"

"No."

People still came back groggy and with a slight case of tinnitus which took a few days to dissipate, but they came back.

"Desires to return?"

People came back, but sometimes longed so much to return to what was, to what their mind remembered of the Before, they cracked into sullen shells which threatened to hinder the productivity of the Colony.

Sometimes they'd go back in just to get lost, refusing to find the door. Too many close calls and their HMM privileges would be revoked.

"You know, Daniel," the attendant said, leaning forward in earnest. "You saved my life."

Daniel patted the chair and nodded; a humble smile forced across his lips. He had heard it all before. Although he had not invented the Mind Mapping, he had made it safer. But in his mind, he'd only served to mass market FC47's newest drug: one he was equally addicted to as well.

"No. I mean in the Before. You worked at my school, and I came to see you. I was just an awkward kid. Not smart enough to be a geek. Not popular enough for the jocks. I just never felt like I fit in."

Daniel had worked briefly as a high school guidance counselor when he was fresh out of college. He had liked the job; enjoyed feeling like he was helping the kids. He'd even encouraged them to call him Danny thinking it would break the ice and help them open up to him.

"Anyway. You told me that life wasn't about fitting into some mold. It was about finding what you loved, whatever interested you the most, and pursuing it with all your heart. Gaming took me to coding which took me to VR and that got me in here. You gave me direction. And purpose. I'm Lincoln Dunnwater."

Daniel smiled, more sincerely this time, and swallowed. He wanted to say "a lot of good that does you." He wanted to say "that wasn't me; I'm a different person now." He wanted to tick off the talking points of the Apost that had been squashed a year and a half ago yet still lingered in faint whispers in some of the air ducts. He missed his family so much, all of the under-breath horrors posited about life inside the snow globe in the sky were starting to get to him, particularly in the wake of an HMM outing.

"How about your family?" he asked. As an unspoken rule, it was a question not meant to be posed in the Colonies but coming out of the HMM tended to rearrange one's priorities toward the nostalgic.

The attendant stared at the floor briefly before pulling a happy face back on, one he could wear like a mask. He was still an awkward kid; no more than 28 at the most, with gangly arms and legs that buckled slightly at the knees. He wore the same hard-lived expression concealed by happy compliance on his face that the bulk of the other citizens wore. The smile that signified survival. A sort of happy-go-lucky camaraderie meant to stifle thoughts of the Before, of the Below.

"My sister was on the west coast for grad school," he said. "And my parents are still down in Atlanta. It's rough sometimes, not being able to contact them, but it's—what?—just another six years until we're down there again. We're over halfway there. I do miss them though."

Daniel nodded. He wanted to hug the kid whose name he couldn't remember, but instead placed a firm hand on his shoulder. "My family didn't make it in either," he said.

"Is that who you go to see?"

"Sometimes," Daniel confirmed. For just a moment, a brief visage of Paul snapped into his brain. He was standing by the kitchen island with their Go-Bags at the ready, holding tightly to the twenty-four-month body of their newly adopted Samantha. "Sometimes I just want to watch the seasons change."

"I get that," the attendant nodded. "It's a little disconcerting when it's always Summer." Daniel could see he was pulling himself back together, resetting his professionalism and getting ready to show him the door. "That's a lot to fit into two and a quarter hours, Daniel. I won't report it this time but remember to give yourself extra time to reach the door on your next journey."

Daniel's biometrically assigned living station on Sub5 was little more than a lofted bunk above a multi-service chest meant to serve as chair, couch, table, desk, and entertainment area. There was just enough space alongside the bunk to form a clear pathway from the door, but even turning around to exit was difficult without the use of the bed or chest below. While other loners had decorated their quarters with photographs or lewd drawings of folks from a variety of genders, Daniel kept his bare, with only the blue-grey tones of the structure to stare back and question him. His own memories were kept stored beneath the bench, deep down in the chest, under blankets and clothing: a series of printed photographs nestled beside a single, silver rattle. When he'd first arrived, his station on Alpha3 was larger, with room to spin or to even dance if he desired, but dancing was the last thing on his mind.

"This is all I know," he told himself. "This is all I can know."

Sometimes he believed the over eight years—nearly nine now—spent inside FC47 had made him as hollow as his unit. Each of the Floating Colonies had been designed with practical efficiency and nostalgic utopia in mind. Six floors—Subs 3-5 and Alphas 3-5—served as living units where all daily needs were met within its one square mile radius. Laundry and Showers and Waste Centers and Classrooms. The Office—more of a booth really—where Daniel filled the hours others weren't waiting with their notebooks to listen to and calm down the citizens missing their loved ones, having regrets, going insane. Patients became fewer and fewer as the years went by. It was shocking how swiftly the human mind could get used to altered circumstances. Though a new psychosis seemed to be creeping through the corridors, it was largely considered status quo, and no one sought help for it unless escorted by the Guard.

Restaurants on each living level featured different preparations of the vegetables and lab-grown proteins produced on Subs 1 and 2 where nearly twelve hundred and eighty acres worked year-round to sustain the 2,048,000 people now living above the clouds. Alpha2 housed the lawmakers' offices; the scientific and engineering labs that kept the Colony alive; and the Guard who kept the Colony in order. Residents of the Subs were only allowed to Alpha2 with work orders for the labs or Guard escorts to the doctors except during special occasions when the massive festival centers there and on Alpha3 were opened and the Sub citizens got to feel like they were welcomed into the upper echelons. But it was just as well. There was a cold sterility to the level that reminded anyone who stepped between its walls that they were no longer of the earth.

Below that, Alpha1 provided a buffer level between the castes. The massive machines and generators needed for oxygen production, power, water reclamation and recycling (of both water and waste), and the backups upon backups required to maintain a normality for the Colony packed the floor. Until recently, it had remained largely unpopulated save for a few engineers or mechanics tinkering with the wires and knobs. As year eight rounded itself out and flattened along the timeline that ticked digitally on every level, the number of small bodies shadowing large computers grew higher and higher. No need to be alarmed. Everything was routine.

In true center, with numbers ascending or descending in either direction, sat Ground Floor Zero: the Neutral Zone. Originally imagined as a recreation space for all the Colony's inhabitants, it had taken just three short years for the floor to devolve into a den of iniquity where anything was possible, and everything happened. Moonshine and sex, newly created powders smuggled from the chemists' labs, and the traded belongings of the Dreamers—as the Subbers affectionately called those who hadn't woken from their Mind Trips—were all on full display in the unsanctioned yet unthreatened black market. It didn't help that a third of the floor had already been converted to a space to store and process the bodies of those who had died. Even behind a screened wall digitally evoking a beautiful sunny day with a slightly gentle breeze in Piedmont Park, the bodies did little to invite the joyous recreation the architects had intended the floor to evoke. Eventually, all the LED lights were busted out, and a permanent night descended upon the floor that was always packed despite "no respectable citizen" ever setting foot there.

Floating Colony 47, like all things in Atlanta, was situated slightly north of the city proper, as if even the structure designed to save humanity from the onslaught of climate change was a victim of white flight. Originally posed as FC13, the motion to build the Colony had failed to pass the State Congress Budgetary Committee. Eventually, the city of Atlanta financed it on its own. In the end, it would be only one of two in Georgia. A marvel of construction 1 square mile and 11 stories tall situated 10 miles above the surface of the earth, nestled snuggly into the ozone layer of the stratosphere. High enough to let life, as it were, carry on below—planes could still fly; weather could rage on below the base—but low enough to allow the stratosphere to continue filtering, as best it could, the harmful radiation of the sun's rays. Though the thick walls with zero access out took care of that as well.

Of course the Floating Colonies weren't actually floating. Their name wasn't even actually "Floating." It was "Forward" (as in "forward thinking" the young congresspeople who had pushed the agenda had said), but the name that the commoners use is what sticks. Nine columns housed support for the Colony—four of which were the chutes upward—to form a strange sundial wherever they were placed. Though, by the time Daniel entered, leaving the ground in a much faster twist than he had foreseen, the social media videos of long eerie shadows cast over great swaths of America's epicenters had died down. Even the site of the columns reaching skyward as far as the eye could see had become commonplace.

It should have been beautiful, the flattened solar cube perched on the backs of two preposterous giraffes, but try as he might, Daniel had never been able to let go of the forced cheer and utopic masks of the place. It felt, to him, like a theme park designed to keep the cattle happy. And he wasn't the only one. That was why the HMM had been created. Why thousands had risked their lives in testing. Why even now it was one of the most popular, and most expensive, attractions in the Colony. The Powers that Be had even offered to return Daniel to his Alpha3 dormitory when he solved the exiting conundrum, but he had declined in exchange for unfettered access to the chair. It had become a biweekly habit for him—

the maximum amount of time the law (for those with money) allowed. He had even started to overcome the headaches in a shorter span, though the tinnitus kept his ears off kilter for a good three days.

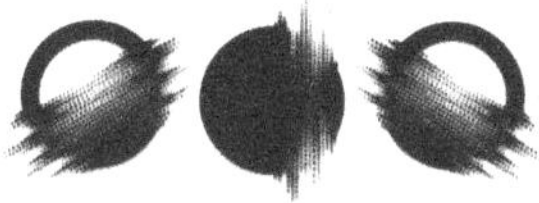

Giving up on sleeping away the migraine, Daniel rolled from his bunk. He pulled on a t-shirt that had already begun to unravel at the collar and bulged slightly in places it hadn't before. It no longer smelled like Paul, but Daniel still felt comfort with it pulled tight against his skin. He watched himself in the floor length mirror, no more than ten inches wide, that adorned the wall opposite his bunk. His blondish hair had darkened with time and hung in disarray around his face, curling slightly at the ears in festive ricochet trails, spreading out in all directions as if each strand, like himself, was unsure of where to go. His skin had paled greatly over the years, even with the radiant sun-spectrum lights overhead pumping unfelt Vitamin D into his body and looked more vampiric against the reddened brown stubble that lined his jaw. Though he was leaner now than he had been, more sinewy muscles draped his bones from the hours spent in the workout centers trying to quiet his mind.

He imagined, for a moment, he saw Samantha behind him in his reflection. She was sitting on the bench, petting and shaking a stuffed sea creature, swinging it by its tail, and bobbing its head from side to side as it "spoke." It was the same toy manta ray he and Paul had given her at the airport in Ethiopia after the adoption papers were signed and dried, and they were about to board to bring her home. He'd wanted something different for her—some gesture to show her how special she truly was. Nothing traditional like a bear or falsely exotic like the monkeys that lined the airport gift shop shelves. The doll had not aged a day. No sign of wear or dirt or matting graced its brown fur. Samantha, though, would be eight years older, ten—pushing eleven—now. The mirror filled with lifetime of memories never actually achieved for him and instead imagined both in and out of the HMM. He wondered if she had chosen to keep her hair natural or if she had fallen in line with supposed American standards to relax it, if she preferred Sam to Samantha, and if she ever missed the home she could not remember. He hoped Paul had taught her to love and stand up for herself, to be proud of the melanin in her skin. He prayed, to no one in particular, she was still alive.

The corridors on Sub Level 5, and throughout all of FC47, were named for the streets on the ground below. In an effort to showcase commonality and deny any segregative past of Atlanta, the higher ups had decided to layout the space with no regard to the actual mapped design of the original, resulting in a hodgepodge that had greatly confused all the inhabitants upon arrival. Time, though, and quickly produced touchscreen maps had solved most of the navigation issues. Daniel wondered, if he were once again land-bound, if he would even remember how to drive across town. Great floor to ceiling LED screens shone in street view images of Atlanta's landmarks, and the ceiling always displayed a clear blue sky with a marigold sun reflecting a pale imitation of true southern heat from any angle with jet streams and clouds just over at the horizon. It was designed to simulate normalcy, but to Daniel, it made the entire space feel stretched and forced, like a Disneyworld of the sky.

He wondered if Orlando had made it, or if the state of Florida was now submerged, bulbous black half circles peaking the waves like glaciers instead of ears. Hurricanes had been battering the peninsula for decades, but retirees and spring breakers still migrated there like swarms of seventeen-year locusts: loud and destructive and hungry. Saving the planet from mass overpopulation was the reason for the Colonies in the first place—to try to mitigate the damage done by too many consumers consuming just because they could. Maybe the Colonies had done their jobs. Maybe the world outside was resetting, refreshed and anew, with each passing dawn.

Turning left on Ponce, Daniel did his best to acknowledge everyone he passed with a gentle nod, one that was polite but did not invite conversation. Though few on Sub5 had had the privilege of experiencing the HMM, everyone had witnessed enough to recognize the Haps when they saw it so, like true Southerners, would smile courteously and steer clear. Those moments when the digital memory and reality blurred, the airborne version of the bends, were tricky to navigate, and trickier still to insert oneself into. Once recognized, most people would avert their eyes or shift their gate suddenly toward Euclid to take the long way around.

When he arrived at the Mess, Daniel saddled up to the shortest line. It was still about a half hour before most people arrived for dinner rations, so he would be able to eat in peace. The red and white Varsity sign above the cashier had once reminded him of the single worst date he and Paul had ever been on, but now he could barely remember the taste of their long, greasy french fries or smothered chili dogs.

"What'll you have? What'll you have?"

The cashier spouted her greeting with the same urgency they always used, a holdover from the surface, even though no one was waiting behind Daniel. He ordered a Heavy Weight with Strings. He tried to tell himself the protein pods really tasted like beef, as if proximity were close enough in the way that the Haptic was real enough to feel family. He ordered a Coke and was asked what kind.

"Twenty-three units," the clerk said, and Daniel held his wrist up to the scanner next to the till.

Commerce had not ended with Utopia. Work was required. Credits were earned. And you got what you paid for. Although sustenance was still rationed, meals monitored by technology, the tiers of preparation and costs associated varied wildly. Rumor was some of the fanciest restaurants in town had lost their chefs to Alphas 5 and 6, but that had never been confirmed or denied. Who could afford it anyway?

Units were processed through a chip implanted in all citizens' right wrists. Initially, the tiny bits of silicon had been placed in the web of skin between the thumb and the index finger, but when the Aposts had begun to remove them, recognizing them as a tracker alongside their wallets, the orders came down to relocate all chips to the wrist. Placing them in was easy. Taking them out was suicide.

A group of diners bristled as he walked past, a sudden closure Daniel squinted to take note of. He found a spot, alone, far enough away, but still within earshot of the others in the pre-supper-rush dining space. Curiosity had always had its way with him. It was eight tenths of the reason he was where he was now. He caught himself freezing between bites as he tried to decipher the low whispers behind him.

"You got a hearing problem, Doc?" one of the diners called out. He was thin, with stringy black hair pulled back into a bun. Grease and dirt etched the outline of his fingernails and sliced in exasperated wisps across his forehead. The holes in his tank top looked cut more than worn, and he couldn't seem to manage to keep both feet on the ground. One foot or the other constantly found its way to his stool, his lanky knees floating first on one side and then the other of his angular face like a toad at attention, ready to leap at the first sign of trouble.

"Just minding my own," Daniel said, refusing to turn around to even acknowledge the man.

"Why don't you mind it somewhere else?" one of the other men laughed. The two could have been brothers except for the rounder features and the blond locks. No, not related. It was identity through familiarity, Daniel decided. Chosen family had influenced them as greatly as any bloodlines, as was the case with most of the residents inside.

From the corner of his eye, Daniel spotted a lone man in a Guard uniform studying the situation intensely as he poked through the mush on his plate. He would at least have backup if things got out of hand. So many of the youth in the Colony had grown stir-crazy as the years passed by, teenage rebellion giving in to tiny ant hills of power struggles with anyone older than them. And these guys seemed ready to bite the toes of all the elephants. Of course, another side effect of the Haps was paranoia.

"It's still a free Colony," Daniel said.

The men huffed to begin their retort but were silenced by the calming voice of the young Asian woman sitting with them.

"Let him eat in peace," she commanded, and the two boys quieted and poked at the vegetable purée on their plates.

Without turning his head fully, Daniel glanced slightly to his left and behind. The young woman met his gaze and nodded to him, making him, for the first time that day, actually smile. She was young—twenty-four, he thought—with an oil slick of hair hanging to her lower back and short, choppy bangs scattered across her forehead. Her oversized pink sweater and casual jeans looked disparate beside her companions' unwashed garments, but a sly twinkle in her eye foretold that she was capable of the same mischief as the boys. He marveled at how kept she was. Most people had long since converted to the Colony garb, the three outfits each were allowed to bring in having long since begun to wear out to the point of un-wearing. But most of all, her quiet confidence conveyed a power beyond her years, one she obviously wielded over her more disorderly companions. She returned Daniel's smile and nodded again for him to get back to his meal.

The lines were beginning to grow as he finished the last few bites of his meal. The din was already beginning to agitate the soft ringing circling his eardrums. He needed to return his tray and remove himself before too many others arrived. As he reached to pile his trash atop his empty, wheat-plastic plate, a softly manicured hand slid a folded piece of paper across the table toward him. A peculiar scar poked from her pink sleeve, like a broken arrowhead—three lines that merged to a single point, a half-moon that disappeared behind the wool. The young Asian woman did not even look at him or break her stride as she passed, but Daniel could feel a sense of urgent privacy emanating from her. The Guard officer eyed them suspiciously before following the young woman out. Daniel slid his tray atop the paper and nestled it between his fingers and the plastic. He swiftly deposited the paper into his pocket as he placed the tray in the return center. He didn't dare to look at the paper until he had more privacy.

The walk down Boulevard to his quarters felt long and syncopated, himself a salmon struggling upstream against the flow of people food-bound. Everyone who smiled at him was a potential grizzly waiting to swipe him from the waves. The Haps were hitting him hard.

When he finally made it home, he unfolded the paper with his breath held, though he was not sure why. Something about the tight, purposeful lettering felt familiar, but he couldn't place it. He had no idea why, but he found himself eyeing the clock. He read the note once more to lock it to memory.

Expose the lies. / Nowhere. / 2AM

"We have reached a literal boiling point. And since the time to act has long since passed, we are given only now."

The young woman on the screen retained the animated look of urgency on her face as she paused for the applause of her party. She kept her eyes straight forward, locked behind the stone-thick frames she kept as a matter of pride although corrective surgery was quick and easy, but noted the stoic and unimpressed faces still peppering the Chamber. She didn't look directly at the camera, but it was obvious she knew it was there. She played to it, attempting to rally the court of public opinion as she knew the opposition in the room would refuse to budge unless their seats and the pensions were threatened. The soft hum emanating from one of the seven tiny drones allowed to buzz around the hall ticked in place a few feet from the podium. It was ironic, Paul thought, the white noise they produced which should have influenced a calm, collected conversation amongst the representatives had instead created an animated barbarism, a grandstanding soapbox once reserved for rallies and exterior steps.

"This is not about party or creed," Representative Collins continued. "This is not about faith, and this is larger than science. This is the survival of the human species!"

Paul clicked off the television as he heard the chime of the lock pad granting entry at the front door. The morning had gotten away from him, but he couldn't turn his head away from the arguments proceeding at the Capitol. The unmitigated passion and hope alongside the denial and vitriol was intoxicating. The US Congress had fully become the Roman Colosseum. Whichever side of the argument the public fell on, the drones giving unfettered access had made each new session the most-watched reality show on tv. Paul told himself it was a necessary evil. The outcome of the arguments would, after all, affect his work for decades to come. The so-called criminals he spent his life rehabilitating and re-placing into society would, indefinitely, become some of the hardest affected as resources continued to dwindle and oceans continued to rise. Nearly half of the rural farms most of his clients ended up tilling had become defunct as increased temperatures burned the soil. Most grocers didn't have the stock to necessitate the overnight shifts the larger corporations were comfortable placing the ex-cons in, out of view of the public, but still ripe for governmental subsidies. *The outcome of these debates is essential,* he told himself. *Watching it all unfold is simply research.*

He swept into the kitchen and busied himself pulling items from the cabinets, shifting containers left and right in the fridge.

"Lunch isn't ready yet," he apologized. "I got caught up in the hearing. Have you been following this shitshow?"

"That's okay, babe," Daniel smiled, dropping his satchel bag on the table and clutching a large manilla envelope to his chest. "My next appointment isn't until three fifteen."

He flicked the envelope with his index finger to make a crisp, clean pop. Paul, though, was too engrossed in his task to notice. It was one of the things Daniel admired most about him; Paul's dedication to the thing in front of him. He was a completionist above all else. Dedicated and determined. It was a trait that served him well in his nonprofit work. Plus, when trained on him, it made Daniel feel like the only other person in the world, which, after long hours dissecting and aiding those othered by society, was a welcomed sanctuary.

"It's insane," Paul laughed. "And, I mean, I don't know if these

'Forward Cities' are the solution, but at least they are something. Moving three to five million people out of every major metropolitan into a self-contained ecosystem seems crazy. But it would go a long way in reducing environmental impact and giving us all a fighting chance at real change that could sustain us. Or at least buy us some time to right and heal the planet."

"Paul…"

"I know, I know. Social Justice Warrior. But I'd totally live in one of those for fifteen years."

"Paul." Daniel's voice was more forceful this time, a clap against his subconscious. "It came."

"I mean, it's not like you're totally cut off from the world. Satellite and radio keep you informed. Camera drones piping in the news of the world. You're still part of it all, just ten miles away."

"It came, Paul."

"Ten miles up instead of ten miles over, true, but, I mean, what's the difference really? It's not like we visit your parents very often anyway and they're only twelve miles outside the city…. What came?"

Daniel laughed as Paul blushed. He had a tendency to ramble when he was focused or nervous. It was one of the first things that had endeared him to Daniel. By the end of their first date, Daniel was well-versed in Paul's thoughts on color theory and at least three movies he had yet to see. Paul's eyes widened at the envelope clutched to his husband's chest.

"Oh. *It* came," Paul said. "Did you open it?"

"Not yet." Daniel inhaled deeply as he placed the envelope on the kitchen island between them. "I wanted to do it together."

Both men's breath caught in the throats as they locked their gaze on the envelope. It was odd in and of itself, receiving snail mail, when everything had long since been digitized and delivered instantaneously. But the agency had insisted on it, despite the excruciating slowness. *Gestation happens faster,* Paul had lamented. *The icecaps shift and melt faster.* Yet now, here it was. The envelope that could change the course of their future.

"Are we ready?" Daniel asked.

"For their answer or for parenthood? Yes." Paul gestured toward the folded yellow paper and Daniel reached to grasp it. "No! Wait, wait!"

Daniel dropped the envelope as Paul rushed to the cabinet. He pulled out two flutes and placed them on the island, then popped the cork from a fresh bottle of Prosecco from the fridge.

"What if it's bad news?" Daniel asked.

Paul smirked sheepishly as he returned to the cabinet. He placed two rocks glasses and a bottle of rye on the other side of the envelope.

"Now we're covered either way," he said. "Are we ready?"

"Let's find out," Daniel sighed the excited breath of anticipation. One of those airy, exasperated exhales when the lungs couldn't quite keep up with the fear, the thrill, the want, and the wait of it all. He leaned forward and kissed Paul. Their lips pulsed. "Together?"

Daniel started a small rip at the top corner of the envelope. Paul's fingers joined his as they pulled the imagined cork from the bottle, both hoping for a genie inside. One single piece of paper was ready to tell their future. One slip of pressed wood imbued with all of their hopes and nearly every single dream they'd shared for the last two years. They understood, looking down at the envelope, both fearful of peeking inside, that this was only the first step of what would be a long journey. Should there be a journey. Otherwise, it was the last step for this path. It was an intoxicating mix of expectation and dread.

After what seemed an eternity, Paul pulled the letter from the counter and flipped it to study the type. Daniel held his breath. Paul's chest heaved as he read, then he closed his eyes as he placed the letter back on the island.

"Remember that little place over on the east side that you liked so much?" Paul asked. "The one with the old school, 2020s architecture?"

Daniel's brow furrowed. It was bad news. It had to be. Why else would Paul be changing the subject. He felt his lungs melt, sticky and slumping into his gut like ice cream on a hot summer day. Sickening in its sweetness and churning. The cone of his heart was hard but cracking, threatening to crumble completely.

"We should maybe put an offer in on it," Paul sighed.

It was fine. Paul was seeking an alternative to soften the blow. Something else he knew Daniel had set his heart on. So what if it had been hours of paperwork and interviews, months of hope and longing. They'd understood it was a long shot anyway. Plus, Daniel wasn't sure he was ready for that sort of massive change to his lifestyle anyway. He didn't think he could handle it, really. A massive change like that. At least that's what he told himself. Besides, it wasn't like they had exhausted every avenue.

Daniel's head flushed with a thousand scenarios, steps they could take, reassessments as to whether they even should. His eyes shot over all of their belongings as if appreciating them for the first time. The antique kitchen table had been passed down from his great grandparents from back when they were made of solid wood with chairs to match. Its corners were sharper than he remembered. He let his vision grace the low, hard edges of their coffee table, all the kickbacks and tchotchkes—too many of them really—strewn atop it, and finally, the sharp lines of the smile that had broken across Paul's face as he spoke. "We're going to need the room."

"We're approved?" Daniel asked, a dizzying combination of relief and disbelief colliding across his chest as all the beauty in those hard edges became corners needing softening.

"We're approved," Paul confirmed.

Daniel could not contain himself as he lifted Paul off the ground in his embrace. They were going to be parents. And though nearly two years would pass before they would hold their daughter, it would feel like no time at all.

Now, seconds felt like eternities. Not simply the dull whine of simulated night ticking towards 2am, but every moment of his separation from his family. Daniel knew it had turned him cold. He walked the Colony as a hollow husk of a man most days, save for when he adorned his friendly professionalism in his sessions, and, at night, he glimpsed fantasies of the mundane daily life he was missing. In his dreams, Paul had not aged a day. He had the same black hair, shortly cropped, with a mischievous cowlick that sent the locks at his widow's peak feathering out like the plumage of the grey crowned cranes they had seen on one of their many visits to Samantha's village in Ethiopia. His jawline was hard, but a soft stubble softened the edge and gave his smile a manly gentleness. And his smile: all ripe apples and wide as the Oldsmobile in his great great grandfather's photographs. Still, none of that compared to the electrified intensity of his eyes. They were storm clouds ready to burst with lightning. They were eager oceans waiting to swallow the world whole. In Daniel's dreams, Paul loved him unconditionally and no time had passed since their last embrace.

Samantha, though, had grown in leaps and bounds. Each night there seemed a need for another tiny notch on the doorframe in his mind. Daniel found himself modeling her after the older sister he had met: the one whom he had promised—through the translator app on his phone's earpiece—he would give young Sam a better life. Her skin was deep and smooth like a calm river at night, reflecting back the moonlight of her eyes from her soft umber cheeks. He felt his fingers, even in his sleep, practice through the memorized motions of doing black hair he had studied for months with his friend Rachel, even though, in reality, he had never really gotten to do her hair. In his dreams, Samantha was a ferocious little girl, an outspoken young woman. She had gone through a pink phase and a blue phase. She hated broccoli but adored carrots. And the tiny stuffed manta ray she kept hold of constantly had intensified her love of animals. Daniel and Paul would take her to the sanctuaries to see all of the birds and beasts they could and then sit with her at the long kitchen table and pour through books to point out pictures of all those creatures long since lost to extinction. Her favorite was the red fox, and she'd made Daniel promise her, if there happened to be one left, somewhere deep in an unknown wooden area, untouched and undisturbed, that she could take care of it and keep it safe. In his dreams, Samantha was everything, and when he woke, he felt such a deep loss sink into him he worried the weight would shift the entire Colony downward, send them all crashing back to the surface.

By midnight, Daniel had given up on pacing back and forth between his quarters and his office like a wayward ping pong ball leaping from the table and lost under the bench in the corner, ticking up and down between the floor and seat. That was all he was, he thought: a lost game piece ignored as the action raged on. He had only seen maybe six people over the last two hours, shadows slinking past the LED Moonlight to meld with the night and lift off to the Neutral Zone. He had never been there himself, at least not after it became what it became. During the first year or two locked inside the space, he had attempted to set up shop with his books and his papers there, trying to get lost inside words that swirled more than they swelled. That was back when the screens that lined every hallway and ceiling had shown an approximation of the weather going on below them. *To help our citizens adjust. To keep us connected to our home below.* They had even, for a short time, pumped a drizzle of water to mist down on people as they hurried through their daily routines whenever the screens showed rain, but the cleanup, waste, and overdrive of the water reclamation system had put an end to that. Not long after that, Alpha2 had decided to keep their world to a breezy, but not too windy, summer day followed by a crisp, cloudless summer night. *For morale.* The growing lawlessness of Ground Floor Zero had been overlooked as a much-needed outlet that would constrain any further resistance. Especially since the radio to land system had failed almost immediately and no one could contact their families. Especially since the population had been rounded up so swiftly—and months ahead of schedule—on land and hurried onto the decks so that too many expected souls were left beyond the airlocks. The only thing that had stopped an instant rebellion was the firm stance of the Guard and the mayor's reassurance that, "You are doing a great service for your loved ones left on land. Your sacrifice of the life you knew is what allows them to live on below us."

"Hey, Doc. Midnight stroll?"

"It's just Daniel," he said. Jessica had been a patient of his for about eight months around year two. He'd told her a hundred times he did not have a doctorate, not the way she was thinking, but now it was just easier to insist on his first name. It had actually been Daniel who suggested she apply to the Guard, seeing that she craved structure in her life. It seemed to have paid off.

"You know I can't call you by your first name, Doc," she said. "Just seems too informal."

Daniel tried to smile sincerely, but he was too out of practice. Except for when he donned his therapist persona, he rarely tried to control his face anymore. He waved his wrist toward the scanner to call the elevator.

"Not headed to the Neutral Zone, are ya, Doc?" Jenny asked, a sly smile spread across her lips. "Can't protect you there. No Guard allowed. At least not on duty, am I right?"

She let out a cackle that echoed down the corridors like a hurricane, picking up speed and velocity to smack Daniel from all sides.

"I'll be alright," he assured her. "Just doing some research. For the practice."

"Hey, man. To each their own and then some." The doors opened slowly, and Daniel stepped into the chute. "I hope you find what you're looking for."

He wasn't quite sure what to expect, but it certainly wasn't this. By all descriptions, the Neutral Zone was a flurry of chaotic frenzy. Black and sullen, a grimy silt settled over seedy handshake deals and discarded syringes and baggies. Each face saddled with the hard-earned lines of desperation: to sell; to buy; to feel; to forget. He had been told to imagine the darkest corners of the city below and magnify them to a three-block radius. Instead, what spread out before him was a series of make-shift booths amidst a barrage of shoppers like a flea market for every medicinal or carnal need.

He tapped the wall to activate the digital clock, but the screen remained black. Strange. He tried again, more forcefully this time, but the LED was unresponsive.

"No clocks here," the man in the booth closest the elevator called to him. His voice had a smooth roughness to it, like an oil slick coating a gravel driveway. He massaged his thick thumb and stubby fingers across his jaw as he sized Daniel up. "You get off on the wrong floor?"

Had he? Daniel wasn't sure. He had assumed this was where he'd find the young woman from earlier. But now, he wasn't even sure he wanted to find her. What was he getting himself into?

"Where you s'posedtobe, Bub?" He said "supposed to be" like it was one word, a catechism whose only response was meant to be "somewhere else."

"Uh." Daniel stammered as he attempted to regain his composure.

He uncoiled his serpentine spinal posture to seem as if he belonged. "Nowhere?"

It came out more of a question than he'd intended. The man's eyes tightened as he again surveyed Daniel. Daniel, in turn, thought it only appropriate to return the favor. He wasn't as tall as he positioned himself, not when comparing his torso to his belt line. He was using his booth to hide a crate or a step stool. And though his fingers were still fat and short, the appropriated rations that kept the Colony functioning and its citizens healthy had lowered his body mass substantially. He still carried himself as if he had more heft, but now his cheeks pinched in stark contrast to his bulbous nose and chin. He wore a modified version of the uniform—don't call it a uniform!—everyone was issued on Day 1 for when their own garments ripped or disintegrated with age or the impulse to conform to the new normal took over. It frayed at the shoulder from the removal of the sleeves. The tank top was inside out, displaying the seams proudly, and the pants had been pinched at the hip and wrapped across the front before they tucked into the elastic band.

"Look, man," he finally said, "I don't care what you Alphas get up to up there. But if you're here to grab your boy by the ear and cause some sort of ruckus 'cause he likes a little of the powder or the cooch, you need to keep that shit upstairs."

"I thought the rule of the land was 'anything goes.'" Daniel thought he'd found the perfect amount of mocking in his voice to garner respect.

"Anything but that," the man said, and, as if satisfied he'd played his role, turned away to leave Daniel to his own vices.

Aside from the occasional "hell no" or "fuck yes," the screams of ecstasy or exclamations of disbelief, the Neutral Zone was quieter than he'd expected. He held his breath and heard a low rumbling noise, like an engine turning over but stalled right before ignition. It took Daniel too long—he thought when he thought of that moment—to realize that sound was the din of voices muddling from booth to booth. That it was, indeed, a match struck but not yet sparking, kindling attempting to burn the whole house down, but stuck, instead, in the pit. All the voices combined to heat the air into a low hum like a chorus of scavengers waiting to devour whatever came their way, a choir of precocious children clamoring for more, more, more.

Daniel slid through the throngs, feeling himself surrounded, and, for the first time in years, sensed a flutter in his gut, a slight tingle on the back of his neck just below the hairline, as if from a too warm breath on a too cold day. There was a wonder to the Zone—one that Daniel did his best to prevent his eyes from absorbing in its entirety. A sense of freedom permeated the air, and he marveled at its existence within captivity. Or rather, *because* of captivity, he corrected himself. He was sure nothing like this could have ever happened on the ground, not since the surveillance drones had "cleaned up" the streets of New York or San Francisco or Bangladesh. Something about the finite walls made the danger seem necessary.

"Excuse me," Daniel said, bracing himself on the shoulder of a man twenty years his senior as he stumbled. The old man scowled, barely moving his head, and heaved himself free of Daniel's grip. When Daniel turned to see what had tripped him, another man stared blankly at him from the ground. He was perched on all fours, cocking his head slightly to the left as if trying to assess new information that confused more than it cleared. He wore what amounted to little more than a loin cloth diaper, a dusty brown fold of fabric wrapped just below his navel, and a matching collar around his neck to which a chain was sewn. No more than seventeen, he would have been just a child when they were locked inside.

A foot found purchase on the man's back, and Daniel followed the leg up to a petite woman well into her 40s. He thought he recognized her and prayed she had not been a patient. One hand held dried bits of something—Daniel guessed sweet potato from the tanned leather coloring—and she wrapped the leash tighter across her other palm. Daniel felt his mouth go slack as his eyes bounced between the pair.

"What?" She slinked closer and lifted herself to Daniel's ear. Her voice was smoky, thick and breathy, with tendrils that tried to wrap through his hair, around his neck. "He always wanted a puppy before this. Now, he gets to be one." She dropped a treat to the floor, and her pup leapt to devour it. She wrapped her free hand around Daniel's thigh and stretched in closer still. "What do you want to be?"

"Gay," Daniel squeaked. He had tried to give a polite decline, but it seemed the only word that would form.

The woman dropped away quickly and called over her shoulder. "Got another one for you, Gary." Her voice shifted so suddenly, Daniel wasn't even sure it was she who had spoken at first. What had, moments before, hung in the air like heat lightning was now brisk and clipped, like a diner waitress yelling code words to a sweat-drenched cook: "axle grease" for butter; "dirty water" for coffee. Daniel now recognized her from the Sub3 Waffle House. His face twisted into the awkward smile of an apple peel, stretched and thin and too long compared to the white flesh beneath, and he slipped away into the crowd, not wanting to wait around to see what Gary had in store.

Daniel wasn't a prude: he and Paul and spent their fair share of 2ams wrapped in studs and leather, dressed in more sweat than clothing, pulsing on an over-crowded dance floor. They had been predators, circling the trinkets that caught their mutual attention; and they had been prey, the two-for-one deal for the eagle-eyed tourist. So what if that woman's touch was the first he'd had in nine years? It didn't change who he was at his core. And that didn't make him a killjoy. He told himself he belonged in the Neutral Zone. He could blend. His body just needed a moment to catch up, and then he might be able to get somewhere.

He fell into a casual gait which mimicked the relaxed posture of those around him. Soon, he was able to tell the difference between the booths with only a quick glance from the corner of his eye. Most seemed legitimate if a bit sketchy. Tables were lined with clothing or extra rations or tech cobbled together from spare parts. Other areas, usually the spaces with drapes extending back to cordoned off imaginations, teemed with scantily clad people, calling and smiling as if they'd seen too many old movies. But that was part of the ploy. And the customers they attracted seemed to eat it up. The powder pushers were less obvious, smiling from behind tables strewn with books that ripped from their bindings, less worthy remnants of the world below, or bulging mounds of piecemeal fabrics no one had bothered to take a needle and thread to yet. It was their customers who always gave them away. Daniel immediately recognized their vacant stares, their need to be filled; each of them waiting there, ten miles above the surface, not quite ready to start falling down, hoping to float for just a little while longer. Most of the booths were on a barter system, but a few, particularly those whose proprietors dealt in flesh, were equipped with pirated scanners and cobbled together tech to form a unit transfer system.

"Perfectly legal. Perfectly safe," they swore to the other wide-eyed first timers timidly approaching the preening figures, eyes carving comfortable forms from their marble.

As they gain access to your entire account, Daniel thought.

He had wandered the floor for over an hour, he thought—it was hard to tell without the digital reminders programmed into the walls—but he had yet to see anywhere that could possibly be Nowhere; he'd had no glimpse of the lady in pink. Punks trumpeted around like a marching band. Subs waddled like ducklings behind their Doms. And every so often, a flurry of hands and tunics rippled, like dark petals opening, as the powder took hold and those very same leaves drifted to the ground to puddle in an all-too-temporary euphoric bliss.

Maybe he had misunderstood the message. Maybe it was all some joke, and they were laughing at him, the forty-something square wandering in Bedlam. It hadn't seemed like a joke: the prudence of it. The stealth in her gesture had felt intentional and sincere. Perhaps it was more a directive: a call to arms. Nowhere was Everywhere; Everywhere was Nowhere.

Besides which, he thought, *what sort of Truth could the children playing at adulthood—those stifled in the arrested development of Colony life—actually have to offer?* He tried to make himself believe it was research, that, for his practice, he needed to understand the mindsets of every subset on the inside.

A weight exploded out of him as he laughed at himself. He had not even realized he was holding so much tension in his chest. He wanted to howl loudly—an expression that nestled like a puzzle piece amongst the angst and the anger, the pleasure and the excitement of the Zone. He stifled his amusement and began to make his way toward the elevator.

Then he noticed it. Embroidered on the fabric overhang of a booth in shaky and thread barely darker than the burnt gray, almost imperceptible unless the light hit it just so, unless the person looking knew what they were looking for. A line shot like an arrow across the center as two others bowed and curved, above and below, to join it at its tips. A circle nestled inside them, centered, and three alternating triangles spread above and below. It looked like the extrapolated angles of something organic and common. It looked like the full expression of the young woman's broken arrowhead, which, Daniel now realized, was an even more archaic weapon: an eye.

The booth keeper paid no mind to Daniel's cautious approach. Arms swimming in black fabric and folded across his chest, a nebulous hood surrounding his face, he stood at languid attention even as he faded quickly into the darkness. Daniel hovered before him, his fingers skipping across the rough fabric swatches laid out there. *Canvas,* Daniel thought. *Probably from mess hall bags once filled with rices or dried beans.* Something caustic had dyed them black, almost as if they'd been scorched. Crudely illustrated garments, each similar to the cloak of the shopkeeper, rested between the cloths.

Daniel cleared his throat and tried to meet the man's averted gaze. "I'm looking for Nowhere."

"I sell garments," the man said without looking. His voice was feathered steel, that of a feeble man who had been hardened by time. It held the rasp of unexpected news, the grit of growth by force. "That a book or something?" He would have been a feeble man in another life. Here, he had adopted the strength that came naturally to others, wearing it like a winter coat to swallow him but keep him warm.

Daniel lingered, hoping for some secret word to be revealed, to grant him passage to Nowhere, but the tailor's eyes stayed fixed somewhere in the distance. Or, rather, *on* the distance. They seemed as unfocused as they were intent. He sighed. Wrong again. He lingered for a moment, willing the path to reveal itself, but the night carried on without him. He rapped his knuckles on the table to say goodbye—to trigger a magical passage—and steadied his course back toward the exit.

The wonder of the Neutral Zone was fading, and Daniel suddenly saw the vile and debris. The orgiastic puddles of people lovingly quieted to corners were heaving mounds of fluids and flesh, dripping venom from a massive maw, desperate to find enough powder to dry itself out. Sellers were swindlers; as serpentine as any above-the-board capitalists as they writhed around their prey, squeezing tighter and tighter and promising their own necessity to breathe. At least the sex work was legitimate and to be taken at face-value. What you saw was what you got, and they made certain you saw it all. And it, occasionally, even provided pleasure.

He noticed so much more now that the magic trick was exposed. There was such desperation in the digital role-play which surrounded him. So much putting on of airs amidst the hedonistic fear and lust. And that damn emblem.

He'd seen the eye on at least five other booths now. Some of them embroidered, like the first—the artist's hand given away by the thickened jumble of thread on one line or the other—while others were painted on or carved into wood, all of them unique; all of them the same. He had stopped by the first couple booths to try his luck again, but each time had been met with the same puzzled look, the same annoyed dismissal.

Daniel felt his resolve evaporate. He had been so sure he was onto something. Though, if he were honest with himself, he had no idea of what. He wasn't even sure why he'd attempted to interpret the note; what lies he was expecting to be exposed. What lies he was willing to expose for himself. But nearly nine years of solitude would do that to anyone. Hell, most people were chomping at the bit for some sort of adventure. *Imagine life in a three-mile radius,* Daniel chuckled to himself. *Four if you're lucky.* If that had been the pitch, he imagined the folks clamoring to apply for the chance to live in the Ten Mile City would have been vastly different. Home and monotony could only bring complacency when there was still an entire world within reach. The world of the Colony was finite, and, despite the onslaught of LED screens at every turn, surprisingly dark. He was actually looking forward to his quarters, his tiny uncomfortable bed.

A firm hand gripped his shoulder, the thumb and index finger applying pressure to the tendon in his neck, threatening more at any moment. "I hear you're asking after us."

It was a statement, not a question, but Daniel felt compelled to reply. "I'm not... I wasn't..." He stammered as the man took him into the crook of his firm arm and diverted his path from his beeline toward the elevator, left and then left again, back into the dingy market. Daniel tried to see who had taken hold of his night, but the man's cloak shrouded him in secrecy.

"No, you've been asking," the man said. He sounded almost jovial. He was enjoying this. "And, thing is, we're more about seeing than hearing. Which makes this even more ironic."

"What's ironic?" Daniel asked, but the answer came in burlap and blackness.

"Follow me," the man said as if he had a choice. Daniel felt his excitement return, coupled with a stiff anxiety, as he was pushed forward into the abyss.

B*uilding a Better Tomorrow... For Everyone!*

It had been over a month since the columns began to plant themselves in half-mile intervals that straddled the Chattahoochee River on the northwest side of Atlanta. Giant pillars of steel and titanium and concrete, they stretched nearly as far into the ground as they did skyward and sprung like crocuses from the harsh southern winter to send frigid shadows of chilled air in slowly creeping sways from west to east as they attempted to counteract the sun. The city, and 46 other cities like it, were left with rippling goosebumps as if filled with restless ghosts, as if too many people were crossing over the graves left seeded by the massive tombstones. Someone had already spray painted a black X across the construction signage and scribbled *Stairway to Heaven* above what would become the elevator access points.

"It looks like the Tower of Babel," Paul said as they bounded up 75 to meet the realtor.

They had seen the newsreels and video footage of the other Colonies, in various states of construction, but having the columns physically there was a totally different experience. They loomed as half mile markers, a chess game for gods, checkmate just around the corner. Atlanta should have been the 13th Colony, but the state congressional fund had shot down Bill FC13 on a largely partisan split. Despite all tangible evidence to the contrary, the contrarians when it came to climate change were vast, and somehow, all ended up in politics. The City of Atlanta—the City Too Busy Sprawling to Hate or to Love—was never one to miss an opportunity at expansion though and had approved a tax that would start construction of the Colony only a few months behind the others.

"This Colony is for everyone!" Mayor Lewis had parroted as she cut the ribbon and ceremoniously broke ground on the first pillar. "Those who reside within and those who stay on the ground!"

It had taken some doing—nearly a year and a half—but Rep. Collins and her team had done enough to convince the public that the columns and adjacent Floating Cities were a necessary solution. "In fact," she droned, "they are the only solution we have left," with her stiff hyperbole intact. She maintained the Colony represented hope for everyone. The movement of nearly 4 million people per Colony—down from 5 million and still higher than what the actual number would be—for only fifteen years would spread the resources and offset the carbon footprint of each major city long enough to give the planet a chance to catch up, to give Earth a moment to heal. Paul had urged Daniel to apply for a family position in the sky.

"They're gonna need therapists," he said. "You're on the list of preferred professions. And they've already got some of the best educators from around the state on board. Wouldn't it be an amazing place to raise our little BTB?"

Ever since they'd received their approval letter from the adoption agency, their lives had centered around their Baby To Be. Paul was already falling headfirst into full stay-at-home-dad mode, and Daniel smirked as he averted his eyes briefly from the road to look at his partner while trying not to glance toward the bulging and raised fabric at his midriff. "My sympathy weight," Paul called it. "You never know, you know, the birth parent of our child could be pregnant right now."

"You still think it's a good idea to live up there?" Daniel asked. "A whole city perched on these chicken legs and surrounded by ozone?"

"I do." Paul smiled and rolled down the window to give him a better view upward to where the columns narrowed and disappeared into the clouds. "But I always wanted to be a Lost Boy when I was little. Flying around the sky without a care in the world. This is the next best thing. Plus it's only for fifteen years."

"Then why are we even going to close on this house?"

"Because you love it. And we can afford it. There's three years until the Colony's ready, and we'll need a place to come back to once the experiment is over. And maybe we rent it out for some passive income while we're there." Paul was matter of fact, as if desire necessitated actualization. "Also, you haven't even filled out the application to move up there, so we have to keep our bases covered."

"Over half the region has already applied. It's a long shot anyway."

"So what's the harm in turning in the paperwork?"

Daniel was an advocate for change, but within, he was learning, a very narrow set of parameters. He had always prided himself on his adaptability. At 18, he had moved to Atlanta on his own to study psychology at Tech. And he'd done that entire year in Berlin when he barely knew more than conversational German. But all of that was charted territory; unknowns he could research because they'd already been figured out by someone else much smarter and more adaptable than him. The Colonies were something completely new, something utterly virgin and unknowable. The idea of leaving the surface for fifteen years, even with his husband and their would-be child, terrified him. These were the types of missions astronauts trained for years to accomplish, not meant for swarms of lay people to try their hand at like ants storming a picnic. Hell, even ants had a more structured life than what was supposedly being offered. How could he not be scared?

"Besides," Paul said as he rolled up the window, "'Space Baby' will be a hell of a thing to put on a college application one day."

Daniel knew Paul had set his mind to it. He knew there was no getting out of it. So when the day came--abruptly and months earlier than expected--for the men and their daughter to ascend, he could not believe it when Paul and Sam did not appear in their family quarters. So what if the argument they'd had the night before had been so intense? Did it really matter what Daniel had said--screamed really--when fifteen years of their lives together hung in the balance? Could Paul have been so impulsive? So cold? So heartless? So done?

Paul groaned in exasperation and shoved the papers from the table. Another dead end. He should have been used to them—it seemed everything was, at the very least, a dirt road into the ocean—but this lead had held so much promise. He turned off the crank generator and listened to the fans in his laptop whir and wind down. The network, or what was left of it anyway, was patchy and filled with sporadic bursts of hope amongst all the false information. He coughed hard as he bent to pick up his notes and caught himself on the desk as his lungs threatened to seize.

"Figs and toast, Dad!"

Paul heard a thud as Manta dropped her pack to the floor and rushed to his side. Her hand was gentle on the small of his back, but he could feel the power in her grip as her other hand guided his shoulder to stand.

She let her eyes dart around the office. She was so rarely allowed inside. Except for when Paul attempted to use the old computer her other father had left behind—and he usually did that while she was asleep or out on the hunt—the room was kept closed-off and sacred, a shrine to the man who would one return to clear away the cobwebs and dust that had accumulated in its untouched sanctity.

"Language, young lady," Paul wheezed, and Manta stood back with a defiant smirk. She had seen more than any ten-year-old girl should have to. She had had to do more than anyone should ever be asked to do. But she had taken it all in stride. Children were remarkably resilient that way. Still it broke Paul a little when he thought about how this was the only life she'd ever known.

He had done his best to give her a normal upbringing—as normal as an upbringing could be during the end of the world. Archery practice was intrinsically tied with mathematics: *Hit the third post from the left.*—or—*If there are five targets and you miss three, how many targets do you hit?* English and foraging went hand in hand. *And how do we spell mushroom?* Science was handled by knife skills. *The neck bone's connected to the rib bone. Be sure not to puncture the stomach so you don't contaminate the meat.* At three, she couldn't pronounce her h's, and so her name had been formed. But by five, she could count to twenty-five before spearing a hare with an arrow from thirty yards. By seven, she could skin and prep the rabbit in under twenty minutes. Those were their happy times together, both father and daughter learning survival skills as he tried to show no fear. He tried not to think about the darker times.

"I'm almost eleven!" Manta exclaimed.

"Oh, are you, Princess?" Paul mocked her to hide the wince as his lungs recalibrated from the dusty air in Daniel's seldom-used office. "I hadn't realized. You're practically an adult. No need for birthday celebrations, right?"

"It's still three months away." Manta folded her arms across her chest. She was as stubborn as Daniel. Paul wished she could have really known him. "I'm sure we can figure out some reason to celebrate. I got two hares today and a heap of mushrooms. I almost had a boar, but I wasn't fast enough. But I saw one. So that means they're back. We can celebrate that."

"I will always celebrate you." Paul cheesed, and Manta laughed at the saccharine honesty of it. Her laugh, the twinkle of a waltz from a jewelry box, warmed Paul in ways he had never dreamed possible before.

She was tall for a ten-year-old, Manta was, even for one who was almost eleven. Her limbs were like Black Cohosh, long and lanky and born anew each Spring. They carried her lithely through the Georgia mountain underbrush. And when the sunlight hit her cheeks, Paul saw a glint of quartz in the rich forest loam, ready to explode with so much life it both surprised and invigorated him. She was a daughter of the new Earth as much as she was his.

"How about we celebrate tonight?" Paul smiled.

Manta's eyes widened, two of the brightest stars against a midnight sky, as she released her soft curls from her tied fabric headband. "Did you find him?"

Paul did his best to mask the pain in his eyes as he shook his head from side to side. "But I did find something. Go grab a couple tomatoes from Daddy Dan's garden. Let's get dinner going before it gets too dark."

Since before she was old enough to understand, Paul had told Manta stories of Daniel: her brave other father who had been lost in the Great Wave but was—even today—doing all he could to make his way back to her. He was tall, and he was jovial, and he was as compassionate as Paul was focused. It was Daniel who had given her the stuffed manta ray she kept in her room: the one bit of fabric that would never be cut and swatched and repurposed as her body grew and their needs expanded. It was Daniel who had started the garden that kept them fed when the animals were sparse, and the heat had dried up all the flowers and fungi.

Though she had never met him—not that she could remember anyway—

Daniel was as much a part of her life as Paul. He was the sassafras leaves that had cured them both when the deer meat had spoiled and inflamed their stomachs. He was the black bear that had scared off the marauders from taking their cabin while she and Paul hid inside below the darkened windows. And, though she hadn't told Paul about the incident, she was sure he would tell her that Daniel was the branch that had miraculously appeared for her to grip when she lost her footing on a hunting trail and nearly plummeted down the side of the mountain. She understood the hours Paul would spend each month winding up the generator to power up his computer, and the hope upon hope he had for some new piece of information, some bulletin or lead, that would bring Daniel home. He held his breath in the dust-filled room for any news of the Colonies. He prayed to whatever gods were left for the word to spread that those on high had returned to regain control of the ground. The truth was it had been years since any signals had actually been active. But he refused to give up hope. Manta joined in the wish for Daniel's return but not for any change in the world. It was, after all, the only one she had ever known. She liked it. The solitude bred closeness. The wild spawned adventure.

She chose the two beefiest tomatoes she could find, the purple red of their skin both firm and fragile in her palms.

"Thank you for your fruit," she whispered. She'd heard Paul say it once, and it felt only right each time she came to harvest.

She noticed the cucumbers were coming along nicely and hoped that the apples they had saved—even though it was hard to not ravage their sweet, honeyed flesh—were fermented enough to make a new batch of vinegar. She'd only had real pickles a few times, but she thought of them often: the sour tang that sparked like lightning bugs across her tongue, the sweet spice that exploded in layers like dahlia blooms in early summer. She remembered the way her lips puckered when she first tried one and how her dad had burst with laughter as he placed his own pursed lips on her forehead.

Paul had already stoked the fire and speared two of the rabbits she'd brought home to the rotisserie. Their red muscles sizzled and popped with moisture and were beginning to gray at the edges. The hares were smaller than she would have liked, but it was early in the season still, and soon the woods would be hopping with tufts of their silver-white fur. She placed the tomatoes on the stump beside Paul and squatted to stare deep into the raging fire.

She imagined the flames were a lot like the Great Wave, leaping and sudden and all-consuming. But, where the fire was contained within a circle of stones, the Wave paid no mind to spatial constraints, moving where it deemed necessary, carving out new worlds in its wake. Paul had promised to take her to Atlanta one day to see the ocean, but it was over a three day's walk, and he didn't like to leave the cabin unattended for longer than a few hours even though it had been over a year since the last travelers had happened across their home as they searched for remnants of what they called "civilized society" and stated that their "hunt must continue." Manta had not been able to control her laughter as she removed their empty cups of dandelion tea. Food, shelter, and good company. Wasn't that the definition of civilization? She was still giggling as she and Paul waved while they passed over the horizon.

A branch shifted in the fire and broke Manta's gaze.

"So what'd you find?" she asked.

Paul's lips curled like kudzu across his face, and he held up a finger as he leapt to go inside. Manta settled on a stump and leaned back to take in the sunset through the trees, its neon blues and yellows streaked the ordinary greens and browns of the forest with the magic of coming night. Paul told her that, once upon a time, before the Wave and the Break when the composition of chemicals in the air were different, the sunsets were even more beautiful with kaleidoscopic tangerine and fuchsias, but even now Manta could not imagine something more beautiful than the space between the dog and the wolf.

Her father emerged triumphantly from the house, presenting a platter as if it contained all the extravagance in the world. And it did. A golden honeycomb still dripping with nectar rose like a mighty oak around a jumble of pecans soaked in the stuff. Marta's eyes widened as she reached for a praline and Paul snatched the plate away.

"Not until after dinner," he said.

Paul tried to be firm, but Manta knew his weakness was her smile. If her lip quivered just enough to parrot the shaky legs of a newborn foal, trembled in excitement and wonder, she could get most anything she wanted.

"Fine. One. But the rest after we eat."

The honey-hardened nut weighed heavy on her tongue, and she wondered how long it could rest there exciting her taste buds with a wildflower field of sweetness before she bit to release the earthy dust of the pecan. Honey was such a rare treat, but more and more bees were returning to the area with each passing season. Soon, they would be able to swim in it if they wanted. Manta could create her own ocean of the stuff.

"What was that?" Paul asked, alarmed.

"I just bit the nut," Manta said around it. She tried not to swallow, wanting to keep the flavor alive inside her for as long as possible.

Paul held a finger to his lip and Manta fell into his seriousness, swallowing hard and immediately missing the taste. The soft crack of a twig snapping in the distance echoed in the sudden silence of dusk. Leaves rustled without the wind.

"Probably just a squirrel or something," Manta tried to assure her dad. She'd been out there hunting all day and had not seen anything other than the critters of the wood. Surely, she would have noticed people passing through or ravagers if they were there. But something in the sound worried Paul who was much more accustomed to the differences between man-made and natural.

A moment later, a high-pitched whoop sounded followed by guttural growls and fast running sprints through the brush. Paul and Manta burst into their own immediate action.

"Get inside," Paul commanded.

From his position on the floor, he craned his neck to peek through the window. He made himself as small as possible. He hoped the whites of his eyes would go unnoticed.

"What's happening?" Manta whispered as he held up a hand to silence her.

He counted six men and two women, ranging in age from what seemed to be fourteen to maybe sixty. They clamored around the fire, pulling half cooked meat directly from the rod and downing it in massive bites. One of the younger men bit a tomato and spit the mouthful into the fire before tossing it over his shoulder. Another retrieved it and shared it with one of the women. The pralines and honeycomb stuck to the fingers of the others. They seemed, at least for now, more interested in food than stealing shelter. It was possible they'd eat and move on.

Manta had stationed herself on the opposite wall where her bow and quiver were already at the ready. Her bay was quiet: even the birds that normally hopped to peck the beetles and worms that crawled out of the soil as the cool night set in over the garden were staying clear of the ravagers. Paul kept one hand trained on a pistol. He only had two bullets, but usually the threat of a firearm alone was enough to sway the situation.

"Eight total," he whispered. "They know we're in here, but they're staying near the fire with the food. Maybe that's all they want."

"Maybe."

Paul heard the quiver of hope to fear to hope to fear in her voice and closed his eyes to center himself. They'd promised her birth parents they'd give her a better life, and here she was, a child defending her home with potentially deadly force. But where most of the Horn of Africa was underwater, she was alive. She *could* protect her home, her self. *There is that,* he told himself.

The scavengers outside looked feral in the firelight. He searched their clay-streaked faces for remnants of humanity. The blood-soaked red of Georgian soil covering them made it seem like the earth itself had swallowed them up whole before excising them all for their violence. They were wild creatures equipped with only the malice of survival, the destructive fire of Prometheus. They were cats staring down a canary. And he, he told himself, was the coal mine that would claim them all. *If it comes to that.*

He watched them carefully as he tried to break down the individual elements of the pack. The eldest man, the bushy white of his beard stained with rust, seemed to be in control. A woman Paul imagined to be of a similar age—it was difficult to determine under the makeup of red clay— snatched the honeycomb from a younger guy with a large scar on his left cheek and handed it to the boy of fourteen. He was small for his age, but the elongated limbs of puberty had taken hold, manipulating his stature into a Salvador Dali painting. To his left, another man—thin and sharp with hair matted to his chin, a wet rat in the flames—reached to pull a leg from a hare. Two other men—one a long-billed pelican whose nose hooked to the left to cast bulbous shadows, the other a kangaroo hopping east to west to an unheard music—stood a few feet from the fire looking outward as if on guard while the other woman, younger and blond beneath the clumps of dirt, moved back and forth with bits of meat for each of them, nibbling off her own portions as she went. All of them looked sanguine and wild beneath the darkening night.

Nine years ago these were just people with jobs and homes and daily rituals. They were grocers or lawyers or students. They brushed their teeth, and struggled with monthly bills, and smiled when they saw the chalk drawings left by children on the sidewalks. Paul may have even known one of them somehow. Or, at least, someone who knew their cousin. Everyone in the South was connected through at least one cousin.

The Wave had changed all of that.

It had happened so slowly and so suddenly. Decades of warnings erased by a sudden shift in tectonic plates, a release of gasses, and an ever-threatening storm season. The melt, the wind, and the tsunami as the ocean tried to reclaim what it had birthed. Whole cities were washed out in a breath, and suddenly Atlantis didn't seem so farfetched. Governments had tried to carry on—the US, having lost all the metropolises along the east and west coasts moved to Chicago—but the destruction was too great, the loss in infrastructure and resources to vast to overcome. People were left to fend for themselves.

Most did. They found community that had been lost to centuries of economics. They discovered neighbors were allies and the soil of their yards worked as well for eggplant as it did for grass. They mourned their losses, and they tried to carry on.

But when the newly submerged reactors at the nuclear plants failed, a little more than a year following the Wave, everything changed once more. The waters absorbed the bulk of the radiation, but the fish were no longer a food source; salt could not be harvested for preservation of meats; the water could not be boiled to palpability. Those who weren't as fortunate as Paul and Manta were driven hungry and then mad, though not always in that order.

"I'm only counting seven now. I think they're leaving."

A sharp *thwang* sliced the air into two opposing forces: the before and after along the sharp divide of life and death. It took a century for Paul to turn to see Manta standing, fingers still firm at her chin, her bow string a hummingbird wing as furious as her expression.

"He was going for Dad's garden." Her eyes pierced the dusk as sharply as her arrow.

He'd trained her to be an excellent shot. He knew she'd gone straight for the jugular, taken him down quickly with as little pain and sound as possible. He knew that bought them some time, but it would only be a few moments until...

The banshee cry joined the far away croon of a heron to briefly silence then excite all the night creatures to action. Cicadas and katydids and whippoorwills rose to provide the soundtrack to the coming mêlée. Manta nocked another arrow as Paul readied his pistol. They had learned early to take it to them first if a fight needed to happen. It gave them the upper hand. It helped to prevent destruction to their home. It was a last resort.

Paul swallowed down the fear that raged in his throat as Manta slipped silently through the front door and replace it with awe of her bravery. He watched as the ravagers tumbled toward the front of the house and moved himself through the side door. They had them cornered. Their only place to run was away.

"There doesn't need to be any more violence," Paul called.

The men turned swiftly, and the wailing woman silenced briefly giving Paul enough time to see the body of the young man—a boy really, not too much older than his own daughter—at her knees, his head cupped into her lap. Dali's great elephants now melting like clocks. Paul steeled himself. Death was the natural outcome of war and the ravagers attacked first. He had to keep reminding himself of that.

"Dad, watch out!"

Arms surrounded Paul from behind, slamming down on his elbows with such surprise force the gun shot to the ground. The Patriarch of the ravaging clan squeezed and pulled as the Pelican, the Rat, and the Kangaroo took advantage of the distraction to rush toward Manta. Her very own menagerie. She trained her arrows just above their kneecaps, hitting the fleshy part of their legs with a hawk's precision, her talons slicing through to stun mobility. The Rat went down, clutching at his new appendage in terror, but the other two men kept their pace. Another arrow whizzed between them as they spread to flank the young girl.

Paul squirmed to break free, ramming his head back toward his captor just as sharpened teeth found their way to the tendons in his neck. The Scarred Man stumbled to pick up the pistol, but Paul's managed to kick it away. He pulled both feet from the ground and kicked off from the man in front of him, pushing back with enough force to ram the Patriarch into the side of the house. He felt the wooden shingles of the cabin slam in undulating waves through the old man as the breath shot out of him from the impact. He was free. He left his assailants, still attempting to catch their breath, to rush toward Manta.

She was crouched between the Pelican and Kangaroo, her bow steady as she moved it back and forth, keeping the men six feet away. When she saw Paul coming, she turned her back on the Pelican and let her spear fly to the Kangaroo's right foot. Paul's leg swiped the Pelican's just before he leapt, sending him face first to the ground. Paul placed a knee on his back to keep him down as Manta nocked another arrow.

"Stop!" Everyone turned to the Matriarch. Her voice was grated across barbed wire—ancient and rarely used but a forceful deterrent when called upon. Her palms were turned out like white flags. She tried to stand up straight, as if she were remembering what it was like to be human, an animal trapped and mimicking her captor. Even the wailing woman ceased her noise, sobbing quietly as she continued to cup Dali's head. "Leave!" she commanded.

Paul raised a hand to stop her as Manta aimed her sites toward the woman. The snap of arrows sounded as the men broke the bolts that had struck them close to their wounds. Scar pulled Dali into his arms. No more words were spoken as the ravagers limped into the tree line, the Matriarch nodding to Manta's raised bow as she brought up the rear. The circus defeated, it packed its rings and left for better grounds, somewhere the townsfolk had pennies to spare, luck to try at the ring toss, and were still enamored by magic.

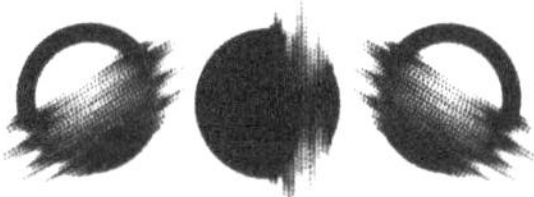

"You look disappointed, Dad."

Paul felt his lips slip inside one another as he eyed the darkened trees for any sudden movement, any swift retaliation. He wanted to tell her how much he wished she had had a normal childhood, not these days of violent reckoning patched, like old jeans, atop the toil and the need and the want. How he hoped for a life for her where death was not so immediate, so slow and so quick. So normal. He watched her settle into Daniel's tan chair with a worn-out copy of *Alice Through the Looking Glass*. Her long legs swung over the arm, and the candlelight flickered its halo across her face.

As soon as the ravagers had passed deep into the trees, Manta had dropped her demeanor nearly as quickly as her bow. Her childhood joy had returned so immediately, it seemed as much an act as her warrior mode: something she wore when the mood struck her, when what the world had become demanded it.

"I'm not. I just..."

"He was going for Dad's garden. They would have destroyed it."

"I know."

This was all Manta had ever known. All she could know. The violence of daily life was as common as the sun, as milkweed or mosquitoes. Manta flipped through her book to find the roughly dog-eared page—one fold amongst so many that had accumulated there—and escaped to the world she preferred. That she could so deftly move from the kill to the quiet disconcerted him. He watched her read and prayed to whatever gods were left that he could one day show her a better version of what life once was.

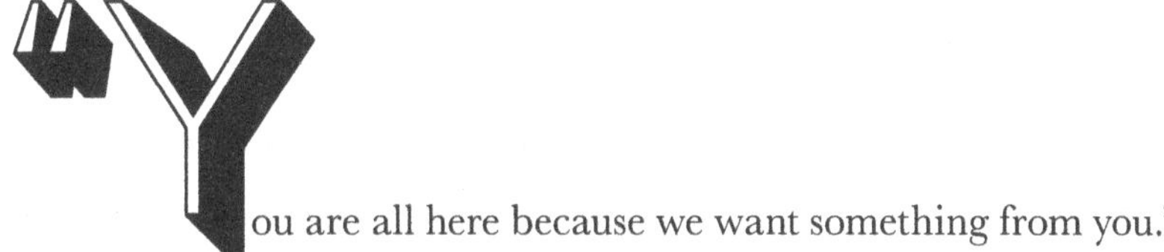

ou are all here because we want something from you."

Daniel recognized the soft trill in the woman's voice, but the burlap sack still blocked his view. Her location sent a waffle of slightly less dark around the black of the twine the way light reflected off the sinewed muscles of a leopard on the prowl. His new friend had guided him here and pushed him down to anxiously fumble until he found the seat of a hard metal chair. His grip stayed firm on his shoulder although Daniel had not put up a fight.

"Everyone wants something from everyone," she continued like Jesus finding his way to the mound, like Athena spilling out from Zeus. "What sets us apart from those that run the Colony is that we will tell you so directly."

A murmur wove through the crowd like a river meeting resistance before carving a serpent. As the sound mixed with the not-too-distant rumble of the Neutral Zone it was impossible for Daniel to tell if it was an enclave of fifteen or fifty. The twist of his head as he angled to parse together the puzzle pieces of his view was met by a tightened grip on his clavicle.

"We have new souls amassed with us tonight, people who can help our cause, but—as is our custom—they will remain masked for this meeting. This allows us to speak freely without fear of retribution. This allows them to make their own decisions on whether to join us or not, free from the pressures of societal need."

Daniel stifled a laugh, nearly choking as he forced the lilts of humor back into his lungs. As with any society, it seemed the counterculture movement had found new means to take root in the dingier layers of community, writhing there, the amalgamation of sweat and sex and drugs pulling up from the dance floor. Even those who decried xenophobia needed some "other" to fight. This was different than the Apost of years past, but, Daniel was certain, would turn out the same way.

He imagined the young woman. Her bright pink sweater meant to evoke a sense of safety and innocence only served to make her stand out in the sea of dismal tones that banged the shoreline rocks, never quite clean no matter how the currents forced their way over the fabric. She stood, somewhere ahead of Daniel, probably at a podium of some sort that was starting to evoke a pulpit, spouting off the same introduction she used for every meeting, one that was meant to be unscripted to fit with the freedom of the movement, but had been parroted so often the words fell out like bulbs on string lights, one after the other, each needed to complete the circuit.

"Fawn?" the woman was saying. "Will you speak in freedom; will you tell in truth?"

Daniel was surprised to hear a gruff rumble in the affirmative in place of the nimble beauty the moniker invoked. The man's voice was low in volume and in tone, the distant moan of a ghost cursed by the lockstep repetition of unending habit. But weren't they all those ghosts? Every person in the Colony spent each day repeating the one that came before, even more so than they had done on the surface. It was required for the efficiency necessary to keep the Colony running. Rats in a cage in the sky, they were. A well-oiled machine ticking minutes into every second lived.

Fawn, he realized, was a code name.

"Thank you, Adrasteia," Fawn said. Adrasteia—the Greek goddess of rebellion. Quaint, if a bit obvious. So *Fawn*, Daniel realized, was most likely

Faun. That made more sense. Daniel could picture the voice spilling from the hairy jowls of a satyr, rich in excess and desire. "We," he continued, "are the Watchers. The Omnipotent Eye."

"We speak in freedom. We tell in truth."

Daniel's shoulders stiffened as the collective voice surged around him. Why had he come? They were children playing at magic, hoping black capes and top hats and a little sleight of hand would bring them power.

Faun continued the mantra. "We are the Seekers of Justice; the Archeologists of Lies."

"We speak in freedom. We tell in truth."

Whatever lies Daniel had felt, gnawing at the back of his mind, batting his gut like moths against a streetlamp, would remain buried, covered here amidst the partial relics of newfound religion. Tablets translated to pomp and circumstance in place of understanding. The hallmark of a people in need. He felt a smirk stretch his face and was grateful for the burlap that blocked his amusement even while cursing it for staying his exit.

The Aposts of a few years ago may have borrowed their name from religion, but their practice was simple anarchy. Driven by presumptions—though often true—of class and caste, they destroyed two weeks' worth of crops or overloaded circuits or promoted the removal of chips. By the time they realized it was only they who would suffer, they were in too deep. They went hungry for a month while the Alphas continued to dine and their friends worked overtime in the fields. The managing engineers relaxed as the mechanics rushed about in a frenzy to replace screens and lights and circuitry. They removed their only means of commerce alongside their ability to be tracked and failed at bartering with the unamused faces in the mess halls. The Guard had been instructed to let them be their own destruction; no use in making martyrs. And as the rest of the Subs began to turn on them, the Aposts clamored for any sense of underlying purpose. They landed on the communications issues that had plagued the Colony since soon after the doors were sealed. All the promises of regular tete-a-tetes with their kin on the land had been squashed. Word from the Alphas was an irregularity in the satellite connection had occurred and, as they waited for the people on the ground to perform repairs, the lines and equipment must remain open for governmental communication. "But don't worry," the mayor had proclaimed, "I've received word from Below and all of your relatives and friends are happy and proud of the work you are doing here."

The Haptic Mind Map was rushed into production testing to quell the desire to reconnect with the ground. Once Daniel had fixed its major flaw and Ground Floor Zero had given way to the Neutral Zone, the rebellion was finished, fizzling out like flattened Coca-Cola on a too hot summer day. Everyone had expected a second wave to come, and here it was: a parlor trick of ritual and inaction.

"For nearly nine years," Adrasteia was saying, "we have lived in this tomb. We know now that we will die here. No one, in six years' time, will return to the surface. We will not embrace again our loved ones we left behind. We will not till and sow the red soil of Earth. We have become the sacrifices of the planet, and when the last of us burns we will be no more. So now we band together to watch, to learn, and to discover why. In freedom. In truth. We ask now for a report of your findings. We ask those new here to listen with open hearts and minds. Absorb what you can and leave if you must."

One by one the people spoke.

Dionysus reported a disparity in crops moving up versus down. "I've seen it with my own eyes," he promised, "while working the fields. Though there are fewer people inhabiting the Alpha levels, more cases of fresh produce are packed to go there than to our much more highly populated Subs. We must do something!" His voice was ardent, raising in pitch as he progressed.

Adrasteia remained calm. "We watch, we learn, and we inform. The time for action has not yet arrived. We must gather all we can to know when and how to properly strike."

Hephaestus, a low-ranking engineer, had heard whispers of Alpha members taking unsanctioned treks to the surface. "They leave us here, praising us for our sacrifices, screaming their solidarity, and yet they leave to visit the ground. To breathe air that has not been recycled by machines. To embrace their children and feel the actual sun on their faces."

"Then it is our job," Adrasteia replied, "to watch and to learn when and how these trips occur. Only then can we know the truth. Only in truth can we demand freedom."

And on and on. Demeter and Apollo reporting rumors that the seed crop was becoming strained in its lack of diversity, each new harvest yielding less than the one before. Eris stating the medical offices were watching a slow growth of a new and unknown disease. Persephone relaying that three more of the Dreamers had moved from stasis to the pyres. A laundry list of fearmongering, gossip, and grievances. The Watchers—that's what Adrasteia had called her gathering of souls—seemed to simply need a place to speak their stresses, to cease their anxieties through expulsion. *But that can quickly grow into outright conspiracy theory,* Daniel thought. Laundry line words and like minds combining to create falsehoods as real to them, and thus to the entire Colony, as their own flesh and bone. Daniel wanted no part in it.

He settled back in his seat and crossed his leg over his knee as he cupped his hands in his lap, taking on his best concerned therapist pose. But behind the itchy twine of the sack, he closed his eyes and let his mind wander.

Sometimes he had nightmares about Paul moving on, about the daughter who would not know him. He saw himself, over a decade older, testing his sky legs on the ground like a wobbly sailor after too long at sea chasing his elusive white whale. It was the same feeling he'd get while riding the escalators up at Hartsfield-Jackson International Airport, escaping from the hungry maw of the earth like Persephone returning home in the Spring. Only, as the crowds behind the cordoned off line—grandpas in wheelchairs with bobbing heads jarred awake by the roaring of jets outside, newlyweds returning home from days of sandy beaches and nights of honey to embrace their friends and future lovers, rambunctious toddlers hopscotching on the tiled floor and attempting to break past the ropes as Mommy cleared the landing—all of them embraced and dispersed with the business travelers who expected no welcome, he's left standing there alone. No disaffected teenager who has only seen him as the digital ghost of photographs. No tentative smile of the man he'd married—grayer now at the temples—hoping amongst hope the spark was still there.

Or, worse yet, the dream in which they were there, standing still and statuesque as the sea parted.

Samantha, bright and full and beautiful, looking right through him in the way that only teenagers and house cats could do, like she had been expecting something better, some god served up on a seahorse or a half-shell. Something that had yet to appear. And Paul, an old, jagged pain that curved to hatred in his eyes, like sand can become a pearl, hardened and perfect and iridescent, as he speaks.

"You left us," he accuses. "We only came to say a much too late goodbye."

Sometimes even his happiest memories became tainted, and he fought his brain to avoid losing them, fearing all the while the very fight of it all was erasing details, picking away at them like children swipe at their grandparent's candy bowl. A few of the red ones first. The ones wrapped in loud and crinkly foil and colored to look like a cubist's dream of a strawberry even though the sweet hard crunch inside tasted nothing like the fruit. Then a few of the orange ones, even though no child has ever liked the orange ones. They're necessary to steal if only to balance the bowl out. To hide the swindle. To cover the loss. And finally, they go in for the kill: the caramel they know will stick to their teeth and muddle their replies as Grandma calls them in for the dinner they've just spoiled.

He'd see Paul, beautiful Paul, laughing from the passenger seat as they careened up 575, watching the highway whittle and expand its lanes through thickets of pine needles and kudzu. Paul would point out the derelict outlet malls that backed up to the road—vast one-story stucco structures whose bright red and blue and green signs had faded in the harsh sunlight to syrupy tans; the burial tombs of a lost civilization still holding onto the last vestiges of community. Or together they would count the crosses mounted to the hills. Once a symbol of hope, of a promised return to the garden, now they were simply the hilt of a sword drove deep into the earth, searching out oil or rewriting history and calling it "God's Will." Daniel would drive, and Paul would laugh, and they would feel closer in those moments than Daniel ever believed possible. But his brain would still be picking away at the bits. Was that freckle on Paul's left cheek or his right? Did his laugh really go up at the end like that? Daniel could have sworn it went down, falling into a guffaw that had made him feel warm and protected. That was one of his favorite memories, but his brain said it wasn't true. It stuck and stretched like caramel. The highway split in two.

Sometimes he lost himself in the night before the Guard came and swept him from his office, promising his husband and daughter would be gathered, allowing him only a moment to grab the Go Bag he'd been instructed to keep on his person at all times. He couldn't even remember what they had fought over. Something as benign as burnt okra or whose turn it was to change a diaper. Something as great as a cancerous doubt as they inched closer and closer to lockdown. Whatever it was, it was certainly exasperated by the lack of sleep created by newfound parenthood. Though, he always reminded himself even though there was no need, it was never nor would it ever be about Samantha.

What he did remember were the tears welling like hesitant waterfalls—each singular and abundant—in Paul's eyes as he said, "Can you live with her not knowing you?" The surging red inside of him as he proceeded, calmly, to the door. He remembered how his heart had soiled for only a second, how the rage he thought he'd left behind in his youth had surged to bear its apple, golden or poisonous, offended it had taken so long to be invited.

Daniel shook himself to the present. He was not Eris. And no matter how many names they gave themselves, the people around him, heaving in discord beyond his burlap mask, were no Greek Pantheon.

"We go forth armed with the knowledge of what you've all witnessed. We will watch and collect and challenge the lies," Adrasteia said. "We thank you for your watchful eye. In freedom and in truth."

"In freedom and in truth."

Daniel started to rise but was pushed heavily back into his chair. The scrape of metal on tile shot through his spine as he adjusted himself to a more comfortable position. He listened to the rumbling murmur of people leaving, the swishing of heavy fabrics grinding together as they prodded toward the exit. Lemmings so proud of their cliff.

"It's okay, Hermes."

Adrasteia's voice was closer to Daniel now, sweeter too, lacking the caged ceremony of before like coffee muddled with too much sweet cream. The man beside him removed the burlap sack from his head and Daniel blinked his eyes to adjust to the still-dim light. Adrasteia was indeed the woman he had seen at the food hall, the one who had slipped him the note. Hermes was not one of her companions there as Daniel had expected, though he was somehow familiar. This man was more polished. He was wiry but held a strength beneath the billowing tunic he wore to hide his slight frame. His walnut hair curled in extravagant waves as if the sea had taken him to bed one night and forgotten to let go. Amusement filled his eyes, seeming to collect all of the light that should have been in the room into a wry twinkle in his iris, and he winked at Daniel before taking a seat a few rows of fold-out chairs away.

Adrasteia had straddled the seat in front of Daniel. Her arms rested on the back of the chair as she leaned forward, revealing the brand that stretched from the back of her hand to the middle of her forearm. She smiled.

"I didn't think you'd be one to ask so many questions," she said. "Not with all the signposts hidden in plain sight. Isn't that what you do? Discern the obvious from the symbolism?"

"Time was running short," Daniel replied. But in all honesty, it had taken him too long to figure out the arrows of the eyelashes as guiding marks. He squinted his eyes and fought to not return her contagious smile.

"What did you think?"

"Honestly?"

"In freedom and in truth," she laughed.

"I think you're a goddamn cult."

Daniel smirked as he braced himself for the sharp hiss of Hermes' chair ripping back, legs scraping the tile like nails across a chalkboard as he burst forth to put Daniel in his place. Instead, Hermes leaned back and laughed. Adrasteia cocked her head to the side as if Daniel was a precocious child, a puppy barking viciously but too damn cute to fear.

"Is that really what you think?"

"The cloak and dagger. The call and response. I'm surprised the sea nymphs didn't break out into an orgy in the end."

"Would that have made it better for you?"

"No! I—" Daniel stammered. He was confused by the joy and amusement that beamed from Adrasteia's face. Her fingers rapped against her bicep in quick succession. Pinky to index finger. Pinky to index finger. A trill on a flute. Four solid notes. A Morse Code message Daniel just couldn't decipher.

"So why did you come?" she asked.

"Curiosity." Daniel was smug with his answer, but when she didn't speak, he quivered to fill the silence. "And I'm a therapist. A psychologist. I find it interesting to explore what mysteries incite the human mind."

"And is that why you're still here?"

"I'm still here because the Greek fucking messenger god over there held me captive."

"You aren't captive now," Adrasteia said. "You're free to leave whenever you want."

"With a burlap bag over my head?"

"As you are."

Adrasteia clutched the back of the chair and leaned away to stretch her arms to their fullest. Her fingers never stopped their tapping, each hand a mirror image of the other. Daniel sat, paralyzed. He wondered if she was hypnotizing him. Adrasteia cleared her throat and shrugged, leaning forward once more.

"You," she said, "are here because something doesn't seem right to you. There is a little tiny caterpillar crawling around in your head, gnawing at your gray matter like leaves, its furry little wormy body tickling you whenever anything just doesn't add up, but never quite letting you figure it out. You're here because truth is more important to you, however comfortable the lies may be. And you know those caterpillars crawling through your brain will turn into the butterflies that keep your gut on edge."

"I'm here because, lie or not, I'm not very comfortable. Period." Daniel rose to his feet and pushed his chair back to put some space between him and Adrasteia. "But whatever I'm seeking, whatever truth is out there, I'm not gonna find it here."

Daniel turned to leave, gathering his bearing as he searched the dim room for an exit. It was like scanning an old sepia photograph for something brown. He could see the shapes but could not make out where they began or ended, where one thing became the other.

"You're right." Adrasteia words stopped him in his tracks, and she smiled broadly as he turned around to face her once more, her lips thin strips of night around a Cheshire moon. "Join me for a drink?"

She posed it as a question, but he could hear the command. Even though she was twenty years his younger, she spoke with the casual confidence of someone used to getting her way. Questions were simply formalities for the inevitable. Daniel missed that confidence within himself. It was intoxicating. It was a firm hand on his shoulder, a burlap sack over his head.

aul rose with the sun and wiped the sleep from his eyes. The morning, wet with dew and promise, slalomed across the mountain to search out survivors and offer them one more chance to get it right. Manta was curled asleep in Daniel's chair, Sleepy Beauty awaiting the return of her King. Daniel was, after all, the knight in all her fairytales. He had wanted so badly for Daniel to be a part of her life, he had told great tales of the times before the Wave, when life was mostly just, mostly right, and Daniel, a great wizard or a chosen prince was but a humble servant called to powerful heights. Whatever the story called for, Daniel would appear as savior. It was natural for her to cling to the fantasy of him and the life he promised upon his return. A return, Paul realized, was unlikely to happen. The stilted base of the Colony was still submerged in water, over eight years later, and it showed no signs of receding. Too, the remnants of society, whose borders continued to shrink as need continued to grow, would not be communicating safe returns to the Colonies. Paul wasn't even sure it was safe for them to return.

He was quiet to avoid waking Manta as he closed the door and stepped out into the chill of the sighing earth. Dali's blood stained the rock path to the garden, and Paul held his breath as he attempted to scrub the red from the stone. Though Manta was accustomed to death in the way that children, too, were accustomed to birth, the bloody aftermath—the wails and shit and depression—were the few things he could still attempt to shield her from. Where the blood would not wipe clean, he shifted soil to cover the blame.

The fire pit was a mess. Soot and ash sprayed across the ground like so many wishes on a dandelion seed. Their rotisserie was bent but still functioning and Paul settled it back over the pit. He replaced the granite and slate they had cobbled together to keep the flames contained: a mini fortress in man's ongoing attempt to control the elements. Though the wood was still damp with dew, he used twigs and underbrush to start a small fire and boiled a kettle of water from their collection bins. Manta emerged from her slumber slowly just as Paul was muddling the leaves from their yaupon holly into the water. It wasn't coffee, but at least the caffeine helped his morning ritual. She sat on the stump next to her father, and he offered her a twice diluted mug of the brew.

"I dreamed about the ocean last night," she said between timid sips, blowing across the top to cool the tea in concentric circles. "It sang songs about all the treasures it had consumed, like a dragon in a tower guarding its gold coins."

"Oh yeah?" Paul mused. He was grateful the night before had not rattled her sense of safety. "What does the ocean sound like?"

"You've already told me it roars and crashes. So it sounds like that. Like a wet landslide missing all the notes. And it can't keep a rhythm. But it's still beautiful."

She smiled wide, her sleepy voice still halfway in the dream.

"That sounds nice," Paul said.

"It was." She sighed and closed her eyes. "I'm gonna see it one day."

"I know. You will. When it's safe."

Manta had been obsessed with the sea since Paul had first told her of the Great Wave. Its vast calm, its roaring ferocity: the consuming All of it both terrified and excited her. She had seen pictures in their books and even a short video clip on the computer before the grid had completely collapsed and they'd made the decision to reserve the generator and what little fuel they had for Paul's monthly information dives in search of Daniel. Waves foamed against a rocky shoreline, pure white against the slick black boulders and left in each indention a tiny puddle which teamed with life and possibility only to be washed away and replaced by the next crash of water. And out in the distance, a lone boat floated along, safe and secure and far away from any of the dangers of dry land. If she had a ship, she thought, she could master the waves and see the world. She could be an explorer, Noah finding his olives atop Mount Ararat, she and Paul the Aloadae dodging Apollo's arrows to actually reach Mount Olympus this time around.

Paul wished he could give it all to her. He longed for the immediacy of the planet he had so often taken for granted in the Before to be bestowed upon her—the girl who'd had no choice but the learn the land; the girl who could truly appreciate its wonders.

She broke from her trance. "Can we do sausage this morning?"

Paul wrapped his arm to pull her close and kiss her forehead. "Sure, sweetheart."

Whisky at 7am had less of a bite without sleep to contain and renew the senses. Or maybe it was the quality. Daniel swirled the amber-gold liquid in his glass, hefty and sturdy at the bottom with a shine like actual crystal, and let his eyes wander around the room. Thick with decadence, the place was filled with panels and screens from the Tokugawa period. Playful depictions of bold waves or fish markets packed with citizens so intrigued by the catch of the day they could not help but to dance, all of them emblazoned in gold or silver or black or blue. Though, where Daniel expected to see *Red and White Plum Blossoms*, he instead found the gentle pink petals and alluring red stamens of a peach tree blossom. There were other inconsistencies as well. Magnolia blooms and Antebellum structures in the place of tree peonies and sleek tea houses as if Feudal Japan had wed the Confederate South to create a history free of the ugliest parts of the land. A sand and rock garden larger than his entire quarters rested to one side of the space, and knickknacks and tchotchkes—porcelain vases, ornate boxes, and figurines—covered every open surface aside from the table they were sitting at. It seemed the southern American penchant for baubles and hoarding had overcome the sleek simplicity of Japan.

"Americans may have invented this stuff," Adrasteia said, savoring another swig, "but the Japanese perfected it. And in half the time."

Hermes huffed from his post at the door. He had downed his drink in two sips, the first tentative and whetting, the next destructive and final, before moving to stand there as if on guard.

When she'd asked him to join her for a drink, Daniel had not expected the pair to lead him up to Alpha5, much less to a five-room suite Adrasteia seemed perfectly at home in. Even on the elevator, as they rose slowly, he expected Hermes to produce some system hack to gain them access. Or the Guard to be waiting as the doors slid open. Instead, they'd moved freely and unashamed down the corridors, the LED screens displaying a slowly leaking sunrise amongst the hills and large homes of the Morningside district below them.

"My Dad's the Head Engineer of Life Sciences," she explained. "He's basically a glorified accountant, pushing pencils and plotting numbers on charts to plan out food production, waste processing, and energy generation versus consumption. It's pretty much his job to make sure we don't all die while we're locked up in here. Like you, Daniel, whose job is to keep us from going mad."

"You got the wrong guy. There must be three hundred other mind docs on this ship."

"Four hundred thirty-seven. But none of them solved the pesky little coma problem with the HMM. Not a single one of them gave up their A3 suite to live in the basement so a family could have more room to spread out."

Daniel leaned back, intrigued. She had certainly done her homework on him. He wasn't sure if he should be impressed or worried.

"Look," she said, a sudden seriousness to her voice like a record had flipped in the jukebox. "Let's cut to the chase. All that down there, it's the pony show to keep the people pacified. People need a place where they can air their grievances and voice their theories without fear of retribution. Hell, that's what your entire profession is based on. It helps them cope. Makes them feel like they're doing something. And keeps them from mucking up the gears where the real work is being done."

Daniel leaned back in his chair and let his eyes scan the room once more. So that's what this was: the government sanction coup led by the Alpha Princess who could keep them off course and away. The prodigal daughter, still supposedly out on her rampage, who would let them eat cake. He bit his lip and sighed, disappointed to be proven right, but decided he could play along.

"And the real work is?"

Adrasteia considered Daniel for a moment as if suddenly unsure she'd brought the right person into the fold. Her eyes scanned his, but he sat blankly, unwilling to give himself away.

"Freedom," she said. "And truth."

Daniel rolled his eyes as he placed his glass on the table and moved to stand. Hermes laughed from the doorway.

"Sit back down, Daniel."

"This isn't my thing, *Adrasteia*." He hoped the sarcastic contempt was evident as he spoke her chosen name. "Y'all can play out your little fantasy coup without me. We're over halfway through, and I just want to keep my head down."

Hermes balanced in the doorframe and looked to Adrasteia for guidance, but Daniel continued to walk forward.

"There is no ground anymore," Adrasteia blurted.

Daniel turned swiftly, an incredulous glare on his face, but she met him with a stubborn quiver.

"Do you know why we were gathered up? Why they rushed us in here two months early? Or why the communication satellites that had been installed and tested for years prior suddenly failed the moment the doors were closed?"

Daniel stood, prone. His body fought to leave, but his mind was captured. The curious cat slinking headfirst toward his death trap. Adrasteia poured him two more fingers of Japanese Whisky and motioned for him to return to his seat.

"I don't know what happened, what caused it," she said, "or why it didn't happen sooner. But August 9th, 2056, something scared the shit out of our so-called leaders." Her eyes were far away, staring past Daniel, and filling with tears. "Maybe it was another pandemic, an endemic this time. Or atomic war. Or nuclear explosions. Whatever it was, the Guard was sent to gather those deemed essential and brought us all here. It hadn't even breached the news cycle and we were up here, doors closed tight behind us. That's why you're here, and your husband and daughter are not. And the ones in charge are terrified of ever going back down. They're never planning on letting us out of here."

Paul and Samantha. If they hadn't fought, if he hadn't slept at his office in the city, he would have been with them, all of them would have been saved. The image of his husband and infant daughter fighting for survival, crying for him even as they succumbed to the fate of the world plagued his mind. He closed his welling eyes and tried to choke back the picture. He felt numb. He wanted to riot.

"Why"—he cleared his throat—"why not tell everybody? They deserve..."

"They deserve to know everyone they've ever known is probably dead? That we are isolated here, and they will never see actual sunshine or breathe in that ozone scent right before the rain ever, ever again? You understand the human mind, Daniel. You really think that's a good idea? You think it's worth the chaos it would create?"

Daniel could not believe what he was hearing. She was wrong. She had to be. A rich girl playing games with the peons for her own bored amusement.

"So if that's all true, and I'm not saying I believe you," Daniel stammered, "there's nothing to be done."

"Except find a way out."

"You said yourself there's no 'out there' to go back to."

"I said the world ended, and it did," Adrasteia nodded. "But the part we don't know is what actually happened on the surface. We don't know who or what survived, just that we are cut off and no contact has been made. And I, for one, would like to know."

When he didn't respond, Adrasteia continued:

"Look. We either die in here or we die out there, and I'm not ready for this tomb. The crops on Sub1 are already failing. And there's no fucking way they'll last us longer than the fifteen years we are supposed to be trapped. Hell, we will be lucky if we even make it that long. Besides, I haven't seen the moon since I was fourteen years old. Fuck that digital copy on all our walls. Always the damn harvest moon, lying to us in pixels. I'll be damned if this is my whole future. We want out, and we think you can help."

Daniel tried to respond, but all he could see were the accusing faces of Paul and Samantha, bloated and water-logged, gaunt and grim, swirling in the whirlpool his mind had created. It wasn't true. They would be there when he got out, the world and his life reset.

"You know no family ever got your suite, right?" she asked. Daniel could feel her smirk as she stood and crossed the room to a locked wooden box. "It's being used as a by the hour booking for the Alphas who want the flowers of the Neutral Zone without having to bring the bouquet back up to their wives."

She fished a key from her pocket as Daniel continued to focus on nothing, arguing with himself as reality and belief quarreled in his brain. She palmed a metal cuff—one of several in the box—and moved to touch Daniel's shoulder.

"This is not a good place, Daniel. I'm not even convinced they didn't know the flood was coming when they were picking us for the Colonies. You know how that really happened, right? Politicians made it in first. Someone would still need to lead. And then church leaders who knew it was more about power than god. They even convinced their flocks that it was God's Will—that they were entering the camps in order to Spread the Word, to convert, to chastise; but everyone else needed to submit to God's Plan. Like it had a capital P and so—obviously—was the Way with a capital W. It seemed overnight the majesty of stained glass, ripping and tearing the increasingly intensifying beams of sunlight, became the symbols of suicide cults, bright and obedient as Kool-Aid. But, of course, once inside, it wasn't about God anymore. But I digress."

As she spoke, Adrasteia twirled the ramshackle bangle in her fingers. It caught and reflected, it trapped and muted the dim light of the room. She kept her eyes trained on the cuff as Hermes watched Daniel from the doorway, searching out any moment of acquiescence.

"After that were the scientists and doctors, based both on experience and age—the younger the better as it meant a longer period of service. Then the psychologists and therapists. And engineers. And farmers. And finally, a few hundred thousand commoners per unit because they needed someone to mop up the shit and tend to the fields and slap the swill between hamburger buns to keep us docile and normalized. People they could rule and control."

"How is that any different than what you're doing?" Daniel asked. "You're choosing your followers. Setting them up by what they can do for you. Collecting souls for your own wants and needs with stories of evil and greater good. Hell, you're even naming yourselves after gods."

Adrasteia looked disappointed for a moment before a sly smile returned to her face. It felt to Daniel like she had expected his reticence, like it was all a part of her plan. That the smile was the true reaction while her disappointment was an act.

"You need time to process," she said. "And to explore the truth on your own. Here."

Daniel looked at the bracelet she placed in his hands. It was cobbled together from various pieces of tech like the scavenged collection of a magpie welded together. Metal bits of circuitry with crude connections where the metal was heated soft and left to harden again in smooth and rounded mounds. Crushed soda cans still conducting energy. He looked at her questioningly.

"It scrambles the chip," she said. "It still reads as a chip being present, but the identifiers come back as unknown. Which happens all the time up here. Especially now. Random glitches in the system. So no one's the wiser, and you can move about freely to test my version of the truth and see that I'm right."

"But the Guard..."

"The Guard knows. Well, some of them. Hermes over there included."

The man nodded at Daniel who toyed between slipping the cuff into his pocket or placing it on the table and laughing at their joke.

"Take it," Adrasteia said. "Do your own research. And come back when you're ready."

The fire was ready to cook on. Paul had found the grate they used as a grill top a few yards away in the thicket of blackberry brambles, kicked and toppled during the hootenanny of the night before. It was settled atop the stone ring and Manta had run off to gather garlic bulbs and tomatoes to roast alongside the salted meat they preserved in their smokehouse out back. Animals, except for rabbits and mealy birds, were less and less abundant so meat was more often reserved to help them get through the Winter when the garden was dormant, resting and awaiting the radiant first light of Ostara.

He could sense something was off as he made the trek to the smokehouse and scanned the tree line for interlopers—ravagers or otherwise—scouting for food or sanctuary. Aside from a few rustles in the brush, the morning was a serene counter to the chaos it had witnessed just hours before, like it needed to balance the ruthlessness with solace. He trod forward timidly, eyes squinting through the beams of light that broke through the trees as sharp and true as Manta's arrows. Instinctively, his hands reached for a nearby branch, broken and dried on the ground. He gripped it like a baseball bat, twisting it in his palms, and let it hover over his shoulder as flecks of dried bark whispered from the rod to leave it solid and smooth.

He heard the hissing first. Low and guttural like a cornered tomcat, it came in sharp warnings punctuated by grunts, by scraping talons. There were at least three of them, Paul decided. Maybe four. His own scream surprised him as he burst forward, primal and urgent, aimed steady on the southern wall of the smokehouse. His staff made blunt contact with the burnished wood, hard and fierce, his war drum nearly drowning the sudden rustle and flap of the creatures inside. Manta tumbled around the corner of their cabin as three vultures escaped the broken door of the smokehouse, rising awkwardly to the trees to no doubt circle and await a safe return to their bounty.

"Buzzards!" Manta yelled. Their bald red heads and gray tipped wings were unmistakable in their departure. By the time she reached him, Paul was standing in front of the broken door surveying the damage. What had not been stolen or scavenged by the birds was already teeming with ants and beetles. "It's all gone. How?"

Paul had seen the reports on the message boards he used while looking for information on the Colonies, on Daniel, but he hadn't believed them true. The new legends of human sacrifice were too far detached from modern society, even seven years removed, to be real. But now he stared down the aftermath of the stories he had read: groups of ravagers sending the weakest or the sickest of them off as a distraction for the homesteaders under attack, sacrificing them as a diversion while the others slipped unnoticed to ransack the food stores, taking whatever they could carry while the rest were consumed by the easy attack and defense of their property. It had seemed too easy—the death, the retreat; them running off with the spoils as he and Manta were left with the spoiled.

They stepped inside slowly. The door was splintered in two, the blow to do so no doubt shielded by the wail of the woman falling by Dali's side. The low burning embers used to smoke the meat had died in the chill of the night. Snaggled chunks of venison and hare still clung to the hooks and ropes dangling from the ceiling where the preserved meat had hung. Their entire winter food store was lost. It would take days to remake the door and properly seal and vent the smokehouse; weeks to hunt and replenish. Paul closed his eyes in disbelief and inhaled deeply to find his resolve for the coming tasks.

"Uh... Dad?" Manta held up a burlap bag she had fetched from the storage bin in the corner. A thin trickle of white, sparkling like falling stars when the light hit it, made its comet descent to the ground from a thin slice in the sack. The cloth was open and unwoven from the jagged edge of a blade. "The others are gone."

Paul bit his lip. It had been years since a traveler had passed through selling wares. That's how they'd gotten the bags of salt in the first place, trading a night's sleep and two old hiking backpacks for a few sacks to sparingly get them through the next few years. It helped them to live instead of simply survive. And now it was gone. In one brief moment of life and death—one they believed themselves to have won—they lost their winters, their too near future.

Manta dropped to the floor, the faerie counting salt granules, gathering them up to pile in a pyramid atop the blood-stained butcher table Paul had cobbled together from an old cutting board and the salvaged legs of the desk he had once used for such simpler tasks. The semi-translucent white glowed against the blackened red, making the dark remnants of grizzled meat and dirt mixed throughout it all the more evident. She did her best to salvage what she could, her face distressed and hopeful as she stared at her father. He looked on the verge of tears, as if he could replenish the salt they had lost from his own eyes: Zeus calling forth Athena with the will of his own mind.

"We still have the garden," he said, and Manta nodded, unable to relinquish the stress she felt sieving from her dad. "We've made it through worse," he said, more for the gods of the new world than for himself or his daughter. But doubt singed the edges of his words like blood on a stone, dark and boldly visible no matter how much water was applied.

"I can hunt," Manta said. "While you fix the door, I can. And there are plenty of fish in the river. I saw them jumping the other day."

"No fish," Paul commanded. He'd made that mistake once before, when Manta was still too small to understand the world she had inherited. Even years later, he was too timid to attempt it again. The radiation that had seeped into the waters had poisoned the fish and left him sick for days.

"But Dad, all the books say stuff about short half life and dissipation and—"

"All the books are from before. When humans thought their dominance superseded any natural laws. Before the earth decided it was time to fight back."

Manta nodded. The planet she had read of had its fair share of treasures, but so many were now out of reach. In her books, there was so much abundance and extravagance, so much exploration and discovery. Still, it seemed to her that before the Wave everyone was always craving an escape—to another world, to a better life. Even with all the More, they longed for an Elsewhere. In her mind, Manta had her Elsewhere. Everything she needed was at hand. She didn't mind the work. Yes, she wanted to see the ocean, but that was out of wonder, not necessity. And though she loved the stories—Alice's fantastical adventures, the brave undertakings of knights, Peter's flights of fancy—she was happy for the solitude and self-reliance life had given her. People, it seemed to her, were the problem. The common factor in all the stories was other humans. Their hatred. Their selfishness. Their destruction. Even in the world that stood before her, it was other human beings who seemed to destroy the life she and her father had built. She understood his longing for Daniel— she, herself, could not wait for his return, his rescue—but she had no understanding of his other nostalgias. But every now and then she caught herself wondering what others must be like, others unlike those who had wandered into her sanctuary the night before.

Paul swallowed hard and crouched to join her on the floor. He cupped her hands in his and smiled the artificial smile she'd long since learned to see through. The nearest settlement was a two day walk northwest, near where Chattanooga had once stood. But it had been months since anyone there had posted to the message boards. It could have been abandoned as cities continued to lose their resources. Or fallen to ravagers who failed to see blood as a deterrent. There was no guarantee they would find what they needed. No, the only sure bet was to move south: to fill their jugs and evaporate the liquid. But that would require fortification to ensure they had a home to return to. That would require preparation he wasn't sure he had in him. Not anymore.

Loss had become so commonplace. First Daniel and then the world. He didn't think he could cope with losing his home as well. And yet, in leaving, that was a very real possibility. Too much time away could mean there would be nothing to return to. At least he had not lost his daughter.

He looked into Manta's gold-brimmed eyes, filled with a hard and hopeful resistance, the onward march of youth stabbed through with more harsh reality than a child should have to abide.

If she had faith in the new gods, then he could too.

"Do you want to see the ocean?" he asked.

"She turns seventy-three today, and I'm not there. And I wasn't there when she turned seventy. Fuck, I don't even know if she *turned* seventy. I just wish I could talk to her. So she knows I'm thinking about her. So she knows I'm doing this for her. You know what I mean, Doc?"

Daniel barely heard the man sitting across from him in his office. He should have been exhausted—the bags under his eyes proclaimed him as such, he was sure—but his mind was aflutter with the morning's revelations. If they could be believed. He had his doubts. Something so massive, so life altering, would have been disclosed to the public. If only to bring the citizens of the Colony closer together in their shared tragedy. If only in the form of political pandering or religious righteousness: Noah leading the huddled masses two by two through the ark that had saved them all. No, it couldn't be true.

He was an easy mark, he told himself. The poor, desolate psychologist who lost his family and his home. The weak, sobbing man—an affront to manliness itself—who had begged on hands and knees to be moved to Sub5 where he could be lost in the sea of nobodies heaving at life like barnacles on a ship. The bored and the powerful too often fell to nefarious trickery, he told himself. And whatever Adrasteia wanted from him— her words, not his—she would not get. Still, his fingers fumbled stodgily against the metal bracelet she had left in his care.

"You leave any family behind, Doc?"

"We all left family behind, Mitchell. But that doesn't negate what you're feeling. However..." Daniel paused as he attempted to square himself in the present, to present his patient with the careful reality he deserved. Not what Adrasteia and her ilk were offering. "Can you do something for me? Can you try to reframe your thinking? That doesn't mean you have to let go of your pain. You shouldn't. It's a part of being human, of feeling life. But you should remember that the pain is also hope. We are over halfway through this experiment. You are ensuring your mother has a world to grow old in. I mean, that's probably the best birthday present I can think of."

"I guess." Mitchell frowned. "Though she told me before I left she'd rather just have a hug."

Daniel nodded as he pulled his ankle from his knee and leaned forward atop his planted legs to look Mitchell directly in the eye. "You're saving the world," he said. "That's something to be proud of." But Mitchell's expression remained unconvinced. "Have you tried the HMM? Spending time with her that way? It's proved to be very beneficial for people who are experiencing homesickness."

"I ain't homesick, Doc," Mitchell said, and Daniel knew it was true. None of them were, really. They all seemed to enjoy the regulation of their days. The knowing that be-fraught their existence was comforting. No, it wasn't the pangs of nostalgia. They only desired the other. The grass was always greener. There was grass at all. "Besides. It's not like I could afford a session anyway. Or the Haps putting me out of work for even a day after. My daughter is in college on the surface—she's the first of us to actually make it through all four years—so I'm sending almost half my units upstairs for her tuition. And you know my wife is one of the Dreamers. Let me tell you: it's fucking crazy how much a coma costs."

Now that Daniel had made it less deadly, the Haptic Mind Map was the go-to prescription—for those who could afford it—for any and all psychological ailments. By and large, the manipulated memories of the machine felt real enough to return people to a feeling of comfort, of connectedness. Or, at the very least, some sense of solace that could get them through until the next time the helmet was hooked up to their heads. Daniel was there so often the Haps were just his constant state of being: a dull ache in the back of his mind, the ongoing vertigo of time spent with his head above the clouds while pretending with all his might it was below. Ever since word came from the higher high to prescribe the HMM whenever possible, Daniel had petitioned to make it more affordable, but supply and demand would always prevail.

"I understand," Daniel nodded solemnly as he settled back into his psychologist pose: ankle balanced gingerly across his kneecap; shoulders back against the fabric of his high-backed chair; head cocked slightly to the side while his chin jutted forward. "How about we bring your mother to life right here? Tell me your favorite things about her. What is it you remember best?"

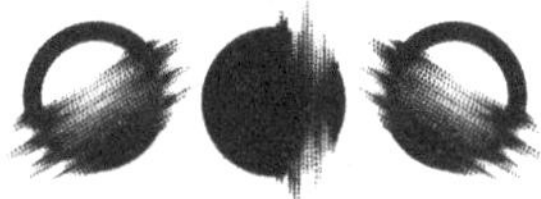

Adrasteia could barely remember her mother's smile, but she knew it was one of the things she missed the most about the land. Not that she would find it there. Her father, when he had been tapped to shift his knowledge from teaching at Emory to practice in the Colony, had told her to imagine their new living situation as a step in the right direction.

"Dear Hiromi-chan," he had said, patting her fourteen-year-old head as if she were still a child. "Do not think of this as a departure from the Earth. Consider it, instead, as a great adventure. One that simply brings us closer to Heaven. Nearer to your mom."

She could remember her mother's hair, silky and steel, made of the solid threads that wove to hold the universe together, hanging to just below her shoulder blades as she turned to check the blind spot before pulling her car into the drop off lane at the Academy. She could smell the gentle lilac of her perfume mixed with the crisp bite of radish and sour tsukemono that still wafted from her hands for hours after she pickled the vegetables from their own backyard. She knew, without a doubt, the curve of the scar on the back of her hand: the tiny crescent moon punctuated by radiating stitches she had promised to tell Adrasteia all about when she was older. But every time her mother would turn to wish her well on her school day, her face would blur amidst the full light of the cosmos so she could never quite take it all in. She replaced it in her mind with stardust and diamonds, with the ancient beauty of a forever lost, temporarily, to the mundane.

There was one face she could remember though. Forever frozen at fourteen, it slipped into her memory when she least expected it and laughed an enticing music which sent ripples of excitement down her spine even still. She knew every twitch, every smirk, every golden tenor in their voice.

"Romi, don't cry," they said. "We've still got three months before you leave with your dad. And once you're back, we'll have all the time in the world!" They cupped her face with their hands, fingers newly calloused from picking out chords on their acoustic guitar, and held onto their optimism even as their lip trembled softly. "Hell, we'll have the world itself."

"I'd rather have right now, Kris. I don't want to go."

Young love was hopelessly immediate, desperately sacrificial. And when it wasn't allowed to run its course, it could cling onto memory like cigarette smoke on a windshield, leaving a haze nearly impossible to wipe away.

"I'll wait for you," they said. "I promise."

Even as she imagined the horror which could have unfolded below, Adrasteia sometimes imagined Kris was still down there, waiting. Maybe they were. Maybe they had found higher ground. Maybe they had grown gills to breathe in the newly toxic air. Or developed an immunity through their unique otherness which somehow made them all the more original and all the more human all at once.

She had brought Kris up to the Colony twice in the Before. Her dad, being who he was, had had early access to supervise construction and check notations or whatever it was he did once the chutes were intact, and the air was stabilized. Mostly, from what she remembered, he'd used his access to slowly bring in all the things he had amassed over the years in an attempt at making a home, she didn't realize until much later, meant to remind his daughter of the land and her mother. Kris had been amazed by the extravagance of the upper levels, but, when the two of them snuck away to explore the subs, had really come to life.

"This is the real deal," they said, spinning with their arms wide to gesture at the narrow, coupled doors of the living units, the long tables in the cafeteria that looked like feeding troughs compared to the exquisite private dining areas being installed above them. "This is where the people will be."

Adrasteia knew from the emphasis Kris placed on "people," they were teaching her something about real life in that moment. Sure, Kris attended the Academy too instead of the Public School closer into the city, but they were almost fifteen, and even a few months at that age were enough to engulf entire worlds in angst-ridden understanding and rebellion. Kris considered themselves an anarchist and an Other, in that way that otherness consumed the whole of humankind. She had tried to convince them to stay in the air with her, to stow away and get lost in the crowds so they could be together, but Kris had declined.

"Somebody's got to get the ground ready for your triumphant return," they smiled. "There's work to do down here too."

"Still in bed?"

Adrasteia's eyes popped open, and she groaned as she craned her neck to bore her crown into her pillow.

"What happened to you, Hiromi-chan? You were always such a well-behaved child."

"Until you chose my twenty-first birthday to tell me everyone I'd ever loved was probably dead from some unknown cause below us. And had been for seven fricking years." Adrasteia rolled to her elbow and settled her face into a haughty smile. "I'm sorry, Father. I meant to say, ' Please excuse me, for I am but a girl, and we are nothing if not well-behaved.'"

Her father shook his head solemnly as he bit his lip. "You can only use that excuse for so long, Romi. I told you because I thought you were ready to put that brilliant brain of yours to work with me. The Colony, while self-sustaining, needs adjustments to enable growth."

"'And without growth, the human race will cease to exist as we all die off.' Blah blah blah."

"There is no 'blah,'" her father said as he crossed the room to sit at the foot of her bed. She pulled her knees under her chin the way she used to when he would read her bedtime stories, and, for a moment, the two were lost in memory. "We have to reimagine the Colony with only what we have here. There is no help coming from the outside. There is only us."

"But why, Dad? Why don't we just leave? See what is left of the planet."

Her father shrugged, exasperated. "Radiation levels. Lack of communication. Right now, returning to Earth is the equivalent of landing on Neptune. We have no way of knowing what we will face."

"But, most importantly, the mayor doesn't want to give up the power she has here."

She almost felt guilty as she watched the heave of his chest. "Ours is not to question," he said. "Ours is to solve."

"Is this my dad or Dr. Saito talking? Doesn't matter either way. I'm still in my gap year," Adrasteia chided as she crashed back to her pillow.

"Years," he corrected, stressing the "s" into the "tsk, tsk" sound he always used to show disapproval.

"*Years*," Adrasteia aped. "You know, Dad, you're the one who taught me to question everything. 'To question is to seek god,' you said. Now you're just stuck on the solutions, but you're answering the wrong thing."

Dr. Saito cleared his throat as he stood and tapped his toe against the floor.

"Polk," he called, and Hermes moved from the front room to stand at attention in Adrasteia's doorway. "Make sure she gets out of the quarters today. Maybe bring her to Sub1 around 4pm." He turned to his daughter. "You used to love the gardens. I'll be there this afternoon for inspection. Perhaps we can walk them together."

"If I just say 'yes' can I go back to sleep?" she asked, fluffing the pillow over her ears.

The girl who had been so full of live on the surface was still there, he was sure, somewhere beneath all the sorrow and grief which had surrendered her countenance to the sullen. She had been through so much—the death of her mother, the death of the world—but he knew she would re-emerge. Somehow.

He was silent as he stared at her scrunched-closed eyes. "I didn't mean to break you," he whispered.

He nodded to his daughter's guard as he left the quarters to return to work. Hermes, as any well-trained guard, like any spinning dancer, kept his gaze trained to a single spot on the far wall.

"Sorry, sir. It's not registering any credits."

The boy behind the counter smiled awkwardly at Daniel as he tried to look straight past him at the growing lunch rush line.

"Can we try it one more time?" Daniel asked and the boy groaned as he nodded. It was bad enough telling a grown man he was broke, but doing so at seventeen with the looming frenzy of substitutions (despite the sign), impatient people (still taking their own sweet time at the counter), and wrong orders (even though everything on the menu was made with the same damn stuff) was just brutal.

Daniel pulled the cuff from his arm and held his wrist back to the scanner.

"Must've been a glitch," the boy smiled. "Sorry about that, sir. Here's your order."

Daniel grabbed his tray and found an empty table on the far side of the cafeteria near the Big Chicken which, in this brave new world, was remarkably close to the Fox Theater. The cuff bore into his thigh through the rough fabric of his pant pocket. It had worked exactly like Adrasteia said it would. Maybe there was something to her story after all. Still, he could not understand why she wanted to recruit him. There was nothing he could do from his chair with his pad. His job was to listen, to attempt an understanding, and to help those he now realized were trapped like beta-fish in plastic bags at the county fair to find some sense of solace in their new surroundings. Not exactly the skill set required to execute a ten-mile drop. Besides, he refused to believe her story. Paul and Samantha were down there, dreaming of him just as he dreamed of them. They had to be. That dream was braided so tightly with the guilt he felt from the Before, and together, those thoughts were all that kept him going.

But are they? he thought. *Is the fantasy really letting me live? I slalom through these halls like the dead. I eat alone. I smile. And I nod like a lover who's long since lost interest in anything other than casual companionship. I jump at the first opportunity to discover something that feels like feeling. Entertaining wild notions just because they hold the promise of something different.*

He knew what he was doing. But even the understanding of the process did not preclude the mental gymnastics he had to undergo; the somnambulist ricochet of thoughts on auto-drive, bouncing through the caverns of yes men and naysayers he held within to arrive at the already foregone conclusion. Adrasteia had hooked him with her story. He had one foot in. The full Hokey Pokey would depend on verity.

Excitement crept through him in undulating waves, radiating not from his head—where he had so long ago trained himself to place his trust— but from the depths of his gut. An instinctual electricity cascaded to the balls of his feet, to the tips of his fingers, and shot back to settle inside his chest with a burning notion of soon. It felt like his first excursion into the HMM, when, for a split second, he could believe it real and actually take his daughter into his arms, look Samantha in the eye, and tell her he loved her. It was his first date with Paul.

Back then, barely out of college and still green, Daniel thought himself as hard and sharp as a thistle. He knew he could put forth a beautiful front, but underneath the facade was a harsh spike of a stubborn self-reliance. He was, after all, the product of parents of the Raging 20's; subject to the overindulgent free love that resulted from years of pandemic-based isolation. But where his parents, like so many others, had spent his upbringing embracing anyone they could touch, Daniel had erected a fend-for-himself armor from all the times he felt too lost in the crowds to be on the receiving end. When Paul asked him out, he would have said no if his own therapist had not insisted he make an effort to connect with someone other than her.

He couldn't remember exactly when he felt it; but sometime between the whiskey and roasted beer nuts and the decision to have dinner together after all, the nervous jolt in his stomach had exploded, shifting slightly higher to light in his chest. He was in for an adventure. But what surprised him most was that he was ready. Still, that didn't mean he didn't need to talk himself into it just as he was now. The vulnerability associated with the unknown was as intoxicating as it was terrifying. It swelled within him in unbound glory the way a gentle whiff of lavender and sweat would center him at eight-years-old, holding his mother's hand on laundry day. All those years of mandated moderation, of step ball change motions through the Colony had felt safe. Now he found himself centered on nostalgia and rebellion once more. On the thrill and stimulation it could offer. This was the feeling the Alphas had diligently worked to subdue. These were the ideas he himself had, in his practice, trained out of his fellow citizens.

Shame pierced through him, splintering his perception and leaving a call to action in its wake. He retrieved the cuff from his pocket and slipped it onto his wrist. When he closed his eyes the different metals collected there, their varied reactions to temperature and contact, felt electrified against his skin. He pictured Paul; that mischievous glint he would get in his eyes when he encouraged Daniel to be bold. The way the skin at the corners of his mouth would stretch and fold in vicarious elation. He pictured Samantha; an infant still, or all grown up, solid and proud and strong and surviving. If, as Adrasteia said, the world had truly ended below them, Paul and Samantha had found a way to survive. Daniel refused to believe otherwise. And, he told himself, if they were down there, they were waiting for him. He had to get out. He had to find them.

He would.

"Dad! They aren't here!"

Manta inched through the crawl space under the cabin. Tiny spotlights from the vents and rodent holes guided her across the hard, compacted dirt as she wriggled from box to box of goods too painful to keep inside but too valuable to throw away. Spiders scrambled into the shadows as she moved. She imagined them there like the inhabitants of Wonderland, watching in their many-eyed wonder as a giant invader destroyed the sanctity of their homes.

"Are you sure?" Paul called from the hatch, straining to peer into the darkness after his daughter, willing his eyes to adjust to no avail. "The box would say 'Winter: Dan' on it. I could swear I shoved it down there."

"Wait!" Manta cried. "Maybe...." She shoved a box in front of her as she made her way back to the hatch. "It doesn't have Dad's name on it, but could this be it?"

Paul shifted the box aside and helped his daughter to her feet. The hopeful expression on her face was at once so innocent and earnest and Paul kissed her forehead. He was proud the world had not hardened her so much she lost her sense of wonder. He wondered how she had kept it when so many adults who had been through so much less in the Before had lost it so quickly, so willingly.

The box was surprisingly well kept. There was a corner or two where the cardboard was slightly dented and a darker spot where it had gotten wet and then dried, but it still seemed sturdy as they knelt to inspect it. Paul's fingers traced the all-caps WINTER scrawled in marker across the flaps. It was Daniel's handwriting, the one he used when he was actually trying to be legible, careful and exacting but with a faint curve of whimsy where the corners of his letters met. He hesitated to open the box, as if doing so would release whatever bit of Daniel's soul he had stacked and stored inside and Paul would lose yet another piece of him, like all the hope left inside Pandora's chest seeping from the skeleton keyhole.

Manta slipped her fingers under a flap and lifted right where Daniel's "R" curled upwards and looped in descending circles toward the corner of the box: a whispered wish, decadent and extravagant. A testament to one of the few times Daniel had allowed himself to be so reaching. Paul could still see him sitting there, sprawled on the floor of their West Midtown apartment, sorting piles into Keep or Give and weaving lids atop the futures they would have at the mountain with the little girl they would soon fly off to meet.

"I don't even know her yet," he'd smiled as he packed away the multi-colored lights and glass ornaments of the holiday, "but I want her future to be as magical as we can make it."

Paul had swooped in behind him and kissed his cheek and promised it would be. He hoped he'd kept the promise, even if it wasn't anything like they imagined it would be. There was magic in the earth. That's what he had taught his little girl. And it was as powerful and unrelenting as it was unpredictable. That's what made it magic, after all. In fact, Paul believed, that power was the one everyone had been striving for all along but had somehow forgotten.

"Nothing," Manta sighed as she peered in. "It's just a bunch of colored balls and lightning bug butts on a string."

Paul knelt beside Manta and placed his arm around her shoulder. His fingers crept through the memories in the box. "Solstice used to be called Christmas for a while. Your dad loved it. These are how we decorated for it."

Manta pulled a tray of carefully collected porcelain from the box and inspected each ornament, tugging at the tiny, hooked barbs with her fingers to watch them spin first clockwise, then counterclockwise in her grip. Errant rays of sunlight caught the snowy scenes in kaleidoscopic bursts like a guiding star to lead them to the valley.

"They're pretty." Manta smiled at her father with such innocence he wished he'd taken the time to show her the unbridled joy of the holiday. It had seemed excessive. He had shown her beauty elsewhere, not trapped in fantasy. "Can I break them?"

She stacked the ornaments to one side, stretched a strand of lights taught in her grip, and sent a cacophony of bells ringing as her foot came down on the box. Paul smiled at her ingenuity even as he suppressed a heavy sigh. He wanted his daughter to know magic. Instead she'd found a trove of trip wire, flesh piercing shards, and alarms.

Leave it to a child for unsurpassed ingenuity. Leave it to a child of the After to find weapons in what was once frivolity. Manta held an ornament up to the light. Dainty and fragile, Paul remembered when his mother had gifted it to him the Christmas after he'd told her he was gay. Society had moved further into acceptance as a whole, but interpersonal relations were as complex as ever. She had tried to show her acceptance—presenting him with a rainbow snowflake enshrined in a clear glass tube—and though he had smiled and thoroughly appreciated her attempt, it only served to show him how she had forgotten who he had been—how much one bit of information could control what was. He watched the light catch the ornament and prism its way across his daughter's face. He reminded himself Manta was a little girl. His little girl. No matter what this new world had done to her—no matter how much it affected her, she would always be a gentle, wondrous child.

"Okay. So we've got trips, sharps, and louds," she said. "It ain't fool proof, but it could be a deterrent as an outer perimeter. Right?"

Paul nodded. He stifled a grimace as he looked over the crumbling past at his feet: a history left to landmines and shrapnel. A joy too glib for such a cold new world.

"It's better than immediate deadly force, right?" she urged. "At least it'll give whoever's passing a chance to turn around."

Paul looked at the pile of bear traps and sharpened sticks waiting by the front porch. Maybe Manta was not so lost in this new Earth after all.

"You're right," he smiled. "Why don't you start setting all that up. I'll go check inside to see if I can find that box of Dan's leather jackets. We might need them for the nights."

"On it, Dad!" she exclaimed.

Her excitement was palbable as she shoved the ornaments back into the box. It reminded Paul of all the simple things he had taken for granted from the Before. The trips to the fairgrounds or to grandparents or even just out to the supermarket. His world had become to small, so insular, as a means of survival. And it was all Manta had ever known. He watched her eyes alight at the prospect of leaving home and felt a rush of sadness.

Manta grabbed the box and disappeared behind the tree line to pace out a perimeter. The broken ornaments clanged against one another to create disjointed carols as she moved, like the Wave had disrupted the very core of music too—made it rusted and sharp and something best left to better times.

So maybe she'll never know the wonder of Santa Claus, Paul thought. Her unbridled passion for seeing the Ocean Where the City Used To Be would have to do.

he key to any covert mission, he knew, was purpose. He had
seen it in his practice time and time again. Those with something to hide
held a heap of nervousness in their chests, twitching and hemorrhaging
along as their eyes darted with each ecstatic burst. Or they glided with
an over-confidence that did nothing but betray them. It was that quaint
middle ground of assured nonchalance, of knowing reticence that fooled
the onlooker. Daniel knew to train his gait with a steady reluctance to
match the expression on his face. He had to do this—he was supposed
to be here—but he didn't really want to be. The whole of the human
condition was displayed in each stride.

As he reached the elevator bay, Daniel swung his wrist toward the reader.
An error message flashed across the screen. "Unknown citizen. Please try
again." The voice was the same pseudo-real, pseudo-electronic one that
had been used for decades. It was meant to bring comfort, to add a sense
of normalcy to life in the Colony. Folks could not have their cell phones,
but they could still hear the helpful tone of voice which promised them
The World as they moved through their new lives. On the third attempt,
just as Adrasteia had promised, the call box switched to override, and he
heard the stuttering sigh of gears shift as the chute came to greet him.
Casual, but not too casual, he reminded himself as he stepped on and,
three swipes later, was bound for the farm level on Sub1. The vines were
failing already, Adrasteia had said, growing yellow and limp even as their
roots struggled to take what they could from the processed waterbeds.

Resources had been diverted to produce enough to get them through next month, and the replacement of diverted resources was a problem left for a different day.

Sub1 was a flurry of motion when the doors shifted open. They parted like the Red Sea, like Daniel was Moses left to wander the arid landscape for forty years. Or maybe longer if his recruiter was to be believed. And he had only signed up for fifteen.

A steady mist sputtered from a roadmap of pvc piping which crisscrossed the ceiling. It gave the entire expanse the familiar stick of Georgia humidity, sharp and wet and pulling the moisture from his pores to balance his inside with the out. The digital screens featured a just before midday sun that glared from all directions within a blue-gray sky. Poorly rendered stratocumulus clouds skipped across the scene to add a bit of texture and depth, but they glitched out when they passed too closely to the edges where the walls met, even the idea of nature unsure of what to do with such cornered delineation. The twenty or so engineers he could see from the elevator bay did not even acknowledge Daniel as he gawked at the variegated rows of green and brown and wilt. The fifty farmhands never looked past their peas.

The thriving jungle of the South swam out to meet him as he stepped closer to the rows of raised beds—some soil-filled but most a swampy mixture of root and water with unseen nutrient packs hidden and dissolved in the liquid—and hid the gawk from his parted lips, from the shallow space beneath his eyes. It looked like so much food. Decades of freshness. The symptom and the cure for Southern Consumption. That was something the South had always been good at: combining cause and effect to propagate the cycle, to keep the circle round and closed and dizzy.

A good portion of the field was relegated to an algae mixture a laboratory muse had dreamed up to provide protein and amino acids in its whitened, curd-like state that was meant to resemble the flesh of a chicken—usually— though it would sometimes be colored and crumbled into the proximity of ground beef. It was joined by the staples of any Georgia Grandma's kitchen: the bubbling leaves of collards so green they were almost black beneath the artificial sunlight, the ashen green of beefsteak tomatoes waiting for their reds to be allowed, corn to cream and potatoes to mash and cane to grind to sugar to pound into cakes or sprinkle in coffee or tuck into the buttery folds of biscuits. Robotic arms tested the pH levels of the water and the moisture levels of the soils. They waved back and forth across the beds of yellow-green protein-slime like wands sporting the red uv light of magic. They built trellises for beanstalks or dug trenches for peanuts. They declared: EVERYTHING IS UNDER CONTROL.

Hands though were where the real power was at. Farm Level employed nearly two thirds of the citizens on the inside. From engineers to scientists to field workers, people milled about the station like ants focused on a singular task. They worked in shifts, overlapping every six rings of sixty: Farmer's Hours. They were doing the work of gods, and, for that, the Colony was forever grateful. The restaurants on the other levels proudly proclaimed things like Hand-Picked or Hand-Sorted next digital pictures of smiling farmers with straw hats and wheat teeth clutching dirt-coated carrots in their dirt-stained hands. They wore dark denim overalls with gold-yellow stitching and waffled shirts underneath the loosely fastened bibs. They stared with eyes so blue Daniel could almost remember them from the films they'd been in before they'd gotten too old and gone to catalogue modeling.

The people working on Sub1 wore a microfiber specially designed to prevent them from sweating, specifically produced to stop them chafing in the steady moisture of the air. Motorized carts followed them on impulse, collecting produce in various baskets until the worker hit a button to send them speeding off, and a new cart emerged in its place. Irregular produce was washed and sent downstairs. Only the tomatoes that were perfectly round were placed on silver platters and carried to the chefs above.

Daniel worried his own clothing—brown linen slacks more worn around the pockets in the seat than at the knees, a light blue polo Paul had gotten him one year for his birthday that had fit his broad shoulders a little more tightly only a few years before, and shoes not purposed for the slick tile that puddled in spots like the oceans left by tiny bare feet at the public pool—would betray his smoothly calculated walk, but in addition to the regular workers, teams of technicians or scientists or managers— all the people brought in to cock their heads to one side or scrunch their mouths in a thoughtful direction or offer platitudes like *great job* or *keep that production high* bounded about to leave him as just another aberration normalized and ignored: a yellow spike on a cucumber; a turnip with an extra leg.

As he rounded the tubs marked Kentucky Wonder, with pods just beginning to form as white flowers withered against their trellises, a vent released a rush of cool air to twist the mist into a calming ballet around him. It was all quite beautiful. Peaceful even. Despite the teeming of workers and robots. And everything seemed to be in order. Sure, there were a few beds of yellowed vines; others where dark soil spit out tiny husks of browned fingers that would crawl no further, but that was certainly to be expected. He'd discovered you couldn't always count on a seed while toiling away in his own little garden back home at the cabin he'd shared first with Paul and then with Paul and Samantha. What was started was not always guaranteed.

A sudden splash surprised him, drawing his attention to a row of raised beds he had thought simply dormant before. He leaned to watch the sinewy smooth bodies of catfish glide like flattened hippos, like the tails of sirens through the tank. So there was actual meat on the Colony after all. A filtration system at either end of the cubed expanse collected the waste from the water, no doubt pumping it out as nourishment for the leafy greens and vines along the other rows. It was a thoroughly beautiful and self-sufficient ecosystem. But the fish, he thought, were no doubt served in the higher end restaurants only available to the Alphas. That alone made him angry, but it did nothing to corroborate Adrasteia's tale.

He wasn't sure what he was supposed to be looking for, but he had come anyway, if only to test Adrasteia's technology, he told himself. Maybe to prove her wrong. She had to be wrong. Time was ticking. The entirety of the Colony was simply a giant countdown before he could see the people he loved again. Before he could have them back, if they would take him. He pushed the thought from his mind. He tried to figure out where to search for any proof that she was wrong.

His eyes moved from the plants to the workers—to the people in lab coats and glasses with clipboards and silver pens making more notes in the margins than in the lines provided, noting the peripherals in place of the important stuff. Or maybe the important stuff in place of the expected. Worry clinched itself like sand in the corner of some of their eyes, tightened and dried into pearls, but surely that was normal too. When one cared for their job, there was always worry. Feigned or real, it didn't matter. It was there.

"So, Dad. Why is it that we're attempting to up production output so rapidly again? The current rate has gotten us here, hasn't it? And we are halfway through this experiment, are we not? Seems like the current rate plus the prohibition against reproduction could sweep us easily through the next half of our journey aboard this tin can."

Her voice was loud and pointed, a sharp blade of fine steel that already knew the answer and wanted only to slice deep. Daniel froze in place as he watched Adrasteia through the snaking limbs of a tomato plant. She stood, cross-armed and defiant in a cluster of lab coats staring pointedly at the jaw-gaped older gentleman whose eyes matched her own. The bleached white of the coats made the fuzz on the tomato stalks glow an unnatural neon. Her smirk broadened into a smile as she caught sight of Daniel. She couldn't have planned this any better.

"My daughter raises a good point," the older man with his daughter's eyes said. The clench in his jaw betrayed the calmness in his response. "As the old saying goes, 'if it ain't broke, don't fix it,' right?" He chewed the word "ain't" with the over-pronounced excitement of someone who'd moved to the South later in life and had swallowed the new vocabulary like Brunswick stew. He combatted his daughter with a sword of his own.

"Can anyone offer an answer, class?"

"Increased production equates to better efficiency, Dr. Saito," squeaked one of the white coats.

Adrasteia's leering smile faltered, and she rolled her eyes as her father urged the student on.

"If we can produce more at a faster pace, we can create stores of supplies to get us through any system failures which may occur." The student was bolder now, his voice earning an assuredness as the falling mist wet his tongue. "Additionally, if we increase efficiency, we can divert resources being used throughout Sub1 to other areas of the Colony for a better overall experience."

"You've been locked in here since you were eight," Adrasteia wanted to say. "What do you know about any overall experience?" Instead she bit her tongue so hard Daniel could feel it in his own mouth.

"That is correct, Mitchell," the instructor said. He squinted his eyes at his daughter with the same mocking hint of defiance she had inherited in her own.

"So that's the only reason?" she urged, unwilling to accept defeat.

"No answer is ever the only reason," he responded.

Daniel watched the tension zizz between their eyes. Defiance challenging stubborn love. He wondered if Samantha would ever look at him with that sort of confrontation burning on her face. If she would ever love him enough to be so irreverent.

Adrasteia's dad sent the class a few rows over to watch one of the automated skimmers remove the blistering top layer of algae that would be fermented into food meant to resemble something it was not. "Your homework," he said, "is to prototype three ways of making the system more efficient. I'm seeking actionable items, not theoretical ones. These are for now, not some hypothetical future. I want you to work as a team to invent, develop, test, and execute your models. You have three weeks."

The class attempted to hide their disdain at yet another group project. After all, hadn't their parents already enrolled them in the largest group project of all? And one from which they could not escape.

As the students moved away, Dr. Saito slipped his hands atop his daughter's shoulders.

"Hiromi," he sighed, forcing eye-contact to ensure she was not only listening, but that she actually heard him. "I invited you here so you could see the drive in your peers. I wanted you to know how hard they are fighting to build this into a better world. Even the younger generation that is now coming of age. You have one of the brightest minds in the Colony. The work you could do—"

She eyed Daniel over her father's shoulder. He was studying the yellow pistols of the Cherokee Purple Tomato plant buds as if they were the only thing that mattered, but she knew he was still listening from the other side of the heirlooms.

"They deserve to know the truth, Dad. You're towing the company line and still pitching Utopia while the rich get richer and the workers work harder. Call me crazy, but I think they deserve to know what they are truly working for."

"They are working to create food. To survive. *That* is the truth. Does the reasoning behind the truth—as you call it—change anything? Must they not still produce the same outcome? Why use fear as a motivator?"

"We came here to give the surface a chance," Adrasteia said. Her voice was flat and low, but still held the urgency of a flashing siren light, the spinning call to arms amidst the warning. "If there is no humanity left on the surface, we have already failed. We should be focusing on a way to go back down. To start over."

"We came here," her father corrected her sternly, "to save humanity." Even in a whisper, his words were serrated. "The Colony is the best way of doing just that. That is why we are here. This is what is left of humankind. Safe in a box in the sky. There is no humanity left on this surface. This is how humanity survives."

He opened his mouth to speak again, but Daniel had already departed. His casual gait ambling faster until it was almost a sprint by the time he neared the elevators. He pushed his wrist erratically toward the sensor like a young child just learning to say hello. He sank back into the elevator and wished for the blue to surround him. The words still stung his mind: *there is no humanity left on the surface.* They repeated, this time as a whisper from his own tongue. *There is no humanity left.*

"I think someone is out there."

Manta's arrow was nocked before she even completed her warning, and Paul held a palm up to steady her. They were two nights out from the cabin headed in a direction that was mostly south but veered with the organic rise and fall of the Appalachian Hills, meandering like the horses that had paved the winding streets of Atlanta before a planner superset their grid.

He had been surprised by how quickly their house had faded into the background, swallowed up by the vast chasm of trees and kudzu like the natural world was a great gaping maw with pinecones stuck between its teeth. He was pleased to see Manta's child-wonder still intact as she pressed forward through the unknown, the exciting, the yet-to-be-consumed. Still, he had kept one eye swerving backwards at every new bend until he could no longer even pretend to see the splintered shingles of his roof, the glinting shards of broken Christmas ornaments they'd strewn in a circle around the perimeter to catch the bare feet of intruders. His home. The place Daniel would know to find them if Daniel was coming back.

He would be back, Paul assured himself. He would return when the Colony opened up and spilled its children back to Earth. The exodus from Noah's ship. The real rapture as the other had been too rushed. The folks in the sky, they would return, and they would set the world straight. Even in his head, Paul knew the thoughts sounded like the fantasy of a religious zealot—the Great Ones returning from above to make it okay—but he didn't care. Daniel would return; and home would no longer be just a word.

A second twig snapped, and Paul rolled from beneath the lean-to as quietly as he could. He squatted and peered through the crisscrossing branches they'd used to camouflage the distinctly unnatural brown and green blobs that compiled the shiny plastic of their tarp. His palm cupped the taut and agitated shoulder of his daughter. The tremble there showed the fear that lingered just beyond her strong exterior. His daughter; the warrior. Manta; his baby girl. Her pupils dilated to hide her irises and replace the whites in her eyes as she shifted them slightly for a signal from Paul.

A third popping sound, and Manta's arrow flew. It thwipped past Paul's ear like a cut string, like a scalpel in its precision.

"Fuck! You almost hit me."

The voice was gruff and unpracticed, like it had not been used in so long a time, but fear had reactivated the muscles, had pushed the air from the lungs.

"That was my warning," Manta retorted, trying to make her voice sound deep and experienced. "The next one will meet flesh."

Paul looked at her quizzically, and her shoulders shrugged. She'd wanted to use that phrase since she'd read it in one of Daddy Dan's old fantasy books. Those days of dragons and knights and princesses and epic battles didn't seem so different from now. The dragons were always there in the dark. She and her father were warriors even if they didn't fully realize it all the time. The only thing missing was the magic, but Manta was sure they'd find some when they reached the ocean.

"Are you alone, little girl?" was quickly replaced with "Fuck. I mean, shit. I mean, I'm sorry. That sounded creepier than I wanted it to. I— It's been a while since I've— I'm alone. I'm safe. I promise."

"She is not alone."

Paul made his voice as thick as the southern air. He pushed into the deepest black of the night and tried to find the rough edges of the mystery contained there. He spread himself out so that this alone and safe man would not know exactly where they were.

"I'm leaving," the person assured them. "I'm leaving," the person assured themself.

Another snap and a golden green glow fizzed to life about thirty yards to the west of their lean to. An awkward body appeared in its glow, silhouetted and cracked into place like a paper doll. They were lean, the kind of lean that came from hunger instead of exercise, and—somehow—a gleaming kernel of hope peered out from around the edges of their horror-filled eyes like the last grain of sand in the hourglass that contained humanity. Paul noted the freckles that flecked their face and tried to picture them before the Wave. A sunny-faced student maybe—they would have been about that age then—or maybe they had just finished college and were getting ready to actually begin a life that had other plans. Hair as pitch as shadows curtained their angular jaw. Their clothes were worn, but cared for, with patches and stitch-jobs drawing the torn bits back together, scarring them in raised, thick, circular motions as the fabric attempted to mend. They carried a small bag that now spilled its contents at their feet.

They blinked their eyes against the light. A peace offering. They'd cracked a flare—maybe even their last one—to show Paul and Manta they were harmless, to keep their wandering body away from the camp and Manta's arrows away from their neck. Paul saw the first arrow Manta had fired, perfectly perpendicular and emerging from the rough bark of the pine tree to the right, inches from their jugular.

They looked tired and lost and confused. Paul understood. He knew tired and lost and confused all too well.

"I'm sorry," they mumbled. Their voice strained as they repeated the apology, louder this time. Paul got the feeling the regret was not directed at them.

Manta had lowered her bow at the first sign of light, and now her hand slipped gently into her father's. He felt their palms touch, tender and taut, as if reborn in the cool of night, washed clean of the clammy humidity that left them nervous and wet through the days. Her eyes searched his in wonder. They asked the hard questions—questions she herself could never enunciate. They wanted to know if this is what humanity was now. They asked where the line between compassion and survival was really drawn. Paul knew whatever answer he gave would affect her forever.

"Wait," Paul called, and the person froze in their slow-moving tracks. Their lip quivered. Paul had half-expected a smile. That part of him that still distrusted earnest behavior wanted to see the smirk twitch across their cheeks as they realized the con was working. Instead they locked themself in vibration. Pulsing in frenetic energy. They squeezed their eyes tight as if waiting for the firing squad to aim, for the guillotine to fall and slice its peace across their neck.

"Are you hungry?" Paul asked.

He hoped the smile that brightened Manta's face would be worth it.

When he held up his hands, the lather slipped into the curve of his nail beds like the tiny crests of ocean waves. It made sense: his mind was as restless as the Atlantic. Though physically, nothing had occurred, everything was new; changed. Novel information was reforming his mind. The daughter he did not really know was now the daughter who did not know him. The husband who was waiting was the husband who had watched the world end. Fifteen years was now a life sentence.

No matter how Daniel's mind chose to rearrange to center within the newfound facts of his being, it refused to conjure any images of his family deceased. Not for longer than a few dismal seconds at a time anyway. When they emerged, he closed his eyes beneath the shower head to wash them away.

It didn't work. Nor did the shower realign the discoveries he had made on Sub1. Adrasteia had been telling the truth. If he did not act, he may never see his family again. If he did act, he may never see his family again. He braced his outstretched arms against the tiled wall and let the water cascade over him hoping it would wash it all away.

The sharp droplets licked down his back, slightly colder than he wanted them to be, but he had gotten used to it. Like most everything else on the Colony, bathing was tied to the chip in the wrist. Everyone was allotted a specific number of weekly showers with a specific amount of water determined by body mass and working position. Daniel had an office job which allowed him only two each week, though he received a third shower as a form of hush money when he moved from his Alpha level living quarters with its own private bath and shower he could have used as often as he desired to his Sub5 station. Adrasteia's tech had not worked to initiate bathing though. So, his hopes dashed of a potential drowning, Daniel willed the tile walls to crack open, the waterfall to burst forth and carry him all the way down to Paul's arms in its forceful, god-be-damned embrace.

He eyed the cuff poking out from his crumpled polo on the bench in the corner. He considered heading to his old Alpha home, but he knew Adrasteia would be correct, and its current usage would only send him back to the showers.

He also knew Adrasteia would be waiting for him to return and join her merry band of rabble rousers. She had timed her revelation perfectly, made her father complicit and kept him innocent. If any of them could be called innocent. Maybe innocence was a trouble for later. Right now, they needed a way out. If he ever wanted to see his family again, he needed a way out. And the path out needed to be safe. He felt in himself his own urge to chisel at the outer walls; to bang and push and open up the Colony to the ozone outside. He knew he'd freeze if that happened; he'd suffocate. He knew the mob would not think that far ahead if they found out. Adrasteia was right. What they needed was twofold: a smokescreen to quell the mass hysteria; a carefully selected few who knew the truth behind the lie of truth to actually do the work.

But can I do it? Daniel thought. *Can I join a cult that's disguising itself through revolution?* He let his thoughts dance around the question like so much recycled water from a shower head. To replace the visions of Paul, of Samantha, of the question he didn't want to ask—the one that worried him every single day: Who would he be when it all ended?

olographic fires lit up barrels in the Neutral Zone. Crude tech, Adrasteia thought, but it definitely added to the ambiance as she slid through the forever-night in her darkened robes. She held her pinky extended over her heart, tapping her chest twice to greet those aligned with her cause. Most of them were peripheral figures, grandstanding and longing to be involved. They were the folks who knew instinctively that something was amiss but couldn't quite figure out the exacting whole of what was wrong. They had questionable ideas about what was going on or anarchist ideals on overthrowing the government—any government—the extensive psychological tests for acceptance to the Colony had failed to filter out. They made up tales so tall they could have been fables of giants and beanstalks, and they convinced themselves—and more dangerously, those around them—the stories were just crazy enough to be true. They had vivid dreams that sometimes got the answers mostly right even if they missed the how and the why. They chose the names of the greater figures of the Greek and Roman pantheon—Zeus or Poseidon; Jupiter or Neptune—and left the lessor gods and demons to those who were actually doing the real work. Adrasteia understood that desire to belong, to be a part of something. She'd figured out the means of controlling the mob mentality while still inciting the horde. She gave them a place to voice their opinions as facts and prayed just being heard could quell their more actionable tendencies as they waited for her cue.

It had been five hours since the stars had aligned on Sub1, and she'd gotten her father to admit what was actually happening within earshot of Daniel. If she'd tried to plan a coalescence like that, it would have crumbled. Left to chance, it couldn't have turned out better. But not everything could be left to chance.

She'd spent the last three hours wandering the Neutral Zone in her cloak, an urgent expression chiseled across her face to ensure her other gods that she was working, she was busy, and they were making progress. She expected to see Daniel at every turn. She'd practiced her I-told-you-so smile, its gentle pucker and ever so slight squint of the eye so many times she could feel her face slip into it without warning. Perhaps that was the cockiness her father had warned her about, a piece of the know-it-all mentality that he swore would one day find her in the brig. Or worse. Not that it mattered.

Not that anything mattered except escape.

She caught her reflection in the warped and polished metal tchotchkes displayed across one of the makeshift booths that made up the entirety of the Neutral Zone. Even in Forward Colony 47, where the Powers That Be had considered everything from images of the city's favorite streets to light up the LED pathways or their favorite restaurants to serve the slop that counted as nourishment, people's innate desire to make, to build, to create (and to shop) had won out. The Alphas had seamstresses and tailors and milliners—staffed by the Subs who longed to literally reach a little higher in life—and the Subs had the Neutral Zone. The Alphas had the Neutral Zone too, but only when they felt like slumming.

"Adrasteia fits me better than Hiro. Right, Hermes?" she asked, tucking a lock of her too straight, too black hair behind her ear. Charcoal black floated around her eyes—like a raccoon, she thought, or a superhero— making the brown of her irises turn gold. She was short, she knew, and the curve of the mirrored metal inverted her posture, even as the robes she donned whenever she did her real work swallowed her whole: the hollow cavern of a throat; the deepest black of her mind. It engulfed who she was, she'd said, until all that was left of her were the extremes of her skin pulsing out in escape.

It always came back to escape.

Hermes grunted and nodded his affirmation without even looking at her. He'd been her chaperone since she was fourteen but had known her much longer. He remembered her from before, on the ground, where he was a janitor in her father's laboratory at the university. He remembered her at six and smiling and visiting with her mother. So excited, she was, to play with the microscopes and uncover the hidden worlds pressed between two slabs of glass. He remembered her at eleven, sullen and dressed in all black, becoming a woman even as she lost the person who was meant to show her how to be one.

"You have always been so kind to my daughter," her father had said once, years before, when the Colony was only six shafts leading to an empty sky, devoid, as it was, of ozone or the migrating birds of his youth or gods. Her father had handed him a paper application to join the Guard, and he'd laughed at the idea of paper in a digital world, shrugging and shaking his head at the redundancies of government. "I can get you in," he had said, "but you must have a purpose there. And your purpose will be Hiromi."

"You seen Daniel yet?" she asked.

His eyes scanned the crowd as he moved his head from left to right and back again. He wondered if she remembered him from before, when he'd lifted her onto the stools to press the buttons on the Bunsen burners while her parents reviewed test results in the corner, when she'd giggled and clapped her hands at the sudden flame from behind the safety of her goggles. He thought she must remember when he'd handed her his handkerchief—the black one he'd bought especially for the occasion—the second time she'd visited after the test results became life results, when she didn't even look up but accepted the gift with a muffled sob and an unspoken goodbye to her mother. He had never had children himself. He'd never really wanted them. But the bright-eyed girl with the jack-o-lantern smile and the squid ink hair had vicariously filled a space for him he hadn't even realized was there. All the years in the Colony had dulled her visage a bit, but there was still a mischievous slant to her grin. And, through it all, he certainly still loved her as his own.

"There," he said.

"Finally!" Adrasteia gathered her robes like so many petticoats to free her legs and stormed through the crowd.

Daniel looked exhausted and afraid and strong as triplicate copies of himself emptied out into the Neutral Zone. It was the perfect combination—the one Adrasteia needed him to have if they were to get any real work done. She had shown him the door, and he had burst through a new man: a god.

"So, Asclepios," she said. "I see you've decided to join us."

He scanned what he knew of Greek mythology to remember the man-god worshipped for his healing capabilities; the son of Zeus—who wasn't?—whose followers formed a cult. He smirked at her choice for his pseudonym. He knew she was playing with him.

"I can just be Daniel," he said. "But yes. I want to see my family again. I know they're down there. And you, like it or not, are my best chance of getting there."

Adrasteia's lips pouted in an immature smirk Daniel immediately read as sarcasm. She appreciated his honesty. Besides, all the other recruits felt pretty much the same way.

"The name's for your protection, bud. But you can choose another if you'd like."

"I'd rather be less caught up in the naming of things," he sighed, "and more centered on the how we get the fuck out of here."

Dawn brought with it a crisp stagnancy that chilled the morning air, making it feel even colder than the night. The air held its sticky breath as the earliest risers woke to lap the dew from the tips of the blades of grasses. Paul smothered the remaining embers of their fire with decay-wetted leaves and wafted away the remaining tendrils of smoke that curled and twisted through the air like spirits. Manta slept, still and smiling. He loved watching her sleep, seeing the restful solace that washed over her. He thought he'd understood it when parents talked about it before—after all, he felt something special when he'd wake up before Daniel and sit up in bed and look on at the wonderful escape of his lover's face—but this was something altogether different. It spread a warmth from his extremities to the deepest hollows of his soul. Manta seemed so peaceful when she slept—so happy—and he ached to give her those moments in her waking life.

The wood around them was not the same they'd fallen asleep in. At dusk, the sharp fingernail shingles of the shortleaf pines had been claws of uncertainty, threatening their skin with gashes as deep as childhood wishes. Now, he noticed the soft green of the moss that flowed through their edges like blood through veins, tempering them like life undeterred. The broad leaves of cucumber magnolias that had offered them shadows of violence were now lush pillows presenting the beautiful white and gold of their fruits, haloed and radiant as they opened to meet the sun in their pollen-filled approximation. The slashed and peeling bark of beech trees were now more paper than cut skin, letters from a world that wanted—more than anything—to survive. The world had ended and yet life was all around them. The only beings that seemed to be having trouble in adapting were the ones who had attempted to change it all to their liking in the first place.

"You need any help with that?"

Toni knelt beside Paul and helped him roll his sleeping bag tightly to fit into the straps of his backpack. Their shoulder length black hair shone nearly white, like spider silk, as the rising sun caught it. Paul noted the thin black bands that wrapped their tanned skin around their fingers and forearms, sun-faded tattoos that degraded like the torn pages of a calendar to mark every moment since the Before. In the morning light, he looked at them with the same wonder Manta had summoned in the dim, small fire of the night before.

"Are you a boy or a girl?" she'd asked in the unabridged candor of a child.

"I'm neither," Toni had smiled. "And both."

Toni was calm and collected, crouched there by the flames opposite the father and daughter. They seemed as excited as Paul and Manta to be around other people. And filled, too, with as much dread.

Toni had grown up on the Cherokee Nation Reservation in northern Oklahoma. They'd had a good life there, for the most part. They were employed as a social worker for First Nations youth in a variety of tribes, and their telling of their time helping souls—young and old—find better footing in an ever-waning world made Paul miss his own days helping folks in the Before. They were asegi—"strange-hearted" they'd translated, "though most of the textbooks would say 'two-spirit'"—and identified, simultaneously, as both male and female and as something altogether different.

Manta was captivated by the magic in that. She had always assumed there was so much meandering in the becoming and the being, in the flux that seemed as constant as it was malleable. In the wisdom of a child who'd only ever fantasized about the lives of others—and too often imagined those lives as scary, dreadful things—she'd said, "I always thought real people were so much more than any one thing. That's how Dad tells it anyway." She'd crossed her arms over her chest and gave a knowing nod against the firelight as if satisfied her brighter interpretations had been correct.

When The Great Wave hit, Oklahoma, like much of the midwestern United States—the parts far enough away from the good ol' M-I-Crooked

Letter anyway—had been left largely unscathed. At least by the water. It wasn't long, though, before the scarcity of supplies and the influx of white people had chipped away at the Native Lands. Again. "There's a precedent for this," their Chief had sighed, too embittered to battle anymore. They watched history repeat itself for the umpteenth time as the tribe welcomed in the wanderers, provided what little shelter and sustenance they had, and felt the harsh whip of colonial imminent domain strip away their pastures and forests.

"It wasn't all bad, though. They didn't feed the people like me to the dogs this time," Toni said. The half-joke of fear and humility. "I guess that's something learned, right?"

"They ate the dogs instead," Manta whispered and placed her hand on Toni's knee.

Food waned as land was pillaged and destroyed. Vast acres of wheat and corn and soybean were decimated and subdivided into camps, sent to pasture to feed the cattle and the sheep and the pigs that were then wiped out faster than the plants. Normal people turned wicked, turned mad, turned feral. Eventually, Toni had set out with eight others.

"The 'Reverse Trail of Tears,' we called it," they said. "If the world was ending, if our lands were being stripped once more, we wanted to experience our ancestral home in North Georgia at least once before it was all gone." Toni looked around into the night and shrugged as if to say this is it. "We knew it was less a destination than just something to do in place of watching the world burn."

Only Toni had made it this far. Paul did not ask what happened to their eight companions. He clasped his hand gently around Manta's knee to prevent the words from escaping her as well. When he'd first invited them to stay, Paul had wet a scrap piece of cloth for Toni to wipe what he had mistaken in the dim light of the flare for freckles. The blood smeared when the fabric hit it, dry, but not quite so underneath, as if it had just happened. As if another night had not been kind. He wasn't sure if Manta had caught the exchange, but he took it as an unspoken answer to his unspoken question. He thought of his own daughter cleaning the blood from herself as she defended their home and wasn't sure she would have cared if she had seen the remnants of carnage spread across Toni's cheeks.

Toni's eyes grew wistful in the slowly dimming fire as they looked above the gentle billow of smoke into the starlight that peaked through the canopy. Like Paul and Manta, it seemed they had somehow managed to survive with most of their humanity intact. It felt good to speak, however briefly, with someone else who had endured what they had, a person who could remember the Before and not let the After drive them to desolation or madness. Even the sorrow felt special there by the fire. It heartened Paul. Perhaps there was more hope in the world than he'd assumed.

Now, in the dim light of morning, that hope seemed even more present. The timid, half-smile that cocked Toni's face to one side as they handed Paul his compacted sleeping bag was almost whimsical. It held within it so much pain amidst so much happiness, so much contentment within so much longing.

"Do you know where you're going from here?"

"Toni's coming with us."

Manta yawned her words like they were the obvious choice as she slipped from her sleeping bag. She stretched into the morning sky like a giant batting away the last of the night to leave the world new and refreshed. She was wide awake and certain, and she did not wait for any objection to her statement. She rolled her sleeping bag into a tight tube and strapped it to her rucksack. She counted her arrows by the fletchings and skipped to fetch the one she'd fired at their new companion the night before. She gave a final kick of leaves to cover the fire pit and nodded south toward the ocean.

"I heard the ocean in my dreams last night," she said as she worked to breakdown the campsite. "" hope it sounds halfway as pretty when we get there."

Paul smiled and shrugged off the pain that brimmed in Toni's eyes. It was overwhelming. But they would make it through. He pointed in the direction Manta had indicated and the three of them set off through the wood. Manta's own eyes were wide as she took in the world anew.

"Tell me about the dogs," she said, quickening her pace to keep up with Toni's long and certain stride. She had always wanted a pet. The idea of domestication, of co-existence, felt like a fairytale to her. ""Did you have one of your own?""

"I did," Toni smiled. There was a steadiness to their voice, like a librarian beginning their once upon a time, in a land far, far away. "A husky named Waya. With the softest white and grey fur and one blue eye and one brown eye. She was a little of both, like me."

"That's the world I want to live in," Manta said. "The one where everybody gets to be a little bit of everything: the princess and the knight that rescues her."

"You seem like someone who's already got it all in you," Toni said, and Manta beamed.

Paul smiled as he marched ahead. Seeing his daughter be hopeful, hearing her be young: it was all he ever wanted for her. Even if it was a fantasy.

"I'm not sure I can go along with this."

"Are you kidding me? After all of that?"

Paul exaggerated the shock on his face as he tossed the card stock samples to the coffee table. Three hours with the designer; countless ricochets between the ivory and the eggshell, the cream and the vanilla;

the languished debate between the charcoal or the obsidian ink, and they were right back where they started. But Paul wasn't surprised. Daniel always had trouble making decisions when it came to their wedding. It had taken him nearly four months to decide on their rings—a simple white gold band with circle cut sapphires dotting out their initials in Morse Code. Eight weeks later and he had narrowed the venue choices down to three and hired four different caterers to handle different portions of the reception. Paul thought it was cute and enjoyed being the level-headed one for a change.

"I know, I know," Daniel sighed. "Our wedding is not our marriage."

"Just like I—and every early 21st Century romcom—have told you a thousand times," Paul laughed. "But it is sweet that you care so much."

"We're going to remember this day forever."

"If we ever get to it."

Paul leaned back on the couch and rubbed his temples as he tried to focus on the white expense of the ceiling. It was endearing—the attention to detail—but it was also exhausting. Daniel closed his eyes and let his hands find purchase on a single card from their coffee table.

"This one," he said, before looking. He opened his eyes and Paul joined his gaze. It only took a split second before Daniel added, "With the copy from this one and the ink choice here."

Two more cards joined the one he had chosen, and Paul laughed as he slipped them from Daniel's grip.

"Done," he confirmed. He wiped his palms and held up his hands to put the subject to rest; to surrender.

Daniel turned to face him on the couch and smiled sheepishly. He rested his palm on Paul's always-agitated knee and slowed its pulsing in his grip. He smiled and let his eyes fill with the strange combination of solace, guilt, and hope he held within. He tried to offer only parts of it to his fiancé.

"I know I'm making mountains," Daniel said, "but one of the most vivid and lasting memories of my childhood is my mother looking at her damn wedding photo album. I mean, I was only six during the first pandemic, but it's so fucking clear. After we lost my dad, she lived in that album. It reminded her of everything she had, everything she would always be grateful for. And that was pretty powerful."

"So you're killing me off already?" Paul joked.

"I mean, how else am I supposed to have my *it was all worth it* survival story?" Daniel laughed, then pulled Paul in tightly to kiss his cheek. "No. In my fantasy, we're looking at the memories together. We're showing them to our one-day children. We're able to live beautifully in the future because of the foundations of our past."

"You really are a hopeless romantic, aren't you?"

"You make me one," Daniel said. He knew he was laying it on thick. But Paul brought out the sap in him. Plus he really felt it too, that unabashed feeling of being in the right place with the right person all those movies had assured him would happen one day. Why would he not want to share it? "We get to build this world together. Shouldn't we make it as magical as possible?"

"We should," Paul conceded. "I just think it's worth remembering there's magic in the flaws too. That's where we live. That's where our personalities are formed. The imperfections are just as rich and beautiful. They're what make us us." He kissed Daniel gently and smiled. "What I mean is: you keep making mountains, darling, and I will move them all for you. See? I can be sappy too."

Daniel laughed. "I guess we both get to be gods, huh?"

Paul shrugged and flashed the mischievous twinkle in his eye that Daniel loved.

"You can be a god if you want," he smirked as he stood and led his fiancé toward the bedroom. "I've always thought the devils had a lot more fun."

"So, I'm a god now," Daniel said. It was more a statement than a proclamation, more a sigh than a statement. "Just like you said I'd be. Asclepios. The God of Medicine. Like I'm supposed to heal the Colony or something."

"That's really cool, Daddy," Samantha laughed. Her beautiful young face was bursting with love and joy and not a glimpse of the pain of missing him. He hoped his face reflected the same.

"I always knew you would be. Slice?" Paul smiled as he offered up another hunk of pot roast with potatoes and carrots and green peas from the garden outside swimming in the lavish juices around the meat.

Daniel nodded but let his dinner languish on his plate as he took in the soft wooden expanse of their cabin. It seemed all too familiar and yet so foreign, so lived in and so forgotten. Outside the evening sky flickered with the brilliance of a setting sun inventing colors like promises offered only to never be seen again. Bands of night pierced through the hues to reveal the hollow gasp of stars—suns setting themselves on other worlds—just beginning to twinkle through the vast distance of forever. Paul's smile carved his cheeks into crescent moons that shone across their family dinner. Samantha giggled feverishly as she toyed with her fork and knife.

"How was school, dear?" Paul asked, and Samantha stopped the soldier-marching of her utensils and smiled broadly with half of her face.

"We dissected frogs in science class," she said and slipped her knife to and fro across her plate, motion memory reliving the experience. "Did you know they are amphibians? They can live in the water or out of the water."

"Just like us, honey," Paul smiled.

"But they have to come up for air," Samantha said, her butterknife scratching triple lines across the sides of her throat. "They lose their gills as they grow up. Whereas we have to grow them."

"Something's not right," Daniel whispered.

"And birds can live in the sky or out of the sky," Samantha said. "But there's not a name for that."

"That's because when they go up to the sky, they always come down," Paul said. "Nothing stays in the sky forever."

"Something's not right."

"Except for gods," Samantha laughed. She was always laughing. Forever happy. But her laughter seemed solemn this time. Didn't it? Daniel was sure it seemed sedated despite the bright and beaming smile.

"Yes, except for gods," Paul agreed. "Like your daddy."

"Something's not right here," Daniel said. "Don't you feel it?"

"It is a bit warm for this time of year, isn't it?" Paul agreed. "Unseasonably so. Slice?"

He held out a fresh serving of pot roast and veggies. Daniel offered his empty plate up on instinct.

"We learned about Icky-pus too," Samantha laughed. "After we cut open the little, tiny frogs. We ripped 'em right across the stomach so we could see what makes them hop. And then our teacher told us everything there is to know about the sun and heights and Icky-pus." Samantha laughed and zoomed her knife closer and closer to the overhead pendant light.

"Icarus," Paul corrected. Gentle Paul corrected gently.

"Right," she said. "Icarus. He was just a man, but he thought he was a god. He had wings like a bird, but when he got too close to the sun all the wax that held him together melted and..." She released her knife, and it zipped down to puncture the table. She released her knife; and it zipped down; and she laughed.

"Something's not right."

"No, that's the right story," Paul said and cupped his hand over Daniel's. "Our little girl. Learning so much. Growing so fast. It's amazing, isn't it, babe?"

Daniel smiled, and Samantha laughed. She grew her years in moments. Her laughter rang through the ages.

"This isn't real," Daniel said. He looked around desperately for an escape but couldn't bring himself to leave the table. He didn't want to leave his family.

"Gods are as real as you make them," Paul said.

"And so are demons," Samantha laughed.

"You can't have gods without demons," Paul said. "Otherwise what would the gods have to fight against? Who would pull you up? And who would pull you down? One cannot exist without the other. And both only ever exist because of the other. Slice?"

Daniel blinked his eyes and leaned back in his chair. A door appeared in the hallway that had not been there before. It captivated his attention, urged him to open it, promised secrets beyond its frame, demanded his full focus.

"I'm in the Haptic," he whispered.

"Slice?" Paul offered.

Daniel shook his head and stood. He kissed Gentle Paul on the forehead and Gentle Paul smiled. He tugged at Sweet Samantha's shoulders and breathed in her scent and Sweet Samantha laughed.

"Slice," said Paul.

"Cut," said Samantha.

"Asclepios translates to 'to cut open.' It's an action as much as it is a name," Paul smiled.

"It's a directive," Daniel nodded. He was lucid, finally. He was within the Mind Map and awake. But it was nearly too late. The door was there, calling. The countdown would soon commence.

"See you soon?" Paul asked as Daniel moved to leave.

"Soon," he promised.

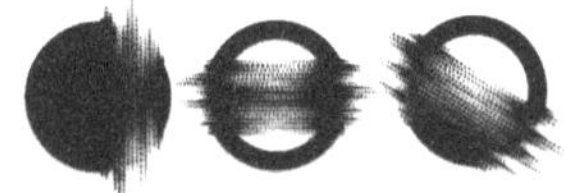

"Did it work?"

The way Lincoln was staring at Daniel from his perch atop the counter made Daniel feel almost violated. It was still so jarring, waking from the HMM, emerging from that place of comfort into reality. Daniel groaned and swallowed hard to clear his throat.

"Yes," he said. "But not until the very end."

"Hmmm..." Lincoln tried to hide the excitement from his face as he scanned the newly written code on his tablet. "I'll need you to take me through what happened. Verbatim."

Daniel nodded and tried to shake the nausea from his body. It was one of the first signs of over-exposure to the Haptic Mind Map. He couldn't let Lincoln see. Even with his excitement at their new project, he'd be forced to cut Daniel off.

Daniel couldn't have that. He wanted more than anything to be with Paul and Samantha again. One way or the other.

"The information came through," Daniel said. "But stilted. Coded almost. And forced. Like my memories were being overwritten."

"I mean, they kind of were." Lincoln tried to stifle his laugh at the unintended pun, and regained his work demeanor. "How do you mean?"

"I knew things," Daniel said. "And Paul—my husband—kept trying to guide the conversation to the information I'd asked you to put in."

Daniel had recruited Lincoln without telling him too much. He'd posited it as a learning experiment: an attempt to figure out if the HMM could teach by osmosis. Lincoln had coded Daniel's session to include the historical information in the database about the Ancient Greek God Asclepios. Daniel had demanded lucidity to ensure the knowledge took.

"Go on," Lincoln urged.

"But I didn't really wake up until the end. Until the door appeared."

"But you woke up?" Lincoln asked.

"Eventually, yes. But too late in the game."

"And the information we encoded was there, presented to you through your own memories as if it was a perfectly natural conversation you'd had?"

"I wouldn't say 'natural,'" Daniel winced.

"And the door?" Lincoln asked. "Did it still urge you out of the Map?"

Daniel nodded an affirmative. His stomach churned, and he swallowed hard to quell its rumbling. The excitement of the situation—the newness of the experiement—overwhelmed him as Lincoln bit his lip and jotted a few notes in the margins of his tablet.

"I can work with that," he smiled.

aul awoke suddenly. A sharp pain burrowed into his side. He felt it there like a phantom, pressing hard against his sleeping bag and the layers of old and ragged shirts that passed as clothing, almost at the skin, almost breaking through. The hardened feeling of suffocation clenched at his neck like the sharpened talons of a childhood ghoul. His eyes fought to understand the darkness, to create the pre-dawn scene with the same sincerity as his dream.

It had been a harsh one—his dreams usually were. What had once been exquisite escapes, moments of clarity and epiphany as his subconscious processed his day, were now anxiety-ridden manifestations of the horrors of the modern world. Though, he figured, they really had always been. It was just that the now could be so much more atrocious than even the evils of modernity had been. In the before there had been a consistency to the madness, an understanding of what savagery awaited, washed in civility as it was. In the now, the barbarism was on full display; the world itself was rising against its inhabitants.

"You may want to be a little faster with the coming to, sweet cheeks."

Paul blinked his vision into focus. The night quelled slightly, and his eyes found purchase on a gruff figure. His shaggy hair met his unruly beard, and his eyebrows did not separate, making his hirsute visage seem more bear than human in the dim light. A beast with matted fur. A serpent caked in scales. Paul squirmed. The blunt barrel of a pistol pierced his side and a stone-sharpened knife rested just above his clavicle. He felt his body tense. His toes pressed against his sleeping bag and pulled the fabric taut.

The goon smiled.

"There you go, Sleeping Beauty."

The man lifted the knife slightly from Paul's throat, releasing the tension while intensifying it. Threat dripped from the tip of the blade, just outside of Paul's vision, ready to strike without warning, with no direct eyeliner to grant preparation. Paul shifted his focus to the man crouched beside him. He was filthy. The dirt that caked him was obvious even in the pre-dawn darkness, and his limbs seemed to slither like the snakes sprung from a gorgon's head as they enveloped Paul in their violence, in their stone.

Paul lifted himself up to rest on his forearms. The crisp pre-morning air licked the sweat on his back, and he felt his skin prickle in undulating waves. His eyes searched the periphery and found Manta, eyes wild and bound with a handkerchief pressed across her mouth. Toni was nowhere to be seen. Their rucksack was gone. They'd left no trace behind.

Seeing his daughter gagged and feral shook the remnants of night from his bones. The clarity of rage ached through his muscles, urging an action his rational side knew better than to undertake. The nightmare of reality drowned any dreams of heroics in the humidity of Southern dawn.

"Take whatever you want," Paul said. "Just let her go."

The man at his side chuckled. It was an awful laugh, phlegm-filled and tight, measured in its frivolity as if, even with his weapons in hand, it was all he had left to control. "You ain't nowhere near bargaining, mister," he said. "We already got everything anyway."

For the first time, Paul noticed his captor's companion. She was small and shared the man's ragged visage. Her blond hair clumped and matted against her petite shoulders like a disheveled nest of leaves turning dead and harsh in anticipation of Winter. Her thin nose exaggerated her profile as she paced back and forth around the perimeter of the camp. She looked like a hawk circling its prey, toying with it before its cool-dark talons find purchase against bone. Her hands gripped a semi-automatic rifle at her breast. Another was strapped across her back. A pistol clung to her hip.

Paul knew it was unlikely—nearly nine years after The Wave—for even the gun-hoarding dooms-dayers to still have ammo, let alone barrels that were cleaned and oiled enough to fire accurately. If they fired at all. But with Manta nearby, it wasn't a risk he wanted to take.

"What do you want?" Paul asked.

"You ain't from near here, is you?" the woman growled. Her voice was as garbled as the man's laugh. When they laughed together it was a nursery rhyme gone sour.

"He talks like he can barter," the man cackled, head high before locking his eyes on Paul's. They were all pupil: dark and cold and lacking in any trace of humanity. His bipedal movements, his language itself were just imagined remnants of something he once was—muscle memory clinging on from the Before.

"What you got here—a week's worth of rations if you're lucky; a flimsy bow and arrow; and a couple ratty sleeping bags. That ain't worth shit to us."

"The real payload is in bodies," the Hawk said. She knelt in front of Manta and reached a dirty palm out to cup her chin.

"Don't worry," the Snake said as he tightened his grip on the knife at Paul's neck. "It's live bodies they want. And its live bodies we give."

"As long as the bodies ain't too much trouble," the woman laughed.

Manta's eyes tightened in fury, and Paul urged her to calm with his own. He'd heard tale of the pop-up societies that traded in people as a supposed civilized approach to life after the Wave. They posited themselves as better when compared to the cannibalistic Roamers, offering shelter and scraps in exchange for a hard days' work. Like a company town. Like a plantation. Leave it to humanity to decide, when faced with the unruly New World, slavery was the appropriate response.

"Kids bring the biggest haul," the woman smiled. It was a wicked and wild and unruly grin, like the stretched snarl of a jackal. "'Specially little black ones." She slipped her filthy fingers under the fabric and pulled down Manta's gag.

"Fuck you!" the girl spat, and the Hawk leapt back to her feet with maniacal laughter.

"We got ourselves a lively one here," she exclaimed. "Bet she gets us a month's worth of batteries."

"All you're getting from me is a bandage if you're lucky," Manta said. "A coffin if you're not."

The Snake laughed again as he moved back from Paul, motioning with the knife for him to rise.

"Get your shit together," he said. "And, iffen you got the good sense of a 'possum by the highway, maybe think about shutting your little bitch up."

Dawn broke across the Colony with an ecstatic smile, like the technological sun was holding a secret only those up early enough could know, the ones and zeros of a life renewed. It sent waves of LED electricity across the hallways, rising floor by floor as if it really could match the outside world. Daniel wasn't sure it did. He'd long suspected the daylight hours had been shifted and altered to increase productivity. He wasn't sure of anything anymore except that he needed to find an escape, that he needed to make his way back to his husband and his daughter. He knew in his heart they were alive. He knew they were waiting. And that knowing was almost too much to bear.

Back when he had thought the outside world was continuing onward, better amidst the sacrifice of fifteen years of his life, he had managed to make it through most days with only a faint, wayward glance into the distance, with simply a marginal longing for what he had left behind. Now, he had no idea what sort of world Paul and Samantha were facing. He imagined great beasts had risen from the seas, or descended from the mountains, or erupted from the hollows of the earth, swallowing whole cities in their wake. His mind pictured the kinds of creatures that littered the fantasy stories he had collected to read to Samantha once she was older. He saw endless scenarios of manic torture and human violence play out in his head. The reality, he knew, was probably much more mundane and endlessly more terrifying. He had to find a way out.

"Is the burlap really necessary?"

Lincoln's voice was muffled beneath the fabric, but Daniel could still hear the fatigue. He was sure it littered the syllables in his own throat as well, coating them with the deep southern drawl of smothering heat and hard work.

"Keep moving, acolyte," Hermes grunted as the triplicate maneuvered their way from the elevators and through the Neutral Zone. It was the one floor the sun couldn't touch, and, as such, its inhabitants pretended the days didn't matter, trudging through the longest night of debauchery they could handle before drifting off to reset and begin again renewed.

Daniel would have thought the entire scene comical if he had it in him to laugh. When he'd been in Lincoln's place, he'd worried the accoutrements of ritual would draw more attention to them than necessary. Now, eyes open and at Hermes' side, he saw the Dominants leading their Submissives by ropes and leashes; the hooded robes pulled heavy across people's foreheads; the sultry striving for anonymity amidst even the forgotten.

Adrasteia was waiting for them inside her makeshift headquarters. The thick expanse of fabric that walled the tent's inner sanctum off from the rest of the Zone hung dangerously close to the open flames of candles strewn around for light, for ambiance. Folding chairs stood like pews, stretched to the sides with a central aisle, and a podium cobbled of wooden crates and plastic boards waited across the room for a speaker to ignite its majesty. It reminded Daniel of the tent revivals which had gained so much momentum as the End of Times drew nearer. *Appropriate*, he thought, seeing it all for the first time without burlap over his own eyes. The idea of a bunch of gods attending church felt strangely perfect for the City in the Sky.

"Lincoln Dunnwater," she said, announcing the name like it gave her power over him. "I hear you might be the key we're looking for."

"That depends," he said, exclaiming his surprise as Hermes guided him forcefully into a chair. His hands moved to remove the sack from his head, but Adrasteia's sharp "tsk" made him stop.

Daniel placed a firm palm on his shoulder to tell him to heel, to give him a sense of comfort and connection. Lincoln went limp, but Daniel could still feel the tension trembling in his chest.

"How much has Daniel told you?" she asked, using his real name in place of his code name. She wasn't quite ready to allow Lincoln into her world of resistance. She knew already what Daniel had shared. Her question was a test of Lincoln's understanding.

"Not much," Lincoln admitted, and Daniel stifled a chuckle. "Just that you are searching for a way to give information to a lot of people quickly. That the information needs to be accepted as truth and needs to be innate. And that the dissemination of said information needs to be covert and total. Secretive and instilled. And, from that, I put the rest together myself."

"And the rest is?"

"Look," Lincoln sighed. The exasperation in his voice was palpable. The fatigue from their night of work slapped against the lack of sleep to settle in beneath the burlap. "I was willing to help Daniel to a point because he literally saved me before we got trapped inside this giant spiderweb. But what he's asking—or, I'm guessing, what you're asking him to ask—has implications I don't think you've fully thought through."

Adrasteia leaned back in her chair and crossed her arms over her chest. Daniel shuddered. He had considered those implications, and they terrified him, but his desire to get out outweighed their possibilities. *It would all happen so fast,* he'd convinced himself, *no one would be able to take advantage of the loopholes they were creating.*

"It's one thing," Lincoln continued when no one else spoke, "to adjust the Haptic Mind Mapping system to implant some facts that just get scattered into the simulation like a dream trying to interpret the day. Writing the code that taught Daniel obscure facts about some Ancient Greek God is one thing. It brought forth concepts that were already there—a subconscious memory of some Eighth grade reading lesson bubbling forth to the surface. Like a subterranean creek that was always there and looking for weak spots in the dirt to come through. But that very same code, when tweaked this way or that, could be used to convince someone that Daniel, himself, is God. That he must be obeyed. And true, not everyone who believes Daniel is God is going to obey him. I mean, that's why we've got so many religious sects to start with. But the point is, tweak it just a little and those 'facts' we put in can say anything, and folks would wholly and truthfully believe them. It's literal brain washing. In the wrong hands, that sort of tech could end the world."

Daniel smirked at the summersaults Lincoln's mind was playing on his tongue. He saw so much of himself in the young man.

"And you think these are the wrong hands?" Adrasteia asked.

Lincoln shrugged. The splintering fabric cascading over his shoulders heaved like straw in a bundler. "I don't know you. Maybe you are; maybe you're not. Thing is: once the technology is created, it's out. It's done. And any grubby little fingers can find it: the right ones or not. One side erodes the separation of mind and matter, once the other side matters more, they get to matter more than mind."

"In that same mode of thinking," Adrasteia countered, "if the technology can be created, it will be. Wouldn't you agree? You did just confirm it is possible."

Daniel could feel the grimace as Lincoln's hooded head hung low. Hermes stifled a smile as Daniel reached to comfort the young man hunched over himself in defeat. The cat was out of the bag, claws still snagged in burlap, but too sharp to be captured again. Adrasteia's hand met his shoulder first.

"Therefore," she continued, "shouldn't it be us—be YOU—who creates it? Get ahead of the curve, so to speak. Wouldn't safer hands be a part of that scenario?"

"That's a reductive form of thinking," Lincoln shot back. "That puts us on a streetcar careening straight towards an end, with no choice as to whom we mow down in the process. The Trolley Problem where everyone dies."

"I like him," she chuckled to Daniel as she removed the burlap hood.

"Speaking of the end where everyone dies," she started. A swift finger lifted the chin of her new recruit as her face steadied its countenance for the story she had told too many times before.

"I'm sorry, sweetheart," Paul whispered, more to himself than to Manta, as they marched through the early morning wood. Their hands were bound at their backs and leashed to the Snake's waist as he guided them through the ill-defined-by-purpose which that slalomed through the trees. He struck his palms like sudden bites at the items inside Paul's rucksack, tossing aside things he didn't need as if basic commodities were not the precious gems they'd become since the Wave. The Hawk did the same to Manta's bag. They were hedonistic scavengers, living only for the moment with no thought to tomorrow.

Manta wasn't sure if the tears that blurred her vision were from fear or anger. Both were so closely related. She trained her gaze beyond the welling water to memorize the backs of their captors. Her father's words bounced around her head, stitched themselves like yarn through the memory.

"What's the plan, Dad?" she whispered back.

"I don't know," he admitted. Manta had never heard her father's voice quiver quite so swiftly. Like her arrows, it thwipped between the tiny, agitated molecules of air, hoping for purchase and finding only more sky. "I—I can't think."

"Come on, Dad," Manta urged. She wished she could reach her bow, but the Hawk was clutching her bag with her talons. "You faced the literal end of the world and came up with a plan to save us. And now you've got a me who can actually do stuff."

Paul twisted his wrists and felt the rope grind against his arms.

His skin tightened against the fibers as his blood pulsed with the struggle. Their captors had seemed inept—kidnappers by happenstance in the new world of the After—but they tied a good knot. He studied them carefully, striving to picture them in the Before. They probably had a house, maybe a kid or two. They were executives or accountants. They worked in construction or checked people out at the local Piggly Wiggly. They maintained a somewhat peaceful existence before the Wave dragged everything they had built into the deepest recesses of the Atlantic. He could play on that.

"Where are you taking us?" he called out forcefully, stopping their progressive march.

The Hawk raised her eyebrows at the Snake as a smirk slivered across his cheeks. His tongue played against his teeth as he spoke.

"Somewhere they don't like questions," he sneered.

Paul was undeterred. Whatever life in the After had turned them into, he still believed in their humanity. He had to. Otherwise what sort of world was he leaving for Manta?

"My name is Paul," he said. "And this is my daughter, Samantha. What are your names?"

They trudged through the forest with sure feet, loud and unafraid of whatever else was out there in the morning sun.

"I'm shut-the-fuck-up, and this is mind-your-own-goddamn-business." The Hawk cackled and turned back to Manta's bag. She pulled the dogeared copy of one of Daniel's books out and snarled as she tossed to it to the ground.

"You bitch!" Manta howled.

Paul felt the rope at his waist tug tightly as she tried to steer toward the discarded novel. She struggled in vain as the Snake tugged back, laughing as he shook his head. The Hawk licked her lips and feigned an exaggerated pout as she walked back to pick up the book. She cocked her head to the side as she held it just out of Manta's reach.

"This mean something to ya?" she asked, flipping through the pages. "'Property of Daniel,' huh? Well, he just told me his name is Paul and yours is Samantha. So either he's lying or you're still dumb enough to think an object can replace somebody you lost."

"He's coming back," Manta insisted.

"Oh, is he, now?" the Snake hissed as the Hawk cackled.

Manta's eyes went wide as he captor tore a page from the book, tossing it to the forest floor.

"We best leave a trail for him then, huh?" she asked. "Wouldn't want him getting lost trying to find you."

She ripped out a chapter and tossed the pages to the breeze. Manta wailed.

"Stop!" Paul pleaded. "Look, you want batteries? You want food rations? If we've got things like books, we've got those too. Let us go, and we'll get you whatever you need."

The Snake shrugged as the Hawk met his gaze with the half-frown of consideration. She looked back at the young girl, and, for a moment, a hint of rememberance, of sympathy, washed across her eyes. She sighed, then laughed, as she ripped another page from the book and hurled it away.

"Don't bother with them, Dad," Manta scowled, the intensity of her voice growing more fierce in captivity. "They're not even people anymore."

"You hear that, Joey?" the Snake asked solemnly, licking the air like he could cry. "She don't think we're people."

"Ain't it funny when the cattle try to talk?" she replied, tugging sharply at the rope to almost trip them along the path.

They marched forward in silence, Manta seething hot enough to burn. Paul tried to calm her with his eyes. He attempted to cultivate a plan.

The trees thinned. Thick, aged and mighty trunks had shrunk to the toothpicks of eight-year-old oaks and maples. Vines twisted across what were obviously once manicured expanses of grass with Japanese Boxwoods or Azaleas still clinging to domesticity. They were nearing the remnants of what had once been civilization. If Paul was going to act, it had to be soon, before the Hawk and Snake were joined by the rest of their menagerie.

"So that's it, huh? The world down there really ended?"

Lincoln sat across from Daniel in his office, eyes frozen open as he stared at the LED approximation of a windswept meadow beyond the false window.

"In some form or another, yes," Daniel confirmed. "I've verified it beyond Adrasteia."

He understood the shock that slipped through every cell in Lincoln's body. All the pain and the loss and the fear and the hope were numbing and unbearable and necessary.

"It actually explains a lot." Lincoln bit his lip as he spoke. He wanted to feel something—anything—to let him know he was still solid. "The early move in; the repeated days; the nix on external communication. Shit! My sister. My parents."

"There are still a lot of unknowns," Daniel said. He did his best to sound sure and comforting. "The other Colonies could be as intact as ours. They could have initiated rescue missions. The folks down there could have acted. Humans are resilient like that."

"We're fucking ants," Lincoln sighed. "Building up our hills, excavating intricate pathways with zero regard for the earth we're pushing and pulling about, and waiting for the other shoe to drop, or the lawnmower to run us over, and collapse it all down to nothing."

"But what happens when someone steps on an ant bed?" Daniel tried to sound hopeful. He wanted to be positive. He had to be—he had to know Paul and Samantha were still down there. "They get right back to the rebuilding."

"Yeah. While trampling all over their brethren and eating the corpses of the ones who got crushed."

Daniel swallowed hard and quashed the fear that lingered just beneath his every thought from surfacing. He steadied his breath as Lincoln tried to find his own. The boy seemed to grow up right in front of him. His gangly arms found the rigor that came with knowing too much about life.

His back stooped from the pressure. The sweep of black stubble along his jawline grew tough, like spikes, and threatened to turn grey.

"I remember you now," Daniel said. "From when you came to me back at school. You've grown so much since then; become so strong and firm and resilient. You are the product of your family, and if they created the man I see in front of me now, they have that same strength and resilience. They've found a way to survive. You can be sure of it."

It was a lie. Lincoln knew it was a lie. But it comforted them both all the same.

The men sat in silence as their brains anticipated the worst and tried to squash it. Human nature versus human hope enveloped them. Deep down Daniel knew it was all the same. Hope begot faith inside man's longing for understanding, yet the same desire that created gods created demons. The search for hope manifested both religion and science. They were the same coin, after all. Not two sides of one—not heads or tails. Both required a blind leap.

Daniel cleared his throat to stifle the inappropriate laugh which threatened to emerge from his chest. It wasn't the time or the place, but it amused him that he was about to take the biggest literal leap of his life.

"Okay. So we tell everyone the truth. Covertly. Leaving no room for doubt."

Daniel nodded as Lincoln mulled over the nuances of her plan in his mind.

"But then we've got thousands of scared souls—scared down to their core in this innate new understanding they can't even place but know is real. All of them clamoring for the exits like they're the entrance to Eden. The motherfucking Pearly Gates. Thing is though: How do we know it's better down there?" Lincoln asked, pulling Daniel from his reverie. "I mean, we're trapped here, but we're safe. Life for us has continued on with as much normality as it can. For over eight years we've had no clue the world we knew ended and that somehow we'd survived. Maybe this is how we survive. Maybe staying here is what we are supposed to do."

"You may very well be right," Daniel nodded. He leaned back in his chair and looked up toward the imaginary heavens, down toward the supposed hell. "But I have to believe my husband is still down there. And that he's raising up the little girl that we had just adopted into a brilliant and powerful young woman. And I sure as hell have to meet her."

He watched Lincoln's eyes dart as competing thought ping ponged through his brain.

"Besides," he continued. "Shouldn't everyone have the information and the choice of what to do with it?"

Lincoln frowned. He wanted to be sympathetic, but the risks were too great. Daniel watched his waver and sighed.

"I know this plan seems rash," he said. "Trust me. I can see that. But now that I know what happened—or even that something happened—I can't wait six more years for the truth to emerge and rally the people to escape. Every day is one more day my family is facing the end of the world alone. Satan himself could be waiting at the bottom of those chutes, and I would fight him tooth and nail to reach them."

"I get that. I do," Lincoln said. The empathy on his face was real. "But how many real, living people are in this thing? People we know for sure have survived. If we fuck it up, we're putting hundreds of thousands of lives in danger just so you can meet one little girl who may or may not even be alive, and, if she is, sure as fuck won't even know who you are. I don't mean to be harsh. But you told me yourself she was a baby when you came here."

Daniel shuddered. Hearing his own fears vocalized had been a low blow, and it froze him in his tracks.

"People should have free will," Daniel said. "We all deserve to be free."

"Free will is what got us here in the first place," Lincoln countered. "We destroyed our own planet with all our fair markets and free will. And then we chose to come here."

"Well, now we have to make it better." Daniel's voice was calm, but he could hear the pleading in it. "People deserve a choice. Or, at the very least, the knowledge to make their choice. That's all I'm asking of you."

Lincoln nodded, but Daniel could still sense his unease.

"Now you have a choice to make," Daniel said. He pulled on his best therapist voice. He tried to make Lincoln understand the importance within his own freedom. "What you do is entirely up to you. I'm sure you have more questions. Why don't you sleep on it tonight and we can meet with Adrasteia again tomorrow. It's a lot to take in."

Lincoln nodded again and stood.

Daniel's breath pulled tight. "I'm sure I don't have to say—"

"I won't say anything," Lincoln assured him. "You have my word."

hy use the HMM? Why not just hijack the Colony's intercom system? Or blast it out in pixels across the LED skyline?"

Lincoln had definitely taken the night to think about things. Daniel let a thin smile slip across his lips as he watched the young man's analytical brain consider, question, reallocate, and spew out everything that crossed through his synapses. It reminded him of his own younger self, back before he allowed himself to linger in the silence of the what ifs rather than chase them down.

Adrasteia, though years younger, was still a product of her station. She tilted her head slightly to the side, and her lips quivered as she tried not to purse them in pity. It was a habit from being raised as always right—with her parents, with the staff at home, at her private school—and one she chided herself for constantly.

"We've tried that," she said. "Twice. Back when I first found out and was an impulsive child. Not that you're impuslive. Or a child—" She tried to catch herself again. "My first instinct, like yours, was to let everyone know. To blow the lid off the whole sardine can. So I stole my Dad's codes and tried to tell the world. The redundancies in place are intense. And they've only strengthened them throughout the time we've been trapped here. They've known since Day One a day of reckoning would come. And they've put a million and four things in place to keep us all blind sheep, jumping fences so that everyone on this ark can sleep peacefully."

Hermes cleared his throat from his post at the door and tapped three fingers on his wrist. Even though no one in the Colony wore a wristwatch, even though most people on the land hadn't worn one either, the short-hand symbolism of human communication was still intact. Daniel knew exactly what it meant. It was nearing 10:30am, the time when Adrasteia's father paused his workday and swooped back to their living quarters for tea. He and Lincoln would need to be long gone by then.

"Plus, can you imagine the chaos that would ensue?" Adrasteia continued as she nodded to her bodyguard. "No," she said, "the HMM is subtle. We can implant the knowledge alongside a calmness. We can target the people who need to know, the ones who can help. Using the Haptic, we can select the right team to lead everyone out of here and to safety."

Lincoln frowned, but he nodded his head. Daniel clamped a hand over his shoulder to comfort him. It was a big ask, he knew. And he hoped his desire to see his family again was not clouding his judgement. The young man was right. The code they were asking him to write could be extremely dangerous in the wrong hands. But for that matter, the Haptic Mind Map had been just as treacherous in its ability to create a virtual reality using a subject's own memories. Still, he'd helped them create the code to add in a door that shouldn't have been there to let them exit. He'd been the first to add in something new, to manipulate the mind into creating a foreign object. The groundwork was there already, just waiting to be exploited.

Hermes grunted again from the doorway, and Daniel pulled himself back into the present. Lincoln's eyes still darted back and forth like he was reading a book, memorizing the scene, as he considered all the new information Adrasteia and Daniel had placed upon him. Daniel knew the roller coaster well, careening through the ally oops of sudden shifts in reality: that helpless feeling of being tossed about at the whim of some thankless god.

"Look," Adrasteia said, the finality in her voice both certain and pleading, "we can do this without you if we have to. But it's going to happen. Just like the decision you made when you joined the Colony, you can be on the side of positive change—the right side—or you can go back to sleep. The choice is yours. But you can't un-know what you've learned. And it will haunt you. Trust me. I speak from experience."

Lincoln's eyes jumped across the knickknacks that lined the room as if they could hold the answer he longed to find, but each ceramic face held a blissful ignorance. He scanned Daniel's supportive face and imagined himself a sophomore at Emory once more.

"I'll do it."

He gulped the words as if simultaneously trying to keep them in and willing them to escape. A smile parted Adrasteia's lips as she nodded to Hermes. The bodyguard moved forward, producing another cuff like the one they'd given Daniel and escorted the pair to the door.

"Daniel can tell you how to work the cuff. Thank you both for doing this. You won't be sorry," Adrasteia promised.

Lincoln sighed, speaking more to himself than the room as they took their leave. "I kind of think we'll all be."

The midday sun was callous, bearing down on them with a sticky intensity which forced them to take shallow breaths as their captors marched them past the makeshift barricade that surrounded the small North Georgia town. It was a strange amalgamation of a past deemed obsolete: old shopping carts and televisions, broken boards with spines of exposed nails protruding from amidst shards of shattered pottery and bricks. Vines of old power cables and computer cords twined around books and children's toys to hold everything in place. Anything that could be spared—which, considering the lack of most necessities was a surprising amount—had been stacked to create both height and obstacle.

There didn't seem to be any people around though. Paul wasn't sure if that was a benefit or not.

They paused just outside a metal gate strapped into place by neon checkered bungee cords that were nearly bleached to pastels by the sun and humidity. The Snake nodded, and the Hawk went ahead on her own. As she passed through the bars, the barricade shifted and heaved but held firm.

A poorly painted sign above the gate read "New Yukon" in an exaggerated hand which did its best to feign elegance.

"She's just got to check on your accommodations," the Snake said, sarcasm dripping like venom from his teeth. "It'll just be a few moments if you don't mind waiting here in the lobby."

Manta stretched her shoulders back as she squared her hips. The air stung as the rope shifted against her wrists, lifting slightly to expose the damp sweat beneath the twine. She eyed her rucksack slumped by the Snake's feet. The Hawk had dropped it there before she'd skirted the gate. It languished limply atop the well-trod dirt. The Hawk had discarded most of her belongings: her favorite shirt and one of Daddy Daniel's books she'd brought along to comfort her by their evening fires. But her bow was still there alongside three sharpened arrows. The Snake followed her gaze a chuckled softly as he dropped Paul's bag beside it, checking their knots with a quick tug of the rope still tied to his waist and daring them to make a move.

Paul lifted his pinky finger to caution her as he studied the situation. The tree line was a good three hundred yards away, with only a sparse outcropping of saplings offering no cover between them and the thicker underbrush. Even if they could break free, it would be a long jaunt to safety. Plus the Snake still held the pistol in his hands, laughing as he twirled it like an Old West caricature and pointed it at his victims with a stuttering ""bang bang."" His knife was tucked securely in his boot.

Both promised impending danger. Still, Paul knew that now was their best chance of escape.

He waved his pinky once more behind his back to catch Manta's eye, then used it to tap out a quick Morse code. Zulu | Uniform.

$$— \, . \, . \, | \, . \, . \, —$$

He smiled as Manta nodded. She had understood his message. *Zulu, Uniform. Tug* and *Run.*

Raising his index finger he counted to three at a slow and steady pace that still felt rushed. They had to act, he knew, but they were facing their last chance at freedom. When his ring finger lifted, the father and daughter heaved quickly away from the Snake, pulling him off balance and pitching his body over. Then, just as suddenly, they burst forward, using the expanse of rope between them to wrap their captor's lanky extremities. The three toppled into a pile on the ground, the gun flinging out from the Snake's grip to spin in the dirt a few feet away. Paul reached for the knife in the Snake's boot and sliced at the rope, freeing Manta from the chain and giving her the slack she needed to worm her way out of her bindings. Paul rested his entire weight on his knees as he perched atop the Snake's chest and throat. Manta took the knife and quickly freed he father before rolling to her bag and extracting an arrow. She held it to the Snake's throat, the sharpened tip of the stone threatening to puncture skin. Fury welled in their kidnapper's eyes as Manta's dared him to move.

"Enough." Paul said. He rubbed his newly freed wrists and reached for their bags. "We are better than them."

Manta did not move. The sinewy muscles in her young arms strained as she fought the urge to plunge the sharpened tip into his arteries.

"They're just going to do this to someone else," she growled.

Paul wavered. She was right. He was proud that she usually was. Yet he couldn't let this world turn her into the monster it was remaking so many others into. He retrieved the pistol and aimed it at the Snake. The metal felt cold against his palm, even in the sweltering heat. It was a heartless piece of manmade destruction: tight and compact and empowering in his grasp.

Manta was right. But she shouldn't be the one to kill him.

He shuddered as he pulled back the hammer and heard it click into place. Manta pulled back as well but kept her arrow firmly in her right hand and the knife at the ready in the other. The Snake laughed, gruffly and maniacally.

"You ain't got enough balls to shoot," he snarled from the ground, convinced still of his own power.

Paul pulled his hands together to steady the shake in the barrel. The gods to his left urged peace, but the devils on his right were louder. Quickly, he shifted his aim to the ground beside the Snake and pulled the trigger. In slow motion, the hammer clamped into place and the cylinder shifted. He braced himself for the noise, for the blowback, but there was nothing. Paul cocked and fired twice more in rapid succession.

The gun was all for show. There were no bullets.

Paul tucked it inside his bag and swooped both his and his daughter's up. Manta kept her sites trained on the Snake as they backed slowly away. Then, once they reached a safe distance, the pair turned to bolt to the tree line. Once there, they could get hide long enough to get lost to the wilderness.

Paul startled as the click and lock of a rifle cocking sounded behind them. He heard the Hawk's voice trill across the field as she screached after them, demanding they stop. *No bullets*, he reminded himself. *Run!*

It sounded like an explosion, loud and sparking and violent, as the rifle fired. A bullet whizzed past them and splintered into the trunk of an oak sapling, sending shards of white wood flying like the flames of fireworks dwindling toward the ground.

"Next one won't miss," the Hawk called.

"Keep running," Paul commanded his daughter as he stopped and stepped between the gun and Manta. He dropped the bags to the ground and held up his hands as he turned around, praying his little girl would make it to cover, wishing her freedom and aching as he turned away.

The Snake was pulling himself up from the dirt to join the Hawk and two new companions from the town. They were just as weather-worn as the animals who'd brought them here, but where the captors were cocky, these men had a submissive fear behind their eyes. Still, their stoic faces didn't flinch as they raised two more guns in Paul's direction.

"I was gonna be nice to y'all seeing as there is a little girl and all," the Snake hissed. "But seems my welcome mat is a little dusty."

"I surrender," Paul yelled, wishing for Manta to run like the Wave.

"You don't have to shoot," Manta said.

Her voice was coming from behind him, but not nearly far enough away. She had stopped, unwilling to leave her father. She still held the blade and arrow in her hands, considering them for what little protection they offered. Her bow was still in her bag. Her bag was yards away at her father's feet.

The Hawk kept the loaded rifle braced on her shoulder as the Snake and the two new townsfolk scurried forward.

"That's more like it," he snarled. "But thanks for the show. Now these two fine folks'll escort you on in and show you around your new home while we collect our rates."

Flowers wilted in vases and sagged, petal-less, toward the dust-covered kitchen table of rounded wood, intricately carved along the edges. Chairs that matched, a few with broken cross rails but mostly intact, sat halfway under the table awaiting the return of loved ones gathering for dinner, longing to hear the tales of homework completed or fingers crossed for that big promotion or upturned, innocent palms slyly feeding green beans to the dog. Families had been here. Families had been here since the Wave. They had loved and lived and strived to move forward with the traditions of togetherness meant to imbue notions of society atop whispering fantasies of home. But the water in the vases had mildewed and dried and left a sticky residue within the clouded glass.

The new downtown of New Yukon spread across the winding street like classic Americana. Identical tract houses, factory built and trucked in just the same as the trailers the sprawling Atlanta transplants had found an eyesore elsewhere, popped up like thistles in a new suburban nightmare. The onward march of progress: nature dotted with the mark of humanity. The neighborhood was relatively new, built maybe thirty years before the Wave, as Atlanta stretched itself to the max as a metropolis and those with means sought higher ground. Now, most of the houses featured the broken windows and kudzu draperies which had become fashionable as nature retook what was once her own. Most of the houses felt hollow, even from the street, appearing as gaunt faces with front door mouths hung open and no memory of light behind their eyes. Others were better kept. In those, the windows, though opened to allow for a cross breeze against the sweltering what-was-left-of-Georgia, held panes of polished glass. Doors remained on hinges. And lawns, though uneven and patchy, were not the jungle-thick yards of sunburnt dandelions and crabgrass and creeping vines. They popped like daffodils against the burning yellow sun.

The house they were in was not well-kept. Furniture, once carefully selected and cared for, ripped to expose its stuffing like the innards of roadkill, splintered in the corners, and heaved the contents of its drawers to the floor. School pictures faded in sharp angles by the sun, bank statements denoting imaginary dragons protecting imaginary treasure, and ripped journal pages from when dreams were things meant to be kept littered the floors like burial mounds. Appliances had been ripped from their alcoves—no doubt now resting amidst the clutter of the surrounding barricade—and the sudden hollow from when life had been denoted by the collecting of things made the space feel ancient and unwelcoming.

"Wait here," the Hawk had told them before clamping the padlock that held the front door in place.

A clump of misshapen bread and a ramekin of butter sat on the counter. Paul hadn't seen either in forever. He wasn't sure Manta even knew what they were. It was an odd display of power: manufactured and perishable food provided for prisoners. A swath of white-green mold puckered from the pores in the crust, fanning out in circles and lines that called an S.O.S.

Manta drew circles in the dust on the dining table while Paul searched the kitchen drawers for anything weapon worthy. The cutlery was gone, but there were pots and pans. There was glass to be broken. But even if they made it out, they'd still have the barricade to contend with. For the first time, Paul noticed the fear quivering behind the resilience in Manta's eyes.

Why didn't you keep running? he wanted to ask her. *Why didn't you get away?*

"I'm going to keep us safe," he said, as if speaking it and believing it could be the same thing.

Manta wiped away her circles and brushed the dust off her hands.

"I know," she said, stronger than any child should ever have need to be. "We'll keep each other safe."

Paul sat beside his daughter and pulled her gaze to his own.

"I'm serious," he said. "When we chose you, we made a promise to always protect you. That's what sent Daniel up to the Colony. And that's what I'm going to keep doing down here."

"But I'm the reason we need protection," Manta cried. "If I hadn't wanted to see the ocean—"

"We would have had to leave the cabin eventually. And the salt stores running out was reason enough. It wasn't your fault."

Manta's eyes fell as she crossed her arms over her chest. Her heel kicked against the leg of her chair, and it skidded harshly against the wood plank floor.

"I'm serious, Manta. You can't blame yourself."

She gulped hard against the humid air, like it's moisture could drown her if she took enough in. Paul held his breath as he placed his hand on her knee, hoping contact could equal comfort.

"It is my fault," she whispered then raised her voice. "Those people—the ones who stormed our home—I led them to us."

Paul didn't speak, and though he tried to hide it, Manta had seen the question cross his face.

"That morning, when I was out hunting, I ended up at the gorge. I know I'm not supposed to go that far out, but I'd done it before, and everything had been alright."

Apology filled her face, but she couldn't bring herself to look at her father.

"When I got there, there was that kid. He was kneeling down by the water, and he had this lizard crawling all over on his hands. It was bright green like an emerald, and its throat flashed red as it bobbed its head and clung to the little boy's skin. And he was dipping his free hand into the shallow of the rocks and catching tadpoles to feed to it."

She looked back at her father, face pleading for forgiveness.

"I didn't think he'd seen me too. But he must have. He must have followed me back to the cabin."

Paul sighed. "It wasn't your fault," he assured her once more and pulled her into his arms. "You, my sweet, sweet angel, do not hold this blame."

He thought his heart was breaking, but he knew that was a lie. It pounded against his ribcage like it could shatter the bones, like it could envelope Manta and take away all of her pain. It had never been more obvious in his life, that beating, that pulsing in his chest. It tried its damnedest to confirm he was alive, even as everything around them faded. She heaved against him with tears untried for nearly a decade.

"Well, ain't that just the sweetest thing?" the Hawk mocked from the doorway.

Paul had not even heard the padlock open. He and Manta turned to see her silhouette fill the doorframe. Her lips her pursed beneath her hooked nose. Her hair frizzed to her shoulder blades. Though she had grown callous to contend with her reality, a sincerity overtook her.

"In time," she said, "you'll realize we did you a favor bringing you here. Three square meals and a roof over your head is a lot better than sleeping on the dirt out there in the woods. And we all got our jobs to do in the After."

Manta growled. "Oh yeah? What's yours?"

"Billy and me? We bring in the riffraff that keeps society pumping. Y'all's essential workers, to borrow a phrase from the early part of the century. You should be thanking us for your new life. Your new home."

Manta scoffed. The Hawk shook her head.

"Do we need the rope?" she asked. "Or are y'all gonna be good little citizens and follow me?"

he road zigs where you think it will zag," the realtor told them. Her voice was bright and bubbly and affected with the octave lift used by most salespeople. "So you two be careful driving up here. But I think you two will absolutely love your new home."

She spoke with an exaggerated southern accent but refused contractions and detested the word "y'all." It all seemed fake to Paul, but Daniel just called it the "tools of her trade."

"She's only doing what she needs to do to make a sale," he said after he'd hung up the phone as they bounded up I-575.

"It just seems so disingenuous," Paul frowned. "And did you hear that? 'Your new home?' Like we've already bought the place."

Daniel nodded in passive agreement as he eyed the navigational map in the dashboard. A tiny pop up next to the address showed a picturesque little cottage, semi-modern and small, but quaint and with room to grow. It would be the eighth home she'd shown them. Each previous one had felt strangely off-putting—too remote or too close to the neighbors; too much space or no room for a garden—and Paul was growing tired of the back and forth. It had been his idea to move in the first place so they could raise the child they hoped to adopt away from the overstimulation of the city, but the struggle to find the perfect space was wearing on him.

"I love you; you know that right?" Daniel smiled, catching Paul's eyes in the rearview as he drove past a roadside market offering fresh produce alongside homemade jams and jellies.

"That sounds like it's got a 'but.'"

"But," Daniel said, stressing the word with a smirk, "you need to remember that no place is ever going to be exactly perfect. And that every place we are as a family is going to be exactly what we need."

Paul sighed his concession and turned his attention to the rolling trees outside the passenger window.

"I distinctly remember having a very similar conversation with you surrounding our nuptials back in the day," he shrugged. "Now it's my turn."

"I'm starting to think you don't actually want to leave the city."

"Don't shrink me," Paul chuckled. "You know the rules."

Daniel laughed with him and zigged where he thought he was going to have to zag.

"I'm just stressed about this whole adoption process," Paul admitted. "And maybe I'm taking it out on the house."

"We're going to get approved, babe," Daniel assured him. He slowed a bit so he could take a hand from the wheel and place it on Paul's thigh. "And we're going to fly to Ethiopia. And we're going to bring Gloria home to an amazing place."

"Gloria?"

"Yeah. I thought we could name her after your grandmother. Call her 'Glory' for short."

Paul's smile widened. A sigh of relief cascaded down his spine. Daniel had that effect on him.

"I like that. But I was actually thinking Sam. Samantha. After your sister."

Daniel smiled even though he could feel his eye well with tears. His sister had died when he was only eight years old. His parents had blamed a rare and sudden illness, but he had found the note. He knew she had taken her own life. It was the reason he had decided to go into therapy.

"Samantha," he nodded and turned onto the dirt road that led to the small, two-story cabin the realtor swore was just "awash in potential" and "only a little over their budget."

He stopped the car in the gravel driveway next to the realtor's cherry red convertible. Even though she drove it almost exclusively on dirt and gravel roads, it seemed to stay forever clean. It's candy coating shone in the afternoon sun.

The house had a tin roof which Daniel knew would be amazing in the thunderstorms that spread so suddenly and quickly throughout the summer. And the land was flat enough for a garden in the front of the house though they were high up the mountainside. According to the listing, a creek ran across the far end of the property, and the bulk of the two-acre plot was still lush with thick old-growth hardwoods. It was the perfect place to build a future as a family.

"It does have a certain charm," Paul smiled as Daniel cut the engine.

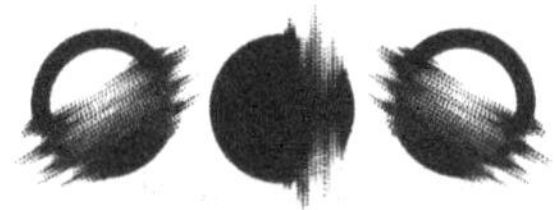

"This is not our home."

A murmur of agreement and concern spread across the group seated between the lush brown curtains of the Resistance's inner sanctum. Daniel and Lincoln sat together near the back and scanned the faces as Adrasteia spoke from the podium at the front of the room. The crowd had grown, more than just Daniel and the HMM technician. He and Lincoln made eleven, not including Adrasteia and her ever-present Hermes. She had been hard at work, recruiting and encouraging.

"Yes," she continued, "this is where we've lived for nearly a decade, but we are just interlopers in an experiment that failed the day it began. The governments of Earth, in their hubris, positioned us here above the clouds in hopes of finding Heaven. They placed us here as if we were the gods created and chosen by a world too far gone to save itself."

She had practiced the speech all afternoon, even proclaiming parts of it to her father, taking note when phrases appeared to puncture the Company Man shell he had donned to function in their new reality. She had finally gathered all the disparate components she needed, but, if she wanted the machine to work, she needed to make sure all the parts fit together. The speech had to be perfect: a rallying cry.

"They wanted gods, so let's give them gods!"

Whoops of encouragement sounded through the room. Fists raised to the air to join Adrasteia's, then fell, silently, with hers.

"We belong on the surface," she said. "The Earth was a gift we were meant to cherish, not control. It is up to us, now, to return. To, this time, get it right!"

"But what if there's nothing to return to?" a woman in the second row asked above the rumbling agreement. "We don't know what's down there. There could be nothing left."

Lincoln was not the only one with doubts. And, Daniel knew, as more people learned the unknowns of their fate, more would join in that fear.

"You're right, Nyx," Adrasteia said, using the woman's code name. Nyx, the goddess of night personified. Daniel wondered if the richness of her skin had inspired the name but doubted Adrasteia would be so obvious. "There are many unknowns we will have to contend with. And too many of them will remain a mystery until we touch the ground. But what we do know is that the Colony is failing. It cannot support us in our current capacity, despite the efforts of people like my father. Like you. No children can be born. No future is available with our resources. We can be the final generation of humanity, trapped in a birdcage in the sky, or, like our ancestors, we can go forth into uncharted territory. We, like Icarus, can decide to fly. And I think everyone deserves that choice."

Daniel closed his eyes. He hoped they'd be more like Daedalus, Icarus' father who created the wings of their escape. In the myths, both men flew, both tasted the freedom of the sky. It was only Icarus who ignored the warnings of his father, flew too close to the sun, and, when the wax that held the feathers of his wings in place heated and melted and stung the skin of his back, plummeted to the sea and drowned. Still, a part of him believed Adrasteia had chosen to site Icarus on purpose.

She left the podium and grabbed an empty chair in the first row, turning it around and sitting eye to eye with the people she'd recruited to her cause. She motioned for Hermes to follow suit, and soon, the entire room had circled up like an Anonymous group awaiting truth and settling for any time away from the terrors of their daily life.

"You," she said, "are some of the brightest minds in a Colony exclusively created with the smartest people Georgia had to offer. That's why you're here. You know something isn't right; that it has to change. You're smart enough to see through the lies of those desperate for power and complacency."

It was an obvious manipulation, Daniel knew. The others in the group knew it too. But it was working. Sometimes nuance was better left to the scholars. Sometimes what was obvious was the only way to get the job done.

"You all know me and Hermes," she said. "It's time you got to know one another. You want to start?"

Daniel sat up a little straighter in his chair. He fluffed the brown robes Adrasteia insisted they wear while in the Neutral Zone and smoothed the fabric against his chest.

"Hi. I'm Da—" he started and quickly stopped when Adrasteia held up her hand in caution. "I'm Asclepios." He stuttered as their leader urged him to go on, wondering what she wanted him to say. "I'm a psychiatrist. So... So I'm available to help(?) any of you adjust(?) to this new reality."

He hoped it sounded less like the question it had in his head.

"Amongst other things," Adrasteia added.

"Y'all heard her call me Nyx," the woman who had spoken earlier said. Her features were deep and stern. Her eyes seemed to hold a world of answers behind their impenetrable pupils. "I'm a part of the team that designed the lifts that brought you all here. Then sealed them and diverted their power sources to keeping us alive inside this steel can. So I'm the one tasked with diverting power back to those chutes and getting us out of Dodge without cutting the life support for the entire fucking Colony. So no pressure or anything."

Daniel chuckled, and she smirked at him, a wicked gleam in her eye.

"I'm One-Eye-Ross?"

Lincoln sounded out the word on the tiny slip of paper Adrasteia had handed him when they entered the meeting. Daniel's chest heaved as he glanced at the metered handwriting which had drawn him into this that evening in the mess hall on Sub5. Adrasteia has been there for him, he realized now, slumming it in the Sub levels and making those in her exterior circle feel like she was one of the people. She had planned the whole thing.

"Ow-Nee-rowz," she corrected.

"Oneiros," he said and swallowed the syllables hard, like they could tear his esophagus and end his speech forever. He shrugged. "I'm just an entry level lab tech."

"The entry level lab tech who is writing the code to save us all," Adrasteia smiled.

Around the room they went, timidly becoming gods—if in name alone—as they tried to discern what powers they held within the young woman's manifest destiny. In addition to Hermes, there were two more members of The Guard—Typhon and Echnida—who would help the team move through the plan undetected and, "in theory" Echnida was sure to point out, assist them if they happened to be caught. Helios, Selene, Theia, and Hyperion each worked with the crew responsible for the sunrises and sunsets, the waning and waxing moons which skipped across the billions of full-spectrum light-emitting diodes that formed the walls and ceilings of every level except for the Neutral Zone. They would be crucial, Adrasteia promised, in carrying out her vision once the code was written and the way down was secure. And finally, Eurynome and Achelous, two of the environmental scientists charged with ensuring the Colony was livable, would, with their gadgets and expertise, determine if the surface had viable air, water, and food sources once they hit the ground.

"You are the chosen ones," Adrasteia said, her face beaming with satisfaction. "You are the ones who will save humanity. You should be proud."

"That's great and everything," Nyx said, her voice dripping with sarcasm like her lungs were filled with the stuff. "But now that you've got your ragtag team all put together, how exactly do you expect us to pull this off?"

"That depends on the lot of you," she said.

The plan seemed straightforward enough, but even she admitted there were major caveats when it came to implementation. Once Lincoln and Daniel had figured out the proper code for implantation, the Light Crew would program orders to appear like calendar reminders, sending the citizens of the Colony Subs and the non-governmental Alphas to the Haptic, giving each and every person in the Colony a time to learn the truth. Meanwhile, Nyx and the Guard would focus on unsealing the lifts to the ground and restoring environmental systems to the chutes so they would be ready when the revolution began. She needed them to work covertly and simultaneously.

"It's really very simple," she said. "But it requires incredible precision. The shit hits the fan, we have to be ready to kick bricks."

She was both smug and dismissive, as if she had it all figured out while she did not have a clue. She shrugged and stood with Hermes, and he escorted her out as quickly as they had all arrived. The remaining gods stared around the circle. They committed one another's faces to memory; they learned the nuances in each person's jaw, in the line of their noses, until they blurred into memories of forgotten crowds. Then each god disappeared into the night, slowly, leaving behind a constellation of directional insecurity in their wake. Perhaps it would take longer than Adrasteia thought to figure out the correct way to go.

"I know who you are," Nyx said, making Daniel pause in his tracks as he folded a chair to put it aside. "You're that shrink who created the door in the Haptic."

"I didn't create it. I just suggested it based on my own understanding of the subconscious's relationship with the physical."

Nyx nodded, slamming shut the folding chair in her hand and leaning it with the others on the rack at the edge of the room. "What's that like?" she asked. "Playing God with people's heads?"

"Can't imagine it's all that different from adjusting the levels of oxygen in the air they breathe," Daniel countered. "Get 'em high or drag 'em down, right?"

"That is the goal. Drag them all down," she winked.

Nyx grinned as she swept from the room. Lincoln stood, dumbfounded and frozen, as Daniel pulled the last of the chairs from his grip, added it to the pile, and slipped, silently, from the sanctum.

The equipment wound down with an exaggerated whirr and a rattling sound that worried Dr. Saito as he ticked off boxes on his tablet. Technicians too young for any real-world practice ran around the room, checking bolts and flipping switches. It was good they didn't have actual experience—young minds fresh out of college were easier to mold, to control. Plus, in three months' time, when the last of the lifts rose and the environmental systems unit was fully activated, the real world would be a thing of the past. This was all that would be left. And it had to be perfect.

"Dad, can I take Kris to see the living quarters?"

Hiromi angled her pleading face to catch the light perfectly through her oversized helmet. It beamed in that innocent light only a fourteen-year-old could manage, as if she'd learned just enough of existence to have not been completely hardened by it yet. She was a far cry from the revolutionary goddess she would become in just a few years' time. Kris stood halfway behind her, her blonde hair—*their*, he corrected himself, *their pronouns are they/them*—their blonde hair shorn shortly, but still wishing and curling around their ears. They were a shy thing, but Hiromi seemed to blossom when they were around, more so than he'd seen her do with anyone since her mother had died.

"Don't go anywhere else," he cautioned absently. "And take those boxes over in the corner to my bedroom. They're fragile but not too heavy. You should each be able to manage one."

The kids were out the door before he'd even turned around. He missed being that spry sometimes.

"Can we get the corridor lights up in Alpha Three?" he asked one of the technicians. Wilson, he thought. Or maybe Lincoln. Some past president.

"It's just a stock photo of Peachtree Street right now," the tech replied. "The motion rendering isn't finished yet."

"That's fine," Dr. Saito sighed and made another note on his tablet.

They weren't behind schedule, but they also weren't ahead of it, and that to him was just as bad. He'd always appreciated the students who read his syllabus and completed projects and papers ahead of time. Those who took initiative were bound to go farther in life, to truly make something of themselves. That was the most important thing he'd tried to distill in Hiromi. She'd floundered so since the death of her mother. Perhaps the Colony was the fresh start they both needed.

"Sir?" another of the techs started, barreling into the room with a swift power walk Dr. Saito found unbecoming despite his insistence on urgency.

"Doctor," he corrected, on instinct. He mounted his stylus and looked up in question.

"Doctor," the tech continued, "you're needed downstairs. Three of the bays are failing to germinate, and we can't..."

Take the initiative to try something new? Dr. Saito finished the sentence in his head before groaning out a: "Yes, I'll be right there."

He finished his instructions to the Environments Team and headed toward the elevator bay. There was so much yet to be done; his list was never-ending. Sometimes, late at night, after Hiromi was asleep and all his papers had been graded, he questioned his decision to take the job. But his daughter deserved a future, and the Colony could give that to her. The irony that the majority of the technology used to create the Castle in the Clouds was nothing new was not lost on him. Energy efficient and low consumption LED lighting; stackable hydroponic growth chambers for food; solar powered generators for comfort: if the surface had just committed to using them for the decades they had been available, maybe the Colony would not have been needed. Maybe their efficacy would have been tested and fine-tuned, and he would not have spent the last several months tweaking them and ticking off little boxes on his lists while circling more in red pixels to note *Further Attention Required*.

"Dr. Saito."

"Dr. Nelson."

The head of the Psychiatry Unit was leading a tour of his recruits through the Colony when Dr. Saito arrived at the bay. The brain to his body. Both would be needed for survival once the lifts were closed and sealed. Fifteen years was a long time to be cut off from the world, even when surrounded by a small metropolis of people.

"The elevators are pretty damn slow," Dr. Nelson was saying. "Doesn't help that the chips aren't ready yet and we have to use the intercoms to call over to the control room."

Ah, yes. The BRIs. Something else to work through on his list. He used his stylus to write out *Biometric Recall Implants* and watched it vanish to highlight his note in the appropriate place on the appropriate page in his forms. He smiled at the efficiency. At least something was working correctly.

A group of twenty-five or so people milled about beside Dr. Nelson, expressions ranging from a childlike wonderment as they peered around the fortress to a stern, eyes-forward practicality. They were young, most of them, with bodies healthy enough to survive the Quarter Hour Quarantine as Dr. Saito had taken to calling the fifteen years they'd be held captive. His job was hard now, but theirs had yet to begin. He did not envy what they were in for.

The elevator arrived and the doors stuttered open too slowly for his liking. When they parted, a blur of motion sprang forth as Hiromi and Kris darted from the lift. They giggled as they passed the waiting scientists as if they were but statues in a museum—a generation too staid and solid to engage, too ephemeral to notice. He remembered the same feeling from his own youth, the disregard for his father's wisdom that he still regretted every day.

Before Dr. Saito could open his mouth to stop them, one of the psychiatrists who lingered near the outskirts of the group held out his arms and knelt to catch the carousing kids. His jet-black hair made his blue eyes look like burning embers.

"Whoa, there," he laughed as he captured them. His voice was calm and self-assured. Like he'd had practice. "You're ten miles up in the sky," he laughed. "Up here, you have to behave like gods, not heathens."

Dr. Saito moved quickly to join them.

"Thank you, Doctor—"

"Daniel," the man said, holding out his hand.

"Dr. Daniel," Dr. Saito finished, shaking his hand as the young man opened his mouth to protest but thought better of it. "Are you a child psychiatrist? You are good with children."

"No," Daniel smiled, shyly shaking his head with a slight blush to his cheeks. "My partner and I are in the process of adopting. We've been working on our parenting skills. Sorry if I overstepped."

"Not at all," Dr. Saito nodded. "It takes a village, as they say. And isn't that what we're building? You will do well as a parent. Hiromi, Kris. You would do well in listening to Dr. Daniel. We must behave like gods while in the sky. Now come. I will show you where we will grow all the food to feed the people once they arrive."

He turned back to Daniel and nodded his appreciation once more as the young doctor smiled and moved to join his compatriots in the elevator.

"Thank you, Dr. Daniel," the children chimed.

He didn't have kids yet, but he completely understood the sarcasm in their voices.

"This is where we grow the food to feed everyone in town, including you two now."

The Hawk had handed Paul and Manta off to a man she'd only addressed as Mr. Madison, and he was busy showing them around the settlement as if they were his guests and he was giving them the grand tour. He was a jovial man, filled with smiles and murder, with thinning brown hair that melted into his sun-stained skin. His chestnut eyes gleamed with the mischievous mirth of newfound power. Paul's mother, who was reared by an Old Southern Family, would have referred to the man as "New Money," if money were still a thing to be had, to be novel.

The field was expansive. Rows of tomatoes burst in vibrant reds beneath jagged leaves, and curling yellow flowers like North Stars promised more to follow. Golden squash and green beans slithered from vines which snaked around mounds and posts in lush, thick tendrils covered in sagging leaves. Peppers in all colors, from the deep, soggy green of moss to a brilliant, regal purple dotted rows like fireworks; and innocent white buds were just beginning to form from the potato mounds. There was okra and eggplant, cucumber and wheat and onion, three rows of nothing but corn, leafy greens and broccoli and rounded heads of lettuce. Ripening strawberries, still green at the base, were turning white to pink to red beneath the polka dots of their dark seeds. And just past the log fence beyond the field, three dairy cows chewed at the cud with swollen udders. The decadence was intoxicating.

Ten or so people kept their heads down as they marched through the rows of vegetation. Paul noticed the cut absences in their clothing made up the patches in Madison's overalls. They refused to look up as they worked, some collecting weeds and others produce. They were gaunt—more so than he would have expected—and their frail hands struggled to pull the fruits from their stalks. Others, probably Madisons from the slopes of their noses, took turns walking the perimeter with rifles stopped to their shoulders.

Manta's eyes widened as she clutched at her father's hand. She had refused to let it go since the Hawk had pulled them from the house.

"We ain't too far off from the Coosawattee, so we got a crew what goes out there for extra water when the rain barrels can't keep up," Mr. Madison said, pointing to the cascading bouquets of barrels angled together in clusters beneath the eaves of the various roofs. "Accompanied, of course." He nodded to a passing rifleman with a sly grin. He did his best to make himself look friendly. "We're all in this together," he said. He said it like Paul and Manta had a choice in the matter. Like they were really just one big happy family, all with a common goal. Slavery had learned a thing or two from Capitalism. "Don't you worry your strong, pretty little head none about that, girl. We take care of each other here."

New Yukon, named for the derelict post office that had been named for the gilded dreams of an ancient gold rush, had formed a little over a year ago by the Madisons and the Coltons. "Two families whose names you'll learn to respect," Mr. Madison said. Abandoned when they found it—no doubt by folks fleeing the radiation that had plagued the new coastline in the years just after the Wave—they'd carved out a haven in the gated community at the foothills of the Appalachian Mountains. "We're a welcoming community," he said. "Long as the workers we put up remember who's boss."

The Madisons occupied the house with the salmon-colored siding and the one with the yellow-tint on the southeastern side of the road while the Coltons took the blue and grey homes opposite them. The houses with the window glass and the landscaping. The spaces with draperies that still billowed in the open window frames when the gentle breeze of summer moved to rustle the clouds of gnats and dandelion seeds. The other buildings were for the workers—"the staff"—to take shelter in after long days spent weeding, pruning, and harvesting in the field or polishing, cooking, and scrubbing in the homes. They let the families stay together as a courtesy—"because we're that kind of folk"—but sometimes another person or two would join them in their quarters.

"Course we do have to keep our little slice of Heaven safe from the outside," Mr. Madison said, shielding his eyes with his grubby fingers so he could watch the storm clouds rolling in from the horizon. "It's a dangerous world out there. We can't let tale of all our riches reach the upstarts and hooligans beyond our walls. Anybody caught trying to leave, anybody refusing to do the work, well, they find their silence at the end of a Remington."

He laughed while he spoke. An awful laugh, filled with phlegm and ferocity. He shoved his hands behind the bib of his overalls like, if he didn't hold onto himself, his body would attempt to escape with the sound. Like he was jostling his heart to service.

"Tomorrow we'll test y'all," he said. "Figure out where to best utilize your strengths. So tonight I suggest you have a little bread and get plenty of sleep. How long's it been since you had either? Really and truly? We ain't ask for much to share our glory with you."

He winked at Manta in a way that instantly infuriated Paul as he motioned them back toward their new home.

Back in the house, Manta fumed with the vitriol she had kept contained during the tour. She stomped the hardwood floors with heaving breaths that left her body gasping for oxygen. Growling, she kicked the soft mauve paint, and a chunk of drywall dusted the air as it skidded to a sudden stop on the floor. Thunder clapped and shook the air outside while the birds sounded their final cries of warning, urging their compatriots to cover before the storm.

Paul lit a candle against the impending darkness. He poured a bit of the yellow wax on the linoleum counter of the kitchen isle and used it to mount the tapered stick into place. The wind cut itself on the jagged edges of the shattered glass windows but forced itself onward all the same. The room grew darker with each flash of lightning, and the father and the daughter huddled together on the island stools around the flame. They made a game of it—*Keep the Candle Lit*—and watched as the shadows cast revealed emotions unseen before in one another's faces.

A small goldfinch had found its way through the glass before the storm and pecked at the moldy clump of bread. Paul shooed it away, and it flew to the exposed rafters to wait out the storm.

"This is bullshit! Is this really what human beings are?" Manta said, and Paul nodded.

It was bullshit. This was not how humanity was meant to survive, collecting souls as bargaining chips to sell to ruthless oligarchs who wanted to feel power. The ravagers were one thing—brutal and animalistic in their instinct-based survival—but this savagery disguised as civility was unnerving.

"I want to say no, but this kind of shit has a way of popping up repeatedly in the history books," Paul admitted. Even still, there was a spark of hope which remained in him, as dim and struggling as the candle between them. Yet it shone enough for him to see it in Manta too.

Thunder roared and pushed a gust of wind through to seize the light. Paul rattled the box of matches: only two left. And the half-burnt stump on the countertop was the only candle he had found. He didn't know when or if they would get more.

Outside, the first thick drops of rain joined the power display of the heavens to splash like bullets against the outside world. The ground sizzled and cracked to welcome in the water with such ease the rivers quaked in agitated fear. The trees spread their branches like arms, pushed out their leaves like the tongues of children attempting to catch the drops, and shivered in the howling storm.

They set out pots and pans to catch the water which sputtered in through the broken windows. They found the bedroom. Sunburnt photos turned sepia showcased smiling faces, posed and frozen like death masks along the dust-covered tops of dressers. The drawers were overturned and emptied except for one ragged and threadbare quilt. The mattress was missing from the bed frame, probably to soften the rest of a Colton or a Madison or to reinforce the barricade that surrounded them.

The whole scene evoked a quiet acquiescence, a place just outside of solemn to leave the captured grateful for what they had—something; anything!—with upturned monuments to a long-lost past which seemed at once gluttonous and forlorn.

Paul spread the quilt across the bedroom floor and welcomed Manta into his arms as they curled, concave into one another. He let her use his bicep as a pillow and did not move it an inch, even when the tips of his fingers began to tingle their militant wishes for blood flow. The lightning bounced their shadows across the wall like flashbulbs staining their silhouettes into permanence. Nature punctuated each electrified "You Are Here" with a growling acknowledgement of its force, a fist shaken at the sky.

Paul tried, but he knew he wouldn't sleep. He listened to Manta's breath and controlled his own to sooth her. She fought it, but eventually the shallows sighs of sleep took their hold.

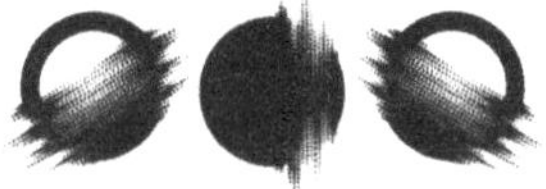

The storm passed with the sunrise. Robins and Jays steamed themselves in the post-rain heat emitted by the tar shingles of the roofs. They puffed out the feathers on their breasts and let the rising mist spread open their wings. Manta breathed in the fresh-washed air and watched the steam lift toward the heavens, wishing it were smoke, wishing all the houses would catch fire.

ater collected in crystal ball orbs, magnifying the sporophytes which sprung from the moss like tiny wishes in the hands of a goddess. Like each one was a hope with the future contained upside-down in its refraction. They pooled, turned white, and dripped from the Earth Goddess' fingertips to join the thousands of others swimming in the collective of the pond before her. She looked on in peace, the ivy and lilac locks of her hair washed and renewed by the thunderstorm. Her expression was pleasant and hopeful, serene, and it changed as slowly as photosynthesis.

It was Daniel's favorite time to visit the Botanical Gardens: right after a storm when the colors were their brightest and the leaves all reached skyward in worship of the majesty they had just witnessed. Plus, the crowds were minimal then—usually just them and the half-sleeping volunteer at the ticket booth—so they were given free rein to traipse about the grounds as they eyed the clouds carefully for signs of another shower.

"She looks like she's sleeping," Paul whispered as Daniel twined his fingers around his and the flush of their skin meeting made the post-rain humidity sticky but somehow comforting.

"I think she's just waiting for the world to wake up," Daniel said. His lips quivered into a half-smile as he kept his eyes trained on her visage. She rose from the hillside, her face tranquil and collected as the water drained from her outstretched hand.

The squirrels and the chipmunks were emerging from their shelters and chittering through branches of the oaks and dogwoods. Brown Thrashers and Mockingbirds swooped toward the ground to feast on the earthworms and beetles that had emerged from the rich soils to bathe. In the distance, children shrieked and howled as they leapt with both feet into the puddles which now shattered the paths of Piedmont Park like portals. It was an altogether perfect day with the altogether perfect person.

"I love you," Daniel said. He said it for the first time, and he held his breath.

He didn't expect Paul to say it back. They had only been dating for a few months. It was far too early for a word with so much power to be uttered, especially in the presence of a goddess. He wanted to look at him—he should have looked at him when he said it—but his eyes would not move from the landscape.

Paul tightened his grip on Daniel's hand. Their palms pressed at one another hungrily.

"You talking to her or to me?" he asked, and Daniel laughed.

Paul and his jokes. Paul and his ability to cut the tension with the precision of a scalpel. Paul and his jovial comfort.

Paul cupped Daniel's chin with his free hand and gently pulled to turn his face. "You should look at someone when you're talking to them," he smirked. Their eyes locked and Daniel swam in the wishes in Paul's irises. "I love you too," Paul said.

Daniel laughed again. All the tension left his body and he struggled to keep himself upright as he felt himself go limp. And then Paul was laughing too, and it echoed out to the ears of the goddess whose eyes remained closed, but her smile seemed to grow.

Suddenly, their giggling chatter shifted, screeched across his eardrums, scraping like the metal wheels of a train on the tracks and moving in the wrong direction, like an ancient modem starting up and a landline removed from the receiver to stop it before it could open to the world. His vision blurred and cracked like a broken mirror. Dark lines sliced across the scene, cutting the frame like claws across his memory. Paul was still laughing. Or Paul was concerned. Or Paul was walking away.

"Wait!"

Paul was laughing. Or Paul was leaning in for a kiss, to touch their lips together in naive comfort. Or two faceless men in black clothes and shapeless bodies were dragging Paul away.

"This is not—"

"Daniel, what's wrong?" Paul's voice was exaggerated, a memory, a ringtone. "Daniel, you must escape."

A doorway appeared where there had not been one. It sprung from the walking bridge in a brilliant white that did not belong. Beside it, Paul howled. His tears threatened to awaken the goddess from her slumber. His tears were another rainstorm, drops free of any hope or future. Daniel's head split as if Athena were bursting forth.

"Daniel, run!" Paul commanded and released his hand.

Daniel stumbled toward the door. His skin blistered and burned. His brain turned summersaults as it ricocheted off his skull. He collapsed through the doorway into a stark white room with only a chair and a helmet emitting a sequence of lights in red and green and blue. Flashing. Pulsing. Promising. He closed his eyes and crawled as the pain tied knots in his stomach. This was one of his favorite memories, and it had been broken.

"Fuck!"

Lincoln tossed his tablet aside and leapt toward Daniel's convulsing body. He reached for the helmet but thought better of it. If Daniel hadn't made it to the chair, removing the helmet could trap him in the liminal space between present and memory forever, sending his body into stasis like the hundreds from the early days of the Haptic. Before Daniel had fixed it. And now, against his better judgment, Lincoln had broken it. He never should have agreed to adjust the code.

Daniel heaved in the chair. His fingers turned pink and then white as he clutched to the arms. His back sought stability but could not find purchase against the cold, polished steel. Lincoln braced his shoulders, then set and tightened the straps they no longer used. Daniel's eyelids opened, but his eyes turned back as he seized. Lincoln set the straps on Daniel's legs and swallowed hard. Thinking quickly, he disconnected the automatic call before the ninety seconds had lapsed and medics were called to the scene. He needed help—Daniel needed help—but how could they explain this?

His worst fears were coming true. He knew better than to ignore his gut. But Daniel had convinced him the ends would justify the means. Even if it meant some sacrifice along the way.

"Bet he didn't think he'd be the sacrifice," Lincoln whispered.

Daniel's body fell limp, but the monitors showed a strong and steady heartbeat. The Haps had him in its grasp and was not letting go. Lincoln readied a receptacle and administered a shot of adrenaline into Daniel's thigh. The man heaved up quickly, as far as he could while still strapped to the chair, and turned to vomit into the container Lincoln had set up. Lincoln turned his back. He'd witnessed it a million times while working the Haptic, but it still made his own stomach turn.

The retching gave way to a ragged, heaving breath, and Daniel groaned, the wilds of humanity obvious as his mind tried to center on self.

"It didn't work," he said. He sounded exhausted. His words barely made it past his lips, extinguishing swiftly in the parched, acrid air.

"Obviously," Lincoln said. "Drink this." He offered Daniel a water bottle to clear his throat, to fool the mind to the calm of hydration even though the IV was keeping his body there already.

"Why didn't it work?"

Lincoln frowned as Daniel swooned again. He had barely made it out of the HMM alive and was already settling into work mode.

"Stop moving," he directed and pulled the helmet from Daniel's head.

Daniel's knuckles whitened once again as he gripped the arms of the chair. His chest heaved in the space between glory and defeat. He swallowed back the bile in his throat, and it swam circles with the acid in his stomach. He needed the face of bravery. He needed to quell his nausea. Otherwise he would lose Lincoln, and the plan would die.

He let his eyelids fall, but that only made the pounding inside his skull worse. It seared against the whites of his eyes. It hammered at his eardrums; tried to saw through his skull. He forced open his eyes and trained them on the barely noticeable seam where the wall met the ceiling in the stark white room. He let his ears focus in on the beep and hum of machinery instead of the throbbing in his head. He attempted to ground himself; to appear normal so as not to scare the young tech to abandonment. He'd had so much practice with the Haps, but this was unlike anything he'd experienced before. His body felt trapped under an avalanche of collapsed bricks. His limbs were still his own, but he wasn't sure he had any control over them.

"I'm okay," he said. His voice was returning. He almost believed the statement himself. "It worked before. What changed?"

Lincoln expelled a heavy, exasperated breath. He retrieved his tablet and looked through the parameters of Daniel's readout. Everything was normal. Not a tic or beat or synaptic firing was outside established parameters. Until the code attempted its information dump.

"I have a theory," Lincoln sighed. He didn't like it, but Daniel insisted on business as usual, and maybe, he thought, it would help to center the man. "Before, when we input the information to the memory, we weren't actually adding new information to your mind. Yes, the conversation changed. But Paul and Samantha were telling you things you already knew. They were conduits for information you'd learned already in school or some late-night internet rabbit hole. Data that was there, in your mind already, even if it was buried inside a different synapse. Please stay down."

Daniel was trying to pull himself upright from the reclined seat. He struggled against the straps that held him there as his brain fought for clarity. A part of him felt still trapped inside the Mind Map. Lincoln turned to the wall as Daniel retched again, willing his ears to pick out any other sound in the quiet lab.

"It could be that new information—really and truly new knowledge—can't be forced into the brain like this without serious consequences."

"We have to go again," Daniel demanded.

"Are you fucking insane?"

Lincoln felt his hands clench into fists. Daniel's desire to escape the Colony was clouding his judgement. Another session like the one he'd just experienced would kill him. Lincoln took a few deep breaths to calm himself and moved to release Daniel from the chair.

"Look, Daniel. I know you want to see your husband and your daughter again. But you've got to be alive with all your mental faculties intact to do that."

The tension in Daniel's body relaxed at Lincoln's words. Rational thought started to find its way through.

"We will find a way to make this work," Lincoln assured him. "But right now, you need to recover. Give me some time to figure it all out, and then we can run some more tests, okay?"

"How long?"

Lincoln shrugged, but Daniel wasn't letting go. "A week?" he offered.

Daniel nodded. His entire body ached. A dull soreness permeated deep into his bones as his muscles prickled with electric shock. He shivered to release the excess energy and it sent his head swooning and forced his eyes shut.

"One week," he agreed. "And then we test again."

The pre-dawn air was thick and black when Trent, the House Manager, wrestled Paul and Manta from their slumber. The clean scent of fresh, wet earth was laced with the green smell of fresh growth from the hyacinth blossoms the Coltons had planted beneath their windows. Under night's thick blanket, the village seemed almost quaint. Perfect little row houses whose flaws were covered by darkness promised Game Nights and Sunday Dinners, Afternoon Strolls and frantic waving hands from Rocking Chairs on Fern-laced Front Porches. Starlight accented the haze from the waxing moon, beamed down to illuminate their path, and caught the muddling of nocturnal animals retreating through the thick grasses to their homes.

Paul felt his heart crack as he looked at Manta. Her eyes darted across the shadows, on guard, searching for any sign of danger that could be a distraction from the very real danger of her present. She trudged— cautiously, angrily—behind Trent as he left them toward the field. The world that was left for her was not the one he and Daniel had dreamed of. All that remained for her was struggle, was war. Paul wished she could know what it was like to play tag in the street with the neighborhood children until the streetlights flickered on like trapped lightning; to smell the wafting joy of freshly baked waffle cones as vanilla ice cream dripped sticky down her fingers; to know what community felt like when it was something chosen and sacred.

Day was just beginning to crest the horizon as Trent ushered them into a small lean-to shed which housed the dairy cows. The black of the sun-forsaken sky had given way to navy, and Paul could just make out a hint of orange above the tree line. The cows' udders shone pink in the dim light, bulging in flesh and promise as Trent lit a wick made of a shredded rag inside a lantern.

"Your first test is breakfast," he said. He had the heartbroken countenance of middle management—glad he'd made it to this point, but fully aware he was yet another cog. He was both casual and stern as he spoke, haggard and resigned. "You can start by milking the cattle."

"I don't get it," Manta said. A simmering rage did its best to hide the fear in her voice. "You caught us already. We're your slaves. Why 'test' us?"

Trent froze for a moment, two steel buckets swinging in his hands. He cocked his head as if considering the girl for the first time and sighed as he placed the buckets near two of the four cows.

"The Families want to see where you'll be best suited," he said. "Think of it like a job interview. You'll want to work in the houses. It's a better life than the field."" He met Manta's eyes as if pleading for her to settle down. "And we don't use that word."

"What happens if we fail all the tests?" Paul asked.

Trent started to laugh and stopped himself as if the sound surprised him. "Well, they don't just send you on your way," he said. "It's best to just fall in line. If you don't do the jobs, they'll spend a few days trying to break you. And if that don't work, there's a group of ravagers 'bout ten miles out. A few live bodies every now and then—hell, even a dead one—keeps them at bay when the crew goes out for extra water."

Manta swallowed hard as Paul placed a hand on her shoulder. Trent shook his head to bring himself back to the barn. He cleared his throat and settled back into a stoic demeanor.

"First few squirts ain't no good," he said. "Give 'em to the ground. The rest goes in the bucket. It's good to empty it into one of the jars every so often in case the cow gets randy and kicks the damn thing over. And don't ever get behind her hooves." He crossed his arms and waited for Paul and Manta to kneel beside the heifers. "You wanna pinch near the top of the udder with your thumb and forefinger. And then massage the teat downward with an even pressure. Not too tight 'less you feel like dying."

Resigned, Manta gave a tentative pull. The cow bristled. The bulk of her much-skinnier-than-Paul-remembered-cows-being body heaved against the chill of the morning air.

"Whoa, girl." Manta instinctively rubbed her thigh to calm her.

Paul followed suit with his cow. Pinch and massage. Pinch and massage. It sounded like fireworks when the milk hit the bottom of the stainless steel.

"Is it supposed to be this color?" Manta asked, peering in at the creamy yellow liquid.

"You ain't never seen milk before?" Trent asked in disbelief.

"That's right, Manta," Paul said. "You're doing good."

The milk began to stream faster as they fell into a rhythm. It smelled sour, almost fishy, as the bucket filled. Soon it overtook the aroma of grass and manure. Trent looked on with squinted eyes.

"How long have you been here?" Paul asked.

"Long enough," Trent replied. He seemed disinterested in small talk, even less so in making friends.

"Why don't you just leave?" Manta asked. "There's got to be more of us than there are of them."

Trent groaned and shook his head. Paul thought he saw a glimmer of hope flash and vanish from his eyes.

"Three squares and a roof over our heads," Trent said. "How different is this than slaving away at some dead-end job before the Wave? Ain't nothing better on the other side of the barricade."

"We don't use that word," Manta quipped, and a brief moment of who Trent had been in the Before pulsed through him, shaking him back to who he was now. He crossed his arms and groaned, letting his face fall back to stern acceptance.

"What'd you do in the Before?" Manta asked. She poured the milk from her ground bucket carefully into the series of mason jars set out on a rough, splintered grey table.

"You gone talk the hide off that cow, girl," Trent groaned. "Worry about finishing that milking so you can have breakfast cooked and ready 'fore the Families wake up."

"What time do they—"

Trent threw his hands in the air in anger, in surrender, and bounded from the milking parlor. Paul smirked at the wicked gleam in Manta's eye. He emptied his bucket and kissed her gently on the forehead before turning to continue the process. The udder was warm and pleasant in his grasp. Soft, tiny hairs tickled his palm as he milked.

"Toni!" Manta leapt to her feet suddenly. Her cow startled and reared back a few feet, narrowly missing the half-filled bucket. "Did they get you too?"

Sure enough, the young Cherokee was silhouetted in the doorway. Their shoulder length hair looked like ink against the slowly rising sun. One arm was crossed awkwardly over their body, hand clutching an elbow as they closed in on themself.

"I'm glad you're alright," they said.

Paul stood and moved to Manta's side. He smiled, but Toni didn't seem happy.

"You too," Paul said. "I was hoping you'd been long gone before those two showed up."

Toni wouldn't make eye contact. They kicked at the dirt with their foot.

"The three of us could make it out of here," Manta whispered as she glanced at Trent pacing in the distance. As quiet as she tried to be, her voice was electrified with excitement.

Toni didn't speak. There was a slight tremble as they cocked their head away to peer behind them toward the yard. Trent was stomping his way back to the barn, re-composed and ready to rate the new "employees."

"I'm sorry, y'all," Toni finally said. Their voice scratched like branches against siding, like gravel under tires.

Trent appeared in the doorway at their side.

"Hey, Scout," he said. "Shouldn't you be out there with the traders?" He eyed the progress Paul and Manta had made and huffed. "Rustling up some others in case these fuckers gotta be put to pasture?"

Manta furrowed her brow in confusion. Paul's face collapsed. He placed an arm around his daughter and slowly turned her back toward their work. Toni had been working with the Hawk and the Snake. They were the friendly face sent ahead to put the prey at ease, to make them lower their guard. They were the bait in the trap.

"I don't... Toni?" Manta's eyes welled as she began to understand the situation. Her chin dropped to her chest as she lowered herself to the cow's side.

Is this really what human beings are? Manta's question from the night before echoed through Paul's head. All of the air left the barn.

He winced. He felt his heart crack once again. He knew it would soon be broken beyond repair.

"You can fix it, right?"

Adrasteia paced her quarters hoping the determination in her step could set things in motion, would put everything back on track. Daniel swooned as he watched her, the nausea still waved through his body. He closed his eyes and spoke slowly from the corner of his mouth. His words marched across his tongue like soldiers following commands they didn't believe in.

At least the residual tinnitus wasn't as bad this time.

"Direct implantation of information is akin to mind control," he wanted to say. He wanted to say, "I went into the Haptic knowing something was coming, subconsciously, and the first attempt nearly killed me. Imagine an unprepared mind attacked like that. Are the thousands of potential deaths worth the risk?"

What he said was: "We'll try."

Adrasteia stopped moving. She took a deep breath to steel herself. The urgency of youth had gotten the better of her. They were so close, she rationalized. After years of knowing the truth, she had finally assembled a group of people who had a real shot at revealing the horrors of their plight, at escape. Daniel's doorway inside the Haptic Mind Map—the possibilities it created—had been the basis of her entire plan. But her hypothesis had been flawed. The scheme was over before it had even begun.

She closed her eyes and steadied her thoughts. This was science. Science encapsulated failure. The point of a hypothesis was to prove it—right or wrong—and adjust the method. They could figure it out. She just needed to have patience.

"Alright," she said as she took the seat across from Daniel. She slid two more ibuprofen next to the glass of water leaving condensation rings in front of his folded arms, his sweating forehead. "Maybe emotional manipulation and direct contact was a little flawed to begin with. We'll have to find another way."

Daniel winced as he lifted his head to take the pills. Even the dim light in her quarters was blinding. His head, heavy and dull, throbbed with a force usually reserved for construction sites.

"What if we take out the 'direct'?" he asked.

"Subliminal messaging?"

"At its base, the Haptic works on two levels. Electrodes send pulses to stimulate parts of the brain and call forth memories and sensations. That's the direct part." Daniel swallowed hard. The more he spoke, the easier the words came. The focus diverted his attention from his pain. "But the helmet also emits a series of flashing lights. Those guide you through the Mind Map. They work subconsciously to continue the story, to send you moving toward the door when time is up. It's the basis of the door. The thing that shouldn't be there but it. The thing that makes sense there, so it doesn't crash the whole thing down."

"So you're saying, skip the helmets and electricity and just send folks toward the light." Adrasteia let the idea roll around her head. It had merit, true. "Subliminal messaging is inconsistent and can take a long ass time."

Daniel nodded. He was breathing easier now. The nausea had passed, but he knew it was only a matter of time before it crashed into his bones once more. He stretched his shoulders back and sighed.

"It's still faster than waiting for a million people to be processed through the Haptic Centers," he argued. "Instead of using the screens for doctor's notes sending people in for appointments, we blast out the information to everyone, all at once."

"Not everyone will get the message," Adrasteia argued. "Subliminal propaganda has long been problematic. And I'm only talking about implementation. This says nothing of the humanitarian issues. With the mind Map, we're giving them actual knowledge. With Subliminal Messaging, we're just giving them fear. We'd have absolutely no way of massaging the emotional reaction around the message."

Daniel nodded and rose to his feet. "Think it over," he started to say as a wave washed over his body, and he ran to retch into the nearby trash can.

"But I suppose it's better than this as the alternative," Adrasteia conceded. "Or no plan at all."

aul wiped the sweat from his brow. His muscles ached. He felt them throb against the sweat-drenched work shirt the Madisons had provided him. Graciously, they were sure to note through their proxy. Aside from Mr. Madison, he had yet to meet a single member of the prestigious, generous Families. As threadbare as the fabric was, the sweltering air was brutal. The sun beat down in harsh beams of yellow gold; sharp, metallic, and heavy as the day dredged on.

He tugged at the leather straps buckled across his chest, and the relatively cooler air that rushed beneath them gave him a temporary relief. The harness sat awkwardly on his shoulders—not at all like the ones he used to wear out to the bars with Daniel. Those were of a soft leather, only meant to appear hard, and meticulously fitted to accentuate his frame. They were meant for an altogether different type of work. This harness, obviously cobbled together from old belts and saddle straps, cut into the skin beneath his arms where the hide was awkwardly joined by punctured stitches of rough twine. The whole ramshackle contraption was attached to what was left of a tow-behind tiller with dull blades which skipped across the soil and seemed to lose their will to turn with every begrudging step Paul took.

"Keep your ass moving," Dart, the Field Manager, growled. Like Trent, his household counterpart, he was not a Madison or a Colton. Like the Madisons and the Coltons, he seemed to relish in the supposed power of his station inside New Yukon. "You and your brat gonna be here, we're gonna need more ground turned over to field."

"We can always leave if that's easier," Paul mumbled under his breath, attempting to hide it under a grunt as he heaved forward.

"What was that?" Dart asked angrily as he marched to stare Paul down.

Dart was a small man, but spry. He stood a good foot shorter than Paul, making up for the height difference with a fierce bravado that puffed out his chest and pressed his shoulder blades together like forgotten wings behind him. His russet skin was the same reddish-brown as the earth Paul turned. His rich brown eyes had a mischievous gleam that was highlighted by the depth of his shaggy black hair.

"You got something to say?"

His tongue slithered across his lips. He bucked at Paul once more. His fists clenched into fireballs at his side. Unlike Trent, he didn't have a gun. He was newer to his position; not yet trusted by the Families. It made him want to prove himself.

"I can't till if you're standing in front of me," Paul said. He tried to make his voice sound passive, like surrender, even as he stood his ground.

Dart's fist met Paul's cheek before he even saw it coming. A second fist to the gut sent Paul to his knees, the heavy tiller creaking and bearing down on him from behind as the harness jerked it suddenly forward. Paul gasped for breath as Dart's knee landed beside his nose. He could feel the skin beneath his eye already beginning to swell and pucker. It reached out as if it could find comfort away from Paul's body but was met only with harsh and sticky humidity.

"Any more words, smart ass?"

Paul didn't answer. He kept his head low and toward the earth. He wasn't crying, but his eye didn't seem to know that.

The steel toe of Dart's boot met Paul's knee. He felt his kneecap shift suddenly and pop back into place as the kick shot up his thigh.

"I can't till shit if you break my fucking leg," he growled, finding his voice in the pain.

Dart's elbow came down between Paul's shoulder blades, but this time he managed to shift slightly and the buckle on the harness took most of the blow.

"Faggot assholes like you don't make it too long here," Dart spat, but he had taken a step back and was cradling his elbow where it had met the metal on the strap. "And don't you forget who makes that decision."

Paul bit his tongue as he nodded. Dart kicked at the dirt and a wave of dust caught the air and filled Paul's lungs.

"Finish your fucking job," he said, turning away as Paul slowly pulled himself to his feet.

Paul felt the whole of Manta's power enter him as he found his footing. His hands worked at the buckles of his harness to release himself from the till.

"Were you a homophobic asshole in the Before too?" he called. "Or just the runt of the litter with a chip on his shoulder the size of Texas?"

Dart spun around, fury igniting his eyes to flames. Paul planted his feet in a boxer's stance as all the other field workers turned briefly too gawk before catching Dart's glare and lowering their heads.

"Put that harness back on," he commanded.

"No."

The word clipped from Paul with such assuredness he almost thought he could win this battle.

Dart surged forward as Paul dodged, spinning to meet the small of Dart's back with his fists. Dart dove face-first into the dirt, barely missing the dull, jagged edge of the till blade. His fists punched at the soil as he pushed himself to his feet and turned. His eyes raced across Paul like he could read him, but Paul knew Dart was seeing something that was not there, something from the Before when the world, or the people in it, had still been cruel and cold, when he had struggled to hold his place in a land that had not been built for him.

"They told me to rough you up a bit," he spat. "Keep you in line and that brat of yours from trying to run off." His knuckles rose like waves, like mountains, as his hands clenched and the Teutonic plates of his bones formed new continents at his side. They pulsed with promise, with death. "But, motherfucker, you best remebering ain't no one saying nothing if you end up dead."

He lurched forward as Paul raised his arms to block his chin, taking another heavy blow to the gut and doubling over. His empty stomach swelled and tried to expand into armor. He swiped blindly and lucked into a jab at Dart's ribs.

Dart howled. Paul could feel the eyes of the field works on him, urging him onward, but no one ceased their tilling or weeding or harvesting. He was alone in this fight. Rebellion had been broken from the others like domesticated dogs.

Pulling back to his full height, or as much of it as the pain would allow, Paul winced. The blood from his busted eye was hot on his cheek, even against the beating of the sun, and blurred his vision as he thought of Manta and centered his focus on Dart. The Field Manager side stepped another swing and used Paul's uncentered state to tackle him. He pinned Paul's arms beneath his knees, straddling his chest, and leering down at him in a halo of dust and light.

"You like this, faggot?" he growled, landing a boxed fist against Paul's ear and sending his head ringing. "I want to make sure you die happy."

Another blow hit Paul's opposite cheek, and he felt it split. The fresh blood burned like fire as it burst forth to meet the humid air.

"This is what you like, right?" Dart asked, forcing his weight downward through his torso to where he sat atop him.

Paul spit into the dust that filled his mouth.

"Seems more like what you like," he groaned.

Dart's eyes shot daggers as he reeled his arm back for another punch. Paul braced himself, squinting as a hand wrapped Dart's wrist. The weight of Dart's thigh pounding into his ribcage made Paul huff as his aggressor turned to see who had stopped him.

"What the fuck, Scout?"

"What the fuck, Dartanian?" Toni bit back.

They pulled the Field Manager to his feet and extending a hand to help Paul stand.

"This is my domain now," Dart growled. "I decide what goes on in these fields."

"You don't do nobody no good by beating down all the able-bodied recruits."

"You mean like you did me? Shoulda known one of your kind would stand up for another."

Paul hung against Toni's shoulder, happy for the support, but wanting to flee from them all the same. He fought for the air to match his lungs, tried to take it all in, to steady him, to let him float away.

"I'd say he knows his place now. Ain't that right, Paul?"

Paul tried to nod. He thought he nodded, but he wasn't sure.

"And now, Dart, you're a man down with a lot of shit to finish and what looks like—maybe—three more hours of sun."

Toni's power over the Field Manager was palpable. Paul wondered what other horrors they had committed in pursuit of their current station.

"Paul here won't be no help in this state, so I guess you'll be dirtying up your hands with soil now instead of blood," Toni continued. Dart fumed but simply stomped once on the ground. "I'd say you best get to it."

Toni turned, pulling Paul forward as he struggled to tell his legs how to move. He tried to force a quicker pace as they stepped back toward the row of homes.

Manta stared through the window with a longing gaze. Though she couldn't see the field from the small kitchen inside one of the cleaner, nicer Colton houses, she knew her father was out there. She'd gotten the supposedly better assignment, but she still wanted to be with her dad. Belinda eyed her from the island counter and tsked the young girl from her distraction.

"Pay attention, dear," she said. She littered her sentences with "dears" and "sweeties" like they were the main ingredients in her baking.

Manta turned back to the island and tried to force a smile as Belinda's fingers worked the dough. She seemed nice enough. But everyone Manta had met away from their cabin had turned out to be the pure evil of the wicked queens and witches in her storybooks. Belinda's grey hair was wrapped and pulled into a tight bun atop her head. Her complexion matched Manta's own and was mostly smooth, but the lines around her eyes and on her hands placed her somewhere in her sixties.

Belinda held her shoulders high and back as she worked, as if she refused to be broken by the state of the New World, as if her place in the Before had been wrought with enough hardships to know that this, too, was fleeting. She was slender, thinner than her bones wanted her to be, and Manta tried not to notice the loose skin swaying as she worked the mixture of flour and water into something new. She spoke constantly, singing her words as if excited for someone to hear them, as if she could conjure a space of normalcy.

"You darling girl," she said between adjusting the power of Manta's knead and telling her how to cup her hands to shape the loaf perfectly. "How old are you? Too young to remember a life before the Wave, I'm betting."

Manta nodded. Her fingers twisted a pinched circle from the dough as she tried to emulate what Belinda had shown her. It was a simple task, and one which felt exotic and foreign, as if she had found herself in a land of excess where food was abundant and grain could be turned, like alchemy, into something new. She wondered if it was Belinda who had baked the bread that had been waiting for them when they were captured. If her hands had worked the dough just like now, imbued it with song, and once the Families had had their fill and left it to mold, it was her who had carried it in for her and her father. She wondered if there was a time in the Before when fathers and daughters regularly made bread together, warmed it through in the ovens, and broken it, hot and airy, together at the dinner table. Or, better yet, they'd simply found aisle after aisle of it, ready and pre-sliced, in the Grocery Stores Paul had told her of. For all of her fairytales, the one most magical to her were the ones that featured the normalcy of the Before.

"You got the good house," Belinda said. "The Colton's Woman House. But, sweetie, you gotta work hard and do things just right or they'll put you out to field faster than a rabid dog meets Jesus."

Manta didn't know who Jesus was or why a dog would want to meet him, but she nodded solemnly. Belinda had spent the morning trying to explain what she called the pecking order of New Yukon. The Madisons and the Coltons were at the top. Each family had three houses—one for the menfolk to do whatever it was that men folk did; one for the women and the children under the age of "knowing what their parts were for;" and a third to bring them all together for supper every Sunday. Manta wondered what it was that "menfolk did" and how that could differ from what anybody else did, but she didn't dare to ask.

There was Mr. and Mrs. Madison, and Mrs. Madison's sister Eugenia who had been called something else before the Wave, but now wore the family name like silk chiffon. They had two boys "old enough to know better and vile enough to live up to the Family Crest." The Coltons, Mr. and Mrs., had one child between them—a daughter—who was pushing sixteen or seventeen but trapped in an six-year-old's mind.

After the Families came the Managers. Dartanion was the Field Manager—an ornery fellow Belinda described as a "Mexican with a chip the size of Napoleon's pocket square"—and Trent—an awful man who "wouldn't know his hind side from his elbow or the curtains from the drapes"—was over all six houses but usually stayed in the Madison Men's House. Below them were the folks like herself who kept on top of individual house upkeep, then the house workers—she said the word "workers" with a bite so strange it sliced the word in two, like she was still trying to believe its meaning herself—and then, after them, the people who tended the fields.

"The Scouts and the Traders," she said, "like the monsters who caught you and your daddy, report directly to Mr. Madison so they ain't exactly on the pyramid. They're like the broken nose on the Sphinx. But most of them came from in here before they proved themselves trustworthy enough for parole."

Manta made a mental note of all the new things she needed to ask her father about. They'd have to play the long con, but she finally saw possibilities for ways to make it out.

"What are the Families like?" she asked. "I've only met Mr. Madison, and he was a fucking full-of-himself asshole."

"Language, dear," Belinda scolded. "But he is a fucking asshole."

Belinda let a slight smile slip across her lips as she stoked the fire inside the stove. The electric burners had been removed from the top and two stainless steel trays now held splintered wood and the residual ash of a thousand breakfasts.

"The Madisons are just trailer trash with a fresh coat of paint. Mrs. Madison must've raided a drug store before coming here and made off with all the electric blue eyeshadow. She slathers that on her face every day and teases out her hair like she's making phone calls to Jesus himself."—There was that guy again.—"She's so stuck up, she would drown in a rainstorm. And those two grown up boys playing at manhood pick a different one of us every week—not you or me, mind you. I'm too old, and you're too young, thank Jesus. But they move 'em into the Woman House and play the devil's hockey with them till they get tired or get in a fight or she gets knocked up, and then no one ever sees hide nor hair of those women again."

Belinda shook her head from side to side in an exaggerated expression of her disapproval. Manta added more questions to her list.

"The Coltons are worse," Belinda said, "but they mostly keep to themselves. They think it's beneath them to interact with us common folk. I tell ya, Jesus loved the beggars and the whores, but even He'd have trouble turning the other cheek on that lot. Downright evil is what they are. Putting Satan to shame. When Mrs. Colton gets mad, she's hissier than a puffed toad and three times as angry. Once I saw her—"

"Ahem."

Belinda slammed her lips shut quickly as she turned to the new woman now standing in the kitchen doorway. Ms. Rose was the manager at the Family House and would use any information she had to oust Belinda from her position so she could take it over. She'd tried it before, several times. But luckily Belinda's bread recipe always saved her.

"Hello, Ms. Rose," Belinda said.

"Hello, Ms. Stapleton."

The women spoke like they liked one another, but Manta could hear the carnivorous undertones that gnawed on their words.

"What can I do for you, Ms. Rose?" Belinda asked.

"I came to get the girl."

Manta instinctively edged herself around the center island, placing the big block of cutting board and flour dust between herself and the sneering woman in the doorway.

"The girl," Belinda mocked, "has been assigned here with me."

"Well, Miss Chrissy says otherwise."

Belinda frowned. She looked to Manta with apologetic eyes.

"Who's Miss Chrissy?" Manta asked.

Ms. Rose strode into the kitchen with a precise, march-like step. She grabbed Manta by the wrist and began to lead her away.

"Miss Chrissy," she said, "is the Colton's precious daughter. And what Miss Chrissy wants, Miss Chrissy gets."

She pulled Manta across the street to the Colton Family House, never letting go of her arm as they trudged along. Manta tried to get a peek at her dad as they walked, but there was no clear line of site to the fields.

The Colton Family House was a mirror image of the Woman House across the street, and Ms. Rose offered no pleasantries as she ushered Manta inside and up the stairs. They stopped in front of a closed door in a cluttered but well-cleaned hallway. Ms. Rose knocked, three firm raps that echoed through the hollow wood.

"Enter."

The room inside was washed in pale pinks and torn lace fringes. Dolls with painted on eyes and poorly cut hair watched from the perimeter of the room. A sheer canopy hung over the bed like it was a fortress of protection for the young girl inside. To Manta, everything seemed exaggerated, like it was someone's piled on idea of what a little girl was supposed to like.

Chrissy crawled from the bed and stood before them in the middle of the room.

She was tall, with dirty yellow hair tied into bunches with tattered ribbons on either side of her head. Her sky-blue dress was a little too short for her, fraying at the hem which fell just above the middle of her thigh. What once were white socks with a band of lace around the top stretched up her calves and stopped just below her dirty knees. The socks had more holes stretched through them than did the lace hem. She looked to Manta like a poor man's approximation of Alice from her books back home. Like someone had done their best to recreate the girl from memory.

Her fingernails were bitten down to the quick and looked rough and ragged as she pawed at the hem of her skirt. She cocked her head and pursed her lips as she took in Manta and the school marm-ish woman behind her.

"Oh," she said. "You're black."

Her nose crinkled, and she scrunched her eyes slightly. Her gaze shot from Manta to the satisfied look on Ms. Rose's face and then back to the young girl with a shrug. Chrissy sighed.

"Oh well. That's fine, I guess." she groaned. "Better than no one. At least it's a girl, right?"

Ms. Rose nodded and moved to the hallway. She pulled the door closed gently leaving Manta inside with the Daughter of the House. Manta opened her mouth to speak, and Chrissy held up a quick finger to silence her. She moved to the door and held her ear to it, listening for the sound of Ms. Rose's retreating footsteps. Her breath expelled quickly as the bottom stair creaked beneath Ms. Rose's step.

"Okay. She's gone."

Chrissy's entire demeanor changed. Her lips curved into a mischievous smile, and even her blond hair seemed to bounce and perk up with new life.

"Sorry. I have to talk like that when Ms. Rose is around. Otherwise she tells my momma I'm not doing right by my station."

Manta's mouth fell open as she tried to understand what was happening. She had never met a girl close to her own age before. She had never met someone so peculiar before.

"So, I was thinking, since you're another girl like me, you could be my personal slave. Though Daddy don't like it when we use that word. But he also ain't like it when we ain't trying to control a body. So that man really just can't make up his mind, is what it is." Chrissy spoke a mile a minute, each word barely breaching her lips before another one tried to swallow it up, like every sentence was one long, run-on word. "So maybe I call you my lady-in-waiting. Like I'm a queen. Momma says I will be one day. I may have to be mean to you in public sometimes, but mostly it'd just get to be us playing together. Do you like to play? Of course you do. We could play princess or brush each other's hair—well, you can brush mine 'cause I don't really know what to do with yours and I bet it'd just snag on the bristles—and we can do tag, and you're it, and hide and seek. Or I've also got this whole shelf of games here." Chrissy pointed to a bookcase housing small flat boxes with names like *Life* and *Chutes and Ladders* and *Monopoly*. "Most of them are missing pieces but we can always just make up how they're supposed to go. I used to play them with my classmates before the Wave, so I mostly remember the rules. But my rules are better anyway, and I'm going to be Queen someday, so... I'm Chrissy, by the way."

Manta's mouth gaped as she tried to form words. She wasn't sure Chrissy even cared about a reply.

"Samantha," she said. "But my daddy calls me Manta."

"Alright, Manta," Chrissy smiled and took her hand to lead her to the bookshelf. "Pick out a game and let's play."

"No, no, no, no, no! We played that last time!"

Laughing, Paul waved his hands erratically in front of the screen, and Daniel knocked the scroller toward another game selection. His go to for Game Night was always Scrabble. He was good at it and had locked a litany of Q words into his repertoire because he liked to win. Alexander and Vanessa chimed their suggestions from the couch while Craig, Alexander's latest boyfriend, poured another glass of red wine in the kitchen.

"Aww, I like Scrabble," Craig said, and Alexander gave an exaggerated eye roll only the four others could see.

Daniel had started referring to Alexander simply as "X." At first it had been an inside joke and jab at Paul, who had once dated the man. But the constant string of new "loves of his life" at their biweekly get togethers had made the nickname all the more appropriate. He'd been seeing Craig for less than a week and already seemed tired of him.

"What about strip poker?" he suggested as the scroller highlighted the option.

"How about when I'm not here," Vanessa said, knocking her elbow into Alexander's ribcage with a loving tap. "This sausage fest ain't as fun for the lone lesbian."

"Aww, come on," Alexander pouted. "You know you've got a drawer full of them beside your bed."

"Vic does," Vanessa laughed. "In shapes and sizes to put you to shame, mister."

"Where is Vic tonight?" Daniel asked. Victoria was usually his fiercest competition at these things. Filled with the same competitive spirit, she helped him rise to the challenge. And together they kept one another from ruining the fun of the evening.

"Working late. She's got some new top-secret project going on that's been keeping her past midnight most days."

Paul slumped into the opening on the couch between Daniel and Alexander. He spoke sloppily around the crumbs of rich crackers and smelly cheese from the charcuterie board on the coffee table. "The never-ending excitement of city planning," he said.

Craig stood awkwardly with his wine glass at the edge of the living room setting and took a heavy swig before sitting in the open armchair off to the side.

"Your girlfriend works for the city?" he asked. "She's not part of that new Forward Colony thing, is she?"

Vanessa shrugged, but everyone in the room knew that was probably the case. The promise of life-saving castles in the clouds were the worst-kept political secret since President Germanotta had attempted to rewrite a more inclusive and less violent National Anthem. It was all anyone could talk about, but, with no solid information coming from on high, everyone also had a different theory about what the structures would be. Some folks believed the Colonies would be giant rafts, floating on the ocean waves as a way to help offset the growing overpopulation concerns from around the world. Others thought they would finally be colonizing Mars.

"I don't think I could live in one of those," Alexander said. He stretched his arms and laid them across the back of the sofa, one wrapped around Vanessa shoulders, the other around Paul. His hand gripped Daniel's sleeve and shook it. "I think I'd probably go insane."

"Like you're not already," Daniel smirked. "In my professional opinion, I mean."

Alexander's mouth gaped in shock as he looked around the room for backup, clutching at the nonexistent pearl at his chest.

"Don't look at me, honey," Vanessa shrugged. "He calls 'em like he sees 'em."

"Well, then, sweetheart. Maybe I should go off to the sky, then. Maybe that is my destiny," he said. "Send me to the crazy house and throw away the key."

"Except you'd last a week before you—literally—blew through all the men and started clawing at the walls to get out," Paul laughed.

"They say there'll be millions of men in there," Craig said, and Paul shrugged.

"Two weeks then," he corrected.

"Have mercy," Alexander laughed. "My jaw is sore already."

Craig took another heavy sip of his wine and peered around uncomfortably. His toes fidgeting inside his sneakers made the fabric bulge and dance.

"I don't know," Vanessa said as she leaned forward to stack another cracker with cured meats. "It might be a nice change of pace to go live in a controlled biosphere. It'd almost be like a vacation. A sultry seventy degrees with zero chance of rain and no more eight to fives. Out here, Summer days rarely dip below a hundred and five now."

"Plus, you can't skip a rock in Piedmont Park without hitting two dozen folks who are unhoused," Alexander agreed. "Even in the frozen Winters."

"One in three children are malnourished and starving," Paul said.

The group stared blankly at the coffee table. The smiles dripped from their faces. It was appalling how the forward progress of time had left so many people behind. Daniel tapped his toe as the controller went limp in his grip. Craig squirmed in his chair and downed his third glass of wine.

"You know those Forward Colonies are just a way for the government to seize control of the rich, right?" Craig blurted when he'd swallowed his last gulp of merlot. "They're the only people who will be allowed in. And they'll put chips in their heads, and try to control their minds, and leave the rest of us all out here to starve or burn."

A short, staccato chuckle escaped from Alexander's throat. He tried to hold it in, but soon the entire couch erupted in laughter.

"It's not a joke!" Craig pleaded. "There are too many people on this planet, and this is the government's attempt to keep control."

His eyes were dark and earnest. He believed what he was saying with every fiber of his being. He had read it online. He knew it was true.

"Speaking of too many people," Paul said. "Daniel and I have decided to adopt!"

"Seriously?" Alexander exclaimed! "Good for you two!"

He pulled Paul into a headlock and rustled his hair with the palm of his hand as Paul struggled to break free.

"Congratulations!" Vanessa added.

Craig reached for another open bottle of wine and bypassed the glass.

"You people are just sheep if you don't think the government has nefarious notions in this whole escapade."

"Ahh," Daniel smirked. "You would've done well in Scrabble, too, huh?"

"Speaking and spelling are two different things," Vanessa groaned.

"You really think anyone on Capitol Hill gives a rat's ass about you? Anyone under that gold dome?" Craig bellowed. "If these fucking space pods ain't built to leave us all behind, they're nothing more than prisons to ship us all off to."

"I think you should leave," Alexander said. "You can find your own way home, right?"

Craig stood, dumbfounded. His mouth gaped. He grabbed another bottle of wine and marched to the door of Paul and Daniel's apartment.

"Fucking sheep," he muttered as he exited.

Alexander pursed his lips in thought. His nose crinkled like a rabbit's.

"What can I say? The crazies are the best in bed." he sighed.

"Tooting your own horn?" Daniel laughed.

"I was trying not to," Alexander smiled. "Hence the crazy. How about five card stud?"

Daniel laughed and selected the game from the menu. The computer dealt the digital cards to each of their hand-held consoles.

"And I won the second round, but she said she let me win, but I don't think she really did because she kept trying to change the rules against me, and I still kept beating her."

Paul had never seen Manta more excited. She had not stopped talking since she'd bounded through the door. She paced back and forth across the floor and made exaggerated hand gestures to accentuate her tale. He was grateful for the poorly lit room. He kept his head turned slightly so the left side of his face remained hidden away in the darker shadows of the den as he listened to her story and tried not to wince. His daughter had made a friend of a sort. Finally, she had encountered someone near her own age who wasn't a roving cannibal. He wished he could celebrate with her, but his body was too broken and bruised.

"Word is, she's sixteen or seventeen, but I swear I know more about the world than she does. It's like she's trapped in this idea of what a kid is supposed to be. But anyway," Manta continued. "She says I'm 'hers,' so my only real job is playing and then picking up the pieces of the game when we're done. She says if I lose any more of the pieces or if she loses any more of the games her daddy will beat me, but I'm pretty sure that's just her idea of a joke."

Manta paused for breath as the door swung open and Belinda stepped inside with a tray. She didn't speak as she placed it on the kitchen table and departed. There were two slices of stale bread, some okra—blanched but still furry and hard to the touch, and the curdled remnants of the morning's milk that were supposed to resemble cottage cheese. The full loaves and butter they were given as a "welcome gift" to set them at ease were now reserved for the Families and the Families alone.

Manta tapped a slice of the bread against the table and shoved it into the wet dairy curd to try to soften it up. The okra felt strange in her mouth: green, and new, and it tickled her tongue with its fuzz.

"Don't you want to eat?" she asked.

Paul nodded. He pulled himself up from the chair and shuddered as his bones snapped back into place. His muscles pulled at his joints, and he wobbled as he crossed the room.

"What the fuck?" Manta exclaimed.

Her face hardened. The fire returned to her eyes. She was once again the girl he knew. The girl too old for her age. Manta, the protector. Manta, the destroyer.

"It's nothing," Paul said. "I'm okay."

His words were strained. The air in his lungs struggled to carry them past his vocal cords.

"Like hell you are," Manta snarled. "If I had my bow, I'd kill them all."

She helped her father into a kitchen chair and shoved his slice of bread into the cottage cheese. Manta, his companion. Manta, his caregiver. She gently touched the bruise welling under Paul's left eye and pulled back quickly when he winced.

"I think I saw some aloe growing near one of the other houses," she said. "I'll be right back."

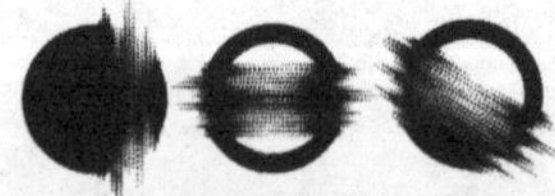

"There's no coming back from this," Lincoln said, firmly, although a tinge of the worry which seemed to always coat his throat was still present.

Adrasteia's team had assembled inside her inner sanctum immediately following the larger meeting she held for the major gods, in all their misguided revolution, to air their grievances. Daniel nodded. He agreed with Lincoln. Although he had survived and the nausea had passed, a steady, tinny hum still haunted his ears. But, when all was said and done, he now knew the precise dimensions and inner workings of the Macintosh 128K. Lincoln had chosen the history lesson as a joke, but now, with no prior knowledge other than the thing's existence, Daniel was an expert on a personal computer from 1984. Now, Adrasteia, along with the majority of the other minor deities, believed that was the proof they needed to stick with the original plan, casualties be damned.

"If we do this," Lincoln continued, "if we send the entire population through the Haptic, we're going to lose hundreds of them. No question. Daniel—I'm sorry. Asclepios has clocked more time in the Mind Map than anyone else inside this damn Colony, and you see what it did to him. Even if we pretend, we don't care about a few hundred lives, what happens when the bodies start piling up and we get found out?"

Daniel blushed. He knew his visits had been a little excessive—he missed his husband and daughter with every fiber of his being—but he was still embarrassed by his time spent inside his fantasy.

"Or," Nyx countered, "my theory is that Asclepios' overuse of the Haptic is what caused the breakdown to begin with. It's very possible that someone with a, for lack of a better phrase, virgin mind would not experience the breakdown he did."

"We can't know until we test it," Adrasteia sighed. She leaned back in her seat and rubbed her temples. The plan, in theory, had been perfection. The details were more complicated.

"The idea of subliminal messaging could actually work," Helios, one of the LED lighting environment technicians, said. "But it is unreliable. It may not get through the everyone."

"And the Haptic, itself, may knock the same number of people the subliminal messaging would miss out of commission. Permanently."

The room erupted into a cacophonous din that merged with the roar in Daniel's ear. The stink of fear and frustration clung to the dark brown drapes like pollen on a Spring day.

"You heard those assholes sharing their conspiracy theories out there at that meeting," Nyx yelled. "It's the Aposts all over again. We can't afford to hedge our bets on a maybe. We know the Haptic works. We need to act before those bozos lose their shit and start cutting their wrists and trying to form picket lines again. And it's our fault for giving them a podium to rant and not acting swiftly enough."

"People need a place to air their grievances and gossip," Adrasteia protested. "It helps to keep them sane."

"It also radicalizes them," Nyx argued. "They find like-minded individuals who believe the nonsense they're spouting, and that leads to them believing more and more insanity, and that—well, that leads to insurrection."

"But isn't that what we're doing, too?" Lincoln asked.

The Gods fell silent. Collectively, they bit their lips and tried to quell the churning in their guts. The pratfall of those on the right side of history was too often the belief that everyone, including the cheats and liars, deserved equal time on stage. The quest for truth was too often mired in insanity. As they questioned their own motivations and actions when mirrored in others, they allowed too much time for the gorge to grow.

"The difference is: we know what is truly happening."

It was the very first time Daniel had ever heard Hermes speak a full sentence. Every eye in the room was on him as he continued.

"We know the Colony will soon be unable to sustain us all. And we know enough history to know what that means. We are already at war. Not on the cusp of. Not doing all we can to prevent its outbreak. We are there. There are casualties in war. The fact that we are even considering those casualties is proof of our righteousness. It's the loss of the few for the many. We need to follow Adrasteia's plan."

The room was quiet as they mulled things over. Daniel was torn. He knew if it was Paul and Samantha he was risking, he would not think twice about pulling the plug on the whole thing. Didn't the citizens of the Colony deserve the same consideration?

"What if it was Kris?" he asked.

"What?"

Nyx was confused, but Adrasteia knew exactly what he meant. Daniel watched as the determination on her face gave way to a crestfallen worry. Her eyes searched her mind for an answer; her mind searched her memory for a clue from Kris that would guide her through. Daniel felt sorry for her. He knew it was an impossible impasse.

"Would you send them through the Haptic if Kris were here?"

"Kris would be willing to sacrifice themself for the good of the world," she finally whispered then let her voice grow stronger. "We all would, would we not? Isn't that what brought us up her to begin with? Something within us was willing to face the unknown to save the world."

"Or to save ourselves," Achelous whispered. It was the first time in all their meeting Daniel had heard him speak, and he swallowed the words even as they formed.

"The Colony offered a chance at life amidst the growing uncertainty of the surface," Nyx agreed. "We can applaud ourselves all we want, but we were being selfish."

The debate had stretched beyond itself, growing out into philosophical quandaries they would spend the next six years trying to solve.

"What if we do both?" Daniel suggested. "We start the subliminals, and we finalize the Haptic. When people show up for their appointments, we ask. If they know, they skip it. If they don't, maybe the subliminal will have primed their minds enough to avoid a major case of the Haps."

"What kind of time frame does that put us in?" Nyx asked.

"Three days to program the lights," Helios offered.

Lincoln said, "Another two weeks to process people through the HMM."

"Best of both worlds, so to speak," Adrasteia said. "Let's do it. Start the process. We'll meet again the night before the implementation."

She wanted to talk to her father once more. She wanted to appeal to his good senses and avoid the smoke and mirrors. She only wanted honesty. Was that too much to ask?

If Kris were there, they'd know what to do. But Kris had chosen to remain on the surface. And this could be her only chance to ever see them again. If she could convince her father to come clean—to defy orders and tell the Colony (and her) what had actually happened on the surface— the whole of it, the truth, they could avoid so many of the less fortunate probabilities.

No, she wouldn't have let Kris near the Haptic. Not in its present state. Not with the trauma it could cause. She had to ask herself what made them more special than everyone else she'd be sending through. She had to be sure, but she carried Orpheus's doubt.

"So we meet again in three days," Daniel said. "Same time. But in the Control Room. We start this process together. We all take responsibility."

Adrasteia sank into her chair. She hated these events. She detested pretense. Every few months her father hosted a dinner in their quarters for the mayor and her underlings. Every few months, Hiromi was expected to be the perfect Southern Hostess, the consummate Japanese daughter. She bowed her greetings with locked shoulders. She ate sparingly and daintily. She ensured drinks remained topped, the ice unmelted, and the rings of condensation were wiped away before the glass could touch down again. The conversation flowed without her input, without any truths beyond pleasantries passing lips. By the time the first course was served, she felt ready to explode.

"For all we know," the mayor spoke to rapt attention from around the table, "we are all that's left of humanity. It is imperative that we forge a path in this brave new world. That we survive."

'We' meaning the elite, Adrasteia thought. The Aldous Huxley reference was not lost on her, though she assumed it probably was on Mayor Lewis. She detested the woman. Her blond bob and perky personality which yielded false promises and fake compassion grated against Adrasteia's soul. Her father, though, was the ever-noble supplicant.

"We are working nonstop, night and day, to ensure food and oxygen production levels can meet the needs of the population," Dr. Saito promised.

"Well," Mayor Lewis said. She stretched the word through four whole seconds as she looked around the table, glancing only briefly to ensure Adrasteia's eyes were lowered, her mind the appropriate elsewhere. "At least ensure production is to the level to keep most of us alive and healthy. Cullings happen. In hindsight, it's how we got here to begin with."

The gentlemen surrounding the table laughed as Adrasteia bit her lip. She thought she would draw blood as she peered at the plates around the table: heaping servings of half-eaten greens, fresh tomatoes and cheeses that would be scraped into trash cans for recycling, real meats from the salted stores only the top-level Alphas had access to. And this woman had the nerve to laugh about production levels, to scoff at the Subs who would die.

"I'm sure you've considered the numbers," the mayor continued, "but I'd like a report on how production needs may be changed or met by the closing of some of the lower floors."

Adrasteia's jaw gaped. She tried to make eye contact with her father. She longed to appeal to his better nature. She knew this was not the man who raised her. That man was compassionate, a humanitarian. He would never laugh at such a cruel dismissal of his fellow man. Something about being trapped inside the Colony had changed him. His survival instinct had kicked in. And though she knew the solutions he sought were for everyone inside, he would ultimately bow to the masters.

It was all the more reason to break out, to begin her revolution. Kris would understand the sacrifices she was forced to make. If she ever saw them again.

Deep down, Adrasteia had hoped this dinner would change her mind. She had wished the politicians and scientists would dine and convince themselves that truth held more weight than survival. No. That truth, in and of itself, facilitated survival.

She was wrong. And it hurt. Even though she knew going into the evening she would be.

As the politicians cleared the chambers, Adrasteia sulked at the table. Her father bowed and thanked each person individually as they left, promising a full report of possibilities to Mayor Lewis by week's end.

"You can't honestly be okay with this," Adrasteia said when the last person exited, and the door had whooshed closed. "Give her a lesson on how much air would be saved if we shut off Alpha5!"

Dr. Saito crossed his arms over his chest and squinted behind the glare on his glasses.

"Not enough people live there," he shrugged. "Thirty at most. There would be no significant impact on our resources."

Adrasteia cried out as she rose from her seat. She had never seen him be so callous.

"You can't be serious. Who even are you anymore?"

"I am your father. And you, child, will respect me."

His voice was harsh and stern, but he softened as he moved to help clear the leftovers from the table.

"Hiromi," he said, "the mayor is just weighing options. It is her job to look at the science and come up with contingency plans to help the Colony."

"Because history shows politicians making decisions around science has been real fucking fruitful. She's only interested in helping the Alphas."

"Lest you forget, you're a so-called Alpha too, young lady. No matter how many Subs you chose to slum it with, you've taken every advantage your station has given you with abandon. You do not work. You do not study. You live a life of leisure only allowed to those of us on the upper levels."

Adrasteia hung her head and she turned away from her father. The bright pinks and yellows of cupcake frosting on the dessert table mocked her.

"People are going to die," she whispered.

"Yes, they will," her father confirmed. "By culling or starvation. By suffocation or by drowning. What do you think would be the better way to let them go? Be thankful you will not be one of the people forced to make that choice."

"Will they be given a choice?"

"Be grateful for what I've given you, Hiromi. No matter how much you pout or sulk or yell, you have privilege. Be thankful for it. For what the gods have blessed at your feet."

Her father stormed from the room into his quarters, and Adrasteia slumped to the floor. Her fingers clenched and released the fibers of the carpet. There was no turning back now.

The following night her gods would meet. In just thirty-six brief hours, her plan would be set into motion. She would yell and shout and cause an avalanche that could not be stopped.

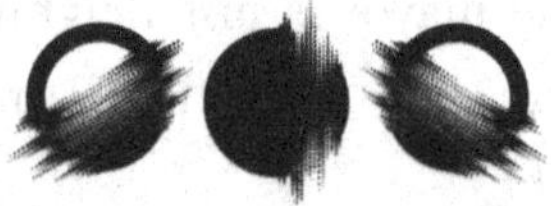

Daniel walked the halls of Sub5 slowly. He wanted to take in the brightly colored sunset over Atlanta streets that would not be the same when he saw them again. If everything went according to plan, he would see them in just two weeks' time. He wondered if the ancient oaks that lined Juniper Street—whose massive roots cobbled and cracked the sidewalk—whose canopy arched gently over the road and fluttered a limerick green hello to the neighbors—would still be there, tall and stately, with a majesty reserved for only what was old and made new with each Spring. If the small restaurants and boutique clothing shops nestled inside the living rooms of old row houses had been demolished to make way for more of the high-tech, glass covered skyscrapers which rose above the tree line of the City in the Forest. He wondered if Paul and Samantha were waiting for him, nestled away in the cabin they had bought in order to figure out family less than two hours north of the city. If they had maintained his small garden. If it had brought them sustenance and growth in his absence.

Other Subs trudged along the hallways on their way to and from their work or quarters, oblivious to the change that was about to occur, secure—barely so—in the knowledge that their worker-ant lifestyle inside the Colony was all for the greater good of those they had left behind. Some attempted the Southern courtesy of eye contact, the brief nod of hello, the "y'all have a good evening, sir." Others trained their eyes on their shoes and bounded through the motion of point A to point B. All of them were oblivious to the machinations at work behind the orange, pink, and purple LED flashes meant to simulate the perfection of the setting sun just on the other side of the 75/85 connector.

He'd spent the last three days dividing his time between the Haptic Mind Map Programming Quarters and the Environmental Systems Control Room. He and Lincoln had made their guesses at standards to reduce the effect of the Haps on the general population. It was all hypothetical. They wouldn't know the true effect of the programming until the plan was set into motion. And then it would be too late. They couldn't make any major changes, not with the onslaught of back-to-back scheduling for their unwilling, but soon-to-be-awakened lab rats. Lincoln had seemed reluctant but resigned, a feeling Daniel had known all too well since long before he'd been ushered into the Colony.

He felt his time in the ESCR had been more fruitful. Helios and Theia had been charged with scheduling the notifications for HMM appointments based on the Venn diagram of those least likely to suffer extensively from the Haps amidst those least likely to fall prey to subliminal messaging. Daniel had used the scrambling wrist cuff to access the Colony medical records with his credentials but, he hoped, no trace of his presence in the system. Helios had set up a server outside of the Colony's systems to hold the digital files. Daniel helped them decipher the medical jargon to determine the best order for the test subjects to undergo their treatment. Meanwhile, Selene and Hyperion had focused their efforts on programming the lights—little flickers of sudden color within the browns of the tree trunks or the grays of the pocked cement sidewalks that were undetectable yet would—hopefully—get the job done. The test on Daniel had not triggered a resurgence of the Haps nausea or tinnitus, but he now knew exactly how many people had visited Dollywood in Eastern Tennessee before the chutes to the Colony had been sealed. He'd had to focus though, standing still and observing the whole of a message he knew was there for nearly two and a quarter minutes as his mind did the work of reading what he could not directly see.

Everything was falling into place exactly as Adrasteia had hoped. If Nyx, Eurynome, and Achelous were able to restore environmental systems to the stilts that kept them aloft, 10 miles in the air, above the clouds and surrounded by ozone, they would be, quite literally, home free. Nyx and the ESCR team were still trying to figure out a means to divert that much power in a way that wouldn't trigger immediate action from the Alphas intent on keeping them trapped. But they would have two weeks to get that sorted after the plan was set into motion. And maybe, once more of the Colony's citizens were aware of the truth, an undetectable diversion of power wouldn't be necessary. It would be required. People really did have power when they had information. Of that, Daniel was sure.

He rounded the corner to the elevator bay to find a group of seven or eight of Adrasteia's secret society huddled together and speaking in hushed tones. Adrasteia discouraged external meetings of the group, especially those away from the Neutral Zone, as it could too easily draw the attention of the Guard. Though many in their ranks knew what was happening, there was always the possibility of some eager young recruit, desperate to earn their stripes, seeing any covert exchange as an Apost-like gathering and reporting it. They stopped speaking quickly as Daniel moved into sight and did their best to appear ungrouped and nonchalant. Daniel smiled and gave them the three-fingered hand tap to his chest Adrasteia had given them as a way to signal one another outside of the inner sanctum. The sigil return was half-hearted, but he thought nothing of it. There were more important matters at foot. The sun had nearly disappeared beyond the LED horizon. It was time for the Gods to meet. They would convene in their inner sanctum and then, like Titans going to war against Olympus, march to the Environmental Systems Control Room. All of them, present and together, would see the start of the Revolution. Soldiers or fodder. Ready to take on the night.

He felt an air of celebration as he stepped off the elevator into the Neutral Zone. The Zone's hedonistic calamity which before had seemed so passé and controlled was now alive and vibrant. Knowing the little sanctuary of the people's revolt had actually been accepted and condoned by the government—"Give them their 'safe space' to keep them pacified"—had clouded Daniel's ability to see it for the revolutionary act it truly was. Tonight, caught in his own rebellion, he could finally appreciate the cobbled tech and fashions, the dog collars and the leads for the gluttonous and freeing expressions they truly were.

He smiled as he sidestepped a grown man in a leather diaper and bonnet throwing a temper tantrum in the middle of the walkway, wailing from around his ball gag pacifier as his Dom threatened a spanking he would not soon forget. He paused to give passage to the patrons rushing to watch the sword-swallowing drag queen perform retro lip syncs to the pop dance hits of the 2020s, the bards of decades past spouting the hopeful, escapist lyrics the population had needed in the aftermath of the first of several modern pandemics which should have been viewed as yet another clue the planet was fighting back against the scourge of humanity. He felt finally god-like as he slipped through the plush brown curtains that made up

Adrasteia's inner sanctum behind the hand-stitched clothing booth.

Or, he supposed, it was his inner sanctum now too. It belonged to the eleven of them—the people's gods, aloft in the clouds, who would, very soon, usher religion back to the surface of the world.

Walking into the room, he could tell his compatriots felt it too. An unspoken, anxious exclamation point filled the room. All of them were upright and ready, teetering tall upon a ball of fire just waiting to ignite. Together, they stood on the precipice. Together they would jump.

"Are we all here?" Selene asked, peering at her wrist as if a watch was there. "Two hairs past the freckle," as her father used to say. Old habits were hard to break.

"Oneiros had some last-minute adjustments to make on the Haptic," Adrasteia said as she looked around the room, meeting each of her god's eyes with reverence and glee. She did her best to quell the anticipation in her voice. "He's going to meet us at the Control Room."

Daniel wondered what adjustments Lincoln was making and why he hadn't been looped in on them. Even though he hadn't remembered the child from before, sitting—awkward and pimpled—in his guidance counselor office, he had developed a real relationship with the young man now fully utilizing his genius, even if still a bit unsure of himself. He thought of him as a sort of protégé. He hoped he thought of him as his mentor.

"System's check?" Helios suggested, spotting the confusion in Daniel's brow.

All the moving parts were in place for the clock to function properly. The subliminal programming was written to surge every thirteen minutes and thirty-three seconds across all the Sub levels, targeting only the people there before the Alphas were involved. Lincoln had also helped them create a redundancy program which would activate if, somehow, the original file was discovered or corrupted. The HMM appointment schedule was coordinated to begin immediately, and "doctor's notes" were ready to send to employers to explain away any missed work, signed by an assortment of medics thanks to Adrasteia's scrambling bracelets, including Daniel himself to avoid suspicion of his name's absence in case the letters were tracked. Though, if all went well, the exodus would have begun before anyone even thought to look. Nyx was making headway on the escape route and assured the team everything would be set for the doors to open in two weeks' time, once the plan was in full effect. The only thing left was to run the code.

They felt triumphant as they entered the elevator. It would be a difficult two weeks ahead, rushing minds through the Haptic, convincing hearts not to act until the timing was right, but the end was finally in sight. Daniel smiled broadly, unable to convince his face to share in the reverence of the situation. Soon he would see his husband and daughter again—finally!—somewhere other than his mind. He would be able to actually feel Paul's embrace outside of the sense memory he sometimes worried had faltered, his brain adjusting the weight of him to feel somehow stronger, lingering, his scent from musk to lavender. He would be able to see the young woman Samantha was becoming instead of the amalgamated person he imagined her to be.

As they exited the elevator, Hermes, Typhon, and Echnida split to stand guard at the entrances to the passageway. Helios and Selene ambled to the break room to set up the decadent cupcakes Adrasteia had managed to steal after her father's dinner with the mayor. She hadn't planned it, but it had worked out perfectly. More proof, in her mind, the gods were smiling on their actions.

Theia and Hyperion entered the Control Room first.

"Y'all won't believe this," Theia said. "The mayor sent cupcakes down for the Environmental Systems crew. Probably just leftovers from one of her big Alpha parties. But they're the good kind. Real milk and sugar from the reserves. Better get to the break room before they're gone."

"Seriously?" one of the techs asked, slowly becoming alert as he lounged in his chair. While the day crew spent their time coding and manipulating the skylines that poured through each of the hallways, the night crew was mostly responsible for making sure the only beeps from the equipment were the ones that were meant to occur. All of the night crew lived on the Sub levels, so it had been years since any of them had enjoyed any sort of real baked good, let alone cupcakes that were meant for the mayor.

"Hurry," Hyperion said. "We'll watch the consoles 'til you're back."

Echnida signaled Lincoln's arrival and ushered him around the corner. Daniel watched as he slunk through the hall, head low and eyes trained to the floors like he was certain every other tile was a landmine ready to blow. His chin stayed cradled against his neck as he tugged at Daniel's sleeve, whispering into his shirt collar so quietly, Daniel struggled to hear.

"Hey, can I talk to you for a minute?" he asked. "Over there?"

"Can it wait? We're about to head in. We've only got a few minutes to load and run the program. And we promised we'd do this together."

Lincoln opened his mouth to protest but was cut off by Adrasteia ushering them all into the room. Hyperion smiled from his seat at the console keyboard. The static in the room was pins and needles, electrifying the air and threatening to blow the machines before they'd even gotten started.

"All set?" Adrasteia asked.

"All keyed up," he said. "We just have to press enter. Want to do the honors?"

As Adrasteia stepped ceremoniously forward, Lincoln pulled again at Daniel's arm.

"Daniel," he whispered. "I really need to—"

Adrasteia pressed the button and watched the code scroll across the screen. Suddenly, the monitor turned blank. With a pop, the hallway outside went dark.

"What the fuck?" Helios exclaimed. "I wrote this code myself. It should have integrated flawlessly."

He pushed his way to the keyboard and typed furiously but nothing happened. They could tell from the hum the machines were still on, but it was like they had gone into defense mode, locking out the myth of gods from their mathematical majesty. The dim red emergency lights clicked on and gave everything an eerie, hellish glow.

Hermes appeared in the doorway. His expression was blank and neutral, but the light hit the sweat that dotted his lips. His arms were raised at his sides.

"Step away from the keyboard," the woman holding Hermes at taser-point bellowed as she pushed into the room, followed by several other members of the Guard, weapons drawn and ready. They were caught, red-handed, red-faced, and in the dark. It was over before it even began. Daniel only wondered how the Guard had gotten there so quickly.

"I'm sorry," Lincoln whispered.

Dr. Saito entered sternly. His eyes met his daughter's, but his face did not move, opting instead for stone and disapproval in the way only a parent could muster. He walked slowly to the keyboard and entered a few swift strokes. The lights flickered back to full power. They burned in Daniel's retinas. Adrasteia opened her mouth to speak, but her father raised his hand in protest.

"Thank you, Mr. Dunnwater," he said. "Guard, arrest them all."

Daniel stared at Lincoln in disbelief as the Guard reached to place his hands in cuffs. Lincoln's eyes welled with tears as they scanned the floor, the wall, the ceiling. Anywhere but the feelings of betrayal on his mentor's face. He turned away, Dr. Saito's hand on his shoulder as they were led, single file from the Control Room: false gods sent to sacrifice.

aul awoke in the dead of night and stretched timidly. His eye was mostly healed with only a slight cut and a yellow bruise as evidence of what had been, but his ribs still ached from the impact they had faced. His subsequent days in the fields had been less eventful with only the occasional whack to the back of his calf to keep him moving or the relentless glare of the Field Manager coupled with his aggrandized smirk. Dart seemed satisfied that Paul had learned his place.

Another noise like the one that had roused him sounded from downstairs. Footsteps. Someone was in the house. His eyes adjusted to the night, and he looked across the bedroom to where Manta's makeshift cot was to find her sitting up and wide-eyed. She clutched at the rough blankets surrounding her, her hands aching for her bow. Paul's finger met his lips as he pulled himself from beneath the scratchy wool. Manta was quickly at his side, her fleet footed strides silent in the crisp night air. Together they slid to the doorway and listened to determine their next move.

"I think you'll find you'll be very happy here."

The Hawk's voice was unmistakable as it wafted through the stairwell, her backwoods southern drawl thick and bounding up the steps two at a time. The venom in her words was forever embedded in both of their memories.

"You get to share the space with a couple others we brought in too. Little black girl and her faggot daddy. They gone make you feel at home."

The silence between her words was as violent as her syllables.

"What? No growl? No snarky comeback? Told you we could tame any beast."

The Hawk's laugh sliced at the air like talons, slashing it into Before and After with only a great gash to form the present.

Manta's fingers twined around her father's, and they held their breath as they listened to the padlock click back into place on the outer door. They stepped slowly into the hallway and plotted each footfall carefully as they made their way to the first floor, careful not to step into the wound, afraid of being stuck there forever.

A man slumped at the kitchen table. A nearly burnt-out candle still glowed in front of him. From the base of the stairs, they were able to make out his silhouette. He had a medium build, with broad shoulders that hunched forward in defeat like he would fold in on himself if he could. Shaggy blond hair that had once been shorn off caught the light in its wild, grown-out and uneven abundance. The haggard wings of an angel slipped up his neck from inside his tattered red t-shirt. Paul thought he recognized the tattoo.

"Alexander?"

The man tensed. He shifted slowly in his chair, as if turning around to face them took every ounce of his concentration. His face was dirty and bruised, thinner than Paul remembered, and covered in a thick, erratic beard. But it was definitely his ex.

Alexander studied the two figures by the staircase carefully. It was difficult to make out their features through the shadows. The man was tall and thin, and he motioned for the young girl to stay put as he inched forward to skirt the ring of light emitted by the last gasps of the flickering candle.

"Paul?"

His voice was foreign even to himself. It cracked through the night air like the dim glow of fireflies testing the darkness for companionship. He swallowed to coat his dry tongue with what little saliva he could produce. He felt his face twist, misshapen from the action of attempting to feel human again.

"Is that really you?" Paul asked in disbelief.

Alexander didn't know how to answer. It had been so long since he had truly interacted with another person, even longer since he had heard his name aloud. Now, seeing Paul standing there motionless in the dim light, he felt his memory hit him like a wave. He felt himself return to his body. Nearly a decade of torture, of fevered attempts at forgetting the man he had been, coursed through the folds in his brain as memories swam to the surface, colorless and dusty against even the blackness set before him.

It was as if he had disassociated from himself in order to survive, and Paul's presence had returned him into being. Suddenly, the weight of all he had suffered stung through his bones, clenched his muscles, and turned his stomach into knots. Years of fight and struggle, flight and foraging forged through him with reckless abandon. His eyes welled with tears as if his body had any liquid left to give, and he collapsed.

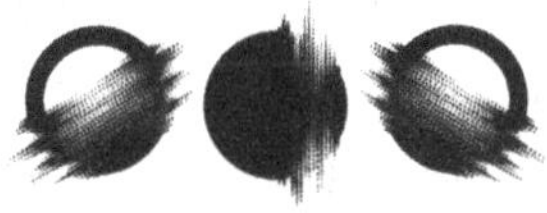

The holding cells in the brig were not too different from the living quarters on Sub5. Long and narrow, with only a mattress built into the wall and a bucket at the end of the walkway, the only real changes Daniel noticed were the lack of a storage bin below the thin bed (for obvious security reasons) and that the white tinted plexiglass that spread the width of the top and bottom of the door had been replaced with bars. His clothing had been switched out for slightly tan linen pants and a pullover.

He'd been denied shoes. The pants had an elastic band with no draw string that dug angrily into his hips.

He paced back and forth, six steps to the bucket, six strides to the door, and tried to center his erratic thoughts on three. It had been hours since he'd seen another human being. He knew the cells around him contained his compatriots—Adrasteia to his immediate left and Nyx on the right with the others dotted out along the hallway like zoo creatures on display—but Adrasteia had urged silence upon their arrival. It was the smart thing to do to prevent further incrimination, but the deafening stillness was already beginning to drive him mad. There was still a chance, if they said nothing, the other elements of their plan could continue. Unless, of course, Lincoln had told them everything.

Of course he had.

Guilt wracked his brain. He had been the one to bring Lincoln into the fold. He'd trusted him and guided him, explained the severity of the situation inside, revealed his own personal, heartfelt motivations, and Lincoln had betrayed him. He'd betrayed them all. Daniel could only blame himself as he marched, punctuating his thoughts with swift, angered footfalls.

The fury at himself was better than the alternative. He tried to keep it centered in his mind. He tried, with each footstep, to slip another brick into the wall that blocked out his other thoughts, but sorrow continued to seep through the mortar, refusing to let it set, threatening to bring the whole thing down. They had failed. But not only that, they had been captured. Even if they made it out of prison, now every Alpha knew their names, every member of the Guard knew their faces. They would be constantly monitored. They would be kept apart to prevent any chance of another attempt. He had lost the only way he would ever see his husband and daughter again.

But maybe there was still hope. The Haptic Mind Map was out of the question, but it was possible the subliminal messaging could reach enough of the citizens to incite a widespread rebellion. Yes, they had been shut down, but it was possible the redundancy code was still operational, the hallway LEDs flashing out an imperceptible message: "We have been lied to. We must escape."

"I'm sorry, Daniel."

Lincoln stood on the other side of Daniel's cage; his face shadowed by the vertical stripes of the bars. They paired well with the anguish he presented there.

Daniel stopped his pacing and faced him. He assumed the practiced, neutral expression he had perfected in his years as a counselor.

"I tried to get you out of there," Lincoln said.

Daniel scoffed.

"You betrayed us all. Not just our group. Every single person in this Colony."

Lincoln's eyes shot to the floor then moved, unfocused, down the hallway. He looked anywhere but Daniel's face. Despite his solid demeanor, Lincoln could not bear the hatred which brimmed the edges of Daniel's eyes. He sighed.

"I saved the people in the Colony," he argued. "We have no idea what the surface is like. If it's even livable. We all could have descended to our deaths."

"But isn't that a choice every citizen here should have gotten to make?" Daniel asked. He tried to keep his professional countenance, but he could hear the bile dripping over his words.

"That's just it," Lincoln pleaded. "We weren't giving them the choice either. We were trying to use the Haptic to control them. We were sneaking messages into the scenery. We were going to use the very walls of our homes to force people into compliance with *our* goals, *our* want to escape."

Daniel shook his head. For the first time in hours, he felt his knees tremble. He felt the knots that had been twisting through his gut throb. All of his efforts to escape his body, to wall off his mind gave way, and he collapsed to a seated position on the mattress. The thin, one inch foam met the board beneath him almost immediately. He rested his head in his hands and the force of his fingers massaged his eyes, his temples, the space behind his ears.

"We were doing what we had to do," he said quietly, as if he himself almost believed it. He chose his words carefully, convincing himself of their pertinence even as they passed his lips. "Gossip doesn't work; the facts change too rapidly from one person to the next. Embellishment begets futility. And had we attempted to hold an assembly or make an announcement; the Guard would have been on us faster than they were when you betrayed us. Even if we had managed to get the message out there, the chaos that would have ensued would have caused more damage and cost more lives than I was willing to risk. Than any of us were. We needed people to stay calm even as they learned the horrible truths of this place. We were doing what we had to."

Daniel heard Lincoln swallow hard from outside his cell. He sensed the young man's hands wrapping the bars as he tried to pull himself closer, as he pretended his own pain made him the one imprisoned. Daniel knew every god in the corridor was listening with rapt attention.

"You're wrong," Lincoln said sternly. His eyes welled with tears as he finally met Daniel's gaze through the bars. "You were doing what you wanted to do, not what you had to. You talk about the horrible truths of this place, but in reality, being here kept us safe. If everything we learned is true, being here—in the Colony—saved all of us from horrific deaths as the world ended below us. This Colony saved humanity."

Daniel hung his head. He heard a gentle sob come from the cell to his left. He imagined Adrasteia there, curled up in the fetal position on her cot, finally grieving her losses. Years of her life had been tied to this very moment, long before Daniel or Nyx or Helios had gotten involved. It had taken so much of her, and in an instant, it was gone.

"Isn't that why we all applied to be here?" Lincoln asked earnestly. "We knew the risks. We knew there was a chance we'd lose the people we loved during our time up here. You talk of choices, well, that was the choice we all made. Every person in this Colony made that choice, signed those papers, and boarded that lift. It would have been wrong to take it away just because you and a bunch of holier-than-thou gods couldn't believe what you were told and wanted to see it for yourself."

Adrasteia's sob caught in her throat. She recognized her father's words in Lincoln's mouth. She wondered how much her dad had known of her plan before he'd stopped them. She wondered when he'd corrupted the young man they'd all trusted.

"I guess we'll see, won't we?" Daniel said. He tried to remain strong, even in defeat.

Lincoln looked confused as Daniel stood and walked to the door. He wrapped his hands around the bars and squeezed, his knuckles white with force.

"It's been what? Seven, eight hours since they arrested us?" Daniel smiled. "The messaging from the redundancy will have had plenty of time to reach people, to get through to at least some of them. And once people know the truth, there's no going back."

He knew he was giving away his hand, the only chance they still had of completing their mission. He knew, if it were running, Lincoln would immediately tell the engineers to find and stop the code. It was a risk, but he had to know if they still had a shot. If enough people had been reached, the war would continue.

Lincoln bit his lip. He slid his hands up to brush Daniel's on the bars but quickly pulled away.

"There is no redundancy," Lincoln said quietly, gulping the words as if they burned his throat. "I put a kill switch in the code. Wiped it out before it even started."

Daniel turned away. He did not want Lincoln to see the loss that ravished his being. Even through the betrayal, he couldn't hurt him more.

"So this was your plan all along? To betray us?" As the words caught in his throat, Daniel paced his cell, refusing to look at the kid who had started to feel like an adopted son. "I brought you in. I vouched for you. I believed in you."

"Daniel, I'm sorry. You knew I had my doubts from the beginning. I made that very clear."

Lincoln wrapped his hands around the bars and wished he could be inside to comfort the man who had placed so much faith in him. He started to wonder if the lump in his throat he'd assumed was sorrow was actually regret.

"I—," he stuttered. "Dr. Saito assured me that the Colony is working as it should. That up here is safer than down there. We— I couldn't risk destroying certain life for potential death. Not on piecemeal information and word of mouth."

"Dr. Saitio assured you, huh?" Adrasteia's voice caught as she spoke, but grew stronger with each word. "Maybe ask my father what the plan is to keep the Colony safe. Ask him how much oxygen, how many resources are saved by sealing off Sub5; Sub4. Because he's done those studies. He has those figures. Ask him what safe really means and for whom."

Even amidst her anger,Daniel could hear the quiet resolve to give up that laced her voice.

"Traitor!" Helios called from down the hall.

"Traitor!" Echnida yelled.

"I'm not the traitor," Lincoln stammered. "I'm not the traitor."

Daniel found Lincoln's welling eyes with his own. He wondered if the kid could hear the fear behind the accusations of his compatriots. The whole block had been listening on bated breath to their exchange. Now, resigned, the whole block knew it was over. Still, there was fight in their voices.

"Traitor," Nyx purred from the adjacent cell.

"I'm not the traitor," Lincoln repeated.

To Daniel, he seemed more trapped than the rest of them.

"I think you better go," he said.

Manta shifted the rag on the man's forehead. The tepid water from their bath which soaked the cloth left streaks of golden soil spreading like tear drops across his face. She had helped Paul move the unconscious intruder to the floor after he had passed out, and they had taken turns tending to him as the night wore on. Now, Paul was asleep on the torn, padded recliner as she watched the mysterious man from her father's past heave with the violence of trapped nightmares.

His wild blond hair was littered with sediment and leaves, tiny twigs that had gotten caught, the ruffle of the unkempt wild. His dirty, clenching fingers and small bulbous nose were human enough, but the guttural growls that emanated from deep within his chest were the stuff of untamed bear cubs and fear. Real things. Not imaginary monsters like her storybooks held. This was present and terrifying. She used the rag to remove more of the dirt from his face and glanced toward the outside world through the window.

Night still held the Earth in her clutches. Rich and deep, she offered little hints to the passing of time. Manta could only assume the hours until the sun poked its sleepy head above the horizon, his mind abuzz with thoughts of tangerine and blue. She was glad she had convinced her father to sleep. Dart would arrive with the first rays of morning to unlatch the padlock and hurry him into the fields. He needed his rest. She was sure Chrissy would understand if their playdate was slowed slightly by her own fatigue.

Miss Chrissy had been a simple enough assignment, at least in comparison to the arduous work of the other captives in the compound. Yes, she was older than Manta, and sometimes that clash between age, hormones, and mentality made her lash out in strange and unexpected ways. But mostly, she just wanted someone to play with, another toy—new and shiny—to toss around until she grew bored.

The man let out an awful wail as his eyes shot open, the whites of them muddled in red and pain. He clutched at his stomach but did not move from the floor. It sounded to Manta like the howl of the ravager mother who had lost her son at their cabin, and she pulled back instinctively, the filthy, wet rag still dangling from her grip.

Paul leapt from the armchair to kneel beside the man. He used one hand to hold his arms down while the other rested on his cheek to quell his shaking head.

"Alexander?" he said. "Alexander, it's okay. You're okay."

A statement had never been less true, but it was not a time for nuance. He turned to Manta, still reeling on the floor a few feet away and asked her to fetch the loaf of bread the Hawk had left on the table. Manta did so quickly, as if on instinct. Her mind was awash with a million conflicting thoughts, but her body had known what to do.

She wasn't sure what to make of the situation. She had never seen her father show so much love, so much affection for someone who was not her or, in less direct terms, the memory of her other father. It was unsettling, seeing him there on his knees, hunched over the hulking mass that had once resembled another human being, trying to cajole him back to sanity. A part of her was happy: perhaps there was finally another person within the mess of the people who had betrayed them whom they could trust. But the part of her which still imagined Daniel—the gallant, brave, and fierce knight Paul had told her of again and again—bursting through the gates of New Yukon on his white steed to save them—that part of her was unwilling to accept the crumpled man before them beyond a basic compassion.

She had never experienced jealousy before. Desire for something else, a longing for the life she was meant to have before the Wave, before the men in black suits ushered her father into the sky: sure. She had felt that. But this was something else entirely. She knew the throat-stopping, wet beast of emotion, caged in her lungs like a cornered hound was not for herself, but for the father who would return. She felt it for him, proof he was on his way, proof he still mattered. And she didn't know what to do with it.

But here was the man who remained, the one who raised her and adored her unconditionally. He needed this, she could tell from his frantic coddling, the feral look in his own eyes as he tried to meet and calm the intruder's. She swallowed hard, surpassing what she felt into the deepest pit of her stomach.

"Water," Paul said, breaking bite-sized chunks of stale bread from the loaf and coaxing them toward Alexander's lips.

Manta poured a minuscule amount from one of the two-gallon jugs they'd been given to last them the entire week.

"More than that," Paul said. "There's three of us now. They'll bring us more."

Manta wasn't so sure. After the initial gift of bread and butter, the Families had been pretty stingy with the sustenance, leaving them just enough to maintain their energy levels to keep them working. Even the table scraps from their lush and lavish meals—roasted and stewed vegetables, fresh bread and milk and butter, and newly hunted slabs of venison or game bird—were placed in a trough like slop, left outside rain or shine for the workers to fight over. Manta didn't believe another mouth to feed would change their generosity. If anything, it would stretch them thinner. Still, she filled the plastic cup to the halfway point and hurried it to her father.

"Drink," Paul urged.

Alexander's eyes grew wide with an escalating understanding as the water passed his lips, a quick fear of drowning replaced with subtle remembrance.

Returning to his body felt like the first great crest in a rollercoaster ride. His stomach pushed his heart aside to make its way to his throat. His thoughts were slow and painful, his mind always four seconds behind where his body was being pushed. He swallowed hard. The bread and the water were beginning to distract the core of him, urging his organs toward autonomous function, and allowing his brain to catch up.

"Is that really you, Paul?" he asked. His voice was weak and not his own. He groaned between syllables to conjure it back into place.

Paul nodded. He could only imagine what Alexander was going through. The shock of the last eight years had been traumatic. Had he not had Manta to care for, he wasn't sure he would have survived. And here was Alexander: the frivolous party boy who had somehow made it through, going feral in the process. The mental journey back would be harrowing.

Alexander smiled, but it felt funny on his lips, more like a wince or a grimace. It had been so long since his mouth had moved that way. It was foreign and disquieting.

"So that," he groaned, trying to remember, "adopted." He sighed. It was slow coming, but it was there. "Samantha," he said triumphantly, eyeing the trembling young girl perched timidly by Paul's side. His words were beginning to come back to him. The memories he had kept at bay flooded past the barriers his mind had summoned to keep him alive. Survival had outweighed living, and he was only now facing the consequence of both.

"It's Manta," she said, placing a hand on Paul's shoulder to divert his attention to the brightening sky outside.

Alexander followed their gaze. "Daniel?" he asked.

Paul's grimace spoke volumes, but the shocked glare on Manta's face screamed.

From outside, they heard the rattle of the chain as Dart fidgeted with the lock.

"Be strong," Paul whispered as he and his daughter stood to start their day. "They trade the bodies who won't work to the ravagers."

By noon, the white-hot sun was calling the moisture of the earth forth with full abandoned, leaving a surplus of sticky, thick humidity where all the morning shadows had been. Paul was moving on adrenaline alone as he weeded through rows of crops. Alexander was a few rows over in the field. Dart had taken one look at the broken, filthy man and decided he was not worth testing. He belonged either in the field or in a cannibal's stomach. Paul had tried several times to catch a glimpse of the man, to see how he was holding up, but the tall stalks of corn had made it impossible. Still, just knowing he was there brought him some comfort.

After the Wave, when Manta was still too young to remember, Paul had attempted to find any survivors of his past life. Society had not completely crumbled in the instant the water struck. There was panic, there was fear, but there was also power—or electricity at least, and the internet, and pockets of unfettered hope. Hundreds of millions had died worldwide, but humanity was not one to give up that easily. What remained of government structures had seized control of all infrastructure and attempted to parse out what the world would become. It had felt safer then to take his infant daughter in search of community. The world had not yet become what it was.

For two weeks, he drove from town to town across North Georgia, only once venturing far enough south to look in morbid fascination at the coastline where Atlanta had been. This was before the bodies had begun to surface, before those not washed out to sea and gone forever had made their way to cloud the shore with their stench and their bloat. This was when the sudden, maniacal twist of nature had made the world seem clean somehow, like there was chance washed in all the grief and sadness.

The rumblings of destruction were already in place, however, and as trade lessened and oil reserves depleted, mankind began to devour itself. Governments were overthrown by the power of the people and then that very power was turned on itself in greed. Paul had gathered as much as he could and retreated to the cabin to create a haven in which to raise his little girl. He'd found no one from his past; and the little girl strapped to the car seat, cooing and giggling at the kaleidoscope of fall colors passing by was his future.

He had given up hope on seeing anyone—save for Daniel, and even that was questionable—especially that was questionable—alive again. Yet here was Alexander. He was a shell of the man he had been, misled and hardened, but Paul could still see him in there, somewhere beneath the grime and the fortitude he had needed to survive. It brought him a strange sense of comfort. It renewed his hope that he would see Daniel again.

Dart released the workers just as the sun began to dip behind the distant trees. That's what he called it. In a grandiose voice, he would proclaim to all the workers, "You are released," as if that could somehow make them feel free. The field workers would have just under two hours to eat and bathe before the sun fully set and their houses were plunged into total darkness unless they still had a bit of wick in their candles. Two hours before Trent and Dart and sometimes Mr. Madison himself would scurry from house to house to click the padlocks tight. The Families treated those hours like they were gifts, as if their care was magnanimous and not forged from control.

Paul's hands were calloused and black from snatching at thorny weeds with barbed stalks, pulling, glovelessly, at ripe produce, and spreading manure and compost about the base of the plants. He put his arm around Alexander's shoulder and helped him stumble to the house. They moved in silence, slowly, Alexander's feet still uneasy beneath him. He felt the ache seep like humidity from Alexander's muscles, pulsing with each sinewy stretch and contraction of a body re-finding its place.

Manta was sitting on the front porch as the men approached. Perched on the top step with her back pressed against the post, she cocked her eyes at Paul's hand resting beneath Alexander's arm. She tried to smile, but it felt forced. Though she hadn't had cause for much practice, Paul had always pounded the notion of politeness into her. The cooling air dried her teeth, and she was disappointed in herself.

"Hello, pretty lady," Alexander said as they reached the house. Civility was coming back to him.

"Manta," she corrected.

"Manta," he replied and nodded his head slowly.

She sighed and bit her lip. Her fists hit the wooden step, and she pushed herself to her feet. She slipped to the other side of Alexander, and, together with her father, they guided him up the stairs and inside.

He sat, exhausted, on the ripped couch and picked at the foam stuffing as Paul and Manta attempted to make the meager dinner—more stale bread and curd, snap peas, and roasted corn—look appetizing. His whole body throbbed, but that ache was giving way to a sudden wholeness. For so long, he had lived on instinct, surviving by brute force or dumb luck or unbridled savagery. For so long, he had been alone. Now, though he found himself a slave to two redneck families who'd acquired a bit of firepower and land, he didn't seem to mind inhabiting his skin as much. Perhaps there was a trace of hope left in the world after all.

They ate slowly. Paul was patient as he coaxed out the story of the past eight years since the Wave from Alexander, what he could remember anyway, punctuating it with his own story from the small cabin farther north. Manta noticed he focused on the more difficult times, afraid to contrast Alexander's horrors with their own happiness. It was a kindness, she supposed. And the newcomer's tale piqued her sorrow for him. Alexander's memory returned slowly, like the notions of a past life resurfacing. Moments of clarity gave way to foggy, cloud-filled dreamscapes serving only to bridge the gaps the mind had chosen to forget in the wake of self-preservation. He tried to capture what he could of his former self. Or release him, he wasn't sure.

"Where is old Danny boy?" he asked. It took him a while to get to the question, though it had been batting the edges of his skull since he'd realized the man before him actually was Paul. He hoped the story would not be painful, though most tales from the Wave onward were.

"He's in the Colony," Paul said, solemnly. He eyed Manta cautiously.

"Oh, that shitshow," Alexander laughed. It came automatically, strange in his throat as it emerged against his will. It was such an awkward sound with no place in the modern world. "Didn't the state round up people like three months early for that thing? Rounded some of them up anyway. And didn't even bother telling the rest of us about the tidal wave that was coming in a matter of hours? You sure he made it inside?"

"It was two months. And he made it in," Manta growled. "My father is alive and strong, and he's gonna come back for us."

Alexander stopped laughing, but he couldn't wipe the smile from his lips. Instead, it trembled, forced and embarrassed, as he watched the young girl's face retreat.

"Of course he is, sweetheart."

"He is. So don't you get any ideas."

"No ideas," Alexander said. "Barely a cohesive thought." He looked to Paul and smirked. "I'm just happy to have actual human beings in my life again."

Paul maintained a genuflecting smile as he gave Manta a "be polite" look. She crossed her arms and leaned back in her chair stubbornly.

"He's coming back," she mumbled under her breath.

It was refreshing to see Manta pout. She had spent so long being strong, being fierce, fighting for survival. Seeing her act like an actual child warmed Paul's heart.

"And don't call me 'sweetheart,'" she said.

Lincoln approached the office door cautiously. In the days since he'd turned in the gods, he'd watched as the Colony had erased them, conveying their absence as being on a "special project" to the few who would have even noticed. A few of the members of Adrasteia's larger, less organized group had whispered through the hallways of conspiracies and retaliation, but even they had mostly resigned to the Neutral Zone and avoided even mentioning their former leader. So, when Dr. Saito demanded his appearance, the tiny ball that had been waiting in his gut grew so large it threatened to choke him out.

He had all the same knowledge as those now imprisoned. He was a liability. Could they allow him to continue walking the halls or would they make him one of them? Another lost member of the Colony; an unspoken name soon to be forgotten.

"Mr. Dunnwater," Dr. Saito said before he was even able to knock. "Right on time. That's a good sign."

The door shifted open, and the engineer smiled from behind his desk. It was a stern smile. Efficient. As if only there because the pleasantry was required. He remembered it from the brief training encounters they'd had when he'd first entered the Colony, cold and obligatory, useful for calm.

Lincoln stepped into the room and stood behind the chair opposite Dr. Saito's desk until it was offered to him. The doctor gestured for him to sit and seemed pleased by Lincoln's gentility. His hands folded in front of him on his desk, and the two sat in silence for a moment. Lincoln searched Dr. Saito's face for any clue as to why he was summoned, but the old man was stoic and calm, giving nothing away. The door opened again, and a young woman stepped inside with a tray, silently moving to the side of the desk.

"Tea?" Dr. Saito offered.

"No, thank you, sir," Lincoln replied.

Dr. Saito took his dainty teacup—white porcelain with a red toile pattern—and poured his own hot water from the matching pot. A fresh, grassy scent filled the room as the boiling water hit the leaves. Lincoln shifted in his seat and did his best to look polite and invested.

"So," Dr. Saito began when the server left the office, her feet but whispers on the tile floor. "How are you adjusting after turning in my daughter and her little band of insurgents."

"I— Fine, sir. Though I did want to tell you I'm sorry."

"No, no," Dr. Saito interrupted. "You did the right thing. You showed initiative, bravery, and a high level of understanding in your actions. My daughter was—unfortunately misguided in her interpretation of the situation facing the Colony. And now, you have that same knowledge."

Lincoln felt his heart bat at his ribcage. His mouth and throat went dry.

"I'm not going to tell anyone," he stuttered.

A sly smile slipped over Dr. Saito's lips, and he slurped a bit of his tea. It was bitter and sweet. The Colony still had not quite figured out how to properly roast the tea leaves, but he was proud for having kept the plants alive, even as other crops were beginning to fail.

"We know that," he smiled. "That you came to us, even after Hiromi had filled your head with her doomsaying, proves as much. You aren't in trouble, Mr. Dunnwater. We want to offer you a job."

Lincoln was shocked, but he felt his shoulders suddenly ease. He had tied himself up into knots all morning. This was not at all what he'd expected. Adrasteia's words rang in his head: *Ask him about the oxygen... As him about the resources...* He could ask, but then he may end up right next to her in the brig.

"Is this just about keeping an eye on me?" he asked.

"Partly," Dr. Saito admitted. "But mostly, we believe someone of your intelligence, with your unique understanding and skillset, would be an asset to our little team."

Lincoln leaned back in his chair for a moment but moved quickly back to attention. Dr. Saito obviously appreciated a bit of formality. He needed to keep it front and foremost. He was basically in a job interview. A job that, if he got, would answer his questions. And if Adrasteia was right, he could stop it from inside.

"What would I be doing?"

"Ahhh," Dr. Saito smiled. "That is classified until you've signed on. Though, with your knowledge base, I suppose I could show you a little bit of what we have in mind."

Lincoln was on the edge of his seat as he watched the small, old man casually finish the rest of his tea and rise.

He did not speak but simply gestured for Lincoln followed him out of his office and down the hallway. They stopped before a door marked Test Lab 4. Dr. Saito scanned his wrist, then entered a code when prompted. The added layer of security intrigued Lincoln. While the leaders in the Colony had not been known to be entirely forthright, all the secrets they had kept had been for the good of the people. They were rebuilding the world. Not everything could be—or deserved to be—common knowledge. Whatever was behind the door must be incredibly important, and Lincoln would see it firsthand!

Dr. Saito paused before entering in the last number in his sequence. He turned to look Lincoln sternly in the eye.

"What you are about to see is highly confidential," he said. "Revealing anything will land you in the cell next to my daughter without a moment's hesitation."

"I understand." Lincoln nodded as he spoke. He tried to fill his words with as much reverence as he could muster. He was overwhelmed by curiosity.

Dr. Saito punched in the final number, and the door slid open behind him. The lights in the lab blinked on, and they stepped inside quickly before the door closed on its own. Lincoln peered around in awe. The lab was well equipped. In the center, a helmeted suit lay across a stainless-steel table with wiring connecting it to a computing system far beyond those he had gotten to work with inside the Colony before now. More suits were sewn and hanging from a rack on the wall behind the table. Filling the far corner was another Haptic Mind Map system, though the helmet was larger, and, as with everything else in the lab, the computer powering the thing was massive. Closest to them, two of the hydroponic chambers used on the Farm Level were pumping and recycling their water beneath three massive bushes.

Dr. Saito grabbed a small pair of scissors and lovingly clipped at the leaves.

"These are my *camellia sinensis*," he said. "Tea shrubs. From these tiny evergreen wonders, one can produce every type of true tea known to man. Black or Green or White. Herbals, dear boy, are not true tea."

Lincoln's confusion was visible as he watched the old man lean in to smell the glossy, lime green leaves, rubbing his fingers over their smooth surfaces as if the wonders of the universe were inside each one.

"We must have our little pleasures," Dr. Saito smiled. "Mustn't we?"

Lincoln nodded but did not reply. His mind was enchanted by the Haptic set up on the far side of the room. He squinted as he imagined the computing power of the massive machines lined up beside the chair. What, he wondered, could a machine so powerful accomplish? Was it possible to add scent memory to the HMM experience? Or even touch? Something like that could keep the citizens of the Colony happy, even if they were not allowed to leave when the fifteen years they had signed up for had ended. Something like that could put the seedier services of the Neutral Zone out of business.

"Ahh, yes," Dr. Saito smiled. "The Haptic Two Point Zero. She's beautiful, no?"

"What can she do?" Lincoln could barely hide the excitement in his voice.

"That, good sir, depends entirely on you."

It was Lincoln's dream come true. After moving from the environmental systems studio to helping in manning the Haptic during his second year in the Colony, he felt as if he'd truly found his calling. The chance to code a person's happiest memories from the deepest recesses of their mind, to make them feel whole and connected to home: it had been a such a satisfying experience. To take that to an entirely new level, to let a person actually feel the things they were remembering... Well, that was the epitome of his existence.

"You look pleased," Dr. Saito smiled. "I'm glad. Only a minor bit of paperwork, and you can get started right away."

"What are all these suits?" Lincoln asked. "Are they a part of the Haptic?"

"No need to concern yourself with those. We're making a few minor upgrades to the Environmental Stabilization Units we used when the Colony was first under construction. Eventually, we may send a team to the surface. Or, in the event that one or more floors of the Colony become unstable and must be locked down, these suits will help us retrieve usable materials. But you, good boy, should keep your focus on the HMM."

Lincoln crossed the room and caressed the chair. The steel was cool but alive beneath his fingertips. The whirr of the machines buzzing idly behind him warmed him to his core. And the helmet—she was a thing of beauty. Large but lightweight, it was like a cloud in his hands. He could not contain the smile that spread across his face.

"What exactly will I be working on?" he asked. "What are we trying to do."

Dr. Saito smiled. "Exactly what you have already been working on."

Lincoln's mouth gaped. He felt his heart sink into his stomach. He had gone from his greatest joy to his worst fear in the span of one simple sentence.

"My daughter, Hiromi—I think you know her as Adrasteia—misguided as she was, actually had a brilliant plan. Which doesn't surprise me in the least. The girl is a genius. If she had applied herself where she should, she would have been unstoppable. A true leader of the people instead of a despot in a cell. But I digress."

The energy in Dr. Saito's words seemed to suck all of it from Lincoln's body. He leaned forward against the chair and was happy for the support.

"The Colony is dying," Dr. Saito confirmed. "Not soon. But it was not designed for a longer span than fifteen years. And even then the science was hypothetical. Experimental. The environmental systems for food are already failing. It won't be long before the air recyclers reduce their ability to produce enough oxygen to keep up with the entire Colony. The circumstances that had us bring people in early left us unable to contact the outer world and ill-prepared for extended survival inside."

Noticing the rising anguish in Lincoln and mistaking it for fear, Dr. Saito extended his hand to feel the soft leather of the suits hanging against the wall.

"These," he continued, "will help us survive on the surface if living conditions are not optimal. At the very least, they will enable us to acclimate to any environmental changes that have occurred on the surface over the past several years, which, as we know, can be extensive. They are a Plan B precaution. We are simply thinking all courses through."

"That's fantastic," Lincoln said. Relief was trying to find its way into his lungs, though they still ached, waiting for the other shoe to drop.

"Yes. Yes," Dr. Saito agreed. "It is very good indeed. With our resources, our team is able to produce nearly two thousand suits based on these fifteen prototypes."

"But aren't there over a million of us in here?"

"That's where your new code comes in, my dear boy. We need you to optimize your ability to input information and emotion to ensure those not selected to return to the surface stay—docile."

"But the code never truly worked," Lincoln lied. "We tried, but it only led to a severe case of the Haps. Only buried ideas were able to be brought forth."

"You haven't tried with the fire power you're standing beside," Dr. Saito said. He was so certain. And he seemed to know more than Lincoln had told them. Had they known of the plan all along? Had they been watching them, waiting to see what they would produce, what they could learn?

Dr. Saito crossed the room and planted his hands on Lincoln's shoulders. They smelled of life—green and new and escaping. The tension in Lincoln's neck reminded him so much of Hiromi when she first entered the Colony. He repeated to Lincoln the same words he'd given her:

"You've got this," he said. "You were selected because you are special. What you're doing has the potential to change the world."

He patted Lincoln's back and closed his eyes as he smiled.

"Ready to sign the paperwork?" he asked. "Then you're free to test that beauty out."

Lincoln tried his best to smile back. He hoped his wide-eyed gaze did not betray him even as his gut turned somersaults of realization. Adrasteia and Daniel had been right. The Alphas were only out for themselves. A mutiny was all that would save them. And, thanks to him, their best shot at it had been revealed and locked into cells.

"So you're telling me you don't believe we could bring enough of us on board for rebellion?" Alexander asked.

Paul motioned for him to keep his voice down, not only for Manta, who was fast asleep on the recliner, but also for fear the walls and broken windows had ears.

As Alexander regained his strength and his humanity, his voice bubbled forth with the wild abandoned Paul remembered, only exaggerated far beyond the scope of normalcy. It was as if he had eight years of talking to catch up on, and he wanted to do it all in one night. Paul, for his part, welcomed the conversation.

"There's food—or something like it. Shelter. And after a lifetime of plebeian capitalism, I guess this almost feels like normalcy for some people, especially compared to the brutalism of the world we've known since the Wave. They don't talk, but I get the feeling folks think at least this is better than what's out there." Paul knew he was making excuses in an attempt to rationalize the situation, to cope with what his life had become, but it didn't matter. A lot of what he was saying rang true. And though the work was rough for him, Manta had it easier. That's what mattered most. "Plus, they have all the firepower."

"You cannot expect me to believe you're just going to take this on the chin. Good ol' Social Justice Revolutionary Paul." Alexander frowned, a mischievous look looming in his irises. "I've known you to take thing or two there before, but never something like this."

Paul mocked Alexander's laugh and returned his scowl. Deep down, he knew the man was right. Life in New Yukon was not good, not sustainable, and most definitely not just. He was just so tired. Tired of fighting against the unknown. Exhausted from waking up each day with no idea what struggles would need to be overcome. Tired of raising his daughter alone. Tired of her being alone.

And Manta, asleep in the chair, curled up into a ball as she dreamed whatever dreams children had been forced to create when all their fairy tales were proven false: how could he throw her back into that struggle? For years he had watched her become a warrior. Now, she had, for all intents and purposes, an actual friend. Someone her own age to frolic through the days with. She got to play make-believe, to play games. And though she wasn't allowed to win them, winning wasn't as necessary as survival. So what if the bread was stale?

"It's been a long eight years since the Wave," Paul said. "Of course this isn't the life I imagined. But after all that time of constant struggle, there's something comforting in not having to think anymore."

"Trust me: I've spent the last who knows how long living on instinct alone. Not thinking isn't all it's cracked up to be."

Paul wanted to continue laughing, but the whole situation was unnerving. He had done his best to keep these sorts of thoughts at bay, but Alexander had broken the wall down and each and every one of them rushed in. All of his resolve to accept his life, all of his release and denial, all of it was laid bare upon Alexander's arrival. He knew he could no longer afford complacency. The reappearance of his past was invigorating. It renewed a glimmer of hope that Daniel would return. He wanted so badly to have hope again. But he was broken. He knew he was. He wasn't sure he could let himself feel it.

"Look," Alexander said. He spoke firmly with a sudden seriousness that shook Paul to his core. "If you can't do it for yourself, do it for that little girl."

As if on cue, Manta stirred from her slumber. She wiped the sleep from her eyes and blinked rapidly to adjust to the darkness.

"What are you doing for me?" she yawned.

"Nothing," Paul murmured. "Everything."

"We're talking about—," Alexander started.

Paul slammed a hand over his mouth to shut it. His eyes widened in warning before he turned to his daughter with a smile.

"We were talking about staying safe. And surviving this. And you getting the things you need to live a long and healthy life. Like sleep."

Manta rolled her eyes and shrugged the threadbare blanket from her shoulders.

"What we should be talking about," she said, suddenly fully awake as she leaned forward expectantly. "is getting the hell out. You really think we're safer in here?"

"The girl's got a point," Alexander smiled.

"And a name," she snapped.

Alexander held his hands up in surrender, and Paul shook his head as Manta rolled her eyes. It would be years before Daniel and the others returned from the Colony. At least in New Yukon, his daughter would have a roof over her head, and, with her new post, a chance at being a child. Life on the outside had been stressful and no less work. Inside New Yukon, if they were careful, Manta could have a better chance of thriving.

"They've got the guns," Paul said. "They've got the numbers. And I've got to keep you safe."

"You've kept me safe my whole life, Dad." Manta stared into his eyes, hoping he could see the strength he'd given her. "You taught me how to fight, how to survive, how to dream. You made me strong, and you made me hopeful. And this place, Dad, is bullshit."

"I like her," Alexander said, interrupting the tension that held tight to the air. "It's crazy how much like Daniel she is."

Manta caught the growl in her throat, but her glare still shot through Alexander's smile. This man may have been from her dads' past, but he was not a substitute. Still, she could use him if she needed to.

"Look," she said, "all I'm saying is that there's three of us now. And those are better odds at getting out alive."

"Careful; careful."

"I've got it."

Paul stood at firm attention as Daniel kicked aside a box haphazardly left in the entryway of the cabin. They had intended to be fully unpacked already, but time was fickle and demanding.

"I've got it," Daniel repeated. "Plus, don't you think it's a little early to start with the helicopter parenting."

He chuckled as he stared down at the beautiful infant girl in his arms. She was an angel: exquisite and loud and mad at the world for the entire flight back to the States from Ethiopia. All fists and fury, she was, and Daniel and Paul loved her immediately. Paul had stayed with her in the back seat the entire drive up from Hartsfield-Jackson-Lewis-Abrams International Airport and had beamed so brightly he was afraid he'd wake her as he watched the gentle hum of the car's engine lull her into slumber. She was a wondrous and majestic thing, this new life that had been entrusted to them. Both men knew, then and there, there was nothing they wouldn't do to keep her safe and happy. All the cliches they had heard about parenting were true.

"If we had actually finished unpacking like we were supposed to before we brought her home, I wouldn't need to hover," Paul bit back. Even in a whisper, it sounded harsher than it should have. But he was tired. They were both going on twenty hours with very little sleep.

"You know what is unpacked?" Daniel asked.

"The nursery?"

"The nursery."

Samantha's bedroom was next door to their own. A solid oak crib handmade by an Appalachian woodworker took center stage with a quilt of lilac and magnolia, hand-sewn and draped lovingly over the side. Surrounding the crib were monitors and mobiles, and a collection of books Daniel had saved from his own childhood stood at attention next to a sweet, padded rocking chair. Shelves were lined with stuffed animals. They'd gone a bit overboard in buying them as the anticipation for her arrival swelled and they wandered through toy stores and daddy blogs like they were religious study. Paul had insisted they be correct, at least in form if not in scale, and the beaded eyes of non-anthropomorphous brown bears and foxes, orcas and manta rays and octopodes stared back at them.

They placed the infant atop the spread of organic cotton and wool and stared down at her, neither man wanting to let her leave their sight. She squirmed in her swaddle—an off-white cotton blanket rimmed in the most brilliant of purples in the traditional fashion of her birth land—and smacked her lips against the humid Georgia night as if she could taste the moisture there like mother's milk. Daniel slipped his arm around Paul's waist and kissed him gently, first on the cheek and then the lips. This was what family felt like. This is what home would be.

Daniel was a bit worried about the commute. His practice was still in the heart of the city and his time on the road meant more time away from his family, but he would have to make it work. Besides, he told himself, two hours on the highway was better than two hours of surface street gridlock. He'd managed to get several of his patients to switch to online sessions, but others insisted on in-person meetings. He could blame them. The planet had become so impersonal; actual connection was a nice thing to have, even if it meant early mornings and late evenings. Plus they only had two years in the cabin before they moved into the Colony. Two years to fill young Samantha's mind with as much of the natural world as they could before the cold steel of the Ten Mile City was all she would know until her eighteenth birthday. They wanted her to know what the earth felt like, how the scent of new buds perfumed the wind in the Spring, the wonder of animals left wild who explored the edges of clearings and made eye contact only when they wanted to. Even if it was in sense memory alone, those were the things she would carry with her to the sky. Those were the things that would connect her to home.

"Come on," he whispered.

"I don't think I can leave her side," Paul said.

"Let's let her sleep," Daniel insisted and kissed Paul's forehead once again. "We have a monitor in the other room. Besides which, you need to rest your eyes too."

"She's waking up."

Lincoln nodded, sighing as he pulled himself from the computer console and grabbing the tablet for the Haptic checklist. His three new coworkers—two coders and a medical officer—flanked the gurney as their latest test subject came to. She was groggy, still, which was to be expected, even after being kept under for three hours.

His third day with the Haptic 2.0 had seen ten test volunteers fail at any new knowledge retention, though that didn't surprise him. He'd purposefully messed up the code hoping to buy himself some time to figure out his next move. What he hadn't expected was the new Haptic placing three of the subjects in a permanent coma. What he wasn't prepared for was the moment, watching them, when the tension in their facial muscles failed and softened. That moment, watching the subjects go limp, was like watching them die. Which, he was sure, in twenty some odd days, they would.

He found himself wishing Daniel was around to talk to, to help guide him through this. But Daniel was in the brig, and it was all his fault.

"This is Officer Two Six Eight A," his coworker chimed into their recording device. "Officer Eight Fourteen Q will now begin the checklist for Subject Eleven."

They were not allowed to use their names, even amongst one another. Lincoln was surprised Dr. Saito had not forced them to wear masks. Father and daughter were not too far apart in their eccentricities, he supposed.

"Did you experience any nausea within the simulation?"

Lincoln ticked through the usual checklist in roboting manner. He marked her answers and braced himself for the end of the checklist. That was when it always happened. As soon as they reached the portion designed to test the implanted knowledge, the subject reacted: some violently, some in anguish, a few going blank. He felt responsible for each life, but he had no other option. He couldn't let the likes of the Alphas get access to his code.

If only he could tell Adrasteia he now understood. If only he could let Daniel know he was sorry. Really and truly this time.

He steeled himself as I reached the last question on his checklist. He kept his eyes trained on his tablet as he spoke: "Who was the ancient Greek goddess of rebellion?"

"She's seizing!" Officer 268A called, but he was already turning away. The medical officer jumped into action, as Lincoln retunred to his console.

"She's already asleep."

Paul did not look up from the table as Daniel bounded through the front door, his work bag heaving from his shoulder. Two plates of food sat cold atop the woven placemats which surrounded the solid oak dining table. Paul could have eaten his when it was still warm, but he was stubborn and wanted to prove a point. His misery hurt Daniel more than it hurt him.

"Damn it. I'm sorry, babe," Daniel pleaded. It was an empty apology. They had been for a while now. "We're two months from the Colony. I warned you things were going to be hectic at the office until then. There's a lot to tie up. And anticipation of the Colony opening is not making it easier for some of my patients."

"I guess we've been 'two months from the Colony' for the last two years," Paul groaned.

Daniel slid his bag to the floor next to his favorite armchair—a rich brown tweed that looked regal and expensive even if it had been secondhand—and moved the few paces to join Paul at the table. Paul was still staring at his plate. The English Peas from the garden outside were pocked like soccer balls as their moisture spilled out to run across the plate. The pile of them there, stacked up and withering and the color of the leaves from a hydrangea, were the only thing keeping him calm.

I just need two months, Daniel wanted to say. *Can you just give me eight short weeks to get a handle on my life on the surface? After that we'll be in the Colony, together, the three of us. And you'll have my undivided attention.* He wanted to say: *Up there, I couldn't escape you if I tried.*

Instead he said, "This looks delicious," as he slid his steak knife into the pork chop his husband had prepared.

Paul rolled his eyes and picked up his silverware. He ate noisily, his fork clanging against the porcelain; his knife scraping across bone. Deep down, he knew why Daniel had been absent so often. But that rationale did nothing to quell his anger in the here and now. He understood that, in his mind, Daniel thought he was doing it all for their daughter. But was missing out on her formative years worth it? He could never get these moments back. Would he find solace in a job well-done when Samantha was off and running, her toddler legs swishing swiftly away from them as age and independence took their hold?

"It would have been better warm and eaten as a family."

"I'll heat them up."

Daniel dropped his silverware and grabbed his plate from the table. He swooped to grab Paul's as well but was blocked as Paul cut another chunk of his cold pork chop. Daniel sighed, gave up, and sat back down.

"I don't know what you want me to do," he said.

"And I don't know when we became a sitcom cliché from a hundred years ago," Paul countered. "You the hard-working, never home Man of the House; and me, the doting housewife who's stuck doing everything as our child grows up without you."

Daniel leaned back in his chair and closed his eyes. He attempted to center himself. He knew better than to speak from anger. He also knew whether he said them kindly or in spite, the words would be the same, and Paul would take them the exact same way.

"You," he said, stressing the words and pausing to gather his will, "chose to quit your job. You wanted to move away from the city to raise Samantha."

"We moved here for our family." Paul's voice was harsh, but he kept his volume low to avoid waking the sleeping girl. "That is what I chose. And you, Daniel. You chose work over your family. You missed her first words, her first steps. Did you even know she's speaking in complete sentences now?"

"Seriously?"

Daniel's anger slipped from his irises, replaced by the excitement of another milestone in Samantha's development. He could see it in Paul's eyes to: the wonder, the pride.

"Well," Paul said, almost laughing, almost letting himself remember the joy of who they were. "Three-word sentences. But holy fuck is she smart."

The smile on his face faded as he remembered they were arguing and his eyes narrowed to force his anger back into place, but the fight was gone.

"I hate missing these things," Daniel whispered, and Paul knew it was true. "I don't want to not be here for Samantha. I don't want to not be here for you."

"You say this again and again. But you are not here. Saying you wish you were doesn't change reality."

Paul could feel his ire begin to ignite once more. He tried to keep it at bay. He knew it hurt Daniel to be so absent. But Daniel had the same choice he'd had and picked his patients over Samantha.

"Two months," Daniel pleaded. "Just two more months. And then it's just the three of us. Up there in the clouds."

It was always the same argument from Daniel. It was always the same promise.

"Right," Paul said. "But I don't believe you. We were selected for the Colony because you're a shrink. And up there, you'll be responsible for the mental health off, what, five hundred people? A thousand? You know you and your colleagues are there as fucking tokens and when the reality of being trapped inside a tin can in the ozone layer sets in, all of you are gonna be overwhelmed. And we'll be right back where we started, with our daughter not even knowing who her fucking father is."

Paul had tried to keep it contained, but the vitriol reemerged, coated in the fear and fatigue that had plagued him while raising a two-year-old and preparing for the world to change dramatically. He threw his words at Daniel like knives from the kitchen drawer, serrated and dull, but still able to get the job done.

Daniel crumpled in his chair. He knew Paul was right; and he hated to be wrong. He wished he could prove to him that family was the most important thing in his life. Make him understand that the lives of his patients were important too. His eyes were red as he blinked them open to look at his partner. He watched him as if it were the first time he'd seen him in years. Paul was exhausted. A broken man trying to keep it together without the support he deserved. He sat there, motionless, his eyes unfocused and wet. Daniel rose and kissed his forehead.

Daniel's mouth twisted into a faint smile, a subtle frown, as he bent down next to what would have been his favorite chair and grabbed the bag with his client files and tablet. He breathed slowly as he slung it over his shoulder and turned to stare back at his husband. Paul blinked into awareness. The hurt in his eyes was unbearable.

"Where are you going?" he asked.

"I'm gonna go sleep at the office," Daniel said. "Give you a chance to calm down. I've got an early day tomorrow anyway."

Paul sucked his teeth and pursed his lips. A million thoughts galloped across the green and gold fields of his irises. He could not believe Daniel, the psychologist, could be so blind to his own selfish, self-serving behavior. He couldn't believe Daniel could be so blind to his family's pain. He chose his words carefully, calmly, but with a force behind them that etched them into law.

"Your daughter is not going to know you, Daniel. You'll be just another absent father like the one behind half your patient's traumas. Like the one you had yourself. Are you sure you're okay with that? Can you live with her not knowing you?"

Daniel couldn't respond. He didn't have the words. In just eight short weeks it would all be different. In two months, he would prove to Paul that he was a good father, a supportive husband. In just two months...

"I love you," Daniel said as he opened the front door. He waited for Paul to reply, but he did not. His eyes were unfocused again. He stared at the chair where Daniel should have been.

The night was quiet as Daniel drove back to Atlanta. The music on the radio seemed to mock him if he turned it on. He drove in silence and tried to focus on the road, how his headlights formed a sphere ahead of him like it could offer a protecting embrace—a bit of light and comfort—that forever pulled out of reach.

Two men in black uniforms were standing by his office door when he arrived at the plaza.

"You need to come with us," one of the men said when they verified his identity.

"I'm sorry, what's going on?" he asked.

"We're filling the Colony tonight."

Daniel's stomach sank as his heart reached toward his throat. He stuttered as he asked to call his husband. His family was meant to all be on board.

"I'm sorry, sir," the man said as they grabbed his arm and guided him toward their van. "There's no time. Other agents are out collecting the citizens. Your family will join you in your quarters aboard the Colony."

He was in shock. What would make them fill the Colony so abruptly with such caustic measures two months ahead of schedule. He was glad he had a change of clothes in his work bag. And that they'd been able to move a few personal items in already.

Maybe this was a blessing in disguise. Now, he could show Paul that it was all about to change. That he would have more time for Samantha, more time for him. This is a good thing, he tried to tell himself. They'll grab Paul and Samantha, and we'll have the next fifteen years with no more interruptions. He tried to tell himself it was all going to be alright. But beneath his bravado, herded like cattle onto an elevator already well above the skyline, he knew he was wrong.

For as long as he could remember, Daniel had preferred to be alone with his thoughts. Now, the silence seemed an eerie torture, beckoning forth memories he'd rather not revisit. He played the night he'd ascended into hell over and over in his mind. Paul's warning, which had seemed a mere admonishment at the time, echoed in the cavernous hollows left in his synapses where his daughter should have been. He hated that Paul was right, this time not because he was, but because of what that meant. Samantha, if she had survived, would not know him if he managed to make it out of the Colony. So many "if"s to send him reeling through his solitude.

He pulled himself to a seated position as the door to his cell whooshed open. Even the silent guard with her tray of daily rations was preferable to the isolation. Her avoidance of eye contact and stiff gait were a pittance to pay to be around another human soul. Even if it was only for twenty-seven seconds, he'd grown to appreciate her twice daily visits. The way she lingered a little and used her body to shield the button sequence when she entered her code to leave. He opened his eyes smiling, expecting to see her tightly pulled ponytail of muddy brown hair beneath her standard issue Guard cap and her vacant eyes averted as she brought forth the tin tray of water and protein-algae slop (they didn't bother to process it into meat substitutes for the prisoners) and the occasional clump of steamed broccoli. Instead, he saw Lincoln striding in, stern and wild-eyed.

"What are you doing here?" Daniel asked, the comfort he felt in seeing someone—anyone—quickly diminished by the feelings of betrayal that still batted at his ribcage.

"Dr. Saito sent me," he said, his voice loud and exaggerated, as he glanced behind him to see the door close, and his Guard escort recede down the hallway. "He needs you to tell us the secret in the Haptic coding required to implant emotion."

Daniel squinted and cocked his head to the side, confused as Lincoln's hand motions urged him to keep quiet. He shifted to make space for him on the cot, and Lincoln stepped forward timidly. They held their breath, Lincoln on purpose and Daniel in reflexive solidarity, as the sound of the door closing to the Guard quarters at the far side of the brig resounded through the passageway. As the last reverberations slipped into nothingness, Lincoln's demeanor collapsed. His chin trembled; his shoulders hunched forward; his stomach turned in on itself.

"You were right," he whispered.

"What?"

Daniel almost felt sorry for the young man. He looked so broken, as if he were, for the first time, learning that Santa and the Tooth Fairy were not real. He had been so young when he entered the Colony, the world had not yet had a chance to tame him to its harsher realities. Suddenly, the relative effects of life were becoming all too clear.

"I got offered a job," Lincoln said.

Daniel cocked his head again and furrowed his brow. That Lincoln could possibly believe Daniel would still care about his daily victories was astounding. Lincoln swallowed hard and continued.

"As a reward for turning y'all in," he said. "They want me to program the Haptic to keep the masses compliant."

Daniel's eyes widened.

"Did you—?"

"I told them you were the mastermind behind the code," he interrupted. "I said you'd kept the most important parts a secret. And that you'd written a self-destruct into the system we'd already implanted."

"Smart," Daniel conceded. He wanted to place his arm around the boy to comfort him, but he did not move. A wave of relief washed over him, but he did not bend.

"They've been planning their own escape," Lincoln said. "The top Alphas have environmental containment suits and were working on their own Haptic coding. You were right on that count too. The technology was going to be developed one way or the other. Now, they just think they can get it faster through me."

Daniel groaned as he rose from his bed. His legs were stiff, but he paced the six steps back and forth in front of the crumpled boy.

"So their plan is to get themselves out and leave the rest of us here to die inside a giant mausoleum?"

"And use the Haptic to ensure there's no push back as they leave."

Daniel shook his head. He understood the myopic qualities inherent in government, the me-first makeup that had formed the political hierarchy. Still he had not expected this. In order to rule, one needed a working class. He had expected the elite to remain, stuck inside their giant tomb, where they could continue to send out edicts and be worshipped for their firm yet guiding hand, even if they deemed half the peasants expendable in their minds. They could not rule without someone to rule over. Things must have been far worse for the Colony than even Adrasteia knew if they had chosen survival over power.

"I tried writing code that just didn't work," Lincoln said. "I wanted to test if I could turn it around on them. But they've got four other people working on it, and they saw through it right away. That's when I told them you had the brain that was responsible for the real work, and I was just playing the same guessing games they were. Bought me a little time. And Dr. Saito sent me here. Told me to work out a solution for this mess. With you."

Daniel stopped walking and looked into Lincoln's pleading eyes. His hands, twined together in his lap, were trembling.

"What do you want me to do?" Daniel asked. He refused to help the Alphas gain that kind of control over the population, even if it meant a pardon for his supposed crimes. Lincoln could not seriously be asking him to do that.

"Escape," Lincoln replied. For the first time, his word was firm and unflinching. He imbued the syllables with strength, with power, as if it were the easiest thing to do. Daniel could barely contain his laugh as an abrupt chortle left his throat joined by those of Adrasteia and Nyx who had been listening in from their adjacent cells. "All of you—all the gods—need to escape."

"How are we supposed to do that?" Daniel asked incredulously.

"With this."

Lincoln bent to pull at something tucked beneath the lip of his boot. A cobbled together cuff of clashing metals was wrapped around his ankle. Daniel recognized it immediately. It was the same cuff Adrasteia's team had built to scramble the chips in their wrists. He turned it over in his hands. Inside, a small scrap of paper featured five digits scrawled in Lincoln's hasty penmanship.

"That's a master override code for the Guard. The new one now that Hermes is in here," Lincoln said. "I could only get my hands on one of those cuffs though. So only your chip will be undetectable. Once you use the code to open the doors to the other cells, you'll all have to move quickly. It's the best I could do."

Daniel stood dumbfounded. He slipped the cuff onto his wrist and twisted the metal to a comfortable position. He stared at it there, the gleaming promise of freedom welded together in its tacky, shiny glow.

"It'll be best to move at night," Lincoln said. "Fewer guards are active then. If you can make it to the Neutral Zone, you should be able to get more bracelets for everyone. I told them Adrasteia always blindfolded us when she took us there, so I didn't know where it was, and they couldn't search the place. But they've been on me like hawks, so I didn't dare go myself."

"You're becoming quite the little double agent," Daniel said, and, for the first time in as long as he could remember, Lincoln smiled.

"The Nine Year Anniversary Festival is two days from now," Lincoln offered. "There should be plenty of distraction then."

Nine years. Daniel had completely forgotten they were coming up on that moment. That the Alphas still intended to celebrate it irked him. But Lincoln was right: it would provide ample cover for their escape as the blasts of LED fireworks echoed through the hallways, and, on the one night a year alcohol was technically allowed outside of the Neutral Zone, all the citizens stumbled in a drunken stupor. It didn't matter though. Daniel wasn't going to suffer through another day in that cell. No, with that cuff on his wrist, they would all escape that night.

"You're not doing it right! Mr. Jingles doesn't talk like that!"

Manta stared at the stuffed animal in her hands. A bizarre, vaguely bear-shaped creature peered back at her through unblinking glass eyes and half a pair of glasses on a chain. A black bow was tied around its neck and a strange, elongated hat was stitched atop its head. All she could think was, *Mr. Jingles doesn't talk at all,* but when she looked at Chrissy's face—bright red and flushed in pout—she frowned and apologized.

Chrissy had been crabby all morning. In one fell swoop, she'd wiped away the player tokens on the board game they were playing—something about escaping from a jungle and being chased by hippopotamuses—when Manta had rolled a higher number of dots than her on the little six-sided cube. Then she got angry—all spit and fury—when Manta didn't know how to play Pretty Pretty Princess.

"All the princesses I've read about were locked in castles or put in sleep spells," Manta said when Chrissy insisted that a princess should be pampered. "I can fight a dragon or something if you want to take a nap. But there's no damn way I'm kissing you to wake you up."

Now she sat, silently fuming, as Manta attempted to raise and lower the pitch in her voice to capture the ambiguous sound Chrissy heard in her head but couldn't put into words.

"Just stop it!" she yelled and snatched Mr. Jingles away.

Manta leaned back in her cross-legged position on Chrissy's bedroom floor and watched as the little girl grumbled to herself and picked at the matted fur on the teddy bear. They were such different creatures, the two of them. From an early age, Manta had learned the importance of self-sufficiency and survival. Her father had taught her to really observe the world around her, to learn from it, to be one with it, and to use it to her advantage when it was necessary. Her own stuffed animals and the other "kid stuff" in her room had become tools to be utilized: fabric to let out clothing, stuffing to refresh mattresses and pillows, crib wood to be whittled into hunting weapons or burned. Everything but the books. Those, she treasured and read again and again until the pages sagged from their bindings.

Chrissy didn't have a single book in her room. Everything there was plush and pink and broken and dusty. She seemed trapped in a childhood from which she could not escape, like it was holding her there in a Never Neverland her parents had named "innocence." Manta understood why she would be frustrated.

"Do you want to maybe play outside?" Manta offered, hoping that direct sunlight could help brighten Chrissy's demeanor, maybe even toughen her up a bit. It just made her lips purse farther from her teeth.

"Momma and Diddy don't really like it when I go outside. They say it's unbecoming of a lady. And that the workers is too dangerous."

"I'm a worker," Manta said. "And I'm not dangerous. Besides which, don't Dart and Trent carry those rifles around with them everywhere they go? No one could get to you without being shot clear in the head first."

"Diddy don't let the help have bullets," Chrissy blurted. She tried to take it back, casually, and smiled when Manta acted like she hadn't heard.

Manta reached out a hand and planted it firmly on Chrissy's knee. She smiled mischievously as she looked her in the eye.

"Aren't you the princess of the Families?" she asked. "Not just a make-believe one. You're a literal princess. No one would dare do anything to you. And, as a princess, you should be able to play outside if you damn well please."

"Yeah!" Chrissy exclaimed, her face finally brightening up a bit after an excruciating morning. "But don't say the d-word. Momma says cursing is a sin that'll take you right to h-e-double hockey sticks in a handbasket."

What if you're already in hell? Manta thought. She smiled, astutely, and took Chrissy's hand as they rose from the floor.

"My dad and I used to play a game called Hide-and-Go-Seek around our cabin all the time before we came here," Manta smiled. "One person hides while the other one counts to ten. And then they try to find the one that hid before that person can make it back to home base."

"So it's sort of like Catch the Slave, huh? My diddy used to play that with me all the time. Said it was better than schoolin'. And I could count all the way up to thirty iffin I skipped a couple of the numbers that don't really matter none."

Manta bit her lip and smiled. Hide-and-Go-Seek or Catch the Slave, whatever Chrissy wanted to call it, was a better alternative to sitting in her musty bedroom all day. While she would much rather have been out in the fields with Paul and Alexander, helping them to convince Dart to add them all to the next water voyage to the river so they could make their escape, playing outside would, at least, give her a chance to explore the grounds a bit. She'd be able to keep Chrissy happy in the game without having to be directly in front of her, not to mention she could keep an eye on her dad as Chrissy practiced her twos, fours, and Ellie-Bens.

"You're right. I can do whatever I want. Let's go!" Chrissy exclaimed as she marched forward and swung open her bedroom door. "Princess coming through, people!"

Thunder rumbled like the bellows of angry gods striking their fists against the clouds. Lightning flashed in white hot pulses to illuminate the thick drops of heavy rain that poured over New Yukon. The Georgia thunderstorms that littered the summer evenings watered the fields and filled the rain buckets, drowning out any thoughts of any voyage to the river any time soon. Paul frowned as he leaned beside the broken window in the living room. Soon, Dart would make his rounds to latch the padlocks on the doors and Manta had yet to come home. He hoped the sudden storm had not trapped her in the Colton Family House for the night.

"If she's there, at least you know she's safe."

Alexander offered the empty comfort from his perch at the kitchen table. His fingers picked at the brown flesh of the bread loaf that still had some give inside the dark, cement crust. He was as frustrated as Paul. Their plan to force an excursion by over watering the field, through allowing the taps in the rain barrels that held the town's water supply to drain just a little too long, and the buckets that moved the water to sloppily overflow had been for naught. And now Manta was missing. He hoped their acts had not resulted in her being punished.

Paul startled as the front door swung open with a clash of thunder and Mr. Madison pushed a drenched and frazzled Manta inside. He did not seem happy, sopping wet himself and glowering from lowered eyes.

"You're lucky Ms. Chrissy says it's her fault y'all were out so late in this storm," he growled. "Next time, me and Mr. Colton won't take so kindly to such insolence."

He said the word "insolence" as if he were just trying it out, like he'd read it somewhere once upon a time and had been waiting for an opportunity to feel it in his mouth. Manta nodded solemnly and kept her head down.

"Yes, sir," she mumbled, slipping into a demure acquiescence she hoped would send him on his way quickly. She had news—the best kind of news—and he needed to be long gone before she burst.

Paul stepped forward and wrapped his arm around her shoulders. They trembled beneath his embrace as water dripped from her clothing to pool on the floor. It collected the dust and debris from the wood like tiny armadas circling in the puddle.

"We're sorry, sir," he said. "It won't happen again."

"Best not. You see to it now."

Mr. Madison slammed the door closed, grumbling as he latched the lock into place. He had barely descended the stairs when Manta turned to her father, a wild gleam in her eye.

"Wanna get out of here?" she asked.

The plan had passed in whispers down the block like it was traveling from cup to cup along a taut string from cell to cell. Daniel had the key. If he used it, Hermes, Typhon, and Echnida would take it from there. As now-former members of the Guard, they knew the hallways and the rounds patterns well. They could get them out quickly and unspotted.

Daniel had spent the afternoon studying the spacing of the numbers on the flat panel lock inside his door. The one outside would be a mirror image. He'd have only one chance to stretch his arm, to crook it around the corner, and to get the sequence just right.

"You'll have to use the outside panel to let yourself out," Hermes had warned him. It had whispered down the line slowly, painfully so, in jilted staccato. "An in is required for an out. Use of the inside panel will immediately set off the alarm. Input the code incorrectly and it triggers an immediate lockdown."

Daniel pushed himself into the corner and closed his eyes. He stretched his arm across his body in his best approximation of what was to come. His fingers traced the outline of the screen carefully to get his bearings. He moved a single digit over the first number in the sequence. It hovered there, mere millimeters between his fingertip and the screen. He opened his eyes and leaned forward, keeping his hand firmly in place. Three. He had been correct. He retook his position and tried again for the second digit. And then the third. Again and again until he could manage the sequence in less than the twenty second window required. If he took too long, the screen locked, and the Guard was alerted. If a finger slipped too far in any direction, the Guard was alerted. He practiced until he had it down without the cuff, then slid the metal over his wrist and worked at it again with the added weight, with the awkward stiffness it caused in his wrist. If the cuff did its job, the initial scan of the Guard on Duty's chip would not be required.

So many "if"s, but at least these were preferable to the ones which had clouded his mind before. He was glad to have something else to focus on, an actionable item that could potentially bring him closer to Paul and

Samantha. He reminded himself escape from the brig was just the first step; escape from the Colony was next.

"It's time," Echnida whispered as she opened her eyes. She had spent the last three hours counting the seconds from mealtime to when the Guard would start their shift change. It had been a meditative experience, but one she did not wish to relive. Her thigh still ached from counting the sixty second downbeats of the ten thousand eight hundred strikes that had passed.

Daniel braced himself and steadied his breath. He could do this. His arm squeezed through the tight bars. They pulled at the skin on his bicep, stretching it uncomfortably and trying to keep him contained. Once the number was entered, the quick recession of the door would leave little time to yank himself away. When he bent his arm, it flexed, and his muscle pounded against the obstruction. The cuff was heavy and obtrusive, awkward as it tried to balance the force of the bars. He listened for the subtle beep as it registered nothing and began counting backwards from twenty in his head as his fingers sought out the edges of the panel. He closed his eyes and began the sequence. He could do this.

He entered the last number and yanked his arm quickly back in before the door could shift to the side. The force of his pull knocked him back a few steps and the cuff slipped off and clanked to the floor. The metal was deafening as it hit, and he held his breath as he leapt forward and cupped it to stop its wobble, sliding in one fell swoop with it still in his grasp beyond the doorframe. The freedom, for as much as it could be called such, was heavy.

The rest of the cells were easy. He entered the code one by one as Adrasteia ticked down the twenty minutes they had before the next set of rounds began. She smiled as she counted. Her eyes conducted a wicked gleam like it was pure electricity, like there was music in the air.

Hermes led them to the far end of the hall, and the gods huddled by the door.

"Once we leave this hallway," he said, "we'll be too far from our cells. The location tracking on our chips will be triggered. Then it's maybe half a minute before the Guard descends."

Daniel nodded.

"The elevator bay is forty paces straight past the door," Typhon said. He tapped Daniel's cuff and looked him squarely in the eye. "You need to call the lift and get it here before we can exit. You got that?"

Daniel nodded again. He took a deep breath and felt his heart beating against his lungs so loudly it seemed an alarm had already sounded.

"The rest of us just pray there's no one on that elevator when it gets here," Nyx said.

"Then it's run like bats out of hell," Adrasteia said.

Daniel stepped forward. He scanned his blocked chip and entered the master override code Lincoln had given him. The door slipped open, and he looked quickly at his compatriots before he shuffled down the hallway to call the lift to their floor. He watched nervously as he waited, scanning from side to side and back to the gods waiting forty paces away.

"What the fuck?"

Adrasteia turned to look at the far end of the hallway. Time was up and an overnight guard had stepped in to start his rounds. His frozen shock gave them a short measure of time.

"Shit," Nyx cried. "Go."

The gods burst forward like lava from a volcano, spilling into the hallway erratically and running toward Daniel. They arrived just as the doors parted, the lot of them tumbling into the empty elevator like lemmings from a cliff. As the doors closed behind them, they heard the night guard calling for reinforcements.

Adrasteia punched the button for the Neutral Zone, and they heaved in silence as they hoped no Guard would be waiting when the elevator arrived. She whispered a prayer to her lost mother, asking her to guide them, to get them to the stash of cuffs she kept there, to give them time to hide themselves, to slip away into the night sky with only constellations left behind.

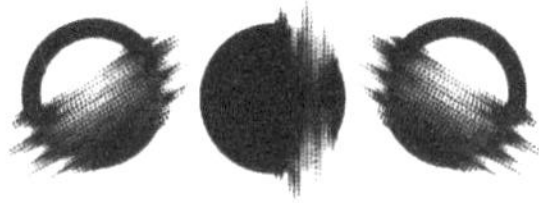

"You're certain the guns are just for show?" Alexander asked and Manta nodded.

"That's what Chrissy said anyway. Not that I think she really knows a lot. But she didn't mean to tell me, and I've heard her dad is kind of a braggart at their family suppers so I'm guessing it's true. Besides, in this storm, the night watch will be keeping under the front porches or in the barn. No way they're marching around in this."

Thunder clapped outside as if to confirm the young girl's assessment. Paul laughed and clapped a hand over Alexander's shoulder.

"She's a pretty stellar kid," he said. "You'll learn to just trust her plans."

Manta smiled sheepishly and shivered a bit. Her clothes were finally beginning to dry. Though her mind was ablaze with thoughts of escape, her body hadn't gotten the message, and the cold of the hot storm made her shake. It didn't matter though. Soon she'd be soaked through again. The weather would provide excellent cover. The downpour would let them slip away undetected until morning and wash away their tracks.

"Okay, then," Alexander smiled. "Let's do this!"

He timed his smash with a lightning clash to push out what little glass was left in the frame of the living room side window. He reached in and began to heave himself forward.

"Wait!" Manta said. "There's a thin layer of dirt over it, but all those shards from the windows are planted in the ground beneath them. 'Slaves can't run if their feet are gashed and bleeding.' Miss Chrissy told me that too."

She grabbed one of the couch cushions and pushed it through the opening to thud gently on the soft earth below. Paul shook his head in pride. He had grown to understand her cunning, but it amazed him every time.

Alexander went first, heaving outward as smoothly as he could manage and tumbling off the cushion with a silent clunk into the mud. Manta followed, deftly landing in a crouch and eyeing both directions beyond the house before she motioned for her father. The rough wood clawed at his shirt, and he felt the bite of a long splinter slip its fang into his shoulder. He winced but swallowed his yelp.

Once they were all outside, Manta led them slowly toward the grove of woods behind the field where she and Chrissy had spent the afternoon together. She smiled. Chrissy had enjoyed her time in the "great" outdoors. At least she was leaving her with that. While Chrissy screamed a disjointed sequence of "numbers" she was obviously proud of, Manta had searched the far recesses of the barrier. That's when she'd found it, off such a distance from the houses and the field the Madisons and the Coltons probably didn't even realize it was there. A flaw in the system. Mother Nature taking back control. A way out.

They moved cautiously, keeping low to the ground. While the storm offered them anonymity, the lightning brought up the stage lights to expose them to the house at irregular intervals. Paul remembered the beating Dart had given him. If they were caught, they were dead, bullets or not.

As they reached the edge of the field, the trio froze. Dim candlelight flickered from inside the barn just ahead. From behind two large barrels, now overflowing with rain, they watched Dart's silhouette as he paced back and forth beneath the shallow overhang by the barn door. He was speaking to someone as he walked, not paying too much attention to the wet world outside.

Alexander struck out first, stooped and moving quickly on Dart's fro pace. He made it to the muddy row behind the taller stalks of corn. From there, they would be able to slip into the wood undetected. He paused a few feet in and turned to watch Manta follow suit.

She was halfway across the clearing when lightning lit up the sky and she froze in her tracks. Her eyes widened as she met the gaze of someone else in the barn with Dart. They stared back at her, mouth agape, a shocked expression on their face. Dart caught their eyes and started to turn around.

"I don't think I've ever seen a storm this fierce," Toni said quickly, pulling Dart's attention back to them. "It might just wash away the whole fucking field."

Manta took the opportunity to bolt with Paul quickly on her tail. He mouthed a "thank you" to the young Cherokee as he scooped Manta up in his arms and carried her quickly behind the corn stalks.

"Good thing we got a whole mess of those fuckers you brought in to clean it up," Dart growled and resumed his pacing. "Tell you what though," he muttered, "these night watches ain't making the extra food and empty gun seem worth it. Especially with fuckers like you."

The storm beat down like it would flood the mountain. The storm carried on as if it would never end.

"Go lay down then." Paul heard Toni's tone shift as they moved between the barn door and Dart. "Look. You don't like me, and I don't like you. That's no secret. And a storm like this, ain't nothing happening. I can keep watch alone."

Alexander breathed a sigh of relief when they reached the inside of the tree line. The rain still fell harshly, but the thick canopy of oak and kudzu shielded them from the worst of it.

"Where to now, little lady?" he asked.

Manta rolled her eyes and shook her head to express her displeasure to her father. Alexander had yet to grow on her, but it was not like they could leave him behind. She rang the water from her hair and stepped forward to lead the way.

They moved slowly still, despite the cover of the wood, hiding behind the great trunks of trees and abundant undergrowth, pausing to listen for calls from New Yukon or footsteps on their tails. They timed footfalls with thunderclaps less they break a fallen twig and alert someone to their location. It was tedious, the whole adventure, but Manta had never felt more empowered.

"There it is," she smiled.

Before them, the wrought iron fencing of the barricade bowed outward beneath the girth of a tree, uprooted by a previous storm as if the gods of nature had wanted them to find their escape. Like a bridge to freedom, they could simply walk across.

"What's on the other side?" Alexander asked, suddenly worried about the extremities he had faced in the outside world. The hunger and the ravagers. The solitude and insanity.

"Only one way to find out," Manta said. She grabbed her father's hand and pulled him forward.

"Room for one more?"

They turned to find Toni standing behind them. Their jet-black hair was glued to their face from the rain, and they kept their hands turned out to show they were unarmed.

"It's your fault we're here in the first place," Paul growled. "How are we supposed to believe you won't just turn us back in?"

"I know the woods out there," Toni offered. "I know where the ravager camps are; what routes the traders take. I can keep you safe and hidden."

The trio held their breath. Rain beat across their faces like teardrops.

"This is not the life I wanted when I left Oklahoma," Toni pleaded. "It was a life of necessity. We've all done things since the Wave we aren't proud of."

"Yeah, well, I never sold people into slavery," Alexander bit back.

"I saved you from the ravagers," Toni started, the old words of rationalization washed false in the rain. "I'm sorry."

Manta could see it in their eyes. They truly were. An apology was all they had to offer, but it was better than currency in their new world. Slowly, Toni reached down to present the two bags at their ankles. They were Paul and Manta's rucksacks. Paul felt the pressure of Manta's unspoken statement as she squeezed at his hand.

"Stay close," he said. "And if any of us think, even for a microsecond, you're pulling a con, we're gone and you're on your own."

"Deal," Toni said as they moved toward the fallen tree.

Daniel knew returning to his quarters was a risk. There was so much open space between the Neutral Zone and Sub5 in which to be caught. Still, he thought, the last place the Guard would expect them to go was back home. He'd stayed in the middle of larger groups, a hat he'd gotten from one of the booths covering his head, and his eyes trained on the toes of his sneakers. The adrenaline high of their escape still fresh within him, he was confident he could make it.

The gods had reached the Neutral Zone quickly and spread out to all corners while Adrasteia retrieved her cuffs. She moved swiftly to grant each one of her crew anonymity while they retrieved new clothing and supplies, leaving the white linen prisoner's uniforms behind as barter. The denizens of the Neutral Zone were only too happy to help. Anything that stuck it to the powers-that-be left them feeling alive. They'd agreed to stay hidden, separately, until Adrasteia sent the signal for them to reconvene. One of the good things in having a larger assembly of lesser gods who needed a chance to vent was having a diverse and expansive network with which to send out code words in a heartbeat. Until Daniel heard the word "Cronus," he was on his own.

He pulled the brim of his hat lower as he turned down his hallway. Ahead, the high-rises of Peachtree Street glistened in the morning sun. Outside his door, a few teenagers were riffling through a muddled collection of fabrics. The Guard had turned his unit, and now the kids were stealing his blankets and clothes. They scattered as he moved forward taking what they could with them.

He didn't care about the clothes anyway. It was just stuff. He searched through the remaining debris and finally found what he was looking for. He smiled as he studied the picture. Paul beamed back at him from in front of a stone structure flying a green, yellow, and red striped flag, a beautiful, swaddled infant in his arms. The photo was taken in Ethiopia, right when she's become theirs, but before she had become home. He pulled the printed photo of Paul and Samantha from its frame and tucked it into his pocket. It was the only thing he had of value; the only thing he had worth saving. He moved forward, disappearing into the pedestrian traffic of Atlanta's morning rush hour.

Manta froze, her ear low to the ground, listening. They had been traveling for nearly a day, as far as she could tell. All she knew was that it was dark again. The wood they were in, the world beyond that, all of it was just one endless night. It closed in on her, its cooing whisper meant to lull her into a false sense of security. But she could clearly see its gnarled fingers, reaching from nothingness to grasp at her flesh, it's gaping maw ready and eager to consume.

"I think we lost them," she whispered as she pushed herself back into a standing position.

Paul, Alexander, and Toni breathed a collective sigh of relief. She looked at the adults in her life and took pride in her ability to keep them safe. Growing up in the wild, she had learned so much about survival. The fact that she poured over Daddy Daniel's various nature and camping guides hadn't hurt either. It made her feel close to him to follow in his footsteps, even if he wasn't around yet. Paul, her present father, had told her once that Daniel had only just bought the books when they decided to move up to the cabin, but in reality, he hadn't even cracked the spines. But Manta didn't believe that. No, Daniel was a true hero who would come back to them one day, his survival skills and a heart full of love in tow.

"We should get moving," Paul said. He had a little of the survival instinct in him too. "We need to set up camp, and I don't feel comfortable doing that so close to where we heard voices."

Alexander agreed. He made the strangest, swooning eyes at her father, and Manta hated him for it. It filled her vision every time. It was all she could see. Paul, though, didn't seem to mind, and that infuriated Manta even more. It had been just the two of them for so long—and she'd longed to have what her father called "community"—but she had expected the first person to enter their lives to be Daniel. Her father. The final piece of her family. She had planned it all out in her mind. And even when she tried to be happy that they now had other people—friends even, if you could call them that—the vitriol crept back in like a rat rutting around in her brain for something to gnash its teeth on.

She kept her bow at her side as they walked, still not quite ready to return it to her backpack. The wood was dense, with trees that had not been there a second ago growing thick and firm and powerful to block their path at every turn. Anything could be lurking behind them. In fact, Manta knew, everything was.

Toni lagged at the rear of the group and Manta kept tabs on them from the corner of her eye. They were a ghost, trapped there and ever present. She watched to ensure they weren't leaving behind a trail of breadcrumbs—like in the story books of Daniel's she liked to read—or snapping twigs to mark their path—like in the camping guides. While it was true, they had saved all of them when they enacted their escape from New Yukon, the previous betrayal still weighed heavily on her heart. The world, it seemed, was not a magical place. Or, maybe it was, it was just that the magic was dark. Tree limbs and brambles snatched at their clothing, barbed their skin, choked the light from their path.

At beats the storm had stopped.

They moved purposefully, Manta becoming more confident with each step. The night grew less dark, less confusing. She was almost smiling as she pushed through a blooming rhododendron and onto a larger path. But her half-smile was short-lived. There, not fifteen paces ahead stood the Hawk and the Snake. Their eyes met and the Snake hissed, his tongue rapid in the air as he commanded his companion to "Get them!"

Paul tugged Manta into motion as the foursome turned to bolt in the opposite direction, but there the path was blocked by Mr. Madison. Then, she saw them: Dart and Trent; Chrissy and Ms. Rose; the family of ravagers who had invaded their cabin homestead. They were surrounded on all sides. She readied her bow, reaching back to her satchel for an arrow only to find it empty. She looked to her father, but Paul had a worrisome defeat in his eyes that shone through the anger and the fear.

It was over. They would be returned to New Yukon, left to toil in the fields and houses for the rest of their lives. Or, worse yet, handed over in trade to the ravagers, their final feelings simply those of fear as they were consumed by the cannibals.

Paul twined one hand into hers, his other into Alexander's. Alexander's free hand found Toni's and the four of them stood firm on the forest path. They were ready to meet their fates.

Suddenly, a humming noise—like the one her father's laptop made when he fired up the generator—broke the silence of the night. Mr. Madison fell first. Then the Snake. Then Trent. One by one, their pursuers fell, each accompanied by the shifting electronic hum, growing louder with each strike, sending a chorus of cicadas into a triumphant song.

And there he was. Daniel. Her savior. Her knight. Riding in on a wild, white horse, a laser gun like in the fantasy books he'd left for her to read at the ready. He looked exactly like he did in all of the pictures Paul had around the house. Tall and strong, with lush black hair and a genuine and glorious smile. He stopped before them and reached his hand down to Manta.

"You must be my princess," he said, pulling her up to straddle the horse behind him.

She heard a groan emanate and turned to see a furious Chrissy pull herself to her feet from between the limp bodies of her parents. A wild rage puffed up her chest as she stomped her patent leather shoes to the ground. Manta smiled.

Quickly, she grabbed her father's laser from its holster at his hip and took the princess out.

She then wrapped her arms tightly around Daniel's waist and breathed deeply to take in the musky, floral scent of him. He smelled like freshly churned earth and fire and vine ripe tomatoes. It was perfect, and glorious, and she knew it was a dream.

"There you are, sleepy head," Paul smiled at his daughter as she stirred from her slumber.

It had been a long night. After scaling the tree into the wood behind New Yukon, they had forced their way through the storm until almost daybreak before setting up camp. Toni's return of their bags had been a lifesaver. Pretty much everything was still intact, so they had their blankets and tarps, and fresh clothes to change into to free themselves from the binds of the town they'd left behind.

"I let you sleep in a bit," Paul said. "Figured you needed it. But Toni was smart enough to grab a handful of tomatoes and some snap peas on their way out behind us. Lunch is almost ready."

He smiled as he watched Manta wipe the sleep from her eyes, yawn, and stretch out her back from a night of sleeping against the hard soil. She was truly an amazing little girl, able to take whatever life threw at her in stride and so efficient at getting herself (and him) out of bad situations. He was proud of the young woman she was becoming and hated himself for being a part of the system that had left her this world to grow up in.

"I had a dream about Daddy Daniel," she said, rolling her blanket into a tight, compact tube.

"He made an appearance in my dream too."

"Must mean we're getting closer to seeing him," she suggested. "You think he dreams about us too?"

"I'm sure he does," Paul said. He tried to smile. He tried to show hope.

It had been nine years since Daniel had disappeared. Nine years since the argument; since the Wave. He'd always told Manta her daddy was living inside the Forward Colony, that he was up there trying to save the world, but the truth was he didn't know for sure. He'd heard of a sweep of the city before the Wave hit, but that was just gossip spread in the aftermath of a world altering event.

"No, they rounded them up," Alexander assured Paul one night as Manta slept in New Yukon. "I was on the phone with a trick when they came for him. That's how I knew something was up. I hightailed it out of the city so fucking fast. That trick saved my life."

So maybe Daniel really had made it. He was either in the Colony or washed away by the Wave, and Paul couldn't stomach the latter.

"Food's done," Toni called.

Paul kissed Manta's forehead and walked with her to the little clearing where Alexander and Toni were busy nurturing the coals of an almost dead fire. They couldn't afford actual flames—the smoke may have given away their location—but a quick fire left the wood chips and leaves hot enough to roast the vegetables Toni had pilfered for them all. The tomatoes were still warm and, when he broke the skin, the hot juice inside stained his fingers. Or maybe it just washed away a layer of dirt where it hit. He wasn't really sure.

"The new shoreline is about a two day walk south," Toni said between bites. "I've never been to Atlanta before, but from what I hear, most of the city is underwater. 'The SWATS to Buckhead' is what they told me."

"Verified," Alexander said. He didn't bother to chew or swallow before he spoke. "Those of us who managed to escape moved inland a bit. But that didn't last long. Once the old nuclear power plant in Albany went and the water became radioactive, everyone started to disappear to fend for themselves." He spoke matter-of-factly, the way only someone who had experienced the trauma firsthand could. There was no mourning in his voice, no fond remembrance or whimsy. "What's the plan when we get there?"

Paul froze. He hadn't considered that. Their original idea had been to collect the sea water to distill down to the salt they would need to cure enough meat to survive the winter. Three days each way to collect and return to their cabin. Now that seemed out of the question. So much had happened and the path back was treacherous, even knowing where the dangers were.

"We have to go back to the cabin," Manta insisted. "It's the only place Dad will know where to find us when he gets out of the Colony. We have to be there when he gets back."

Paul nodded and glared quickly at Alexander before he could speak. Toni hid their frown in another bite of food.

A flock of birds emerged suddenly from a tree in a nearby grove to the west. Something had startled them. Or someone. Toni quickly tossed a blanket over the coals to smother any lingering remnants of smoke and the four of them hunched down on instinct.

"Pack up quickly," Paul whispered. "And be quiet."

They moved carefully, untying tarps from trees and wrapping blankets into tiny bundles in small, measured movements they hopes would not attract attention. They listened as leaves rustled and animals scurried, this time to their north. Then once more to the east. It seemed they were being circled, surrounded. Their voices were low, but they were coming in clearer. And they were moving closer.

"You really think they came this way?"

It was the Hawk. If she was hunting, the Snake would be slithering nearby.

"Fuck," Toni whispered as the group huddled close to the ground. The crunching of leaves sounded nearby to the north, then again immediately to the south. "They're not gonna give up."

"Come out, come out, wherever you are!" the Snake hissed in a singsong voice. He was laughing. He was enjoying this.

"Which way do we go?" Paul asked. The traders were moving erratically, but they were honing in. An unnoticed sprint seemed impossible.

"I can distract them; throw them off the trail," Toni offered.

"No," Manta pleaded. "They'll kill you. We all get out this together."

"Yoo-hoo!" the Hawk screeched. "You can't hide forever. We know all the tricks. We're always gonna find you!"

"They'll kill us all if they do," Toni insisted. "I have to distract them somehow if the rest of you have any chance of getting away. I deserve this. I'm part of the reason all of you were captured."

"They've got a point," Alexander said.

"If I'm injured, I can convince those idiots you captured me. They won't hurt me beyond roughing me up a little bit."

"No!" Manta yelled as loudly as her whisper would let her.

"I can slip away later and find y'all," Toni said. They reached out and grasped Manta's hands. "I promise."

Alexander quickly snatched an arrow from Manta's bag and plunged it into Toni's thigh. They winced but bit their lip to keep from yelping.

"What the hell?" Manta growled.

"They wanted to be hurt," Alexander said, palms out and an unsettling smirk on his face. "I didn't hit any arteries. At least I don't think."

Toni's breath was sharp as they tried to control their pain. They reached a hand out and cupped Manta's chin.

"I have to do this," Toni said. "It doesn't make up for what I did to you. Or what I did to the others. But it's a start."

"It's a stupid start," Manta argued. "A better way would be staying with us, helping us survive out here."

Leaves crunched and beetles scurried as the Hawk and Snake circled their prey.

"I am helping you survive. I'll be fine. I'll find you some day. I promise. We'll get ourselves a dog and get to be a little bit of both. Okay?"

Manta frowned but nodded. She didn't trust Toni completely yet—she wasn't ready for that—but she didn't want them to run toward death like they welcomed it. Paul agreed, but whispered it was not his decision to make to Manta's pleading eyes. He nodded, his own eyes doing all they could to acknowledge the sincerity of Toni's sacrifice.

Alexander led the charge to the south, keeping low through the underbrush, followed by Paul and a reluctant Manta. Toni hobbled in the opposite direction. They made no attempt to hide themselves, breaking sticks with every footfall, and moaning loudly.

"Over here!" the Hawk cried as they rushed in Toni's direction.

"Behold the return of the prodigal son." Alexander laughed as he entered the apartment, surprised at how his voice echoed with the lack of furniture. "Bored of that country life already?"

Paul turned quickly from the window, finger over his mouth to urge quiet, but a sly smirk on his lips. His other hand motioned to the sleeping girl in the baby carriage parked where the entertainment center used to be. Alexander nodded, moving forward in an exaggerated tiptoe as he joined Paul at the window.

"I was surprised to get your text," he whispered. "Figured you'd be nesting and homesteading your way through the wilderness with this little one strapped to your back." He smiled as his fingers hovered over the knitted blanket tucked aorund Samantha, but thought better of disturbing her slumber. "How's it going out there in No Man's Land?"

"It's quiet," Paul chuckled. "Which, after years of your company, is a welcomed change."

"Uh-huh. I'm sure."

Alexander leaned against the window sill and peered out at the sleepy Midtown afternoon. The black of the asphalt below, darkened by a late morning rain, made the perfect backdrop to the pink and fuschia bursts of azaleas and hydrangeas popping out from the front yards. A few pedestrains strumbled along the sidewalks, but it was remarkably quiet and beautiful and majestic.

He turned back to Paul and caught the pained expression in his eye.

"Seriously. What brings you down?"

"Samantha and I decided to surprise Daniel for lunch. But he was busy with clients. So we came here instead."

Paul tried to smile through the statement, but Alexander could hear the hurt in his voice.

"Danny boy's a busy man," Alexander shrugged. "You knew that going into this. And now that you're a stay-at-home-dad, one of you has to pay for the mortgage up there, the lease down here, and that baby right there."

He was trying to be funny, to lighten the mood. That's what he was good at. Plus, Paul and Daniel's move to the mountains had reeked of the impulsiveness they always placed on him. He relished a bit in the turn of events.

He reached out to jab Paul's ribcage, to let him in on the humor he was obviously missing. Paul grabbed his hand and held tight, wiping the smile from his face as their eyes met. Paul looked like he had so much to say, but he shook his head and dropped Alexander's hand.

"It really is great out there," Paul said. He busied himself with checking through Samantha's diaper bag, counting the nappies and the wipes for the fifteenth time that day. "We'll have to have you out soon. Really. I think you'll love it. It's just different."

Alexander nodded as he tappped his fingers, quietly, against the window glass.

"Different is good," he said. "It keeps things exciting."

Paul huffed. "I think that's the problem. I thought it would be exciting. New home. New baby. New family. All these great big moves we made to push our lives forward. And then Daniel's never even around. I just feel like I'm doing it all alone."

"Again, see Exhibit A," Alexander said. He placed his hands on Paul's shoulders and looked him straight in the eye. "Daniel loves you. And I know he loves that little girl. But he also loves his work. And he does a lot of good for those clients. That's part of what made you fall for him in the first place, remember?"

"I know," Paul sighed. He turned back to the window, watching the life he used to lead pass by on the street below.

"You guys will find your balance again," Alexander assured him. "It's just going to take some time."

"I guess. Maybe I'm just tired. Parenthood is hard. But you're right. It's about finding balance. And we will."

Alexander joined Paul at the window. The pain in the man's reflection almost made him faulter.

"In the meantime, feel free to live vicariously through me if you want.

Let's see. Eight dates in two weeks. Three trolls; two bait and switchers; a little bit of fun; and a conspiracy theorist. Wanna trade lives?"

"You do have a type," Paul laughed. It was his first genuine laugh, outside of the joy he felt around Samantha's milestones, in what felt like months.

"Hey, we dated once upon a time too," Alexander reminded him. "Or did you block that part out?"

"I remember," Paul conceded. "You ever think we could have worked out? The two of us?"

"Hmmm," Alexander scrunched his nose as if he were really considering it, looking Paul up and down and squinting his eyes at his aggravated stance. "Maybe. If we were the last two gay men left on the planet."

Paul's laugh nearly woke the sleeping girl. He shook his head as he quieted himself and rocked the carriage back and forth a bit to lull her. Alexander was right. He did have a wonderful thing going with Daniel, with their daughter. They would make it through their growing pains and be stronger for it. He just needed to give it time. And to remind himself that Daniel was working so hard for them, to prove that their family belonged in the Colony. Soon, if they were accepted, they'd have all the time in the world together.

"Let's get out of here and grab some lunch," Alexander said. "I want to hear all about that country life you're leading now, city boy. Tell me, are the bears out there as hairy as the ones down here?"

Alexander stopped suddenly, leaned against the nearest tree, and bent to hold the stitch in his side. They had been running for what felt like forty miles. As soon as they'd made it out of earshot from Toni's distraction, they'd bolted and not looked back. Their adrenaline spent, they skidded to a halt, chests sore and heaving as the late afternoon sun set bonfires in their lungs. Paul held his breath to stop the symphony of his panting from filling his ears and listened closely to the path they had taken. They were not being followed.

He took a swig from his canteen—luckily refilled by the previous night's storm—and offered it to Alexander as Manta nursed her own. The rainwater was warm, but still cooled his esophagus in small doses. Any more than that and he feared his stomach would explode. It churned already from exertion.

Manta was the first to catch her breath.

"Do you think Toni's okay?" she asked.

Alexander shrugged, the roll in his eyes asking "who cares?" better than his words could have done.

"I'm sure they're fine," Paul said. Speaking seemed to help, as if the action was reminding him how to breathe; naturally, slowly, calmly, automatically.

Manta's lips pulled tight as she nodded. She could barely make out the ache in her muscles behind that of her heart. People tended to leave her for her better good. From her limited experience anyway. *Except for the ones who should*, she thought as she stared at Alexander's still heaving body collapsed into a seated position by the tree, legs spread wide and head pushed back against the bark in a sloppy acquiescence.

So far, the world outside the cabin had not been at all as she'd imagined. Of course she knew it held dangers. Even the cabin itself had not been immune to those. But she had hoped for love and compassion. For the morals of all those stories to have finally been learned. Now she realized that fairytales were not real. No forests were enchanted; no gods or godmothers intervened to make things magical. People—in as much as they could be called that if the idea of humanity was the ideal—were selfish and cruel. Why else would there have been a need for stories to be passed down for centuries? Tales meant to remind the whole human species not to judge others, to be kind, to share, to be honest? Lore offered from mute lips to deaf ears. Psalms taken in stride as a sing-along call-and-response.

Paul sat on the ground beside Alexander and the men passed the canteen back and forth between them as Manta paced in front of them. She wanted to sit too, but the run had left her body tight with an agitated, excess energy which she knew, if she stopped, would vanish. And she needed it. Plus, she didn't want to give them that satisfaction. Sitting with them would seem like acceptance of the situation, of Alexander, and she was not there yet. She didn't think she ever would be. Alexander hunched forward and laid his head on Paul's shoulder. Their bodies heaved as one; their deep, slow breaths finally synchronized. Paul yawned.

"I think we're far enough out," he wheezed. "Maybe we should set up camp for the night? Get some sleep? I'm guessing we have a day, day and a half to the waterfront if we're rested. Recharged."

"Fine by me," Alexander agreed. "Besides, I think we deserve a minute to celebrate, anyway."

Manta huffed. "What's there to celebrate?"

Alexander smiled brightly. It felt odd to Manta, exaggerated and out of place. His teeth glistening in the wafting light of the setting sun looked like citrine on a rusted iron band. Everything about him was driving her mad, and she could not figure out why.

"We just escaped a literal human trafficking slave plantation thanks to you," he said. He was trying to win her over, but he could tell it wasn't working. "And we lost our traders several miles back there. And we found each other." He looked at Paul when he said "each other" and Manta's stomach turned. "If that's not worth celebrating, I don't know what is."

"You don't know what is."

Paul watched as Manta mumbled beneath her breath. He grimaced as he gently patted Alexander's leg and rose to join his daughter in her pacing. Anger radiated from her like heat lightning on an otherwise clear evening. She was a storm of emotional confusion. *How could she not be?* Paul thought. Though life had not been easy, he had sheltered her from so much harshness for most of it. Now, on her first foray into the open world, circumstance was whipping her at every turn. He placed his arm around her shoulder and squeezed as he guided her farther away from Alexander, who, for his part, pretended to be enraptured by the contents of Paul's bag: unfurling sleeping bags, setting up tarps.

"Talk to me, baby girl."

Manta froze. Her shoulders clenched beneath her father's arm. "It's not fair."

"No, it's not," Paul agreed. "But Toni made their sacrifice for themself as much as for us. It was their decision."

"It's not just that!" Manta raised her voice to a growl, but quickly reeled it in when she caught Alexander looking her way.

"Sweetie, tell me what's going on."

"That!" she said, pointing at her father as if he'd been replaced with a boogey man, an evil sorcerer, a monster. "All of a sudden you're calling me things like 'baby' and 'sweetheart' instead of my name. Like I'm just some kid."

"Manta, you're ten years old." Paul kept his voice steady even as his heart was breaking. "You are my baby girl. I want you to get to be a kid. To have a real childhood."

"Yeah, well, you let me be a kid but also made me feel like an equal before. Before he showed up. Is he my Wave? The asshole who comes in and drowns everything?"

Her eyes shot to Alexander as he feigned interest in the bottom side of

Paul's canteen. Paul sighed heavily and reached out to take her hands. He hadn't noticed himself doing it, but she was right. The addition of other people to their circle had changed their dynamic. As if on instinct, he had fallen into treating Manta like the little girl he wanted her to be able to be. The entrenched ideas of civilized personhood had outweighed the young woman he knew her to be.

"You are an amazing person," he said. "And I love that. I love you. You have so much strength. You are practically made of power, and that is never going to change."

"Yeah? Well, everything is changing."

"You're still my little girl."

A guttural, animalistic sound sprang from the bottom of Manta's throat. She marched toward Alexander and snatched the canteen from his hands.

"I didn't use to be just your little girl," she groaned. "I was your partner. Until this jerk came around. Now it's like you're trying to play house or something."

Alexander held up his hands in surrender. He did his best to look innocent beneath the barely broken grime of nearly nine years in the wild.

"Hey, now. I'm not trying to change the dynamic of your relationship," he said. "You're a kick-ass superhero in my book. You're the one who broke us out of that living nightmare."

"Then why are you trying to replace him!"

Manta's scream surprised even herself. They stood there, the three of them, in complete silence. Even the jays and grasshoppers, emboldened to crescendo their songs in the rising heat of the argument, held their breath and listened as the weight of Manta's words cascaded over them all. Thicker and more sudden than the Wave itself, silent tears began to stream down her face. In an instant, Paul had her in his arms.

"Manta," he said, "no one is replacing your father. Whether he's here or in the sky, Daniel will always be your dad."

Paul felt his heart ripping as all the pain and love he had held in it for so long attempted to break free, to scurry out and wrap his daughter in a blanket of warmth she had all but outgrown. He had been so concerned with making sure Manta knew Daniel, the love he had had for her, the sacrifices he was making for her. He had told her stories of his bravery, of his beauty, but in doing so he had built him up into a mythical figure in her mind. He had wanted her to feel him, to know him even in his absence. He had needed to make him real for her so he could be real for himself. He didn't want to lose his memory. He didn't want him to be gone. He pulled her close and closed his eyes, fighting the tears from his own realization. She squirmed in his grip, her rage too intense to quell just yet.

"Stop fucking babying me," she screamed. "I can see what's happening. Treat me like the goddamn adult I have had to be since y'all screwed up the whole planet."

Paul shook his head and maintained his grip. They stood, the two of them, like a stone statue in a garden, weeping water in torrents to the ground below.

Alexander wasn't sure what came over him. Perhaps it was never having a child of his own, or maybe it was the savagery of his recent past which overwhelmed him, but he suddenly felt the tendrils of all their sadness and wrath within himself. He knew he was overstepping his bounds, but he would not stop himself. He had finally found a glimmer of comfort and this little girl was threatening it all.

"You wanted to be treated like an adult, little girl?" he growled. "Fine. Are you gonna tell her the truth, Paul, or should I?"

Manta sucked back in her composure in gasps and sniffles. Paul released her from his grip and stood tall, a worried expression on his tear-streaked cheeks as he took a step between his daughter and the wild-ravaged man from his past. His eyes begged Alexander to be quiet, but Alexander was somewhere else. The creature before them was the same that had been tossed into their prison cell all those weeks prior, ferocious and scared and more concerned with fight than flee.

"Tell me what?"

Manta's eyes passed from Alexander to her father's, searching there for answers to questions she hadn't known she'd asked. Questions she hadn't known to ask. The world was changing so rapidly around her. Every step away from the cabin was a revelation. And the bulk of them had not been pleasant.

"Your dear old daddy ain't coming back," Alexander growled. "When the Wave hit, it knocked out communication with the Colonies. No way they're letting folks leave without knowing what they will go back to. And, even if Daniel wanted to leave, to get out of there, Atlanta is gone. Washed a-fucking-way. The Colony is 8 miles into the ocean now. So, little girl, as far as anyone up there is concerned, they got saved, and we're all dead. Ain't nobody coming back. Not even to look for some adopted daughter he barely knew from Eve before he left."

The words expelled from him like a cloud of gnats above a carcass, dark and thick and dripping. He couldn't stop himself. He felt like another person, watching a wraith take hold of his body, ready to lay waste to anything in its path. When he was finished, he inhaled sharply. The thick humidity brought him back to his senses. He immediately regretted everything he had said as he looked at Manta's trembling visage. The adult little girl wavered between belief and fact; the diametric forces poised in war on her skin.

"Is that true?"

Paul averted his eyes. He had shielded Manta from so much, even as he'd taught her to be fierce, to be a warrior, to understand the realities of being born into such a fierce time. The world was horrible enough—a child in her single digits having to learn to hunt, to kill, to scavenge—he did not want to take away her hope on top of it all. But above all that, he had not wished to admit it to himself. The pain of Alexander's revelation echoed through him, paralyzing his body.

Manta thought she would cry again, but the tears would not come. Anger was all she knew. It was calm, calculated, and precise, like the swift thrip of an arrow from a bow, like how it pierced skin and missed bone to puncture straight through muscle and into heart. She blinked slowly as she turned away from the men. The betrayal she felt was holding her heart together. It would not allow her to break. She walked slowly to where she had left her bag on the ground and lifted it up to her shoulder. She bit her lip but refused to look back. Quickly, with all the force of the jackrabbits she used to watch skipping through the meadow near the cabin, she took off into the underbrush.

Paul broke his trance and yelled after her. He started running to follow her trail, but it didn't matter. She was too lithe, too furious. She was gone.

aniel devoured the protein bar Lincoln had offered him greedily. It had been two days since the escape, and, while he had managed some food—scraps, really, from those who were amenable with Adrasteia's cause, though even those were sparse as rations were steadily growing smaller—Lincoln's offering had been more than welcomed. He wondered how the other gods were fairing. As far as he knew, everyone had managed to allude capture. Thankfully, the government could not name their crimes without revealing the cause, and the generic Crimes Against the Colony and Its Government charge that flickered below their Wanted posters next to all the elevator bays and canteens led most of the folks on the Sub levels to turn the other way if they happened to catch a glimpse of any one of them. He'd even gotten a few upturned thumbs and nods of encouragement from strangers he'd passed in the hallways.

He had, for the most part, kept a fairly low profile. After his initial return to his quarters to retrieve the photo of his family, he'd kept to the Neutral Zone except for during the busiest times on the other floors. His thinking had been that it was easier to get lost in a crowd. If he had ventured out when things were slower, the chances of him being spotted seemed too strong. Anonymity en masse was a better mask than the shadows. He hoped the others in his group had been as lucky as him.

The preparations for the evening's Anniversary Festival were well underway by the time he'd moved to meet with Lincoln. After the Aposts failed coup early in the life of the Colony, the Anniversary had become a major celebration, like the 4th of July on land. It was the only holiday the entire Colony celebrated, and people looked forward to the day when debauchery and merrymaking ruled. Even the Neutral Zone emptied out during the Festival. Preparations had also left the labs on Alpha2 mostly unmanned. It was the perfect opportunity for Lincoln to show them all what their leaders had planned, and Adrasteia had sent out the call. The name "Cronus" was whispered through halls alone or merged sloppily into sentences. The father of Zeus, who had separated Earth from Sky, conjured up to unite them once more.

"They think you're some technical genius," Lincoln was saying, though Daniel could barely hear him through the grinding, mealy crunch in his mouth, "so they don't think I had anything to do with your escape. They still think I have something to offer, so they let me keep my job. But they've been tight lipped about their search for all of y'all around me nonetheless."

Daniel nodded, a reflex from his days opposite the couch, though he wasn't really paying attention. Adrasteia and the others would be arriving soon, and he kept his eye trained on the door.

The gods trickled in, slowly, covertly, each with a glaring eye on Lincoln and a wayward glance over their shoulders to make sure they had not been followed or duped once again. Lincoln's face reddened, and he hung his head further in shame with each person who passed the threshold. Nyx was the last to arrive, but they were all accounted for. All of them except Adrasteia. But she had put out the signal. She couldn't have been captured. Daniel breathed a sigh of relief even as the anger mounted in Nyx's countenance.

"If this is another fucking trap," she threatened, her hand wrapping around the hilt of the long blade she had tucked into her waistband.

Lincoln cowered as Daniel stepped between him and the angry woman, hands out to ask her stand down.

"He's the one who helped us escape," Daniel said.

"After turning us in in the first place," Nyx countered. "Ask me, he seems prone to wavering alliances."

"My allegiance is with you," Lincoln stated matter-of-factly. Daniel could sense his fear but was proud to not hear it in his words. "And you'll understand why after I show you what I've learned."

Nyx released the handle of her knife, but kept her shoulders tight, her body poised to pounce.

"Whatever you have to show us can wait," Eurynome growled from the corner of the room. "How the fuck are we supposed to complete the plan when we're now the Colony's Most Wanted?"

Her voice startled Daniel. He had barely heard her speak throughout the entire planning phase they had undergone. Now, the vitriol that laced the voice of the mousy environmental programmer seemed too large for her small, meek frame.

"I ain't living the rest of my life as a fucking fugitive trapped in this sardine can," Typhon agreed. "So we either get out of here, or that brat's gotta pay for getting us into this situation in the first place."

The other gods mumbled in agreement, and Lincoln took a step backwards.

"I'm sorry," he whispered, and then spoke louder, "I'm sorry. I didn't think—"

"No, you didn't," Nyx snarled.

"I thought if the scientists saw that people wanted to leave, that some of us were willing to get out of here, they'd see it as a blessing and let us go. Like they could save the Colony's food production and over-population problem, and we could avoid fucking brainwashing unwilling people in one fell swoop."

"If it had been that easy, don't you think I would have done that? Fuck, the guy you turned us into is my own freaking father. And he threw away the key without batting a single eyelash."

The group turned to see Adrasteia lingering in the doorway. Her face was stern and calm, but not defeated. It sent a wave of hope through the other gods.

"They are not concerned with saving anything other than their feeble hold on power. And the best way for them to do that is to keep us all here, trapped in a maze, where they can keep us quiet and complacent."

"Problem is," Achelous called out at Eurynome's prodding, "our resources are failing. We knew about the food. But the oxygenators are not keeping up. And one of my contacts still on the floor told me one of the water recyclers went completely kaput yesterday. Just done. Gone."

"That makes keeping us all here—alive—less and less practical," Eurynome added.

Lincoln gulped and shook his head. "That's why I asked you to make the call to reconvene. I need to show you Test Lab 4."

He was silent as he checked the hallway to make sure no Guard had rounded the corner, none of the few engineers left working the floor had stepped out for a break and slipped down the corridor to the locked door. He scanned his wrist and entered his unique code before holding the door open and motioning for the group to hurry inside.

The white cube was immaculate. Light seemed to emanate from inside the walls, the ceiling, the floor, as if the room itself contained something holy. Adrasteia knew from experience it was most likely the complete opposite. She stared past her father's tea plants to the white suits hanging like so many wrapped and anointed corpses, then to the modified Haptic Mind Map machine on the opposite side of the room.

"What are we looking at?" Nyx asked, the deep black of her skin glowing with a thousand golden galaxies in the fluorescent light. "I mean, I know what this all is, but give us some context."

"This," Lincoln said as the group spread throughout the room, studying every instrument, every wire and cable, "is Dr. Saito's plan to save the Alphas. Or at least a select few of them."

The programmers studied the sleek lines of the updated Haptic, admiring the craftsmanship even in their horror. Nyx focused on the suits. They were magnificent even if they had been constructed by demons. Lucifer, she told herself, was once an angel.

"They wanted me to program this Haptic to convince people they were happy to stay here and die for the Colony," Lincoln explained. "While those deemed worthy enough escaped with these suits."

"He didn't tell them anything," Daniel said quickly. Despite the betrayal, he still felt the need to defend the kid.

"No. I didn't," Lincoln hurriedly added. "And they're way further away than we were in achieving any results."

"Not judging by these suits," Nyx said. The awe in her voice was tangible. "They are marvelous."

Her fingers traced the tight stitching of a seam, played at the controls on the left arm, toyed with the compact oxygenator built into the back. It was as if they had been culled straight out of her fantasy.

Since entering the room, Hermes had taken a protective stance beside Adrasteia. She stood quietly, unable to hide the worried tilt from her brow. Nyx broke from her trance and turned her attention to their leader, an untrusting squint in her eye.

"So, what you're saying is, the Alphas—lead by her father—had the exact same plan as she did and that's all just some coincidence?"

The fury rose in her voice as she spoke. She took a step toward Adrasteia as Hermes moved between them. Tension filled the room like humidity, and the fluorescents pulsed under its weight. Adrasteia placed a hand on his shoulder and stood her ground.

"It's where I got the idea," she admitted.

"And you didn't think to tell us?"

"Would it have made a difference?"

Nyx stared in astonishment. Her mouth gaped open as she searched for the words.

"Hell yes it would have," Eurynome chimed in, moving to stand at Nyx's side. Others joined her while a few moved to stand by Adrasteia and Hermes. The gods were choosing sides. The Olympians were challenging the Titans.

"You recruited us into something dangerous," Typhon said. "We deserved to know all of the facts."

"You have all the facts now," Echnida countered. "It wouldn't have changed our actions."

"It would have stopped that asshole from turning us in," Nyx said, and Lincoln flushed.

The bickering began in a trickle and then filled the room like a flood. Daniel stepped forward, raising his hands to quiet them all.

"People," he said. "What's done is done. We are where we are. We have to work together now if we're going to make this right."

"I'm not working with someone I can't trust," Nyx said and stormed from the room, Eurynome, Achelous, and Typhon hot on her heels. They were quickly followed by Selene, Theia, and Helios.

"Does she mean me or you?" Lincoln asked, his whisper nearly drowned by their march.

Adrasteia watched them all leave with an inscrutable look on her face. Her head cocked to the side as they disappeared out of site.

"Fuck them," she said. "We can make do without their help. Besides," she turned to Lincoln with a sly smile, "now that you've given us access to this, we don't need them."

She crossed there room confidently and pulled a suit from the rack. She held it against her body as if it were a gown she was selecting for a night out on the town. Casually, she tossed it to the stainless-steel table in the center of the room and grabbed five more.

"We're not leaving them behind," Daniel said firmly.

Adrasteia shrugged. "The suits? No. We're taking those. The rats who jump ship when they get hit by some waves? No, thank you."

"We need Nyx to get us down the chute," Lincoln added.

"All she had to do was open a door," Adrasteia argued. "How hard can it be?"

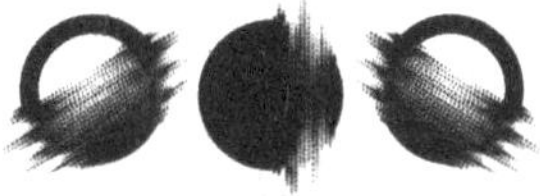

"I'm glad you decided to join us."

Nyx's smile was genuine when Daniel finally found them tucked behind the thick grey curtains of a Neutral Zone booth. He'd been searching for them for hours. He needed to get them and Adrasteia to make up if any of them had a chance of getting out. Opposing factions would only create problems for them all.

The Neutral Zone was nearly abandoned with the citizens of the Colony preparing for the Festival to start in just a few short hours. Without the lively debauchery of its denizens, Daniel found the entirety of it to be rather sad. Suddenly features that had seemed hip and edgy became cobbled together clusters of junk and spare parts. Fabrics were a threadbare stitch away from falling apart; tables a splintered mess held together through spit and wishes alone. It reminded Daniel of the clustered parts of Atlanta which were cut off from the rest of the city by the ever-expanding highways that crisscrossed the land to create pockets of food deserts and disrepair. There, communities were formed and forgotten as buildings succumbed to graffiti and kudzu, broken glass and bated breath. The Neutral Zone told the same tales of the same type of forgotten heartbreak down each clustered and empty aisle.

"I'm actually here to convince you to come back," he said. A direct approach worked best with Nyx. She appreciated honesty.

"Oh, so she sent you." Her voice was calm as if she had expected it, like she had rehearsed her answer several times already in her head, playing out each scenario with a growing hammer of force on her own part.

"No," Daniel admitted. "I'm here on my own because I believe we need to work together to get out of this mess."

Nyx laughed and Typhon answered for the group:

"Fuck that. I'm done cow tailing to some rich kid brat that don't know her asshole from her elbow while she's licking it."

Daniel opened his mouth to respond, but Nyx raised her hand as she finished the last gasps of her chuckle.

"Look, as colorful as his words are, he's right," she said. "Adrasteia is a bored kid playing at revolution to piss off her father. And now the lot of us are fugitives who were already stuck inside a jail to begin with. We either seriously try to escape, or we're toast. And we'd rather work on getting out of here than getting caught up in some teenage rebellion because her daddy loved his lab more than he loved her."

Daniel sighed as he sat, pinching the bridge of his nose. The tension between his eyebrows which he had been blaming on hunger was worsening. The dull ache that lingered there had been joined by a pounding accompaniment, pulsing a 6/8 rhythm with every beat of his heart. It was all too much to take. Weeks of planning only to be thrown into prison. A prison break followed by a disbanding that left no one any closer to any real escape from the Colony. He closed his eyes and breathed deeply.

"She took the suits," he said.

"Idiot!" Achelous groaned. "With those gone, they'll be looking for us."

"They were already looking for us," Selene whispered.

"Just let me be pissed."

"She took thirteen of them," Daniel offered. "Thirteen out of the twenty. One for each of us."

Nyx opened her mouth to respond but paused in consideration. The others in her group were looking at each other. She could see their loyalties realigning in their eyes as they considered the immediacy of the suits, the clean exit they promised, the freedom woven into every stitch. If Adrasteia had considered each of them, Nyx knew they were thinking, grabbed a suit with their name on it even after they had defied her and left, maybe she really was the person to lead them to the ground.

"There are way more than twelve people in this godforsaken place that need to be rescued," Nyx finally said, hoping the altruism of her agenda would win her crew back over. "This has always been bigger than the twelve of us. If she just wants to save her own skin, so be it. But we must be better than that. It may take longer, but some stolen suits to save our own hides are not the answer. Our mission is and always was to save the people here. We must get everyone out."

"But how are we supposed to do that?" Selene asked as Theia adamantly nodded. "All of us are fugitives with no jobs, no money, no food. How are we supposed to live? Let alone gain enough access to support a grand rebellion of the Colony?"

"It doesn't matter how," Typhon countered. "Just that we try. When I joined the Guard, I made a promise to protect the people of Forward Colony 47, not when it was easy or convenient, but when it was necessary.

Well, it's sure as fuck necessary now."

"Typhon's right," Helios said. "We can figure out the how later. This is about right and wrong. And saving our own asses at the expense of others is no better than what the Alphas are trying to do."

Daniel sighed. He knew in his heart they were right. His mind wandered to all the people busy preparing for a festival to forget they were trapped inside a giant steel can in the sky even as they celebrated nine years of it. They were his patients, the smiling faces at the food counters, the masochists searching the Neutral Zone for feeling. They were mothers and brothers and aunts and fathers. They were ignorant sheep whose sense of righteousness had been exploited to get them into the Colony and was being used once more to keep them dumb and moving forward, cogs in a failed experiment while the control group sought, in this case, lower ground.

"We have the suits," Daniel said calmly. "And we're going to use them."

He could see the gears churning in the minds of Nyx's team. Maybe he was getting through. If only a few of them came back, they could encourage the others.

"Even with the suits," Achelous snarled, "you still need us. Me, Nyx, and Eurynome—we're the only Environmental Systems folks in this merry little band. Without us, who's going to figure out the structure for actually living on the surface?"

Daniel shrugged. "We have the suits. And who's to say they'll even be needed once we reach land? And if they are, they buy us time to figure it out. While this Colony slowly suffocates itself."

He wasn't sure if it was a bluff. He knew it's what Adrasteia would have said, but the words felt oily on his tongue. He didn't want to do this without everyone. He didn't want to leave the beginnings of another family behind. He could try to convince Adrasteia to postpone her plan, he thought. But then they would lose the cover of the Festival to mask their escape. He was not sure he was ready to miss another opportunity, let alone what could be their final chance.

"Tell you what," Theia chimed, her voice soft and airy even as the words hissed from her throat, "I ain't no god, and I sure as fuck ain't no martyr. If she got the suits, we got the chance to get out of here. Everybody else can figure it out for themselves just like we did. I ain't looking to die on no cross."

"We have to be better than them," Nyx repeated.

Theia and Eurynome rolled their eyes. Typhon nodded and crossed his arms over his chest, puffing it out and squaring his shoulders behind him. Selene lowered her head. She looked as flustered and afraid as Daniel felt.

"We can't be better than them if we're in jail," Euryonome said.

"Or dying of starvation," Theia added. "Or constantly on the run from the law. Or did you forget that being better than them is what got us here in the first place?"

"Right! Right!" her sister in arms agreed. "Can you imagine it? All of us lurking in the shadows and trying to convince people the big bad government is out to get them in between begging for bit of bread and coffee? Dying slowly of starvation and principle."

"Folks'd look at us like we were crazy. Same way they look at all those hooded crazies Adrasteia keeps in that big group of whiners. Conspiracy theory fuckwads, the lot of them."

Nyx sat and pulled her knees to her chin. She bit her lip as her mind raced, hoping the pain would slow her thoughts to a momentum where she could catch them or at least hop on to see where they went. Daniel watched her eyes slalom through hurdles as she considered the realities of their future. As noble as she wanted to be—as she knew, deep down, they all wished to be—circumstances had pressed their backs against the wall. Maybe saving themselves was the best they could be expected to do.

It broke Daniel's heart, seeing the defeat creep across her features. He knew the feeling all too well, the sacrifice of self for the saving of the very same thing. People were always saving their own skin at the expense of others. It was human nature. Self-preservation was as ingrained as any other instinct. But for those like him, like Nyx, who understood the ramifications, who knew and saw the faces of those they were screwing over when they closed their eyes at night, the succession was unbearable. He took another deep breath that filled the silence of the room and closed his eyes. He searched for the words to make the decision easier for himself, for all of them.

"Paul and Samantha," he said. He opened his eyes to see Nyx and her crew looking at him questioningly. "Those are the names of my husband and my daughter. I don't know if they're dead or alive. I don't know what the hell has happened to the planet out there while all of us were tucked away in the sky feeling like martyrs and nominating ourselves for sainthood. They are the reason I came here. They are who I'm trying to get out of here for. They're the reason I need us to work together to make this happen."

Saying their names aloud suspended the pressure in his brain for a brief moment. It made them real. The lingering fear of loss that had taken residence in the back of his mind vanished. For nine years he had kept them to himself, locked them inside his mind, only interacted with the memories and manifestation of them inside the Haptic. He had wanted to keep them to himself, alive and waiting for him and only him. Now they had re-entered the world. Now, escape was even more urgent.

"We all want out," Selene said. "We all left people behind." She told Daniel of her brother, how he was watching her cats—a tabby and an orange stripe—and how she'd said goodbye to her mother before she'd come up to live there. "She's why I'm here in the first place. Mom's cancer. This position helps pay her medical bills with the money I'm sending down."

Daniel winced as a realization crossed her face.

"No money went down," she said, feeling the truth of it coat her tongue in thick, mossy anger. "We lost contact day one, and they still happily garnered my wages. Goddammit! Fuck all of them."

"I guess if we go down," Nyx considered aloud, her resolves finally shifting, "if we prove the surface is still there and livable, we can somehow get word back to the Colony. That could convince them to let everyone out."

Daniel nodded. Bargaining was an important step on the path to acceptance. He gave her a half smile and patted the back of her hand in encouragement. Her eyes glazed over as she nodded.

"This is not how any of us wanted or expected this to be," he said. "But it's what we have to work with." Nyx nodded her acquiescence. "We should find the others."

Daniel rose to his feet and kept his hand out to help Nyx stand. The others followed suit, Typhon keeping his arms crossed in defiance as he reluctantly joined the crowd.

"Oneiros is keeping them in the labs since they're pretty empty today," he said as they moved toward the front of the booth.

They moved slowly, eyes alert as they looked out for any roving members of the Guard. They were still wanted criminals, even if the Colony was prepping for the largest event of the year. Suddenly, a yell pierced the still air of the Neutral Zone.

"Asclepios! Nyx!"

It was Adrasteia. They exited the rear of the booth and saw her searching and screaming their names. She gave no concern for the Guard. She gave no care to being caught. Something must have been horribly wrong.

Daniel rushed to where she was standing, panting as she caught sight of them. His mind flashed through scenarios, each worse than the last. The suits were duds; the seal on the chutes was impenetrable; the Guard had found the others and was closing in on them all. Adrasteia's eyes watered. Her face flushed with fear, with guilt, as she waited for the entire group to gather near her trembling body.

"It's the Aposts," she panted. "After we got arrested, my merry little band of bitch-and-moaners decided that bitching and moaning wasn't enough anymore."

She looked from face to face, willing their confusion to turn to answers, to solutions for a problem of her own making before she'd even explained.

"Slow down," Nyx said.

"Start from the beginning," Daniel encouraged.

"I left the labs to try to scrounge up some last-minute supplies. I thought we'd need them on the land. That's when Chris Nixon found me."

"Who's Chris Nixon?" Typhon asked.

Adrasteia was scaring them. They had never seen her so visibly shaken. Even at such a young age, her strength and confidence had always been impressive. To see her like this, struggling for her words, quaking in fear and shame, left the rest of them anxious and holding their breath.

"Faun," she said. Daniel remembered the gruff, absent voice of the man who had led the outer group Adrasteia used to disguise those doing the real work in chants during his first meeting. The one where his vision had been obscured by burlap and amusement. It seemed centuries ago.

"Once we got locked up, they decided they needed to take action," she continued. The stress in her voice lingered in the air, thick and heavy, as if it could achieve personhood in their midst. "And they're doing it tonight, during the festival."

Daniel urged her onward. Nyx, wide eyed, grabbed his hand.

"Thirteen explosives," Adrasteia said, the words falling from her lips like atom bombs over Hiroshima. "All set to detonate tonight."

aul stood paralyzed. The world around him, already dark and wild, grew malevolent in its every minute action. The sweet, purple blooms of wisteria withered to dark blood scabs dripping from the vines; wind sawed through the trees, carrying on it swarm clouds of gnats and dirt and death; the cicadas launched into a deafening symphony of screams, lamenting the death throes of the day, a thousand helpless voices being consumed by fire like a choir of lost souls angry at being forgotten.

He had chased her, but she was lost to him. His mind wavered between pursuit and return. He should chase after her. He had to find her. Or he should stay put so that, when she cooled off, she would know where to find him when she decided to return. The world was vast and imposing, spreading out in all directions with the shifting speed of a bullet train. Instead of traveling it, he was tied to the tracks.

"I'm sorry, Paul," Alexander whispered.

The vision of Manta running, of Paul's pursuit haunted him. It was his fault. He wanted to blame his newfound feral nature, but he knew it was his own pettiness that had urged the words from his mouth. And with a ten-year-old girl. How could he have been so cruel to someone who had only known cruelty her entire life. He had haphazardly shoved Paul's belongings back into the rucksack and followed as quickly as he could. Now, he stood four feet from Paul, watching him frozen there with tears spilling silently down his face. The backpack lingered at his feet, sleeping bag and tarp bursting from the unzipped opening as his heart threatened a similar fate for his ribcage.

"How could you do that?" Paul asked. He broke his trance and stared his hollow eyes into Alexander's. His gaze begged for an answer even as his body threatened to attack at the first spoken word. "What the fuck were you thinking?"

"I don't know," Alexander admitted. "I wasn't thinking. I—"

He stuttered as he thought. No response seemed adequate. No answer would come.

"No, you weren't," Paul growled. "And now a ten-year-old is lost in the fucking woods. A child. Out there with wild animals, and cannibals, and slave traders. A fucking ten-year-old."

"She's an exceptional ten-year-old."

Alexander had meant the words to be comforting but regretted them even as they were leaving his throat. The shocked scowl on Paul's face was unbearable.

"What I mean is, she's strong. She knows how to handle herself. And we will find her."

Paul scoffed. Finally, the blood was beginning to return to his feet, to his arms. He could feel it pulsing in his fist and he shook out his hands after thinking better of making contact with Alexander's chin. Remorse coated Alexander's face in a fine silt, the ashen aftermath of a ferocious fire, churned earth finally plowed and ready to be sewn.

Paul crumpled in on himself, but he held onto his fuse. He needed that flame, that explosion of adrenaline, to power through the night ahead.

"You're damn right, we will," he vowed aloud to find her before either of them slept.

Thick tendrils of vines adorned with fat; cupped leaves parted as she leapt fiercely through the wood. It felt like freedom, the reckless abandon with which she cascaded over fallen logs or barreled around azaleas thick with starburst petals. Her feet, alternating with the swiftness of thought, barely touched the ground before rising again to propel her forward. She felt lithe and magical, like the doe she would sometimes catch foraging through the tall grasses at the edge of the clearing around her childhood home. The cabin seemed so far away; a hazy memory dreamed up to reconcile pieces of the past she was fleeing. She wondered if it had been real at all.

The trees broke suddenly into a cleared path that stretched, wide and long, to her left and right, and Manta skidded to a stop. Though broken and crumbling and covered over with vining plants—ivy and kudzu and crabgrass—she could feel the hard thud of the asphalt that had once made the road. The wood behind her was quiet, still reeling from the laceration she had made when she cut through so suddenly. The creatures had fled from her warpath. Her father had given up his pursuit. She was alone.

She pushed down the slight whimper of fear, of regret, that fluttered in her throat. *Alexander was wrong*, she told herself. She convinced herself, through sheer will and stubbornness, that Paul was too. Daddy Daniel would come back for her. And if they didn't believe it was possible, she would just have to find him herself.

Night had almost grown to cover the land, but a few orange and pink waves still coated the western sky. She took one last look behind her and pointed her body south. Staying a few feet out from the tree line, she followed the road, just out of reach of any prying creatures that could grab her from the shadows yet close enough to dive into their cover if she was spotted in the clearing. A few rusted automobiles, like the one Paul had owned when she was a child before they'd pushed it away from the cabin on its frayed rubber wheels in hopes of throwing off passersby who may see it as a sign of life, were busy succumbing to the elements as nature reclaimed their materials. Most of the vehicles had made it farther inland, away from the aftermath of the Wave, before the gasoline pumps had run dry and the charging stations had shorted out. She wondered what traveling in one would have been like: a ferocious rumbling, like the kind the generator made when they wound and fired it at the cabin, echoing all around her, vibrating up through her body as the wind whipped at her face with such exotic force she felt like she was flying. Did the freedom of forward momentum outweigh the forgotten facets of nature? Did the beauty of speed make the lost beauty of the trees and the animals worthwhile?

Metal posts rusted beneath the clinging roots of plants pulling them back toward the earth. They featured words designating directions to cities which no longer existed; ghost towns like tombstones to mark the failed idea of civilization. They proclaimed maximum speeds to establish control and minimum speeds to keep progress moving swiftly in the face of the natural world. As the darkness grew, the signposts becoming more menacing in the distance, like scarecrows dotting her path. Figures that may have been human—or worse yet, not—beckoned her forward to the unknown.

She walked until she was too tired to think anymore of the dangers of sleeping alone. The weather-beaten backseat of an old sedan looked inviting through the rear window, like it could support her in sudden, untold comforts, like the steel frame of the car could protect her from everything that was past. And she slept, a fitful dream of Daniel's return regaling her until morning.

"I think she would have turned south here," Paul said.

They had walked for hours, the night wood thick around them as they searched for the broken twigs and footfalls left in Manta's path. Though

Paul had garnered his fair share of tracking and hunting skills in the time since the Wave, it was Alexander's survival in the wilderness that had really come in handy. He was the one to first spot the wake of Manta's escape. He had measured her gait and speed and each zig and zag she had taken. He hoped it would be enough to make up for what he had done.

When they came to the old highway, he could feel in his gut they were getting closer. He wanted to find her as much as Paul did, not only to assuage the guilt that was burning through his stomach like western wildfires, but to tell her he was wrong. From what he knew of Daniel, the man—if he were somehow safe and alive in the Colony, and who was he to say he wasn't—would stop at nothing to be reunited with Paul, and that same care and devotion would have no doubt passed to Manta. He was wrong for saying otherwise, particularly in a world where hope was a fleeting commodity, a quick-blooming daylily replaced in mere hours by perseverance. He saw the passion which raged in Paul's eyes as they searched. He knew, if Daniel were alive, he would stop at nothing to return to his daughter's side.

He scanned the tree line opposite to where they had exited from the path cut through to the road. There was no sign of her having re-entered the forest. No disheveled vines or flattened earth to follow. Even as the forest regained its ground behind them, slithering in quickly to clot the wound of their pass, he knew Manta had turned to the asphalt.

"She's still headed to the ocean," he agreed.

Paul fished the compass from his bag on Alexander's back and found their direction. He swallowed his fatigue and walked on.

Morning brought with it a strange new world. The dawn chorus of wrens and warblers lulled Manta from her timid slumber. She yawned, stretching her arms toward the lush greenery that had seemed so imposing the night before. The backseat of the car had still been surprisingly soft beneath the withered vegetation that had sprung up from the cracks in the fabric. She peaked out throughout the open window and watched the morning birds soar their great and heaving swoops through the air, ecstatic in the new warmth of sun before it became too overbearing in its march across the sky. They didn't seem to mind the world had ended. Instead they relished in what it had become, circling the bounty of reclaimed nature with sharp eyes and euphoric song. They understood rebirth in a way humanity never could.

As her eyes searched the skyline, she saw something new. No longer clouded in darkness, a large steel circle loomed above the trees, resting against the clouds as if it belonged there with them, as if it had been there all along. The rust-dotted metal featured bucket seats hanging from its spoked posts. Paint in bright, primary colors peels away in places to reveal a thin layer of earthy henna which only made the reds and greens, the yellows and blues look more extravagant, more inviting.

Manta took a sip of water from her canteen and poured a small amount into her cupped hand to wipe the grime of the night away from her face. In the clear light of day, her flight seemed rather foolish. She considered retracing her steps, moving backwards until she found her father who was no doubt searching frantically. A glint of sadness flecked the outer rim of her thoughts, but she pictured Alexander to push it aside. Alexander: that asshole so very desperate to find family, he was willing to destroy her own. Alexander: the idiot who didn't believe in miracles. True, she had not experienced much of the world away from the safety of her cabin, and what she had seen was harsh and unrelenting, and Alexander had survived that, alone, for nearly as long as she'd been alive; but that was still no reason to tell her her father was gone and never to return. She shook away the thoughts. Sympathy was too painful to reflect upon. Besides, the colors of the Ferris wheel were calling to her, a miracle of the sky and what human ingenuity had once accomplished. A bright inviting starting point in her ascent to Daniel.

She tossed her bag in first and then peeled back the chain link gate to slip inside the fairgrounds. Though derelict and overgrown, what stood before her was wondrous. An elevated ring was amassed with miniature versions of the vehicles that had lined the road, with tiny steering wheels centered in their open cavities and weathered rubber surrounding them. Wooden booths were splattered with peeling paints that promised ""Fantastic Prizes"" and ""Family Fun,"" and clowns with white faces and red noses to match their frizzy hair held up gloved fingers to pat the heads of children who stood on tippy toes attempting to gain access to the rides behind them.

She had never seen a fair, but she had read of them in Daniel's books. The stories had been so vivid, she could see the families of freaks erecting tents to perform feats of divine purpose with swinging ropes or flaming hoops, and lions and elephants, and conjoined twins at pianos. She imagined the astonishment alight in all the children's eyes as they scurried between attractions, experiencing what could only be true joy in place of mere survival while they tossed rings at tilted bottle tops, played huntress by shooting metallic fowl for toys instead of food, and swung mallets not to fix their floorboards but to simply test their strength. Weather worn stuffed animals hung inside the booths and she pictured them in their heyday, bright and fluffy and stuffed to the gills with triumph and fantasy.

She pictured herself among the children playing as she explored the tiny buildings which dotted the vast field. Each was a time capsule, a treasure chest. She found plastic bottles of water, glass bottles with orange and purple liquids inside barely bleached by the sun, aluminum cans of sodas whose undersides were still a bright and beautiful red where they had sat in shadows. She pulled the circular tab on a can toward her and startled as the whoosh of air equalized in her hands. The warm liquid met her tongue with an exotic sweetness, thick, like maple syrup, and coated her throat as it washed its way down. She had never tasted anything like it and wondered at the magical potions once made for children as she shoved more cans into her bag.

Another booth was filled with chests of long cardboard tubes. The ones not damaged by water were decorated in exploding neon colors that offered magic unclouded by the smaller warnings printed in faint lettering. They had names like "Magical Barrage" and "Sparkler" and "Saturn Missile" and "Bottle Rocket." They were warning flares meant for fun over function, and Manta smiled as she shoved as many as would fit inside her bag atop the cans of soda. They would come in handy, she thought, if her bow ever failed her. But better yet, they were hers, something from the Before she could hold onto until she held her father's hand.

She spent hours exploring the grounds, drinking sodas until her teeth hurt, and her stomach ached, and a nervous tingle pulsed through her arms. She stood on splintered floorboards pretending she was a carnie. She jumped up and down on foot-packed gravel pretending she was a little girl. She had never felt such freedom. Sure, she had imagined it when she lost herself in her father's books, but even the so-called "playing" with Chrissy had been more of a chore, her soul purpose to be the entertainment for a bored and lonely woman stuck forever in pre-pubescence instead of actually experiencing and participating in the wonder. There was so much to see, so many surprises to get lost in. She barely noticed the sun's saunter across the sky as she indulged in the childhood she had been denied. Now, evening was pressing into the humidity, sending the thick, unseen moisture away to even warmer climes. It didn't matter though, she thought. The texture of joy permeated the past left stagnant all around her. She thought she could live at the fair forever.

"Manta!"

She recognized her father's voice break through her daydream. Her heartbeat quickly as it was joined by Alexander's.

"She's got to be here. Don't worry, Paul. We'll find her."

But she wasn't ready to be found. She slung her bag over her shoulders and grasped to find her grip, pulling herself slowly up the cross spokes of the Ferris wheel.

"See? This is what you get when you entertain people's fantasies. A bunch of conspiracy theorists ready to blow up the world for a cause they've convinced themselves to be true."

Nyx grumbled as she paced the room. She wasn't happy, but at least all the gods had reconvened. If this was their new reality, they would do better to face it together.

"We've got the suits," Hermes said firmly. His thick, golden muscles twitched as he instinctively flexed with his words. "We should just leave and let them burn."

Daniel glanced at Lincoln's worried expression. The boy's brown eyes carried more weight than he should have to carry.

"We can't do that," he said. "There are too many innocents here."

"Do you have a better idea?" Eurynome asked.

Silence struck the room in violent absence. No one wanted to risk their final chance at escape, even if it meant saving the others trapped inside the Colony. At least not anymore, not with the added variable of revolt. But no one wanted to feel responsible for knowing what was about to happen and doing nothing stop it. Nyx wiped her eyes as if it could force a thought, any solution to appear before her.

"Can you just try talking to them, Adrasteia? Convince them this is the wrong thing to do?"

"I tried. They're not listening. This is beyond me now. I think it's gone beyond any single one of them."

"Mob mentality has taken hold," Daniel said. "Even if we convince one or two of them to back down—or, at the very least, postpone—there's fifty more with the means and the knowhow to execute the plan."

"Exactly." Adrasteia nodded.

Her voice was laced with insecurity. It troubled Daniel to see the assertive young woman so at a loss.

"So we warn the Guard," Theia suggested. "Let them do their actual jobs while we get to work to get our asses out of here."

"And which one of us gets captured to deliver that message?" Achelous asked, and Theia sank back into her seat. "No offense, but a bomb threat warning from a bunch of escaped convicts ain't going over well."

"Exactly. I tried that already anyway," Hermes admitted. "With someone I knew wouldn't turn me in. She thought I was lying to take the heat off the rest of us. Building up our story about the danger inside to recruit more people to our cause. I don't know what the Alphas told the Guard, or what they promised to commanders to keep them in line, but we're on our own on this one."

"We have no choice then," Daniel said. "We split into teams. Half of us take the suits to the bottom floor and work on releasing the seal. The rest of us find and dismantle the bombs. Get as many as we can before we reconvene below. Do we know where they are?"

"They're targeting the Alphas," Adrasteia said. "I doubt they'd rig up any of the Sub levels. So Alpha2 and 3, where the Festival gatherings are, those are our best bets."

"I'm guessing they'd want to avoid as many Sub casualties as possible," Selene offered. "So they'd place them near the speaking podiums where the mayor and other officials would be."

"Right where the Guard presence will be the strongest," Typhon sighed.

"More than likely," Adrasteia said. "They want chaos. The want to spur an uprising. And for that, they'll need people on their side. People left with no other choice. So they'll avoid the more populated places to focus on destroying equipment. Use that to force action. Let the fear of another attack force a change in policy."

"They're scared," Lincoln agreed, "but I don't think they're monsters just yet. They feel backed into a corner and are just trying to get attention."

Daniel knew Lincoln's own guilt was adding to his assessment, but it made sense.

"So we search the labs first," he said.

Adrasteia nodded. "Yeah. Chris—Faun was a harvester on Alpha2. He'd have access."

"I'll help with the bombs," Nyx said, the determination she usually carried suddenly returning to her voice. It wasn't a great plan, but it would have to do.

"No," Selene countered. "We need you working on getting us the fuck out of here. I'll join the bomb squad."

"Do we even know how to dismantle them?" Typhon asked.

"We'll have to figure it out when we see them," Echnida sighed.

A quiet resolve was overtaking the gods. The path they had set in motion was coming to a head. They had no choice but to see it through.

"So we take care of the bombs and then meet at the northwestern chute," Daniel said.

"And by sunrise," Adrasteia added, hoping to give even a faint glimmer of hope to the thirteen of them, herself included, "our feet find land."

"Go away!" Manta belted. She clutched the cross bar and settled back into the plastic seat as the capsule she was in creaked and rocked on the beam above it. She was near the apex of the circle. The world spread out, vast and small, before her. She felt like a god, omniscient and able to see everything for miles. Her eyes caught the sudden break in the trees, and, beyond that, the rhythmic pulsing of water arching toward land. She wanted to get lost in it, but the men below her were more important now.

"Manta, I'm sorry," Alexander called up to her. Fear and sincerity tinged his voice as he strained his head back to look up at her silhouette against the slowly darkening sky.

"Come down! It's not safe up there!" Paul added. The relief he'd felt in finding her had been quickly replaced with a growing anguish as he watched her climbing ricochet through the crossbeams of the rickety old ride.

"Leave me alone!" Manta cried.

The men paced around the base of the wheel. Rust had bolted it into place, but also threatened to release it at any moment. The girl's added weight caused the metal to shift and recalibrate, groaning as it faced its first audience in almost a decade. A fall would be catastrophic.

"I never should have said that about Daniel," Alexander admitted. He hoped his words were reaching her. He wished that she was willing to listen. "When you ran off, the determination in your father's eyes to find you— That showed me Daniel would do the same. I know he will. He is."

It was an empty acquiescence that did not change the truth in the rest of his revelation. If Daniel was in the Colony, if the Colony had been swallowed by the ocean, he may never make it back to her, no matter how determined he was. Manta pulled her bag close to her and closed in on herself in the middle of the bucket seat. Deep down, she was glad they had found her, but she wasn't ready to forgive either of them yet.

"I'm going up there," Paul gulped. He reached out a hand to test the integrity of the bars against his grip.

"It's not safe, Paul," Alexander warned. "It's unsteady enough as it is. Your weight could bring it down. Look, she has to come down eventually. It's safer to let her come to us."

"I'm not leaving her up there alone."

Paul pulled himself onto the first line of spokes. He clung tightly as he felt a slight lurch in the wheel, but it remained tall and upright. Another bar, then another. He refused to look down as he ascended higher toward his brave, scared little girl.

Manta shifted to the corner of the car as he pulled himself in with her. Her brow was furrowed but he could see the relief beneath her anger. He settled himself in beside her and turned his attention to the darkening landscape before them. He had been in this same spot once before, long before the Wave. He remembered the joy of seeing the manmade skylines piercing into the sky like testaments to the permanence of mankind. Now, the buildings were replaced by the rolling green of treetops and, in the distance, the gentle swell of the new ocean. What he had thought as beautiful before now seemed horrific compared to the magnificent landscape before him.

"Mind if I sit here?" he asked, an awkward, thin smile pulled across his lips.

Manta huffed in response and pulled her bag closer to her body like a security blanket. But she was glad he was there.

"I used to come here when I was a kid," Paul said. "My mom and stepdad would bring us every summer before it got too hot to bear. They'd buy us each thirty tickets and let us run free to see how many prizes we could win. My sister—the one you're named for—and my little brother made it a competition. The size and shape of the prizes added points, but you could still win with a trove of pencil erasers or little monster finger puppets."

Manta relaxed a little as Paul spoke. He could sense the tension leaving her body.

"I never really played the games though," he continued. "I thought they were all rigged to make sure you won the crappy things you'd lose in the backseat before you even made it home instead of the giant stuffed unicorns. But I loved this Ferris wheel."

Manta almost smiled but caught herself. Paul smiled for her and placed a gentle hand on her knee.

"I'd ride it over and over, around and around. And they'd always stop it when I was at the top like this so I could look out and see how big the world really was. And how small my place was in it."

"It's really beautiful," Manta whispered and Paul's smile grew. "I wish I could have seen it in the Before."

"Somehow it's better now. Despite the shit that's worse," he said. "Back then, seeing it all from up here, realizing how massive it all is, and how limited my experience of it had been, that just made me feel even more important. Like this whole world was trusted to me, and I had to do my best to keep it beautiful. So that one day I could see it all."

"Did you get to?"

"In a way," he said as he moved his arm to envelop her shoulders, and Manta leaned her weight into his side. He squeezed her arm as the last of the tension left her body, and they stared out at the final kaleidoscopic bursts of the sunset. They watched as the nocturnal birds took flight, guided by the first stars that twinkled in the navy sky.

"I think that's what Daniel felt when he chose to go up to the Colony," Paul said. "It's what I was feeling. We wanted to make sure the world stayed beautiful for you. We'd spent so long fucking it up, and now we had this tiny, magical life to care for. And she deserved to see the whole of it. Every single inch it had to offer. All the things that living in it had made us take for granted."

Manta frowned. Paul had long ago explained the night when Daniel was taken to the Colony. How they were supposed to be with him, but it had all happened so quickly, they were left behind. She understood it, but it still hurt. She'd, for the most part, learned to box up that feeling of abandonment inside the glory of her vision of Daniel, but every now and then it crept through.

"Do you think he'll ever come back?" she asked.

"I do," Paul said, and she believed him.

He shifted his attention to the south and studied the night sky until he found it.

"Do you see that there?" he asked, guiding her eyes over her left shoulder. "That dark spot between the stars?"

Manta turned and found it. There, between the great swaths of white speckled light was an emptiness, like the sky had forgotten itself for a moment. A temporary eclipse in the wonder of the universe.

"That's the Colony," Paul said. "That's where your father is right now. Dreaming of you. Counting the days until he can come back down."

Manta focused on the blackness. She wished on it like it was a shooting star. She hoped Daniel knew she was down there, looking up at him, wishing they were together. She wanted him to know, even though years had passed between them, she knew him, and she loved him, and she was waiting to welcome him home.

"What's that?" Manta asked, and Paul squinted into the sky.

Suddenly, a tiny red spark ignited in the darkness, billowing out to a glorious orange and yellow, small, and contained by the distance. And then another. And another. They looked like fireworks in the deep distance, but Paul knew they were explosions. He held his breath. The Colony was being destroyed.

"Let's go," Paul commanded, and Manta followed him carefully from the Ferris wheel car back to stable land.

hree.

Daniel thought he'd heard three explosions, though it could have been more. Their echoes had reverberated through Alpha2, almost drowning out the panicked screams of the masses gathered and watching the animated fireworks on the screens of the floor's concert gathering hall. Safety protocols were triggered automatically with the first blast. Great steel doors descended to seal off rooms. A feminine, robotic voice belted instructions blandly, urging people to remain calm and make their way to their living quarters swiftly and safely. A second electronic voice informed them all that Alpha Levels 2 and 3 were not safe and would be sealed off from the rest of the Colony between a numerical ticking that moved in seconds instead of minutes.

He assumed the rumble of the blast had knocked him to the floor, though he had not felt himself fall. Slowly, the impact of the tile crept into the muscles of his back, lodge itself into his bones and sent his head throbbing as he moved to sit up. It took him several seconds to remember where he was and why he was there.

"The outer walls of Alpha Levels 2 and 3 have been compromised," the robotic voice called calmly through the intercoms. "Please make your way to your living quarters safely and swiftly."

He had heard three explosions. That meant his team had managed to disarm ten of the Aposts' bombs. Though victory was all or nothing, the thrashing beat in his head told him.

"Alpha Levels 2 and 3 will be sealed in forty-two seconds," the announcement warned. "Please make your way to your living quarters safely and swiftly."

His ankle throbbed as he pulled himself up to his elbows to find a large metal case covering his right leg. He pressed it with his palms and heaved, but it would not budge. It was lodged under other debris. He was trapped.

"Alpha Levels 2 and 3 will be sealed in twenty-eight seconds. Please make your way…"

Daniel let his head hit the floor. He listened carefully. The passageway outside the room that trapped him sounded deserted. The screams were now mere echoes in his memory, lingering auditory hallucinations carried on the gentle whoosh of the room's oxygenator unit.

"In here!" he called out. His voice was hoarse, his throat etched in pain, but he wasn't sure why. Had he been screaming already? He couldn't remember. "Anyone?"

Only the pre-recorded voice answered him:

"Alpha Levels 2 and 3 will be sealed in thirteen seconds."

Daniel closed his eyes. Once the floors were sealed, all environmental systems would be shut off, their power diverted to other floors to keep the citizens alive. He pulled once more at his leg. It would not come free, but he could bend his ankle. At least it wasn't broken.

"Alpha Levels 2 and 3 will be sealed in four seconds."

Not that it mattered. He could already hear the oxygenators winding down as energy was moved elsewhere. Where it could keep people alive. People who were where they were supposed to be. Not him though.

"Alpha Levels 2 and 3 will—"

The announcement cut off. Lights flickered their last bit of light, and the sudden black highlighted the dust still floating in the air like ash, like fury. He tried to take shallow breaths, to breathe gently, to conserve as much oxygen as he could. At least the room was sealed. That would help for a little while. At least his final moments wouldn't be the burning from the inside out he'd have experienced from the sudden influx of ozone into his lungs. There was that to be thankful for.

His eyelids were becoming heavy as the flow of air from the oxygenator ceased. The silence left behind in the wake of its gentle hum was deafening. He closed his eyes and thought of Paul and Samantha. He imagined them on the land, looking up toward the sky, and thinking of him. Knowing he loved them and forever happily oblivious to his fate.

He was a god now. Adrasteia had willed it so. As a god, his dying breath would form a great constellation—a warrior in the sky to watch his daughter and his husband and guide them safely through their dreams each night.

Dreams. Now there was a pleasant escape. In his dreams, he could be with the people he loved, the people he was always meant to be with. The souls he had carried with him for nine long years.

Samantha was all grown up now. She was smiling, and opening her arms, and welcoming him into her tight yet gentle embrace. Paul had tears in his eyes when they kissed again. The feeling of his lips, sharp and electric, sent shocks waves through his chest, bolts of electricity like the advent of new life. Stars were forming. His family had been waiting for so long for him to return and make it whole. He was ready to feel their embrace once again.

He closed his eyes.

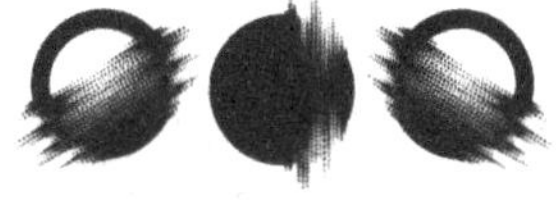

"What do you think that was?" Manta asked. "For real?"

Paul had tried to convince her that everything was alright, but she didn't believe him. She knew he didn't want her to worry as they marched through the night toward the shoreline. His words may have been gentle, but his actions told a different tale. He had not even wanted to sleep. He simply charged ahead, a newfound focus only sharpened by fatigue, as if making it to the ocean could somehow make everything okay. Though Manta didn't see how. She knew those were explosions. And explosions ten miles off the ground could only mean a sudden, inescapable death. But maybe—maybe the colony had already descended, the collapse of the structure a final farewell to the place that had kept them alive but apart from actual living. Maybe her father was waiting where the ocean met the shore, arms wide and ready for embrace.

Paul kept his gait and did not answer, but the shame and pity in Alexander's eyes told her her worst fears were coming true. It was odd: the notion of not getting to meet Daniel, at least not while she was cognizant of who she was, had been so distressing the night before. Now, when faced with its very real possibility, when it had become visible and solid right before her own eyes, even if the distant flames were but a silent spark, a calmness overtook her body. She was sad, yes, but she heaved a relieved sigh as all the weight she had carried in anticipation of a reunion left her body. Rationale swirled in to fill the hole it had left, pushing aside the fear and despondency that had attempted to pool there in the melted icecaps of fantasy.

As Paul took the lead, Alexander matched his pace with Manta's. He held his arms like wings, bent at the elbows and clutching the straps of Paul's bag that was still on his back. He opened his mouth to speak and thought better of it—again and again—until his gaping lips seemed as much a part of their progress as the hard and sudden footfalls of Paul's ravaged boots.

Manta searched the sky anytime it appeared between the gaps of leaves in the canopy but was met with only the pinpricks of stars which dotted the growing night. They told the stories of gods—ripe with betrayal and ascendance—but nothing about her father or his fate. If he had died, she thought, at least he was already up there, close to where it all began in stardust and where it would all end again in silence. She wondered if she'd be able to pick out his soul from the thousands left twinkling through the galaxy.

"I'm sorry, Manta," Alexander finally said. The words rushed from his mouth in a whisper, as if it were all he could manage, as if even that took great force.

Hearing the words made it all somehow more real, but she fought the urge to hold it against the man. He was trying, she knew, and he was just as lost as she was.

"Do you think he's dead?" she asked. Her words were blunt, matter of fact. They almost sounded callous, and she tried to soften the rigor mortis that had set into her jaw.

"I don't know," Alexander stuttered. "That was a big explosion if we could see it from here."

"He's not dead."

Paul did not stop moving as he called back to them. His attention was focused on an ever-shifting goal, drawing them all toward the crashing waves of the ocean. Toward renewal. If the Colony had blown, he thought, surely, they had evacuated the people beforehand. He had to reach the shore. He had to be there when Daniel reached the ground. He had to know he was safe.

Manta could see the tension in the back of Paul's neck. It pulsed, pink and veiny, as his body strained to keep its pace while it batted at the emotions swirling around him. She felt helpless as she tried to make room for his grief, as she reached out to battle the shadows she couldn't touch. She was glad she couldn't see his face. If she did, she knew the threads of truth that were holding her heart together would break their stitches, and they would both fall apart.

She turned her attention to Alexander. He had kept his pace with her the entire last hour of their journey, although she could tell he wanted to burst forth to comfort her father. His legs were shaking with each step, fatigue making his muscles tremble, but his footfalls did not falter. Her gaze moved up his slender frame to meet his eyes. Filled with agony and a feral desire to console, they watered as they shifted to meet her view.

Maybe Alexander wasn't so bad. She tried to imagine him before the Wave, more like her father, but without the whetted edges the modern world had cut into him. He had known Daniel too. All of them—Paul, Alexander, and Daniel—had been friends. And whereas Paul and Manta had each other, Alexander had had no one. He had lost himself to the savagery of the world, its brutal and honest virtue, its twisted new take on humanity, and was only just beginning to remember who he was. Even amid all of that, she could see his pain was more for them than for himself.

"Help him," she whispered, and his lips trembled.

"How?"

Manta grimaced. She wasn't sure. And though she wanted to be the one by his side, she couldn't bear the look in her father's eyes as he came to terms with Daniel's death. She, herself, had only accepted it abstractly. It was a phrase, a notion, for someone else to consider. Not a reality. All she felt was numbness. She didn't know if her feet were actually touching the ground.

Suddenly, Paul screamed: a guttural, primal noise arched from the whole of his being unable to any longer be contained. He stopped his march and leaned against a great oak tree, facing it with his head low, his arm raised above his head and pressed hard against the craggy bark. His knuckles were red, and a tiny estuary of blood flowed from between his ring and middle fingers. He had punched the tree, but that was not why he was sobbing.

Manta and Alexander rushed forward. Manta flung her arms around her father's waist. Her face felt wet. She was crying too. Maybe she had been crying all along. She couldn't really be sure. But she knew her eyes hurt, and her throat was dry, and her lips tasted of salt and misery. Alexander stood by awkwardly. He wanted to reach out, to join the embrace, but he left that to the family.

"I don't know what to do," Paul gasped. The breaks in his voice made Manta squeeze him even harder. She appreciated the heft of his arms draped over her shoulders.

"Do you want hope or acceptance?" Alexander asked, as steadily as he could manage. He wanted to sound strong, sound brave. If he wasn't truly family, he needed to be their crutch.

"Neither," Paul said. "Not right now."

Manta swallowed hard. Everything inside her seemed to quake, to push at her bones and her skin, begging to be as far away from the pain as possible. She felt every sensation individually, as if it were all that mattered in that moment until she felt nothing at all.

"Then we just move forward," Alexander said. His voice cracked as he spoke, but it imbued Paul with strength as he nodded.

Maybe he wasn't so bad after all. Manta reached a hand out to him, took his, and pulled him closer.

His body was burning. He was on fire. Or already plunged into the pits of hell for his sins. It had started in his lungs, slow and simmering and impressive in its ignition, but it was now everywhere, like his body was kindling meant to go up quick. The martyrdom of gods. His eyes still closed, he listened to the fire as it clanged all around him. It sounded metallic as it consumed him. He had not thought a fire would sound like that when it was so nearby. There was so much he hadn't known.

He thought he heard voices yelling, "He's in here!" No doubt his demons, hot on his trail, ready, finally, to punish him after decades of careful planning. They would flash his life before his eyes, remind him of all the wrong he'd done, never let him forget.

Daniel tried to think about something else, anything else. He tried to will his own version of memory to click on like an old movie projector so he could recall the better times instead of the hell he was left to endure. His third date with Paul, the one where he knew he was done searching, when he'd ordered an elaborate meal personally prepared by one of Atlanta's premiere chefs, but then Paul had shown up with a fast-food bag of burgers and French fries. The thick heat of Ethiopia as they barreled down a dirt road in an open jeep, sand and dust swirling behind their sunglasses and into their eyes, but neither he nor Paul willing to close them. And then, arriving there, at that corrugated steel building, the one cobbled together with planks of wood and rusted nails. And all of it looking so very beautiful but also like nothing at all when compared to the little baby girl they were presented with.

"Samantha," Daniel whispered. He coated her name through the dryness of his throat, around the torture that waited. He wanted her name to be free. He wanted a final act of wonder before the fires consumed him completely.

His eyes fluttered open to see her face smiling down at him. She was older now, older than she should have been, and her grin was shielded from his fire behind a pane of glass, haloed in white like the angel she was. She was pushing the cabinet from his leg. She was holding a mask and thin metal tube. She was reaching down to pull him into her.

The trees grew sparse as they neared the coastline. A faint hint of saline and sulphur filled the air, carried atop a somehow pleasant scent of decay. Manta heard it before she saw it. Like a deafening whisper folding in on itself, regenerating in a constant cycle, the ocean spread out before her, clashing against a bed of sunbaked clay and stone. The rocky coast expanded for miles in either direction, licked by rolling waters that seemed to be breathing, heaving their force against the shore as if they themselves could resuscitate life from the land. Offer it another chance to get things right. The rising sun ignited the water to a prismatic wonderland, the waves sending dancing peaks of reds and yellows and blues arching toward the heavens and releasing every ounce of color in the world. This was where it all came from. Everything before, she realized, had been muted and lost.

It was devastatingly beautiful, Paul thought, standing there peering out at what had once been his hometown. Atlanta peeked in the distant waters, a coral reef of skyscrapers, as other parts of the city—broken asphalt and concrete—were smoothed and rounded and washed ashore, leaving the remnants of the City in the Forest to line the thick, frothing sea with stone.

Alexander shifted down the embankment and held a shiny ball of black tarmac in his hands. Like an iridescent pearl, the oily surface glistened in a rainbow smile.

"It's like Peachtree Street decided to go on forever," he laughed.

Paul felt a slight smile curve the edges of his mouth. It felt odd there, like it wasn't allowed. His eyes were set on the horizon where the first of the four massive stilts that held up the Colony plunged deep below the surface, stretched upwards to the gods. It was large and imposing, shooting out from the crashing waters like Venus on her half shell, an obelisk left as a testament to mankind's attempt at salvation. But there were no people; there was no exodus of those who had sacrificed so much to try to save the world. Not one single soul exited the ark for the dry mountains of Ararat. He felt his chest fall as Manta's hand slipped into his. Her touch centered him in reality, gave him love and warmth and light, reminding him it could remain when all else was lost.

"It's wonderful," she whispered. "It makes me think that somehow everything is going to be okay."

"It will be, baby girl," Paul smiled. "I'm sorry. Manta."

Her own smile widened as she looked him in the eye.

"Baby girl is fine," she said.

Together they walked to where the water met the land. There was sadness still. But this strange new shore offered renewal. It pulsed like blood. It said everything would be okay, somehow.

She kicked off her shoes and played at the ebb and flow, jumping back and forth as she discovered the courage she needed to dip her toes into the white, popping bubbles which formed with each whoosh in her direction. Paul and Alexander joined her, and the sound of laughter on the waves hit them like the forgotten lyrics to their favorite song. They splashed, and they played, and Paul kept one eye on the monolithic shaft perched eight miles toward the horizon.

By nightfall, Manta was wide awake. They had taken turns napping throughout the day, recovering from the long journey that had led them there. The ocean spray fought back the humidity and Alexander built a small fire to keep them warm and roast the rabbit he and Manta had hunted for their dinner. Manta fished through her rucksack, setting aside the handfuls of fireworks she had taken from the fairgrounds and pulling out a can of Coca-Cola for each of them. She looked up at the empty spot in the night sky. It was larger there than it had been on the Ferris wheel. The stars around it looked like a halo.

"I'm sorry Daddy Daniel won't be back," she said. "But it's kind of like he's up there watching over us. Like he's making sure we're gonna be okay."

Paul fought the tears from his eyes and forced a smile.

"You know," Alexander said, patting Manta's knee with a warm firm hand as he spoke, "before the Wave, we had a tradition of honoring those we lost. A ritual to remind us of who they were, to celebrate what they meant to us."

"Like a funeral?" she asked.

"Sometimes. Yes. Other times it was people telling stories or lighting candles in their honor. As big or as small as was necessary." Alexander looked at Paul's distant gaze. "It was a way for those left behind to remember what they had. To focus on why those people had meant so much to them. Everything their presence had done for the living instead of just feeling their absence. It was to keep them here. And to let them go."

Manta nodded. She leaned in and kissed her father's shoulder then turned her attention to the pile of fireworks beside her bag.

"I don't have any candles," she said, "but could we use these?"

Alexander looked to Paul for an answer, for guidance. His eyes were as wet as the ocean as he looked to his daughter, to his friend.

"Those are perfect," he whispered softly.

Alexander helped Manta place the fireworks along the craggy shore about six yards from their fire. They used the rocks to create stands that would, hopefully, send the rockets into the sky to burst above the water. He lit the ends of two long twigs, and they rushed to ignite the fuses before running back to join Paul and watch. The first fuse met the gunpowder and fizzled to nothing. But the second, and then the third shot off, exploding is brilliant rays of gold and garnet in the sky.

"To Daniel," Paul whispered.

"To Dad," Manta said.

Alexander watched the last fading ember of the fireworks drift to extinguish in the water. He looked into the distant eyes of his companions as they struggled to hold onto the last bits of fire in their souls.

"So, I remember this one time when Daniel got trapped in the elevator on his way to meet us all for dinner. His cell phone had no signal and none of us could reach him, so we just started eating and pretending he was there, and letting whole gaps in the conversation fall silent like we could hear him responding. He'd missed the whole first course and then just sailed in smiling, but I could tell he was madder than a wet hen underneath it all."

Paul smiled, and Manta leaned into the crook of his arm.

"But that's who Daniel was. Who he is," Alexander continued. "Brave and smiling even when he wanted to scream. That's one of the many things I learned from him, I think. How to be in the moment and move forward even when things aren't going as planned."

Paul closed his eyes and leaned back into the night.

e could stay here, you know?"

Paul squinted into the hot afternoon sun. The glowing yellow orb offered a stark contrast to the gentle blue of the clear sky. It shone brightly, baking a rich sense of solace into his skin as it guided the undulating water toward them and then away again in a syncopated rhythm.

The explosions of three nights before seemed like a distant memory—a ghost in a horror story that had never really been there at all. Listening to Alexander's tales of Daniel, seeing him now in the light of another, made him present again, nearly whole as he wrapped him in the warmth and light of the coastal sun. He felt closer to Daniel now than he had in such a long time.

He could barely make out Manta's figure further down the shore. She sat inside the strandline, laughing as the water washed over her feet and collecting the tiny offerings it brought to her. There were some shells: long and pointed deposits of calcium, spiraling in an intricate nautilus to make Fibonacci blush. She marveled in the nuances of their beauty then placed each one in a tiny pile to her left, not worrying if the tide washed them away again. To her right she collected stones she thought belonged to Atlanta, the City in the Ocean—one of so many now—resting and waiting and crumbling there under the surface like Atlantis before it. She felt a strange kinship to the rock and polished ceramic that made its way to her. She thought the city that should have been her home was sending her pieces of itself to let her know she was not forgotten, that if it could, it would have welcomed her.

"I'm serious," Alexander continued.

He sat next to Paul, reclining under the tarp they had stretched between two of the sturdier trees in the berm. He was smiling. The sea air had been good to him, invigorating him from the inside out. He was closer now to the man Paul remembered from the Before. As close as any person could be.

"It's been three days now, and we haven't seen another living soul. People are still scared of the water, worried it's radiated or that another Wave is on the way. Hell, we set off fireworks, and no one came."

"It does seem safe here," Paul agreed.

"Safer than facing the slavers and the ravagers to get back to your cabin. Which may or may not be occupied by roamers if we make it."

Paul laid his head back down on the grassy clay. His mind drifted to the cabin. Daniel had loved it despite the commute it placed on him to travel back and forth to the city. Even though their time there as a family had been short, they had begun to build the lives they had dreamed for themselves there. Together. He remembered the sweat-drenched smile on Daniel's face as he tilled the tiny patch of earth outside by hand; the ecstatic joy he'd displayed when the first tiny seed sprouted up. And even though that had turned out to be a weed, soon tomatoes were spiraling their furry chartreuse stalks around their wire cages, the puckering flowers of cucumbers and summer squash were singing to the sky. Staying at the cabin had made Daniel feel somehow still with them. He was everywhere Paul turned, and Paul did not want to lose him to a memory. But there was a part off him which felt closer now, as if proximity and memory had conjured him in new form.

"I don't know," he said. "Our life is there. We have a roof. And beds. And a garden. It's where Manta learned to walk, to shoot her bow."

"And it's where Daniel's still alive." Alexander finished the unspoken thought. "Where he could still walk through the door at any moment."

Paul sighed heavily. The gentle breeze the water pushed towards them made him shiver as it caressed his skin, like a ghost passed through his body. Maybe it was Daniel's. "Yeah," he said.

Alexander nodded. He couldn't ask Paul to leave Daniel behind. He wasn't trying to replace his husband. Paul deserved to be somewhere he felt content, solace. He wanted that for him.

He turned his attention to the shore as Manta squealed and leapt to her feet. She rushed towards them with her hands cupped and outstretched before her and presented a swath of ornately painted plaster. The salt water had preserved most of the gold-leaf paint that formed floral Islamic flourishes across what was left of the beam. Manta smiled broadly as she presented it to the men.

Paul turned it over in his hands to study the shapes carefully.

"I think this is from the ceiling inside the Fox Theater," he said. "Amazing that it's so well kept."

"What's a fox theater?" Manta asked and sat cross-legged in front of her father. "Is that like a zoo or something?"

"It was this really old, really beautiful playhouse where live actors would put on shows for thousands of people," Paul said, and Manta leaned closer to look at the piece as he spoke. "I remember once when I took your father there, on like our fifth or sixth date. There was a revival for this classic play, from the 1990s—a musical that he loved—about a group of people in New York who learned to make a chosen family outside of societal norms."

He looked at Alexander who seemed lost in a memory of his own.

"Anyway. We had gotten seats in the upper balcony because that was all I could afford. But even though the play had been out for over fifty years at that point, all of these well-to-do 'theater goers' who had snagged up all the best seats got so offended by the close of the first act, they left at intermission and never came back."

Paul laughed as he thought of that night, the plush red seats and the domed ceiling that looked like an Arabian night sky. It felt good to laugh. To laugh and really mean it.

"So your father grabbed my hand and led me down to the front row. He held up his hands as if he owned the place anytime an usher tried to ask us for our ticket stubs. And he plopped us down, front row center. And we stayed there for the entire second act."

"That sounds really cool," Manta said. "The date. And Dad. But also people performing stories like they meant something real."

Paul thought she would be sad, hearing about a history lost to the depths of the ocean. He thought he would be too, remembering it. Instead it held a miraculous joy, like the sea was a time capsule waiting to reveal his history. *Maybe Daniel could be here too,* he thought. *Maybe he's where we are. Or, at the very least, maybe we can take a few days more to decide.*

"I want to see what else I can find!" Manta said, the excitement rich in her wide eyes as she rushed back toward the water.

Paul wrapped his arms around his knees, resting his head there as he looked out at the ocean which had formed over the land he'd once known so well. It was so violent and peaceful. It contained everything and nothing. On a clear day, it reflected the sky back like a mirror, searching out what was left of the Colony, guiding it down to the old city. Guiding it home.

"There you go," she said. "About damn time."

"Samantha?" Daniel asked, his voice sore and groggy as it scraped across his tongue.

"I think he may have brain damage," she said, studying his blinking eyes carefully for dilation, for signs of a concussion amidst the broken blood vessels of temporary oxygen deprivation.

It was the same face he had seen before, haloed in white. An older Samantha coming to rescue him from the flames, from his demons. At the very least he wanted her to be. He closed his eyes tightly, the tiny particles of sleep in the corners were rough and piercing, jolting him back into his senses.

"Nyx," he said.

"Right," she smiled. "Can you sit up?"

Daniel struggled to pull himself upright. The bright fluorescent lights glinted fiercely off the stainless-steel equipment lining the white room, hurting his eyes as they tried to adjust. A low, steady hum accompanied by a stable, periodic beep pierced his eardrums. An ivory sheet fell from his chest to his lap as he rose, and the fabric pooled there like the petals of a magnolia just opening in the spring.

"Where am I?" he asked.

"A makeshift med-ward on Sub2," Adrasteia said, stepping forward from one of the brighter corners of the room. The light pulsed in his vision, dimming and offering temporary focus before exploding once more in supernova. "You missed a lot," she said.

"Water?" he asked.

Nyx placed a wheat-plastic cup in his grip and helped him guide it toward his lips. It burned as it coated his mouth and slid down his throat, exciting all the nerve-endings as they reached for its liquid smooth comfort. Adrasteia reached out and gently rubbed his leg through the sheet.

"You took quite the fall during the blasts," she said. "Got a nasty blow to the head. But Nyx here found you before your oxygen ran out completely."

Nyx smiled. "We're a team, right?"

"What the hell happened?"

Adrasteia pulled a chair to his bedside and leaned back while biting her lip.

"There was an explosion," she said. "Three, in fact. The Colony lost thousands of people."

Daniel squinted his eyes and scrunched his nose. It was there, somewhere, rattling around in his brain. He knew he could remember if he could just focus his thoughts. He felt he could see his synapses firing; and he could see himself too, chasing them through the darker recesses of his mind, ghosts playing a game of hide and seek, memories no longer bothering with the timeline.

"The Aposts had thirteen bombs. We got to ten of them," he said.

"He does remember," Nyx said, raising her eyebrows to the young woman seated on his right.

"Yeah. It could have been a lot worse. As it stands, Alpha2 and Alpha3 are out of commission."

Daniel startled as his mind caught up with his body, settling in and flexing his extremities as full awareness returned. He pulled himself up straighter and tossed the sheet from his body.

"We have to get out of here," he exclaimed. "The chute."

Nyx laughed and placed her hands on his shoulders to guide him back down to the mattress.

"The chute can wait," she said.

"It's been three days since the bombing," Adrasteia added. "Like I said: you missed a lot."

Daniel's head sank into the pillow. His eyes searched the ceiling, picking out the thin lines which formed where the glowing white tiles met one another like puzzle pieces before the image was added. He remembered being trapped beneath a metal cabinet on Alpha2, staring at what could have been the same ceiling as his lungs burned anyway when they couldn't find enough oxygen to start the fire.

It had been three days. They'd missed their window. He was trapped inside the Colony. He would never see his husband or his daughter again. At least he wasn't back in the brig. Or, if he was, they'd penned the group together versus separately. At least he wouldn't be completely alone.

"Why so glum, chum?" Adrasteia cooed.

He hadn't realized he'd started crying. His eyes were wet and blurry, and the pillow had started to turn cold from the moisture at his temples.

"We missed our chance," he moaned. He hadn't meant to sound like a child, but the sorrow whined from him before he could pull it back.

"And I'll say it again," Adrasteia laughed, a smug, satisfied smirk across her lips. "You missed a lot."

"You should sleep," Nyx commanded. "We've got some things to work through, but then we'll be back for you. Okay?"

Daniel nodded. He didn't understand what was happening. His mind raced through scenarios, turning each to fact before turning them into farce, dismissing them as quickly as they arrived in favor of another. His eyes felt heavy. Suddenly, all he could feel was the pin prick in his forearm, the pulse of the IV in his vein.

"It's all gonna be alright," Adrasteia said. "I promise."

He tried to say *I've heard that before*, but the words would not come out. His eyes were heavy. The lights were so bright. All he could hear was the soft rhythmic beeping of the machines. He had to close his eyes. He'd feel better with them closed. That's where Paul and Samantha would be.

That's where he could see them again.

The doorbell rang again and again, barely chiming through its cadence before it started again. It echoed through the empty apartment, loud as it bounced from the hardwood floors to the bare walls. Daniel had barely opened the door before Vanessa and Alexander bulldozed through.

"No time for pleasantries," Vanessa blurted as she marched toward Paul who was bouncing in the living room, cradling a mess of limbs and blankets in his arm. "I'm here to meet the baby."

Daniel leapt from her path with a flourish and a laugh. Alexander strode in slowly with a sheepish grin.

"Sorry about her," he said. "She's addicted to that new baby smell."

"It's like crack for my ovaries," she called back then returned to cooing at the infant in Paul's arms.

Alexander shrugged. He ran his fingers along the granite countertops in the kitchen and whistled into the empty room.

"I can't believe you're giving this place up," he said. "Moving out to the boondocks like wild animals."

"We've still got the lease for another two months," Daniel said. "With all our stuff moved out, it'll make a great party pad."

"Like we'll have time to party," Paul said. Samantha cooed in his arms while Vanessa played peek-a-boo, twisting her face into funny positions with no worry of them sticking. "You want to hold her?"

"Does a whore sweat in church?"

"I know I do," Alexander laughed and moved to the living room to join the others. "At least there won't be any elevators for you to get stuck in at your new place," he offered.

Daniel smiled as he looked across the scene: his friends, his husband, and the little girl who would forever change his life. They danced through the empty living room, shoes clacking on the polished wooden slats as the sun beamed in like spotlights through the open windows. The air smelled fresh and warm, like cookies just out of the oven. The laughter of a Friday afternoon in the city wafted in through the windows to join the baby talk carousel bubbling through the room. Bottles of wine and fresh formula—and water for Paul who'd be driving—littered the counter to spell out, not a goodbye, but a welcome for the next chapter of their lives. It was an all too perfect day.

Daniel joined his chosen family as they welcomed the newest addition to their ranks. She was glorious. She would be their leader one day, taking them into the future with her beautiful smile. Of that, he was certain.

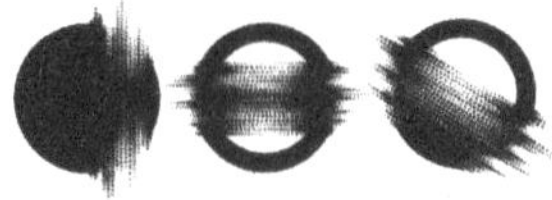

He awoke feeling refreshed, revived, as if a nightmare had somehow ended in his body finding wholeness once again. He pulled himself from the cot, swiftly disconnecting the sensors attached to his chest, and turning off the machine before any alarms could be triggered. His feet were unsure of the flooring, legs wobbly beneath him like a newborn deer, and his right shin smarted from the weight of the case it still felt. It took a moment of leaning against the bed to find his bearings, but he breathed deeply to center himself and twisted his spine upright. The door opened before he even made it across the room.

"Sit your ass back down, mister."

Adrasteia laughed as she spoke, hands on her hips like a scolding child playing at motherhood with her dolls. Her entire demeanor had changed since the bombs. Where she had been intense and mysterious and filled with purpose, she bubbled a light and airy optimism that sat well on her young face. The rebellion was still in there though, that glint of fire which sparked in her irises like lightning bugs or shooting stars. He hoped she'd never lose that.

Daniel sat and craned his neck from side to side, stretching the muscles out from the atrophy of sleep. Her smile sent a smirk across his face, and he pictured her the night they had met, offering him whiskey in a tchotchke-filled room, the glint of sorcery and conspiracy in her eye. Now, she seemed to float across the white cube they were in: gliding, free, and holy.

"Are you going to tell me what's going on?" he asked as she leaned casually against the wall of sleek machinery across from the bed.

"We saved the world, Daniel," she said, then cocked her head to the side. "Well, almost anyway."

Daniel squinted, his confused expression urging her onward. She sighed and beamed.

"I'll start with the bad," she said.

The night of the Anniversary Festival, the Watchers—or "New Aposts" as she called them to distance herself from their creation—had successfully detonated three of their bombs before her gods could get to them. That much he remembered. With most of the Colony spread throughout Alphas 2 and 3, enjoying the party, the casualties had been extreme. Almost 32,000 people were missing and presumed dead. The Aposts had mis-calibrated their placements and blown out sections of the outer wall. Which hadn't been their intention. They were going more for scare than bang, but their zealotry and cobbled together explosives had backfired.

"A lot of folks became shooting stars," she said solemnly, as if the euphemism somehow made their deaths easier to take.

Others, Adrasteia told Daniel, were crushed or suffocated, like he almost was. But Nyx had used the suits to search the floor for him. She had saved his life.

"Luckily," Adrasteia said, still happy and lithe even as she ticked off the horrors of the Watchers' attack like lottery numbers, "none of the outer breaches affected the load bearing structure. Two floors are unusable, but the colony's not going down. Well, not the building anyway."

The reality of his brush with Hades pulsed at his temples, settling into his skull to ache through the marrow. His fingernails dug into his thigh instinctively, checking to make sure he was real, that flesh and bone had prevailed against the cosmic forces which ruled even the City in the Sky. He was solid, at least as solid as he ever was. But with solidity came clarity. An abrupt guilt settled in.

"So what does that all mean?" he asked. "You all stayed behind to save me? I don't want to be responsible for us missing our chance."

Adrasteia shrugged. It was sharp and joyous, amused and sarcastic all at once. She hopped to her feet and opened a cabinet to fish out clothing to replace Daniel's hospital gown. He thought he could hear her chuckling as she tossed them to the cot.

"You're not the only one we saved," she said. "And when word got around about the ten bombs we did manage to disarm, well, there was a slight shift in the power dynamic of the Colony."

Daniel pawed at his clothes and urged her to continue, but it was clear she was done speaking. Her grin widened as she gestured to the shirt and pants she'd laid out and turned around to give him privacy to change.

"You're going to love this," she said to the wall as Daniel disrobed. She seemed to enjoy speaking in riddles that left so much of the story to the imagination. "It's really better than anything we could have planned."

Daniel didn't want to get his hopes up as he pulled the off-white tunic over his head. He wondered how she could be so excited, so cavalier. Over thirty thousand souls had been lost only three days prior. They had missed their opportunity to leave the Colony. He pulled on the pair of shoes that had been tucked beneath the bed and could only see Samantha and Paul moving farther and farther away as he worked the laces.

Alpha5 was nothing like he remembered it. In the hallways, the quiet neighborhood streets glitched sporadically, flashing to solid red or green or black between images of idyllic homes with rich greenery—azaleas, hydrangeas, and dogwoods—planted aside cobbled walkways made perfect despite having succumbed to the roots of great oaks in the reality ten miles below. But no one seemed to notice. The floor that had once housed twenty or so of the most elite governmental figures in the Colony was now abuzz with hundreds of citizens. Several of the vast, multi-room living quarters had been reconfigured to house the multitudes of displaced people in shared units with private bedrooms and bathrooms that felt less utilitarian and more like a home. Other quarters and offices were now equipped with the pods and equipment used on Farm Level to continue the food production necessary for the drastically reduced population. All that space once occupied by The Few was now a lively, robust society. More like a commune than a colony. More like survival than surviving.

Adrasteia walked briskly through the hallway, greeted repeatedly by her three-fingered salute: index, ring, and pinky fingers extended over the heart, middle and thumb tucked beneath in a circle. It seemed the entire Colony had joined her crew while Daniel was asleep. He tried to ignore the whispers, the reverent looks of awe, as he passed through the crowds, but they settled into the back of his mind to shout questions at his subconsciousness. It also seemed, while he was asleep, the godlike status of

Adrasteia's crew had been cemented. The sorcery in the naming of things was powerful. She led Daniel to the doorway for the mayor's offices and turned to him with a sly smile as the door shifted open.

"He lives!" Lincoln exclaimed from behind the large walnut desk centered in the room.

"Great!" Hermes smirked from behind another of the clustered desks throughout the room. "We can get started."

"We waited for you to recover," Adrasteia said, tugging at Daniel's sleeve. "Seemed only right."

The gods were spread throughout the mayor's space, all of them exhibiting an excited, nervous energy. Nyx, Selene, and the other gods of light had equipped a workstation in the corner where enviro-suit materials were spread about like dissected organs removed for study. It reminded Daniel a bit of the Neutral Zone with them pilfering tech to create something new and useful. Typhon, Hermes, Echnida, and Lincoln had set up camp in the center of the room, while Eurynome and Achelous had buried themselves in tablets trying to figure out a way to loop the environmental systems completely around the two derelict floors. Daniel's mouth gaped as he peered around.

"Pretty crazy, right?" Nyx said. "Turns out the blasts created a power vacuum that needed filling, and, well, here we are."

"What the fuck is happening?"

Daniel leaned against the doorframe. The excitement was palpable, but he had awoken into a whole new world. Maybe he had died. Maybe this was his subconscious's sick idea of a dream.

He shook his head in confused amusement as the other gods filled him in on how the world had changed while he was out. In the chaos that ensued, Typhon, Echnida, and Hermes had used their connections in the Guard—those who still believed in them anyway—to restore peace to the Colony. The truth, it turned out, was much more palatable when told in the face of destruction and fear. And in return for that kindness, the people had elected the gods to lead them.

"The mayor and her minions were killed. Some of them anyway. And who better to step into their shoes than us?" Achelous said. "So now the gods are in control. Ready to rule."

"Lead. Not rule," Lincoln added quickly, a wide-eyed gaze betraying his internal struggle between excitement and not wanting to follow the garden path of before. "Leading, coordinating. With honesty."

"Six of one," Nyx shrugged. "But seriously, we are working on ways to make society better. More egalitarian, if you can believe it."

"You're ready to listen to the people?" Daniel asked laughing.

"Adrasteia had some good points with her group," Nyx conceded. "They do deserve to be heard. The important thing is for us to listen. And be honest and truthful about what is really going on."

"We've already begun repurposing tech so that everyone has a direct line to the labs, to these floors," Lincoln smiled. "And you'd be amazed at the ideas coming out of folks who were waitresses and janitors before."

"Would we?" Hermes asked, and Lincoln blushed.

"As you saw," Theia said, "some people have moved up here. But others are staying down on the Sub Levels, keeping those going. Giving everyone room to be. To breathe."

It was a perfect solution. Perhaps, the Colony stood a chance at becoming a sustainable space once again, even with two floors removed from the equation. And, with the Colony becoming sustainable once again, the citizens could make an informed choice about where they wanted to be, what they were willing to risk, how they wanted to live. Everything had changed. The ideas of hope the Colony had once stood for seemed suddenly reborn. It all seemed too good to be true.

Daniel's breath caught in his throat as he peered around the room at his merry compatriots. A vision of Paul and Samantha flashed through his mind.

"So that's it?" he asked. Adrasteia startled at the lack of excitement in his voice. "We're stuck here now."

"Gods no!" Nyx laughed. "You see me working on the suits over here?"

Relief filled Daniel's entire being. As much as he loved the idea of this new utopia, of seeing what the Colony could actually become, he had to get back to the surface. He had to find his family.

"But here's the rub," Adrasteia said, and Daniel nodded solemnly as the other shoe finally dropped. "According to my father—"

"Whom, by the way, she locked up in the brig with the rest of the mayor's lackies who survived," Eurynome quipped.

"Like he fucking well deserved," Typhon added.

"There might not be much of a surface for us to choose to return to," Adrasteia finished. "I know we knew something had happened before. But now we know the full story. And it's not pretty."

Daniel's brow furrowed. He'd been so concerned with returning to the surface, with getting out and finding Paul and Samantha, he had not even considered how much life on the surface could have drastically changed. Lincoln moved around the desk and perched against it in front of Daniel. He watched the fear and anxiety circle in his mentor's eyes.

"If Dr. Saito's to be believed," he explained, "the reason they rounded all of us up early—"

"The reason so many of our loved ones were left behind," Selene added.

"And communication stopped on day one," Theia said.

"—Is that a sudden seismic shift mixed with a solar flare, or climate change, or the planet finally deciding she'd had enough melted the ice caps."

"And not in that slow trickle we've all gotten used to," Helios said. "Like, all at once. Like fucking boom! And whoosh."

The room grew quiet as Helios mimed a tidal wave, arms undulating and vocal cords whirring into a solemn moment of silence. Everyone stopped moving. Every mind oscillated between nightmares of bloated bodies, of silent screams while drowning. Daniel didn't want it to be true. He could not accept that the world had ended nine years ago. That he had carried on with life not knowing everything he had loved had been lost.

"It all happened in a matter of hours," Adrasteia said, almost in a whisper, as if volume gave the statement worth, as if, somehow, keeping it quiet could mean it was not true. "They didn't even warn the cities."

"They just rounded up the people they could find and left the rest to die," Hermes grumbled, the words fighting against his tongue. He did not want to believe them, and yet they seemed so utterly true, so completely what would have happened in such a situation.

"That much water, coastal cities—hell, coastal states and countries may be completely gone," Theia said.

"What that means," Nyx said, her voice strong and firm—bold, as if acceptance was not akin to action, "is that we can leave, but we don't know what we're headed into."

"The sudden rise in sea levels, that shift in atmospheric pressure, ended all communication with the Colonies," Lincoln said. "All of them. Or, at the very least, ours."

"They were flying blind as much as we are," Adrasteia said, a bit of sympathy for her father bubbling to her surface. "But where they let not knowing lead to fear, we're not letting it stop us."

"And we're giving everyone on the Colony all the facts we know," Nyx said. "And the option of leaving." She was determined to see the surface.

Daniel was too. He refused to believe that he would not be reunited with his husband and daughter. His heart broke. He couldn't imagine what they had gone through without him, what life on the surface would be like when faced with a sudden switch of the coastlines. He had to make it back down, to find them, not to make it all okay, but to face the future by their sides.

"The point is," Adrasteia said, "we don't know what's waiting for us down there. But we're damn sure going to find out."

Excitement crept its way back into Daniel's bones. It was really happening. Soon, they would see the surface again, breathe in the air and feel actual sun on their skin. Soon, he would find his family, safe and eagerly awaiting his return in the cabin they had found to start their lives.

"When do we leave?" he asked.

A wave of uneasiness caressed the room. Lincoln bit his lip as his eyes searched Daniel's face for forgiveness, even before he spoke.

"Here's the other thing," he finally said. "Not all of us are."

The ocean lapped its frothy tongue along the Georgia shoreline, thick like saliva, and teeming white against the red clay. Paul peered out at the slowly rising sun and let the liminal space of morning wash him in its hazy mist. He felt like a siren on the rocks, his silent song humming with the vibration of the wine-dark waters to guide the ghost ships home once all their maps were deemed irrelevant after all the stars had changed their plotted course. He felt himself as Orpheus, peering into the bowels of the earth, losing there his love forever. The sea licked his bare feet.

Manta and Alexander were still asleep behind him. Their simple lean-to tarp had grown over the last few days, built up by driftwood and stone into shapes that would one day resemble walls. Walls which, maybe someday, could maybe even form a home. Manta seemed to enjoy the process of building: making something from nothing, a place that was truly her own. Though not in the sense of ownership. That was not how Manta thought of things. Perhaps that was one of the blessings of the Wave. His daughter saw the world differently, in the way that generations had been trying so hard to convince people to view it. Place, she knew, was as temporary as time. Ownership was an idea that was just as brief. The planet would remain: constant and cyclical, connected and wholly its own.

The ocean spray was invigorated by the heat of the sun peeking out from its depths, its droplets aching to join the rising fog washing in to refresh the land before the harsh heat of day pressed upon it in cleansing fire. It pressed against Paul's face, fresh with saline rivulets, tears. He hadn't realized he was crying. He stared out and licked the salt crystals from his lips and did not close his eyes as he let them flow.

"I miss you," he whispered. His message in a bottle; his prayer to be carried out on the undertow. ""I think of you every single day. And Manta does too, Daniel. We tell her stories to keep you alive for her. For me too. You'd be so proud of her, I think. Our little Samantha has become so a determined, powerful young person. Two years or a lifetime, Daniel, you should know you made an impact. She's got your care and compassion. I swear she does. Nurture or nature. I see you in her.""

Paul smiled as the ocean relayed his message, each wave coming in faster, hungry for more words to carry back to Daniel's ears. It felt good to say it all out loud. Maybe he could be like Manta. Maybe he could feel the connection of the world too. He'd spent so long trying. Maybe it was more about giving in.

"Can you believe it's her birthday?" he asked. He asked and he knew Daniel was smiling. "Or close enough to it. We kind of lost track of the actual days when we were in New Yukon. So we chose today to celebrate. It seemed appropriate somehow, doing so here with you. I just can't believe she's eleven years old now. Pretty soon she'll be a teenager, and then—fuck!—look out! She'll be a teenager, and I'll be an old man. Remember the two of us growing old together?"

The ancient waters swirled around his ankles, but they were receding now. He felt them cycle in and out like they were an extension of himself.

"I still hope that one day you will find us again," he told the waves. They answered back in whispers, in a cool, soft caress. They embraced him where he stood, washing him, rooting him into the ground. "But I guess, the truth is, you're always here. I just have to get used to feeling you on the wind."

The sun was warming his face, drying his eyes with the gentle brush of its rays.

"I guess that's sort of what you always were," he laughed to himself. "A brilliant and steady gust of wind rushing into me, filling my life with so much movement and electricity, and then slipping out again into the ether. Too solid to be a ghost. Too ephemeral to be anything short of magic."

It felt cathartic to speak directly to him. He wondered how many prayers he had missed over the years: Daniel calling out to him from the sky. Daniel whispering his name into the darkness. The things he would have heard if he had only thought to listen.

The waves rushed in, and he realized he hadn't missed them at all. He'd felt every single prayer fill him through the last nine years. They'd wrapped him in warmth as he sat near the fire at the cabin. They'd tucked Manta in at night and urged the basil and the snap peas to grow. They were the tendrils of vines that had shaded them on the hottest summer days; the whitewash of pure snow that had blanketed their winter landscape. They were the beautiful rhododendrons and the tree that had fallen atop the fence in the deepest recesses of New Yukon to let them escape. They were the Ferris wheel that looked out on the land and the trails that had led them here. He could feel Daniel's love all around him. If he could keep it there, it would never be lost.

He could hear Manta begin to stir behind him as the sun slipped across the water and glistened across her face. He smiled, a real smile this time, one recovered from joy and not performed in bravado.

"I promise I'll keep her safe," he whispered. "And that she will know you. She will know everything about you. So that one day, when we all meet again, she will recognize you immediately. And you, Daniel, you'll know her too. Because you'll see yourself in her eyes."

Paul let his breath wash out with the waves. He let the ocean return it to him. The in and out. The ebb and flow.

"The southeastern chute was damaged in the blast," Nyx yelled over the hum of her acetylene torch, her voice muffled by the thick, tinted fiberglass of her helmet. "Hopefully we fare better with this one."

She had insisted on unsealing the chutes herself. The buildup had been too dramatic not to want to watch firsthand as the metal burned red and parted to reveal their final path home. She stood with Daniel in the sub-basement. A tiny, barely six-foot-tall space which pulled water and oxygen from above to send to the recycling units in the labs. Here, the massive elevator cars that had once brought the citizens to the sky had been sealed off and replaced with the smaller, commuter lifts above. This was the middle land between them and home.

"The numbers just keep climbing for the initial exodus," Daniel said, checking the listing on his tablet, and Nyx nodded and smiled.

They had decided to move in phases so that those not brave enough to experiment with descent would still have the opportunity to leave if the initial party proved successful. The others would stay in the Colony, some choosing to remain forever, under the direction of the new leadership team: Hermes, Echnida, and Lincoln. Daniel teared up a little when he thought of leaving the young man behind, but he was glad the Colony would be in good hands. The three of them together worked as a balance to ensure the people of the Colony would always remain informed, that safety would be a priority, that people could live instead of just survive. And Achelous would stay to oversee the environmental systems. "No one to return to anyway," he'd said.

Typhon had chosen to stay in the Colony as well, as the new head of the Guard. Except now, the Guard's sole purpose was the neutral advancement of the people, not the protection of the few. Though, with the mayor dead and her crew of conspirators all locked in the brig, it did give him the opportunity to express some of the darker play he'd once reserved for the Neutral Zone.

But the rest of them would soon join nearly five hundred of their compatriots back on dry land.

"That's fantastic," Nyx yelled. "You may want to stand back a bit. And put on your mask."

Daniel pulled his oxygenator on and watched as Nyx turned the gas off on her torch and dipped her crowbar into the white-hot ribbon of molten metal that had been used to close of the shaft. She moved slowly to open it, parting the metal doors only enough to separate the metal from itself. A forceful gust pulled at Daniel's hair, whipping it about his face as the air in the room equalized against the ten-mile drop. As he removed his mask, the stale scent of musty earth and salted brine wafted up to fill his lungs. It seemed so familiar and yet so distant, like a memory belonging to a different lifetime.

"Looks like she's intact," Nyx smiled as she pushed the doors apart and peered in at the vast, metal chute floor. She switched on the generator beside the door and listened as it hummed to life.

It worried Daniel to hear the pulley system groan and creak as she tested the machinery with a three-foot descent, but Nyx seemed to expect the noise after nine years of dormancy. The elevator car was larger than most people's quarters in the Colony of old. Soon, it would be packed to the gills with folks ready to return to whatever the world had become.

"Winner, winner," she smiled.

"Earth by dinner," Daniel smirked.

Nyx laughed heartily. So much weight had been lifted from her chest. And though she was disappointed to not be a part of the first group heading down—she and Daniel had chosen to stay up top to monitor the controls until everyone was safely at the bottom—she was happy to facilitate from above. Selene had volunteered to descend with the first batch of citizens—near sixty-five of them—and weld open the doors at the base. There, they would wait for the rest. Eventually, Nyx hoped, the chute would function freely, connecting the Colony to the Earth, allowing travel back and forth whenever the heart fancied it.

It took nearly two hours to round up the first group of descenders. As they gathered their belongings and said their goodbyes, Nyx allowed the chute to descend halfway and raise back up. Everything was in order. The end was finally near.

Daniel remained in the sub-basement to check in and queue the descendants as they found their way down their stairs, brimming with a newfound hope he'd not felt since their first days in the sky. His feet were just a few short hours away from finding land. And though it felt bittersweet to leave his home of nine years, he had already spoken with Lincoln, with the rest of the gods—his new chosen family—who had decided to stay behind to maintain order for the Colony. He couldn't bear to dredge up that pain again. He was excited to return to Earth, but departure still nagged at his heart.

"Don't you miss it?" Daniel had asked him as they walked the halls of the Sub5 one last time. "Don't you want to feel real grass on your feet again? Hear the clicking buzz of the crickets and cicadas?"

"Get mauled by mosquitos and choked out on dark clouds of gnats?"

Lincoln laughed, punching Daniel gently on the arm to accentuate his joke. "No, I'll definitely go back down someday," he said. "But, for now, there's more that needs to be done here."

"You'll find me when you do make it back to Earth."

It was a statement, an assurance.

"Of course," Lincoln smiled. "I can't wait to meet your husband and Samantha. I look forward to them whipping you into shape. Besides, after you've hugged the life out of them, the next thing you'd better do is work on reestablishing communication with all of us up here."

Like Daniel, Lincoln refused to believe the people they loved were gone. He refused to believe in the finality of goodbyes, so they went unspoken. Still, they echoed through his mind as he counted the travelers arriving, ticking them off on his tablet as they entered the chute.

"See you on the other side," Selene said, embracing Nyx before she boarded the elevator.

"Don't go drinking in all that sunshine before I get down there," Nyx laughed.

Selene tapped the torch across her chest in salute and nodded as the doors shifted closed before her and the fifty-five First Descenders. The murmuring excitement from the elevator filled the sub-basement as Nyx activated the lift and it lurched to a start.

"Here we go," Adrasteia smiled. She had joined Nyx, Daniel, and the other descending gods to watch the Maiden Voyage take off. They would be next. Everything they had worked so hard for, sacrificed so much for, was finally happening! She shook her head in wonder, unable to wipe the smile from her face.

Nyx startled as she heard the lift groan to a sudden stop about a mile downward in the ten-mile drop. "It sounds like they're stuck," she said. "I think the pulley isn't handing off to the next set of wires. We just need to…"

She pushed at the buttons and pulled at the levers on the control, hoping to lodge it free or bring it back to the top, praying the sudden stop had not agitated the citizens and their panic would be held at bay. She closed her eyes and held her breath as a mechanical groan echoed from the hollow canyon.

"There we go," Nyx smiled.

The gods watched as the indicator lights on the control panel turned green and followed the elevator downward another two miles before flashing red once more. Daniel listened in horror as the whipping sound of a snap slapped against the metal tube. Three snaps, in rapid succession, like a machine gun, like a series of bombs. And then it was over.

The gods fought to look away, but the scream of air sliding over the sharp metal of the chute as it plummeted miles in a matter of seconds overwhelmed them. It was everywhere they turned. It was every dream they had, crushed. Their eyes went wide in unspoken grief.

Nyx's lip trembled as she tried to maintain control of her voice. Her hands still hovered over the control panel, willing some magic to turn back time, to make it work again, to save the lives of those they'd just lost.

"That's two shafts gone," she said, the quiver in her voice betraying her. She needed to be practical. When an experiment failed, a scientist knew they needed to move on.

"I'll let Hermes know what happened," Eurynome whispered as she walked slowly to move upstairs.

"We should postpone any other citizen descents," Adrasteia added.

"Looks like the bombs did more damage than we were aware of," Daniel offered as an explanation. Though no explanation mattered. The cause was not as devastating as the effect. "They knew the risks."

Nyx nodded. She bit her lip as she gathered her welding mask and torch. The gods fell in line and walked the mile to the northwestern shaft slowly, searching out purpose with each step. No one bothered to ask if there could have been any survivors. A fall like that, a slip that deep... At least it would have been quick. They had to keep moving, keep trying. The owed it to everyone above, to everyone who had just been lost.

They were silent as Nyx worked her torch along the seal. Eurynome returned with six enviro-suits for them all.

"With our track record," she explained as she pushed the rack to the group. Daniel nodded and touched her shoulder gently. She reached up and cupped his hand.

"We'll do a full descent and lift before we load this one," Nyx yelled above the roar of her torch. "And we go down first. Just us. Even if it ends up being a one-way trip."

She was punishing herself. Adrasteia could hear it in her voice. Perhaps they had all gotten ahead of themselves in their excitement. Perhaps they were not gods after all.

They raised their oxygen masks as Nyx pried open the doors. The sudden rush of ozone dissipated as the air pressure stabilized. Nyx peered into the chute and turned around. Her face dropped, and she refused to look her friends in the eye.

"It's not there," she said. "The car already fell. Or they sent it down when they decided we'd never leave."

Her fingers worked the control panel, and though a few lights flickered on, no sounds emerged from the shaft. The car wasn't coming back.

"So there's no easy way down," Adrasteia nodded as she peered into the vast, dark abyss of the cavern. "But there's still a way."

Nothing worth doing was ever easy though, she told herself. With the weight of the world atop them, this felt to be the hardest thing they would ever have to do.

"**A**nd whatever you do, don't look down," Helios quipped as he finished his impromptu lesson in repelling for the convened group of gods. They were lucky he'd spent his weekends before the Colony rock climbing in the cliffs of the Appalachians. Now, facing a ten-mile drop, the makeshift bungees and clips felt like a much-needed lifeline, an umbilical cord to the past they were desperately trying to be free of. It was like a rebirth, Daniel thought as he tested the harness strapped around the waist of his enviro-suit.

"Not that you could see anything anyway," Nyx quipped back.

All of them were attempting to break the solemnity of the situation. What, only hours prior, had felt so joyous, was suddenly crushed once again by the madness of the Colony. As news spread of the chute collapse, names had begun disappearing from the sign up for returning to Earth. But, with that also came a renewed energy into maintaining the City in the Clouds as a permanent home. People were working together like never before, under the direction of Hermes, Echnida, and Lincoln, to create the utopic paradise they had been promised in the brochure. It was a magical thing to see. Tragedy had a way of doing just that.

"So this is it," Adrasteia said as she stepped toward the opening in the sub-basement darkness. She let her gaze fall on the first jutting rung of the service ladder a foot down from the lip of the floor. "Last chance to change your mind."

In its new light, the Colony had so much potential to become the place they had all wished it to be so many years prior when they had signed up for the experiment. The hope for building a better world, both above and on the surface, was no longer bastardized by the wants and greed of the political structure that had seized upon it for power. Even now, with fifteen years turning into forever, the recouped building of the hive seemed lush with honey. Knowing what they knew of the fate of the ground, it felt a bit like giving up Olympus to reside amongst the mortals, like falling from grace to star in hell.

That five hundred had turned to six felt somehow right to Daniel as the gods moved slowly toward the chute. They had started this all together. It was only right they should end it at one another's sides.

"None of you have to do this," Lincoln said. He'd come down from Alpha1 to see his compatriots off. Or convince them to remain. He wasn't sure which. "We can make this work up here."

Daniel smiled and wrapped his arms around him. It was a fierce hug and felt good in his limbs.

"Of course we have to," he whispered.

"We'll have no way of knowing if you made it," he pleaded. "When you enter that shaft, you may as well be dead."

"We'll make it," Daniel promised. "You'll just have to believe it. Like I believe my family is down there, waiting. Just have faith."

Lincoln smiled, but he wasn't convinced. Still, there was no way he was holding them back from what they'd fought for so long.

"I'll find a way to get word to you," Adrasteia said. "To give you some sign that life has continued down there. So that you'll know, when you're ready, you can come home too."

Lincoln nodded and turned away, not wanting the tears brimming his eyes to sour the occasion. He would miss them—their friendship and generosity and forgiveness—but his place was in the sky. The idea of home was so fickle, so malleable, and so much less about place to him than it had been years prior. The Colony was home now, for him at least. And the potential beauty of its future heartened him even as he said goodbye to those who'd helped to realize it.

Nyx went first, carefully gripping the ladder rungs as she moved down to make way for the others. The light that activated around the helmet of her suit refracted off the gun metal surface to make the hole all the more daunting as it echoed on into the abyss of forever. Eurynome felt the tug of the rope on her waist and followed next. Then Daniel. Then Adrasteia. The gods were rounded out by Hyperion and Helios. One rung at a time. Only ten miles to go.

Daniel tried to focus on the movement of his hands to keep his mind from wandering as he pushed further and further down. Each step was greeted with a tug from below, letting him know when to move his foot lower in search of landing. That was then followed by a pull to let the god above him know when to make her move. *On and on like this*, he repeated to himself. *On and on into eternity.* His arms were beginning to feel the strain as he searched out the eight-thousandth rung. He had tried to keep count. Every 5280 rungs equaled one mile. If he could focus on that, he could make it. If he could focus on anything small in place of the extravagant weight of the fall, he could carry on. They were almost two miles in. There was no turning back. He was closer to his real life than he'd felt in years. One step at a time. *Pull. Step. Tug. Rest. Pull. Step. Tug. Rest.*

"Shit!"

Adrasteia's voice was harsh and sudden over the ragged breath of the gods. Daniel felt a shift in the slack of the climbing rope at his waist, and, before his mind had fully registered what was happening, shouted "Hold!" into the darkness. Hyperion and Helios quickly twined their arms around their rungs and braced the line as Daniel shot out a hand to grasp Adrasteia's falling body. She hung there, frozen, suspended, and terrified until Daniel could maneuver her back toward the wall.

"Okay," she panted. "Got it."

The line heaved in relief. The line heaved in pain.

"Moving on," Nyx said from the bottom of the pack.

Pull. Step. Tug. Rest.

Pull. Step. Tug. Rest.

"Holy fucking shit!" Hyperion exclaimed as their feet met solid ground. He collapsed to his knees and kissed the steel roof of the old elevator car below them. It was still intact, so it hadn't crashed. That was something.

"Give me one second," Nyx said as she focused on the readouts from the left arm of her enviro-suit. The air was thin, as they'd expected, sealed inside the long shaft for so long, but breathable. And now that they didn't have to worry about the excess energy of climbing, they were safe to remove their cumbersome helmets.

Daniel smiled. His body shook and quivered, but, even with only the metal roof of the derelict chute beneath them, felt renewed by the energy of the earth. The same joyous electricity prevailed amongst the other gods, and he beamed widely as they sent out their exhausted expressions of happy relief.

"We fucking did it!" Adrasteia squealed, unlatching the harness at her belt and letting it clang loudly against the steel beneath her feet.

"Almost," Nyx said, excitement tinging the ever-practicality of her words. "We still have to find the hatch, drop the eight feet through the chute car, and weld our way out of here."

"But we're so close," Eurynome smiled as they sat to collect themselves before their final sprint. "What do you think we'll find out there?"

The lot of them crashed down to sit and catch their breath, spread out in a circle with their helmets between them, LEDs still glowing like a campfire for modern man.

"I don't know," Helios smiled. He could feel his second wind taking hold of his haggard lungs. "But the world is too fucking vast. There's no way, even if what Dr. Saito says is true, that humanity just ended."

"If the wave did happen," Nyx mused, "I think maybe they took it as a wake-up call and did something about it. You know, like the Colonies themselves were originally intended to be, at the very least, a Band-Aid over the wounds we had cut."

"One would hope," Daniel nodded.

He looked out at the other gods in the darkness. The dim light still emanating from their helmets cast great shadows behind each of them on the vast walls, making them loom larger than they were. They were cave drawings of the ancients returned, great and powerful myths marking the manmade caverns of forever. Fitting, Daniel thought as he considered all the might and determination spread amongst them.

Nyx pulled herself to her feet. "Y'all rest up here," she said. "I'll work on opening the seal."

"I'll come with you. Keep you company while you sweat," Daniel said.

They left the others to relax and recoup their energy as they searched out one of the six service hatches and dropped into the elevator car below. Nyx's eyes sparkled as she lit her acetylene torch and smiled at Daniel across the red-blue flame.

"Thank you," she said.

"For what?"

"For keeping us all together," she said. "Even after I wanted to give up.

It took all of us to make this happen. I know I can be a bit stubborn."

"Not at all," Daniel smirked. "Thank you for saving my actual life," he replied, and she nodded.

They had come such a long way in such a short period of time. All of them, perfect strangers before, now had a kinship which felt as if it had always been, like chains forged in the fires of Hephaestus. They were forever bonded. They were the gods Adrasteia had created.

Daniel aimed the beam from his helmet like a flashlight as Nyx pulled down her shield and began to torch the thin line of molten metal used to separate the Colony from the natural world. He imagined stepping out onto the soft grass of summer, turning to see the Atlanta skyline welcoming him back into her warm embrace. They were so close. After all they had overcome, they were finally going to make it home.

"Something's wrong," Nyx said urgently.

A thin T-shaped line still glowed from where the torch had met the seal, but she was focused on one section near the floor. She'd removed her welding shield and studied the metal carefully. Water was leaking through. And a lot of it, not just a trickle of condensation. It was powerful, pushing at the entirety of the metal door. Another spurt appeared through the weakened metal casing. And another.

"Helmet's on!" she yelled.

Daniel scrambled to secure his helmet as more water burst forth, a sudden gush filling the bottom of the elevator quickly. He prayed the gods up top had heard Nyx's command as the door burst free and slapped against him. The ocean poured in, filling the shaft and whooshing through the hatch to ascend further. Daniel felt his back slam against the roof of the elevator. It knocked the breath from his lungs, but determination was more powerful than oxygen, stronger than the rush of the sea. He tried to reach the shaft, but the water was flowing with too much force to fight his way through. He thought he saw Nyx float through the opening. She would be able to tend to the other gods. He had about thirty minutes of oxygen left in his tank. Hopefully that would be all he needed for the water to equalize. He tried to slow his pulse to conserve what he had left in his tank. He closed his eyes.

Nyx removed her helmet as the water pressure leveled in the shaft, and she bobbed at the new surface. Dr. Saito had been right. The dramatic shift in the polar caps had changed the coastlines drastically. If her count had been correct, she had risen about fifteen, maybe even twenty feet. The Colony was now in the Atlantic Ocean, though they couldn't be too far from the new shore. The salt water tasted harsh on her lips as she licked them and regained control of her breath.

"Roll call," she yelped. The sudden force would have pushed them all up. She hoped they had been able to put on their helmets in time.

"Here!"

Eurynome answered first, and, when Nyx turned, she could just make out the faint light of her helmet several years away. The water had separated them throughout the shaft, but soon they were all accounted for. All of them except Daniel.

"We're in the middle of the goddamn ocean," Helios exclaimed.

"He was right," Adrasteia sighed. "My dad. He warned us…"

Her voice was tinged in sorrow as Eurynome spoke her fears aloud.

"That means Atlanta is gone," she said. "We were north of the city. If we're underwater here, the whole damn place has been washed away."

The water settled around them. Each move they made sent a trickle of noise to echo back at them in loud, harsh waves. The city they had left behind was truly gone. The world would be a completely different place. But they couldn't afford to mourn it. Not yet.

"I counted maybe a thirteen-foot rise," Helios said. "Plus eight for the elevator. We should be able to handle that pressure with the suits."

"I'm assuming the doors are open," Hyperion said.

"Oh hell yes," Nyx replied. Twenty-one feet. One more death-defying miracle of the gods.

"I've got less than ten minutes left in my oxygen tank," Eurynome noted.

"Same," Hyperion agreed.

"Then we'll have to be fast," Helios said. "Down, out, and up."

"We have no way of knowing how far we are from the shore," Adrasteia said. "But if we can make it out of the shaft, we can surface and get our bearings."

"I think I'm above the open shaft nearest the door," Nyx called. "Follow my voice. We should dive from here."

The gods swam toward her as she spoke, repeating numbers as she counted up to five and back down again to guide them in her direction. Their fatigue from the climb down burned in their limbs, but there was no giving up.

"Where's Daniel?" Adrasteia asked.

"He hit the ceiling," Nyx said, trying to remain calm. "So either he's already made it out, or we'll have to grab him on the way through."

"Assuming he's near the hatch,"" Hyperion whispered.

"Or not already dead," Eurynome said.

Nyx nodded. She hadn't wanted to say that part aloud. She prayed he had made it through the opening before his oxygen had run out. She hoped that the impact of the door, the rush of the water, the slam against the elevator ceiling had not knocked him out. It was so much to overcome. But they had already overcome so much more.

"Whatever happens out there," Adrasteia said, "it has been an honor to work with all of you. We made a real difference up there on the Colony."

Hyperion smiled as the gods reached their hands out toward one another.

"And we'll make another one in the new world out there," he said.

One by one, the gods put on their helmets. One by one, they dove to the depths of the sea.

A storm brewed on the horizon. Manta watched as lightning licked the base of the heavy grey clouds, tempting their thick undersides to open and offer themselves to the ocean. She could feel the electricity in the air, tasting like raspberries and ash on her tongue as she traipsed across the waterline with the spear she had whittled from the limb of an oak tree. Alexander had been teaching her to swim, making her a little more comfortable with moving further out into the water to fish, but she knew how quickly a storm could slide across the waves to engulf her, so she kept mostly to the shore. She trained one eye on the workings of the weather as her other scanned the ever-greying waters for the dinner Paul still refused to eat. The fish were fine now, but he'd insisted that one past bad experience could cloud a taste for life. But that was okay. There were leaves and berries and nuts they had discovered from just inside the tree line. And the sprouts from the seeds she had packed in her rucksack were just beginning to sprout inside the bed she'd made to mimic her father's garden back at the cabin.

They were going to be just fine there, she thought as she plunged her spear toward a scaly flat fish scurrying in the low tide.

"That's some kid you raised there," Alexander said, watching Manta from their shelter as Paul stoked the fire they had started to cook their early dinner before the storm advanced upon them.

"Yeah." Paul smiled proudly. "She's pretty amazing."

Alexander couldn't help but smile contentedly as he leaned back by the fire. The warmth of the flames kissed the right side of his face as he watched the young girl pull a third fish from the tip of her spear and tuck it into the bag tied around her waist. After all the terrible lows of the last nine years, it seemed they were finally building a steady, stable life. The end of the world no longer seemed so daunting. It was surprisingly beautiful.

"Can you imagine if we ever get to take her to a real beach?" he asked. "One with actual sand instead of rocks and red clay?"

Paul laughed as he thought of the sheer wonderment that would cross her face as sand crept between her toes, the joy in her eyes as she wiggled her feet and built sandcastles to look like the real ones that held princesses and knights in all the books she'd loved to read. Surviving could make room for glee, he told himself. He felt Daniel there with them, smiling at them from the fire, kissing them in the excited breeze that pushed against their bodies from the sea.

"Maybe one day we'll get to," he said. "I mean, they have to still exist somewhere, right?"

"It's a big, small world out there," Alexander replied. "I still think anything could happen."

He reached out a hand to caress Paul's shoulder as he sat down beside him to watch Manta hunt. She looked so elegant as she paced the shoreline, her strides beautiful and sure as she disappeared behind a rock.

"I won't eat the fish though."

Alexander laughed. He'd devoured what he'd could when Manta had used her eleventh birthday wish—"well, one of them," she'd said—to convince them to have them for dinner, but Paul wouldn't touch them.

"What about some fresh Gulf oysters?" Alexander laughed. "Or maybe some calamari? Or scallops drenched in oil and butter?"

Paul's stomach churned, but he laughed. He leaned in to kiss Alexander to shut him up.

Suddenly, Manta's voice rang out against the darkening sky.

"Dad!" she called. "Come quick!"

Paul leapt to his feet and broke into a run, Alexander quick on his tail.

Behind the rock, Manta was hunched over the figure of a limp man, encased in white like he was wearing an astronaut's suit. He had washed ashore, wrapped in kelp, from the unknown depths. Manta reached timidly toward his helmet.

"Wait," Paul commanded.

Her eyes met his, and she turned to follow his gaze as five more helmeted figures swim toward the shore. They lurched in the thin waves, and Paul felt his fight or flight instinct kick into overdrive. Whoever these people were, they had technology he didn't think could still exist, let alone function in the harsh environment of the ocean. He wanted to flee with his loved ones before the others could reach the shore.

"Let's go," he whispered. They needed to put out the fire. They needed to hide.

But Manta wouldn't budge. She reached forward and removed the helmet from her stranded astronaut. His breath was shallow, but it was there. He gasped as the fresh air and oxygen met his lungs. Manta cocked her head to the side as she studied his face. It was older, with more hair and fine lines where there had not been lines before, but she still recognized the features.

"Daddy Daniel?" she asked.

Paul froze as she moved aside to let him see the man slowly regaining consciousness on the shore. His eyes blinked open slowly. Paul's hands covered his own mouth in disbelief as he hurried to Daniel's side.

Daniel cleared his throat as his eyes adjusted to the light of the natural world. It was bright; brighter than he'd remembered it being with the natural light of the sun outshining even the UV spectrum bulbs that had given them their vitamin D inside the Colony. The air smelled of salt and soil and green. He was home.

He saw a man leaning over him, eclipsed by the sudden adjustment in his vision. He squinted to make out his features.

It couldn't be.

"Paul?" His voice was harsh and unsure and calm and comforting and real. "Am I—? Is this—?"

Paul's eyes welled with tears. They rushed down his face with the ferocity of the growing storm on the horizon which moved quickly in their direction. All the world was suddenly alive and renewed. The skies cackled with electricity, like fireworks welcoming home soldiers from the war.

"Is it? Is it really him?" Manta asked.

Paul didn't answer, but the tears streaming down his face told her all she needed to know.

He had made it back to them.

He had made it home.

EPILOGUE

"**O**kay, stand back," Manta instructed.

Daniel giggled as she pulled back into his arms and watched the slow fuse of the bottle rockets she'd set up burn to ignite the gunpowder within. The rocket launched up and out over the sea and exploded in a brilliant array of white gold and crimson red. It pierced the night sky like it could create stars there, their impermanence none the matter.

"Do you think they'll see it?" she asked.

"Hopefully they will," Adrasteia replied. She and Nyx were sitting a few feet away, watching the display dance and refract through the sky, reflected beautifully in the calm ocean waters. "Once the sensors are working. And, if Eurynome decides to return from her search of the new world, maybe they'll guide her back too."

For two weeks they had launched a single firework every night, like a safety flare—a "return to safety flare," Manta had said. She hoped it would signal the others on the Colony. She wanted them—all the people Daniel told her of in his stories about his time there—to know it was safe on the surface. She wanted them to know they would be down there, waiting for their return.

"It's a beautiful gesture," Daniel assured his daughter as he wrapped his arms around her.

It was possible Achelous and Lincoln had found a way to reactive the external sensors and detectors on the Colony already. They had made that a priority. So maybe they were up there, staring at monitors that should a deep serene sea, watching the brilliance of human life explode and dance just above it.

It was all so surreal. The world had ended in his absence, but here they were: building a new one, a better one in its place.

Helios and Hyperion emerged from the woods with a fresh batch of cut lumber dragging behind them. In the morning, they would begin construction on a third shelter for the crew. He felt Paul's arm wrap around his waist to embrace his family. His family. Finally reunited. Alexander placed a hand on his shoulder, and Manta smiled brightly as she broke away and ran toward her bag of fireworks.

"Auntie Nyx," she called, "can we light another one?"

"How many do you have left?"

"Six. But there's plenty more at the fairgrounds. And it's only a few hours walk away."

"Then why the hell not?" Nyx laughed.

Daniel smiled, watching as his family expanded into the heavens.

The gods took their thrones on the Georgia shore and watched as the sparks lit up the night. Their fading glow ushered the stars to shine brightly in their constellations. They told their stories of loss and redemption. They shone in glory to guide the lost back home.

ACKNOWLEDGMENTS

There's a peculiarity to imagining the end of the world. There's a sense that it doesn't quite matter how it happens, just that it has. As if, for some unfortunate reason, each of us has accepted its inevitability. We read and we write and we watch the what-aboutisms and the warnings and the denials and hope that maybe someday something will be done. But we will get around to all that tomorrow.

As a child, growing up in the South with bunny ears on my tv and crossed fingers hoping for reception, I was obsessed with TBS's *Captain Planet and the Planeteers*. A cartoon about a love of nature, about fighting against pollution and climate catastrophe, about folks from all walks of life coming together to combine into a superhero: that was some powerful stuff. I still have my "Official Planeteer" patch.

Thirty-three years since the first episode aired, it can often still feel like we're fighting an uphill battle to save the world. In an age of science deniers and "alternative facts," it is easy to feel as if we are going around in circles. But, if there's one thing Captain Planet taught me, it's that "The Power Is Yours."

Humankind—and especially us queer southern folk—have a long-standing history of perseverance in the face of the status quo, fighting for ourselves and those we love, and standing up to those who would do us harm. There's a sense of magic when our "powers combine" that can overcome all odds and stave off or end the climate catastrophe we are facing. We owe it to ourselves and to our planet to do all we can to save it.

Believe the science.

Listen to the earth.

The power is ours.